BARBARA MICHAELS

Vanish with the Rose

SIMON & SCHUSTER

New York London Toronto Sydney Tokyo Singapore

SIMON & SCHUSTER
Simon & Schuster Building
Rockefeller Center
1230 Avenue of the Americas
New York, New York 10020

SIMON & SCHUSTER and colophon are registered trademarks
of Simon & Schuster Inc.

Manufactured in the United States of America

10   9   8   7   6   5   4   3   2   1

Library of Congress Cataloging-in-Publication Data
Michaels, Barbara, date.
Vanish with the rose/Barbara Michaels.
p.   cm.
I. Title.
PS3563.E747V36   1992
813'.54—dc20   92–6852
CIP

ISBN: 0-671-68948-7

For Rebecca Michelle Mertz-Shea
January 3, 1991
with love from Ammie

Yet Ah, that Spring should vanish with the Rose!
That Youth's sweet-scented manuscript should close!

—EDWARD FITZGERALD: The Rubáiyát
of Omar Khayyám

PART ONE

Masquerade

CHAPTER ONE

The Plant of Roses, though it be a shrub full of prickles, yet it had been more fit and convenient to have placed it with the most glorious floures of the world than to insert the same among base and thorny shrubs.

—GERARD'S HERBALL (1597)

The approaching storm cast a tarnished metallic luster over the landscape. The restless, low-hanging clouds glowed greenish-gray, like verdigris on brass; in the fields along the road, the fresh spring growth looked sickly and rotten. Her hands were clenched tightly on the reins and her feet were braced against the floor, but still she was flung bruisingly from side to side as the wheels spun along the rutted road, rushing to reach shelter before the storm broke. It had been raining for three days. Boiling with foam, a stream of rusty water outstripped the racing wheels, rushing down to join the creek at the bottom of the hill. The road curved sharply there; she could see the bridge ahead, narrow and humped, rising out of a swirling pool that had overflowed the swollen streambed to flood the road. And beside it, half submerged . . . The horse was struggling to rise; its flailing hooves, unable to find purchase in the mud, sent up fountains of water over the still form that lay dangerously close to the iron-shod feet.

The approaching storm cast a tarnished metallic luster over the landscape. The restless, low-hanging clouds had a sickly glow, like verdigris on brass. Her hands were clenched on the wheel, but still she was flung from side to side as the car bounced along the rutted road. It had been raining for three days. Along the road a stream of water, boiling with foam, rushed down to meet . . .

11

Diana's foot slammed down on the brake. The wheels skidded sickeningly. Most of the gravel had been washed away; the muddy surface and rain-slicked weeds were as slippery as ice. Cursing, she brought the car to a stop before it slid off into the ditch. What had possessed her to do such a stupid thing? There was no obstruction on the road, not even a confused rabbit.

She negotiated the curve ahead even more slowly than she had intended. At the bottom of the slope a bridge rose out of a pool of water that had overflowed the stream and spread a brown stain across the road. Beside it, half submerged . . .

The driver had taken the turn too fast. The car had slid into the ditch and toppled onto its side. The door on the driver's side was under water. The other was closed. There was no sign of life.

Diana brought her own car to a smooth stop several yards short of the water's edge. As she flung the door open and scrambled out, lightning split the clouds and a cannonburst of thunder made her flinch back. For a moment she clung to the edge of the open door, feeling dizzy and disoriented. Why had she hit the brake several seconds before she saw the overturned car? It was as if she had been warned she would have to stop.

Déjà vu, second sight, clairvoyance—maybe X-ray vision, like that of Superman. Never mind, she told herself. She had no time to waste on theories. The driver might be unconscious, drowning.

Her running feet splashed through the water. It was deeper than she had thought, lapping at her shins as she stood on tiptoe and stretched to reach the door handle. It wasn't until her fingers closed over it that she recognized its unfamiliar shape and acknowledged other unusual details she had been too preoccupied to consider— the curve of the front fender, the elongated fin at the back. Tail fins, for God's sake! The car must be—vintage, was that the word? Bad news for her and the driver. The old cars were heavier, more sturdily built; she'd never be able to open and lift the door, straight up, from her present strained position. Her fingers slipped on the wet metal. How the hell did the damned thing work? Pull out, press in, turn up or down . . . What if it was locked?

As if in answer to prayer, the door opened, with a suddenness and force that sent her staggering back. She struggled to keep her balance, but her water-soaked shoes found no purchase in the mud. She sat down with a thud that sent a fountain of cold muddy water high into the air. Most of it fell back onto her. Gasping with shock, she stared openmouthed at the apparition rising up out of the overturned vehicle.

It was a dog. A large dog. A large *green* dog.

Paws dangling, face set in an expression of benign idiocy, it emerged in a series of jerks and jumps. She was beyond surprise; when she heard the voice she took it for granted that the dog was addressing her, though its manners left a great deal to be desired.

"Move it, you stupid bitch! Get your fat lazy bum out of there!"

The dog was white, not green. The strange light had given its snowy coat that appearance. It scrambled up onto the side of the car, sat down, and stared curiously at her. From the aperture of the open door came the head and shoulders of a man.

If he had been hurt, or even wet, she wouldn't have lost her temper. His hair was disheveled and his glasses hung slightly askew, but his rumpled shirt appeared to be perfectly dry. He didn't see her at first. Squinting past the dog at the half-submerged front end of the car, he looked as if he were about to burst into tears. "God damn it," he said feelingly. "Couldn't you have held together for another half mile?"

Lightning flashed, thunder crashed; the dog let out a howl and tried to force its way back into the car. A breathless, profane struggle ensued; when it ended the dog was wrapped around its presumed owner, clutching him with all four paws, its head buried against his chest; and Diana had recovered her breath, if not her temper.

"If you are quite finished playing with the dog," she said icily, "perhaps you could give me a hand."

"Holy crap," said the dog's owner, gaping. "Who the hell . . . How did you . . . How long have you been sitting there?"

Detaching the dog, he pulled himself up onto the side of the car. He was wearing jeans faded almost white with washing, and fashionably tattered; a bony knee protruded through one of the holes as he slid down into the water and splashed toward her. "Are you hurt?" he asked, extending his hand.

"No. I just can't . . . The mud is so slippery . . ." As she took his hand the abandoned dog launched itself into space with a despairing howl.

After the muddy torrent had subsided, Diana opened her eyes. It gave her some small satisfaction to see that her inept rescuer was sitting beside her. He was even wetter than she. Dirty water streamed down his face and his hair was plastered over his eyes. He sat perfectly still for a moment. Then he spat out a mouthful of disgusting liquid, pushed his hair back, and after an ineffectual attempt to clean his glasses with his muddy sleeve, took them off. The dog was splashing merrily in the water a few feet away.

"Let's try it again, shall we?" said he.

She hadn't meant to laugh, but his cheerful voice contrasted so wildly with his appearance—and, she suspected, her own—that she couldn't help it. Rising to his feet, he gave her a critical stare. "You have a peculiar sense of humor, lady. If we don't drown or die of exposure, we'll probably get fried by lightning. Is that your car?"

"Yes. I saw yours was—"

"So you came rushing to the rescue?" He took her by the wrists and heaved her to her feet. "You should have stopped farther back. The water's rising fast and you'll have to get up a good head of steam to get through it."

"You're damned lucky I managed to stop at all! And people who live in glass houses—"

"You have a point there. Two points, in fact." He hoisted himself up onto the fallen car and dived headfirst into the open door.

"Are you crazy?" Diana shouted. "We've got to get out of here before—"

A burst of thunder drowned her voice. The unknown maniac's long legs waved wildly; then the rest of his body emerged. He was holding an object that looked like a monster from a science-fiction novel. It bristled with sharp spines. "Here, take it."

She managed to grasp the wire that protruded from the top of the pot as he thrust it at her. Another plant followed. It was even larger and pricklier, with needle-edged fronds.

"Okay, that's it." He hoisted the second monstrosity into his arms. "Come on, Fifi. You too—uh—miss."

Fifi didn't want to ride in the back with the cacti. Diana watched in seething silence as the dog wallowed wildly, smearing mud all over her nice clean upholstery. She did not protest audibly, however, until the man suggested she get in back with Fifi. "She just wants to put her head on someone's lap," he explained calmly. "Thunder makes her nervous."

"She can put her head on your lap," Diana said.

"But I'm going to drive."

"Oh, no, you're not. I've already seen one example of the way you drive."

"It wasn't my fault! The brakes gave out. They need relining, but I thought I could—"

"Get in the back."

"You don't have to yell," said her companion in injured tones.

Thunder made Diana nervous too. A particularly reverberant peal startled her, and her foot pressed the gas pedal more forcibly than she had intended. The car hurtled down the hill toward the bridge, accompanied by a duet of horrified howls, canine and human, from the back seat. The water surged up on either side like the parting of the Red Sea, and as they mounted the bridge Diana could have sworn that for an instant all four wheels were off the ground. A thump, a bump, a lurch and a slither, and they were through, heading up the slope and onto comparatively dry land.

"Don't stop, for God's sake," said a shaken voice from the back seat. "It's a straight shot from here—"

"Shut up," said Diana.

After that he was too busy to bother her. The skies opened up, spilling rain like a waterfall. Thunder rattled the windows and Fifi's howls of terror echoed the thunderclaps. The wipers flailed frantically without much effect; only the blurred squares of lighted windows indicated the presence of the house. She took her foot off the gas and let the car glide to a stop.

"I see you have met my son," said Mrs. Nicholson.

It was a statement, not a question, so Diana only smiled and took another sip of the boiling-hot tea. She was swathed in a terry-cloth robe that covered her bare feet and lay in folds on the floor. The robe belonged to her host, not her hostess; Mrs. Nicholson was barely five feet tall and as slim as a boy. There was nothing boyish about her face, however. She was a dainty little lady with pink cheeks and a pair of deep dimples, and her silvery hair was piled atop her head in an Edwardian concoction of rolls, buns, and fat curls.

There had been a certain note of sarcasm, if not downright criticism, in her comment, but the look she gave her son held only doting affection. He grinned back at her and raised his cup in a salute.

When they had burst into the house, saturated and shivering, Mrs. Nicholson had not wasted time in introductions or conversation. She had bundled two of her dripping visitors straight upstairs and into hot baths, leaving her husband to deal with the third. What he had done with, or to, Fifi, Diana did not know. She hoped it had been something unpleasant. Mr. Nicholson was a tall, spare man, with thick gray hair cupping his head like a helmet, and a pair of piercing blue eyes. The look they bent upon the younger man was decidedly critical and not at all doting.

"None of us has been formally introduced," he said dryly. "However, I feel it is safe to assume that you are Ms. Diana Reed, whom we were expecting this evening. I am, as you must have realized, Charles Nicholson. Pray allow me to present my wife Emily and her son Andrew Davis."

"How do you do," Diana said.

"Don't mind him," said Mrs. Nicholson with a girlish giggle. "It's the Victorians. He's been reading them and teaching them all his life; now he talks like them. It's silly to be formal, since we'll be working together for, I hope, a long time. I'm Emily, or Emmie, if you prefer. You can call my husband Charles. I call him Charlie, or Charlie my darling, or—"

"Emily, please!"

"Quite right, Charlie dear. I am digressing. I do that a lot," she explained, nodding at Diana. "I must learn to stick to essentials. Are you warm enough now, child? Let me hot up your tea. Have a cookie."

"No, really, I don't need—thank you. I must apologize for arriving in such a state and making such a mess of your floors and your—"

"Oh, I know who was responsible for that," said Emily Nicholson. "I feel quite certain that if you had been left to your own devices you would have reached my door neatly attired, perfectly dry, and in your right mind."

Up to this point Andrew Davis had remained silent, following the conversation with demure interest and eating cookies. The dry clothing that had replaced his original attire had apparently been rooted out of a ragbag; the T-shirt was shrunk and faded, the jeans had even more holes than the first pair. Now he was moved to protest.

"You always blame everything on me! It wasn't my fault. What happened was—"

"I don't think I want to hear it," said his mother.

"I do," her husband said. "Andrew's stories fill me with a horrid fascination. The fact that they are, generally speaking, true only adds to their charm. I think I can guess at the outlines of this particular saga. The fact that you both arrived in Ms. Reed's car suggests that Andrew's vehicle broke down along the way—a not uncommon phenomenon—and that she was kind enough to give him a lift. The presence of that neurotic canine—which, if I recall, his mother strictly forbade him to bring—leads me to suppose that his vehicle was the one she had also forbidden him to bring—another of his excursions into what is loosely and laughably termed vintage cars."

"Excuse me, sir, but you don't know how valuable those—"

"Excuse me, Andrew, but I do know. I also know the diference between an aged motorcar which is capable of restoration and a pile of junk—a distinction that up to this point has eluded you. The only part of the mystery as yet unsolved is the extent of the mud and water that had covered you both. Since the weather is unsuitable for aquatic exercise, I can only conclude that at some point in the proceedings both of you fell flat on your—er—faces in the floodwaters. The dog may, of course, have had some hand in that."

As she listened, Diana was fascinated by the expressions that passed in rapid succession over the face of Andrew Davis. Its physical structure was regular if unremarkable—brown eyes, eyebrows that tilted up at the outside corners, a broad, straight nose, a wide flexible mouth. But those undistinguished features appeared to be made of Silly Putty. His eyebrows scuttled across his forehead like woolly caterpillars, his lips stretched and contracted and parted in protest, his eyes narrowed in rage and popped in outraged innocence. When his stepfather finished speaking, the whole ensemble settled into a sheepish smile. "Not bad," he admitted.

"I've always said you should write thrillers, Charlie darling," chirped Mrs. Nicholson. "You have such a brilliant analytical mind."

"Please, Emily!"

"Well, never mind," said Emily.

"Never mind? This is the fourth dog he's saddled us with, not to mention the six cats."

"Look on the bright side, Charlie. He may have wrecked the car beyond repair. And I really don't mind the animals, there's plenty of room. Only, Andy dear, I do wish you'd stop using me as a home for abandoned cacti. I hate cacti."

"That is a rare specimen of *Echinopsis eyriesii*," said her son sulkily.

"But I don't like prickly plants, darling. Why don't you bring me roses?"

"That's her job," said Andy.

Three pairs of eyes focused on Diana.

She had known this moment would come; she had thought herself prepared for it. She had memorized names, dates, facts. She hadn't forgotten them, but they huddled in her mind, indigestible as lumps of lard in the stomach—because she had never fully realized that she would have to repeat them to people instead of abstractions.

Charles Nicholson, aged sixty, former professor of history; his wife, Emily, fifty-seven, former Latin teacher. That was how her father thought of his clients—not as individuals but as cases, challenges to his skill in interpreting the complex structure of the law to their advantage and his. There was some validity in that approach, for it was difficult to maintain cool professional detachment when one became personally involved with clients. She had discovered that herself when she began to practice, but apparently two years had not been enough to harden her.

The Nicholsons were not cases or abstractions. With humor and friendliness and trust they had breached the barriers she had unconsciously begun to build against personal involvement, and destroyed the stereotypes she had envisioned. Latin teachers weren't supposed to have dimples. Dignified elderly professors weren't supposed to hold their wives' hands under the table.

Andy's eyes had narrowed—or was she imagining that look of suspicion? He went on, "Roses are prickly too. Even the old ones, I presume. What's with this old-rose thing, anyhow? Who wants a decrepit, tired old flower when he can have a nice new one?"

"Don't tease the poor girl, Andy," Emily said. "If you're as ignorant as you pretend, which I doubt, go to the library and read some of my books on the subject. I will not allow you to interrogate a refugee who is wearing Charlie's bathrobe because you almost succeeded in drowning her. Not till after supper, anyhow."

"I don't mind," Diana said. Emily's interruption had given her a chance to collect herself. If this was a test, now was the time to face, and pass it. "There's considerable disagreement as to the definition of an old, or heritage, rose. Most people would say it's any rose that existed before the introduction of the first hybrid tea rose, La France, in 1867. The hybrid teas have one great advantage over the older roses; they bloom continually, all summer long and far into the fall. Most of the old roses are nonrecurrent. The hybrid teas became so popular that they virtually drove the others off the market. Until recently it was almost impossible to find a nursery that carried them."

"I've always like Trevor Griffiths's definition," Emily chirped. " 'An old rose is any that isn't modern.' "

Diana recognized the name as that of a New Zealand authority, several of whose books she had studied. She smiled acknowledgment, and Emily continued, "The hybrid teas are beautiful, but they're so boring! All the same shape. Some of the old roses are single, some are great fat poufs of petals. And the colors! Not bright glaring yellows and oranges, but lovely subtle shades of mauve and violet and plum, like antique tapestries. Luckily for me they are available again—and I want them all!"

"But how—" Andy began.

"That's enough," his mother said firmly. "No more shop talk till after supper. Set the table, Andy, while I check on the casserole. We keep country hours here in Virginia, Diana, and we call it 'supper,' not 'dinner.' "

Diana's offer of help was refused, with a laughing reference to the unsuitability of her attire. "You can't walk in those trailing skirts, my dear, and the sleeves keep unrolling down over your hands. Just sit there and be ornamental. You look like a cute little girl playing dress-up in daddy's clothes, with those big hazel eyes and your pretty curls hanging loose—"

"You are embarrassing Ms. Reed, Emily," Charles said. "She is not a little girl, she is a grown woman and a professional."

"But doesn't she have pretty hair? Nut-brown locks, a-gleam with golden light . . . Is that a poem, or did I just make it up?"

"Knock it off, Ma," said her son. "You have this awful habit of talking to people as if they were three years old. You do it to me all the time."

This started an argument that turned attention from Diana, to her inexpressible relief. Apparently she had passed. As the conversation proceeded, however, she realized that the change of subject was not a demonstration of tact or of acceptance; the others were just doing what came naturally. They liked to argue. They loved to talk. There were no strong silent types here; conversation flowed like the running water by the road, sometimes witty, occasionally brilliant, always articulate. It ranged from politics to poetry, with side excursions into movies and TV, baseball, the essays of Ralph Waldo Emerson, the color of the new draperies for the library, and Andy's diet, which, according to his mother, consisted solely of various forms of pasta—an allegation the accused denied vehemently and at some length.

Diana couldn't have gotten a word in even if she had wanted to. Having overcome her brief outbreak of conscience, she reflected cynically that the loquacity of the Nicholson family might prove to be her greatest asset. The more they talked, the less she had to say, and the less she said, the less chance of a blunder.

Supper consisted of a mushroom-and-chicken casserole and a tossed salad. Andy finished the casserole and ate two pieces of apple pie à la mode with a gusto that contradicted his mother's accusations. Presumably he was one of those annoying people who never gain weight; he was lean as a scarecrow, and his elbows were as bony as his knees.

They moved to the library for coffee, and by then Diana was composed enough to be amused at the absurdity of the procession. Andy carried the tray, with his step-father dogging his footsteps and criticizing the way he held it; Diana had to use both hands to lift the hem of the robe, while Emily circled her like a friendly puppy out for a walk, snatching at loose folds and making admiring comments about Diana's pretty feet and ankles. By the time they had settled into their chairs she was braced and ready.

She managed to fend off the inevitable for a time by admiring the handsome proportions and the potential of the library. The potential had not yet been realized; the furniture was comfortably shabby, the bookshelves were a motley lot, and the walls had been stripped and replastered but not painted, except for a basic undercoat. The fireplace was Victorian—handsome enough in its Gothic outlines, if one cared for that sort of thing—but quite inappropriate for a house that had been built in the late eighteenth century.

"That's coming out," Emily announced. "We found the most gorgeous marble mantel at an auction. We'll have bookcases built as soon as we can decide what to do with the walls. We're torn between simply painting them, or finding a contemporary wallpaper, or perhaps antique paneling—"

Naturally this statement started another argument, with Charles recommending paint and Andy, whose opinion had not been asked, insisting on paneling—preferably something that had come from a "stately home." Where they were to find this rarity he did not explain, nor did he have any sensible answer to his stepfather's claim that since the wall surface would be almost entirely covered by bookshelves, paneling wouldn't show.

Emily finally ended the debate, announcing firmly, "Diana isn't interested in the house, you know. She's a landscape architect, not—"

"Oh, but I am interested. I love old houses."

"Indeed?" Charles responded to her inane statement with more interest than it deserved. However, Diana's attempt at distraction didn't succeed. Emily enjoyed playing the role of giddy little old lady, but she could stick to a point when she wanted to do so.

"She's here to work on the garden," Emily insisted. "I do hope it stops raining, Diana, I'm dying to show you the grounds. You'll be horrified, I expect; there's so much to do. But we've been reading and studying all winter, and we have a lot of ideas."

That Diana could believe. The Nicholsons appeared to own every book on landscaping and gardening that had ever been printed. The books covered the tables and many of the chairs and they bristled with slips of paper.

Diana picked one up at random—an expensive "coffee-table" book filled with colored photographs—and opened it to one of the pages that had been marked. The photograph showed a perennial border ablaze with color—daisies, pinks, delphinium, and a dozen other flowers she didn't recognize—framed in boxwood and partly shaded by trees. Behind it rose the chimneys and thatched roof of an English cottage.

"I thought you wanted formal gardens," she said in genuine bewilderment. "Especially roses."

"I want everything," her hostess cried, with a giggle and a sweeping gesture. "Perennials, shrubs, roses, herbs, trees—big trees, Diana. I haven't time to wait for an acorn to grow into a stately oak."

This morbid comment was accompanied by another giggle.

Charles gave his wife an enigmatic look and then turned his piercing blue eyes on Diana. "But it was your knowledge of roses that convinced us you were the one we wanted. The old roses are increasingly popular, but in fact few horticulturists know much about their care and propagation."

"As we learned from bitter experience," Emily added. "We interviewed several firms before we found Walt, and he was the only one who was honest enough to admit that he didn't know a thing about restoring Colonial gardens. He's very good at conventional landscaping, but he said we'd need an expert to direct him in this project."

"I'm grateful to him for recommending me," Diana said coolly. "But I hope you haven't raised your expectations too high. The old varieties aren't easy to find. Even today there are only a few nurseries that carry them."

"We know," said Charles.

She had expected he would. He might not be an expert on old roses, but he was a scholar, trained in the techniques of research, and the sort of man who liked to find things out for himself. Charles Nicholson was going to be a problem.

His wife said, "Walt has done some of the preliminary clearing and terracing, but I'm not entirely happy with the plans we drew up."

"They were okay until you started changing them," her son grunted.

"My horizons keep expanding, darling. I want a rose garden, a lily pond, a white garden, a night garden, a pergola, a ha-ha—isn't that a wonderful name? I wanted one before I even knew what it was. I pictured myself showing it to guests—'And over there, of course, is the ha-ha.'"

She gave a wriggle of childish amusement, and her husband beamed at her. "Diana will design all the ha-has you want, my dear."

"If the terrain slopes steeply enough," Diana said, pleased to be able to display her familiarity with at least one exotic term. "We can't build a retaining wall—which is really all a ha-ha is—without a sharp drop."

"We have over a hundred acres," her hostess said happily. "I'm dying to show you and get your ideas, especially about the roses. I want to order more plants, but the most important thing is to preserve the ones we have. It's the most astonishing thing, my dear. You won't believe it till you see it. I couldn't believe it even when I did see it—like a secret garden in the middle of a wilderness, surviving heaven knows how, and for heaven knows how long. It wasn't an impressive spectacle when we first saw it last September. The leaves had been withered by black spot and eaten by beetles, and there were only a few blooms. I didn't know then that the majority of antique roses bloom only once, in early summer. Then I saw it—a single spray of crumpled silken petals—and smelled it, the elemental essence of rose perfume—and I remembered Virgil's Paestan roses and their double spring—'canerem biferique rosaria Paesti.' "

Her cheeks were flushed and her eyes shone. Diana's inconvenient conscience stirred protestingly. If she had been the expert she pretended she would have shared the older woman's delight and known how to add to it. She had only the vaguest recollection of the rose Emily had mentioned, and the meaning of the quotation completely eluded her.

"That's right, you were a Latin teacher, weren't you?" she said.

"For thirty agonizing years, my dear. If we hadn't struck it rich, I'd still be drumming past perfectives into the reluctant heads of youth. But how I do run on. It's late; you must be tired."

Diana snatched at the excuse. "Yes, I really ought to get to the motel. My clothes should be dry by now."

"My dear girl, you can't possibly leave here tonight," her hostess exclaimed. "It's still pouring, and the creek is probably up over the bridge. Where are you staying?"

"I haven't checked into a motel yet," Diana admitted. This was one of the (only too many!) weak points in her story, so she went on quickly, "Motels aren't usually crowded in April, it's not tourist season, and I was delayed by the weather. I didn't want to be late for our appointment, so . . ."

"Oh, good, if you have your suitcase with you, that solves the only remaining problem," Emily said cheerfully. "Charlie's pajamas would be too big for you, and Andy never wears them—at least he never used to, and I gave away those pretty striped ones his Aunt Kay kept sending him for Christmas—a new pair every year, I can't imagine why—"

"Mother, she's not interested in my wardrobe or my personal habits," said her son. "I'll get your suitcase, Ms. Reed."

"I take it that you are also spending the night?" his stepfather inquired dryly.

"Now, Charlie, what else can he do? You aren't going to offer to drive him home, I hope?"

"Home," Charles repeated. His tone implied a number of things he was too wise to state. Diana got the impression that Andy was a more frequent visitor than Charles would have liked. He went on, "No, I'm not especially keen on driving sixty miles in the rain and the dark. At least I won't have to lend him my pajamas," he finished, with a smile that brought a relieved answering smile to his wife's face.

Diana made a few token protests, but allowed herself to be overruled. After all, she had a valid excuse for not wanting to risk flooded country roads and unfamiliar territory.

After saying good night to Charles she followed Emily upstairs. As she mounted the curving staircase, skirts held high, she had another flash of déjà vu—or whatever it was. Memories of history lessons and historical novels, most likely; the lovely staircase, like the central portion of the house it adorned, dated from the eighteenth century, and the women who had ascended and descended its shallow treads over the long years had worn flowing gowns and ruffled petticoats. Daughters and wives and sisters of the aristocratic owners, maidservants . . . No, the servants would have used the back stairs. Despite her caution she tripped halfway up, and her hostess turned to steady her with a surprisingly strong little hand.

"I tripped on that same step the first few months," she said with a smile. "It must be just a little off-scale or something; we'll have to have a carpenter look at it. There's still so much to do! We've lived here only a short time, and the place had been terribly neglected by the former owner. Poor thing, she was over ninety when she died, and quite dotty."

"Alzheimer's?"

"That's what they call it these days. It used to be 'senility.' It's horrible, whatever it's called. To feel yourself losing control of your thoughts and your actions . . ."

"Did she live here all alone?" Diana asked.

"Most of the time." Before Diana could pursue the subject, Emily said, "Wait a minute and I'll turn on some lights. I don't want you to fall."

Bulbs blazed in a row of sconces on the wall of a landing as large as a small room. Hallways led off to right and left; Emily turned to the left and led the way.

"I hope you'll forgive a certain Spartan air about the furnishings, my dear. The bed is comfortable, at least, and the bathroom is functional—and adjoining—but we're planning to furnish the whole house with antiques and we've just begun. The search is half the fun, don't you think? Charlie and I have become auction junkies."

She opened a door and flicked a switch inside. The room was indeed austerely furnished, but the bare bones of it were quite beautiful, for it had the ample proportions and high ceiling of stately homes of the period and moldings framed the juncture of ceiling and walls. It contained only two pieces of furniture—a handsome walnut four-poster bed, and a rocking chair. The windows were uncurtained.

"There's nobody out there except rabbits and deer and foxes," said Emily, gesturing at the black night beyond the window glass. "So don't be self-conscious."

"I'll feel like Marie Antoinette in that bed," Diana said.

"Martha Washington, my dear. Or Mrs. Jefferson, perhaps. It's supposed to be a genuine eighteenth-century piece," Emily added, studying the bed doubtfully. "Not that Charlie and I really know, we're happily blundering around and crowing with delight when we think we've got a bargain. If that bed is authentic we got a bargain; if it's not, we was robbed. I think the auctioneer was honest, but there are a lot of frauds around, aren't there?"

The arrival of Andy with her suitcase saved Diana from replying. Emily bustled around, supplying towels and sheets and blankets. Finally she left, and Diana knelt down to open her suitcase. She selected the warmest of the nightgowns she had brought; the air felt dank and chilly, and rain still beat against the window.

All at once her hands began to shake uncontrollably. She sat back on her heels, her head bowed, and took a deep, steadying breath. It had worked out even better than she had hoped. She had not given herself away; she was accepted, and actually in the house. Now all she had to do was find a way of remaining there.

CHAPTER TWO

*Neither the world nor the imagination can comprehend the
rose.*

—RUMI (Persian poet)

Spring sunshine is a lovely thing, guaranteed to cheer the most
hardened pessimist, but the sight of it streaming through the uncurtained windows brought a sleepy expletive to Diana's lips. She
had hoped for a longer spell of bad weather. Brief but concentrated
study—a skill honed by the horrendous demands of the law-school
curriculum—had packed her memory with a considerable amount
of information about gardening in general and old roses in particular. With fast talking and a lot of luck she might conceal her
relative ignorance of the subject on which she was supposed to be
an expert, so long as she didn't have to *do* anything. The kind,
considerate Nicholsons wouldn't expect her to start measuring and
surveying in a pouring rain, but now she would have to fumble
for unconvincing excuses to explain why she wasn't using the
instruments and techniques of her supposed trade. That kind of
knowledge couldn't be acquired in a couple of weeks; she had not
even tried.

A sound outside the door made her stiffen defensively into a
counterfeit of sleep. Through her lashes she saw the door open
and, after a few moments, close again. Footsteps tiptoed away.

Diana pulled the covers over her head and cursed her employer's
enthusiasm. At least Emily hadn't burst in shouting jolly slogans
like "Rise and shine." A few more hours, Diana thought cravenly.
It was still early; the angle of the sunlight told her that. And she
was so tired . . . even after eight hours of dreamless, undisturbed
sleep.

26

Her fatigue was not physical. The evening had been a strain, forcing her to stay constantly on the alert for potential pitfalls. She knew better than most how difficult it was to invent a long, elaborate lie and stick to it, without a blunder or slip of the tongue. Often it was not the details of the lie itself that tripped up a witness, but some small unconsidered trifle. Like looking over your shoulder when someone addressed you by a name that wasn't yours. She had tried to guard against that by using her own first name and a surname that started with the same initial as her own. Or the license plates on the car. She had considered that potential danger, but unless she did something stupid to arouse suspicion, the Nicholsons wouldn't be likely to trace them—and Pennsylvania was a big state. Lots of people, unrelated people, lived in Pennsylvania . . . Wearily, for the thousandth time, she went over her mental list, trying to think of something she might have overlooked. A useless exercise; she could probably talk her way out of casual errors, it was ignorance of her supposed profession that would betray her eventually.

On the floor, next to the door, was a tray. So that was why Emily had come—not to call her to work but to offer a gesture of hospitality. Diana got out of bed, shivering as her bare feet pressed the uncarpeted boards of the floor.

The tray held a thermos of coffee, a cup and saucer, a spoon, a cream pitcher, and a folded note, which read: "I forgot to ask whether you are one of those sensible people who refuses to face the world before you've had your coffee. Leave it if you aren't; enjoy at your leisure if you are."

The note was unsigned, but despite the bold, dashing handwriting, more suited to a man than a dainty little lady, she knew who had written it. Diana frowned—her task would have been a lot easier if Emily Nicholson had not been so damned Nice—and then smiled as she noted there was no sugar or sweetener or napkin on the tray, and that cat hairs floated on the cream. Philosophically she scooped most of them out with a tissue before adding the cream to her coffee.

She dressed for work, in worn corduroys and a long-sleeved shirt to protect herself against brambles and poison ivy, toxic even in semi-dormancy—and, of course, the thorns on the roses. There would be no need for her to bring out the dreaded surveying instruments today; she could reasonably claim she wanted to spend some time just looking over the area and making general notes.

When she opened her door she found herself facing a phalanx of cats. They were of all sizes, shapes and colors: tabby, calico, black, white, and gray, and one lordly Siamese. The Siamese and two of the others slid between her legs and headed purposefully for the bed. Several others sat still and stared at her expectantly. One, a small fuzzy white feline with blue eyes, jumped up and attached itself to her pant leg. When she pried it loose, it transferred its grip to her sleeve and swarmed up onto her shoulder.

An unexpectedly poignant memory came back to Diana. Her beloved, long-dead Fuzzy (eight-year-olds are not noted for the originality of the names they give pets) had loved to sit on her shoulder. After Fuzzy died there had been no replacement. Her father didn't care for cats.

The three invaders of her room had settled down on the bed. They looked as if they had every right to be there—but then cats always do look that way. After hesitating for a moment, Diana decided to leave them in possession. She started for the stairs, accompanied by a mewing entourage. They seemed to know where they were going, and she suspected their destination was the kitchen, so she followed.

The stairs curved to a landing halfway up, which was lighted by a tall window; the curve continued beyond, to the hall below. The principal reception rooms opened up on either side of this central hall. Through open archways to right and left sunlight illumined areas that had been darkly invisible the previous night. Presumably they were parlors and sitting rooms and a dining room, but at present their function could only be surmised, since they were virtually empty of furniture. All the walls had been freshly papered or painted and, presumably, replastered. Flooring and stairs had been refinished and polished to a golden glow. She supposed wiring, plumbing, and heating apparatus had also required modernizing and/or replacement. Those basic requirements would have to be done first, before the luxury of decorating and furnishing. It was no wonder the house still looked bare, but the few pieces of furniture she had seen were exquisite—a Chippendale-style lowboy in the lower hall, a few rugs of obvious antiquity and value, a low carved chest that might have come out of a medieval palace. However, it was no wonder the Nicholsons preferred to spend their time in the comfortable, book-lined shabbiness of the library.

When she reached the kitchen she was relieved to find Emily alone, seated in a rocking chair by the huge stone fireplace and rocking vigorously as she sipped her coffee and read the newspaper. She flung this aside when she saw Diana, and jumped up, dislodging a cat that had been on her lap.

"Good morning, good morning! You aren't late, the others are early. At least Charlie is, he always is, he's in his study. Andy is still asleep. He was up half the night, as usual. It's a pity he can't find a night job, he's a nocturnal creature like an owl or a cat."

"What does he do for a living?" Diana asked, taking the chair at the table Emily had indicated.

"A little of everything. At the moment he's working for an insurance company in Warrenton, but he's been a reporter, a travel agent, a real estate salesman, and a construction worker. They're a restless lot, these young men, aren't they?"

She had turned to the refrigerator, so Diana was able to get her face under control before Emily turned back with a glass of orange juice and a carton of eggs.

"Please don't fuss," she said, taking the glass. "I never eat breakfast."

"Toast or a roll, at least," Emily insisted. "You need something in your stomach if you're going to be tramping around all morning. My dear, are you aware of the fact that Miss Matilda's tail is in your orange juice?"

"She won't get down," Diana said helplessly. "Why did you name her Matilda?"

"*Miss* Matilda. Doesn't she look like a Matilda?" Deftly Emily detached the cat and put it on the floor. "She belonged to the old lady from whom we bought the house. Nobody seemed to know what her name was, so we called her after Miss Musser. She's deaf, poor little thing. The cat, I mean, but so was the old lady, come to think of it."

"Deaf?" Diana looked down at the cat, which was indignantly licking the tip of its tail. "She doesn't look that old."

"A lot of blue-eyed white cats are deaf. Something to do with genes," Emily said vaguely. "But Miss Matilda is older than she looks; four or five years old, the vet thinks. She's small because she was malnourished in kittenhood."

"But I can't imagine that . . ." Diana stopped herself, on the brink of one of those unexpected pitfalls. "That any decent person would neglect an animal," she finished.

"As I told you, the old lady was very absentminded toward the end. But Miss Matilda—the cat—dear me, I didn't realize how confusing the names would be—the cat was probably a stray. It wasn't the old lady's fault. Now here's your toast. Butter or jam? Sit down, I'll get you another glass of orange juice."

Emily was dressed in a practical ensemble of grubby pants and a wool shirt that had obviously been stolen from Charles; the tails flapped below her hips and the sleeves kept unrolling over her hands. When Diana indicated she was finished, Emily rolled her sleeves up again, pulled on a pair of knee-length boots, and tied a scarf tightly over her head.

"You do have boots, don't you?" she asked. "The pasture is still muddy in spots."

"They're in the car."

They went out the front door and Diana saw the facade of the house for the first time.

The previous night it had been only a Gothic presence, a looming bulk whose outlines were uncannily blurred by curtains of rain, and whose lighted windows glared like watching eyes. Now sunlight warmed the soft red bricks, over which a tracery of Virginia creeper had begun to climb. The central portion was . . . Georgian? Mercifully she wasn't supposed to be an expert on domestic architecture! It was three stories high, with a dormered roof and a severely balanced facade: a pair of windows on either side of the arched front door, which had a fanlight transom above. On either side a two-story wing had been added, connected to the central block by a low, enclosed passageway, so that the roofline seemed to undulate—rising and falling, then rising to a higher point in the center before repeating the pattern on the other side. Tall chimneys punctuated the roof outline. The house showed the effect of recent (and undoubtedly expensive) renovation. Glass glittered, fresh white paint covered door- and window frames, and the pointing, though skillfully tinted to blend with the faded brick, appeared to have been newly repaired.

"You really have accomplished quite a lot in a short time," Diana exclaimed. "That is—I mean—I saw photographs last fall, in the newspapers."

"Yes, we were only too prominently featured in the newspapers," Emily said with a grin. "If I'd written a best-seller or inherited from an aged aunt, the reporters wouldn't have been so interested, but I suppose there is something intrinsically comical about a pair of aging academics like ourselves hitting the lottery. It's usually some worthy housewife or blue-collar worker. Can you believe neither of us had ever bought a lottery ticket till after we were married?" She laughed, her eyes bright and reminiscent. "We've done a lot of things together, Charlie and I, that we never did before. His former wife is as boring as my ex-husband."

"You're having fun, aren't you?"

"Hard to believe, isn't it, that old people can have fun?" Emily's understanding smile removed any suggestion of offense, offered or taken. "Believe it. We were thinking of retiring in a few years anyhow when we got this windfall—settling into a sedentary stupor in the suburbs of Baltimore. After we talked it over, we decided to go for it—do whatever we felt like doing, without regard for age or common sense. Finding this house was sheer luck, though. At least that's what Charlie calls it; I'm not so sure . . . We were visiting Andy, who was working for a realtor at the time, and he insisted on showing us the place. He thought we'd like it, he said. It was love at first sight. I can't explain why. The roses may have had something to do with it . . . Oh, dear, I'm talking too much, as usual. Get your boots and let's begin the tour."

She didn't stop talking, though. As they descended the steps and walked toward Diana's car, she went on, "This is the front of the house now, but in the old days the river entrance, at the back, was equally important. We found the remains of a stone pier, so apparently the stream was deeper and wider two hundred years ago. That's where the gardens were, and that's the part I'm really excited about restoring. This approach, for people who came by road, wasn't so elaborately landscaped. All we need to do here is lay fresh sod, plant more trees and shrubs, lay out flower beds, pave the driveway—it won't be authentic, but since we don't (thank God) have slaves to rake the gravel twice a day, it will be easier to maintain—rebuild the stone wall and find antique gates for the entrance . . ."

She stopped to catch her breath, smiling at Diana, who could only say feebly, "Yes, well . . . I'd better start making notes. My briefcase is in the car."

At the far end of the curving drive, where tottering stone pillars marked the location of now-vanished gates, a pickup truck appeared. Emily shaded her eyes with her hand.

"That's Walt's truck. I wonder what he wants? He can't be meaning to work today, the ground is too wet."

Diana knew what he wanted. The driveway was three hundred feet long; by the time the truck stopped and the driver got out, she was able to meet his gaze unflinchingly. He was tall and broad-shouldered, with a head of unruly brown hair and eyebrows as sharply defined as if they had been drawn with a single stroke of charcoal. His eyes were a curious shade of gray-green—cat's eyes, she thought absurdly. It wasn't their color that reminded her of a cat, it was the unblinking stare that seemed to measure her with a cool appraisal that demanded . . . something she wasn't able or willing to give.

"I needn't introduce you two, need I," Emily said innocently.

"I guess I can figure who she is," said the man named Walt. He offered his hand. The skin of his palm and fingers felt like coarse sandpaper.

"You mean you haven't met?" Emily asked.

"Phone calls, letters," said Walt. "Especially those impressive letters of recommendation."

"I was just about to begin the tour," Emily explained. "Poor Diana arrived last night, in the middle of that raging storm, so she hasn't seen anything yet. I'd love to have you join us, Walt. You weren't planning to work today, were you?"

"No, ma'am, it's too muddy. Tomorrow, maybe, if this wind keeps up. Good drying weather. I just came by to see what damage the storm did, and— if it's okay with you—to pick up a check. I want to rent a front-loader and my cash flow is down to a trickle, as usual."

"Of course. I'll get my checkbook." Emily trotted back into the house.

Diana braced herself. The request had only been an excuse to get rid of Emily.

"Well, hello, Mata Hari," said Walt Slade with a slow smile. "You don't look anything like I'd expected."

His eyes moved over her, from her windblown hair to her shabby sneakers. Diana's lips tightened. Her youthful appearance had always been a handicap when it came to dealing with clients, and even some other attorneys, but when she was on her own turf she could take steps to counteract it—high heels and a built-up chair to increase her height, severely tailored suits and careful makeup to minimize a round face and rounded figure, hair pulled tightly back into a chignon. She had even bought a pair of heavy horn-rimmed glasses which could be whipped out of a desk drawer when the situation seemed to warrant it. Walt's amused, appraising look told her how she must appear to him, with loosened tendrils of hair escaping from her casual ponytail, in jeans and shirt that were shrunken and faded from frequent washings. In her flat-heeled shoes she was a good ten inches shorter than he.

"What did you expect?" Her voice was deliberately belligerent. Walt's smile faded.

"Somebody more . . . formidable."

"I can be formidable enough."

"Don't I know."

Vocabulary and accent were not those of a laborer, she thought, and then reproached herself for snobbery. Just because a man chose to work with his hands didn't mean he was an ignorant semiliterate.

And just because he had been sympathetic and cooperative didn't mean she could afford to lower her guard. Experience had taught her that friendliness could be interpreted as weakness and an invitation to be dominated.

"You were under no compulsion to do as I asked," she said crisply. "And it was you who mentioned that the Nicholsons were looking for an expert on old roses."

"I should know better than argue with a lawyer," Walt said. His voice was as cool as hers and his smile had vanished. "I thought . . . well, you're not interested in what I thought."

"Have you changed your mind?"

"Don't see how I can now. You've boxed me in rather neatly. Anyhow, you convinced me you have a case, and I'm not . . . Watch out, she's coming back. Where are you staying?"

"I haven't decided."

His heavy brows drew together. "I need to know how to reach you. We have to talk."

"I know how to reach you," Diana said, scowling back at him.

There was no time for more; Emily was back, waving pen and checkbook and asking how much Walt wanted. Was she always that trusting? Diana wondered.

He accepted the check and took leave of them. "I'll be seeing you, Diana," he said. "Quite a lot of you, I expect."

"Such a nice young man," Emily said, as the truck rattled off. "You'll have to be firm with him, he has decided ideas about how things ought to be done. Some of them quite good, really; I told him he ought to go back to school and study landscape architecture. Now then—your boots."

Diana had taken the precaution of scraping them on the cement steps of her apartment house and smearing them with mud and dried grass so they wouldn't be conspicuously new. Apparently they passed muster, for Emily made no comment. Removing a clipboard from her briefcase, Diana announced she was ready to begin.

Once again Emily's loquacity came to her rescue. Emily often asked for her opinion, but seldom let her complete a sentence. Nodding and smiling and—for the sake of variety—sometimes wrinkling her brow as if in thought, Diana realized that Emily knew exactly what she wanted. She and Charles, and the other landscapers she had consulted, had had months to work out plans for the driveway entrance. The area between the house and the gateposts was fairly flat; no reshaping of the terrain would be required, only flags to outline flower beds and mark the spots where trees were to be planted. I can do that, Diana thought with rising optimism. It's partly a matter of personal taste, after all; they may not like what I suggest, but they can't prove it's wrong!

They followed a flagstoned path around the left wing—the one that contained the kitchen—and Diana's optimism received a sudden check when she saw what lay behind the house, on what had once been the riverfront.

A square area approximately half an acre in extent had been cleared and planted with grass and shrubbery. It was defined by a stone wall from which a flight of wide stone steps led down to a wilderness that seemed to stretch off into infinite distance. Part was pasture, part woodland. At the base of a slope to the north she could see a belt of trees and hear—in the brief intervals when Emily stopped talking—the rush of angry water. It was, Emily told her, a stretch of the same stream they had crossed on their way to the house. "There are all kinds of possibilities there," Emily added, her eyes glittering with a look Diana had already learned to know and dread. "Paths through the trees, stairs at intervals— the bank slopes quite sharply down to the stream—wildflowers all along the paths and in the little hollows, rustic benches and tables . . ."

"You haven't—uh—drawn up any plans yet?" Diana asked.

"Dozens!" Emily laughed merrily. "I'll show you them. You'll despise them, and come up with far more brilliant ideas. This planted area was Miss Musser's backyard; but it's evident—don't you think?—that originally it was the first and highest of a series of descending terraces, like the ones at the Villa Farnese. We found the remains of the lower walls and steps; most of the stones had been taken away and used to build foundations for outbuildings. I haven't decided yet whether to restore the terraces or do something more informal—a slope with winding paths and perennial borders and . . . But you'll have suggestions, I'm sure."

Diana nodded. "I'm sure," she echoed. "Someone's kept this area—the backyard—well tended. I'd have thought Miss Musser was too old to take care of it."

The answer was not the one she had hoped to elicit. "I've tried to keep up with the weeding and pruning and so on. Charlie and I both enjoy messing around with flowers. But I suppose all these trees and shrubs will have to go, won't they?"

"Uh—yes." Diana decided it was time she made a positive statement. "It's easier to clear everything out rather than try to work around existing—er—plant material. None of this would fit into a formal garden."

It was a pretty little patch, though, and testified to the greenness of someone's thumb. Daffodils swayed in the neatly weeded beds along the back steps. A huge pussy willow, taller than any she had ever seen, had bloomed and faded; the soft gray catkins had sprouted long ugly yellow whiskers. Emily's pruning had not been aggressive. Forsythia and spirea sprawled across the grass, and a gnarled old apple tree had flung itself into an extravagance of frothy bloom, as if it knew this might be its final outburst.

The same thought had occurred to Emily. "I hate to cut down trees," she mourned. "I don't suppose we could save the apple?"

"It's awfully old," Diana said. "It probably wouldn't last much longer anyway."

"Maybe we could just wait till it falls down. Euthanasia is all very well with mammals, but . . . It isn't suffering!"

Diana laughed and shook her head. It required little expertise to see that the apple tree was in its dotage.

They started off across the pasture. It had been mowed the previous year, but not raked. The layer of yellowed fallen grass was still wet, and very slippery. "I'd have thought some of the local farmers would have wanted the hay," Diana said.

"I gather cows have more delicate stomachs than one might suppose. Thistles are especially bad, and we had a bumper crop of them."

"Oh, yes, of course."

"No 'of course' about it," Emily said placidly. "Cows and their habits are outside the ken of a horticulturist. That's where locals like Walt are so useful. We were lucky to find him. He found us, actually; turned up at the front door shortly after we moved in, and said he figured we'd be wanting some work done. He wasn't the only one to offer his services. It's a small town, and they were all agog with curiosity about the crazy couple who'd bought the old Musser place."

She stopped, her hand pressed to her side; the slope they had just climbed was steeper than it looked. "Now. What I had in mind was . . ."

What she had in mind sounded like the gardens of Versailles, only bigger. Gazing out over the stretch of rough pastureland, Diana felt her mind reel. "It's going to be a big job," she said when her hostess paused for breath.

"That's why I want to get started as soon as possible. Oh, and I want a gazebo. I thought here, on the top of this hill, would be a good place—such a wonderful view—but Charlie wants it at the bottom of the slope, so we can see the waterfall and the lily pond."

"Waterfall," Diana repeated numbly.

"And a huge pond. With a bridge over it, of course."

"Of course."

"Now," Emily said, her eyes aglow. "Now comes the part I really want you to see. We haven't figured out what was here in Colonial times; it's been rough pasture for years, probably centuries, and there are no traces of earlier plantings. But on the other side, toward the stream . . ."

Having recovered her breath, she plunged recklessly down the hill. To Diana's bewildered eyes the rough surface appeared little different from that of the upper pasture, but Emily's running commentary indicated that either her experience, or her imagination, was more developed. "... an allée of trees ... parterres ... this hollow may have been a pool ... remains of a knot garden ..."

Suddenly a green wall barred their path. It rose high above Diana's head and was so thick she could see nothing beyond it. At some time in the not too distant past its sides and top had been roughly trimmed, but new green growth blurred the perpendicular lines.

Emily mistook Diana's bewildered silence for admiration. She beamed and bounced with pleasure. "Have you ever seen boxwood this old? Oh, but that's a silly question—of course you have. I hadn't, though, Charlie and I never took garden tours. It must be two hundred years old. It's a solemn responsibility, we feel; you can save it, can't you? I know it needs trimming and feeding and all that sort of thing." Mercifully she didn't wait for Diana to answer, but went on, "Now come inside. It wasn't meant to be like this, of course; the boxwood was a low border, not a barrier, and there were several entrances. Only one of them has been kept clear. It's just like the secret garden in the book, isn't it?"

She squeezed through a gap in the foliage that barely admitted even her slender frame. Diana followed, edging sideways. What she saw was so remarkable that even her untrained brain responded with astonishment.

The enclosed area was about forty feet on either side. Weeds were everywhere, covering the ground with a carpet of green and a sprinkle of colored bloom, but they were this year's growth. Rising from the weeds were prickly stems whose identity was unmistakable to the rankest of amateurs. None had blooms, or even buds, but they were beginning to leaf out. They sprawled in exuberant abandon, some forming tangled mounds almost as tall as she.

"It's hard to make out the original design now," Emily said. "Some of them have died, and others have growed like Topsy. But I think there were graveled cross-paths meeting in the center, where there may have been a fountain or a bench. That was typical of eighteenth-century garden design."

"You don't mean that some of these rosebushes are two hundred years old?" Diana exclaimed.

In her astonishment she had fallen headlong into one of the dreaded pitfalls—an inexcusable error, for her reading had told her that such cases were not unheard-of. In fact, those survivals

answered the question Andy had started to ask the night before—
how had the old roses been rediscovered, after virtually vanishing
from catalogs and nursery collections?

Again Emily saved her from the consequences of her carelessness.
"It has happened; you remember Abigail Adams's roses, and those
wonderful roses in New Zealand—Anaïs Ségales, wasn't that the
name?—Nancy Steen discovered on the graves in neglected cemeteries; some of them had to be a hundred years old. And the ones
American rose rustlers found near abandoned houses and in old
graveyards. Thomas Christopher has an enchanting account of
that in his book." She sighed longingly. "I'd love to think that
some of these bushes are contemporaneous with the house. But of
course—as you saw—this garden wasn't forgotten. It would be
completely overgrown if that had been the case. Possibly the oldest
roses died and were replaced over the years. I know there's at least
one classic rose here, the Autumn Damask I told you about, but
I don't suppose we'll ever know for certain how old it is. It was
certainly available to Colonial gardeners, along with a number of
other varieties. Lady Skipwith had marble and cabbage roses at
Prestwould."

Diana stopped herself, in the nick of time, from asking who
Lady Skipwith was. She'd have to do some quick private cramming
to identify that name and the others Emily had casually tossed off.

"I'd love to find some of the marbled roses Lady S. mentions,"
Emily went on. "I suppose she was referring to the striped and
splotched types."

"Yes. Right."

"And this," Emily said, "is the Autumn Damask—the one I saw
in bloom last fall. I'm right in the identification, aren't I? You see
the loose-growing habit."

"It could be," Diana said cautiously.

Emily laughed. "You're being very tactful, my dear. I know
there's no hope of identifying any of them until they bloom, but
I get so excited when I imagine coming out here one morning and
finding a bush covered with big double pink-and-white-striped
flowers—Lancaster and York, perhaps—and thinking, that shrub
is even older than I am! Now the question is, what are we to do
here? Obviously I want to keep as many of the old ones as possible,
and replace them, when necessary, with old varieties."

She beamed expectantly at Diana, who gathered her wits and

prepared to sound like an expert. "Well. I would really prefer to wait until the roses are in bloom so that we can see what we have. As you know, it's sometimes difficult to identify a particular variety even when it flowers. I wouldn't even want to prune these bushes now. They'll have to be cut back and shaped, but I gather from what you said that most of them are nonrecurrent. That means they bloom only on canes that matured the year before."

Seeing Emily's face fall, she paused, wondering how or if she had blundered. But her hostess was not suspicious, only disappointed. "I knew you'd say that. You're quite right, of course, but I was so anxious to get to work here . . . We can pull out the weeds, can't we?"

"Oh, certainly." That seemed safe enough.

"And feed them?"

"Uh—I don't see why not."

"Wonderful!" Emily looked as if she had just been presented with a diamond parure. "I've started a list of the ones I want. Actually, the timing is perfect; some of the nurseries ship in the fall, and by then we'll know what we have and what we need, isn't that right?"

"Oh, yes."

"And of course we can plant roses in other places. I want one by the gazebo, and another one dropping down into the pond. Graham Thomas has a picture in his book . . ."

They retraced their steps and squeezed through the gap in the hedge. "All this was garden," Emily said, waving her arm in a sweeping gesture. "We keep finding traces of banks and terraces, and I'm sure an expert like you can find more. Do you think we should rent a helicopter?"

This was such an astonishing non sequitur, even for Emily, that Diana staggered. Emily reached out to steady her.

"I should have warned you, there are some fallen stones here, hidden in the grass. We'll have to wait till the end of the summer for the helicopter, I suppose, they say that's when the patterns of underlying structures show up best, in hot, dry weather."

Diana fumbled frantically through the file cards of memory for a clue as to what her hostess was talking about. "Oh! You mean aerial photographs."

"Yes, that's right, isn't it? As I understand it, grass grows differently in areas where the soil has been disturbed, so that even

after a long time you can make out the places where there were
flower beds, and raised terraces, and so on. Fascinating! I've seen
pictures—just like a map. Oops, watch out, there's another stone.
We left them undisturbed, because I think they belonged to a fallen
wall. They seem to run along three sides of a square, so this must
have been a walled garden."

Diana prodded the stones with her toe. They were rough and
untrimmed, but comparatively flat. "Could be. You want this restored as it was?"

"Yes. I wish we could locate the original plans. I'm sure there
were plans, or at least sketches and descriptions, like Lady Skipwith's, and the ones in Jefferson's *Garden Book*. They were enthusiastic gardeners, those eighteenth-century gentlefolk, and
much more sophisticated than one might suppose. Did you know
there were garden catalogs available in the seventeen-eighties, and
that the 'seedsmen' imported plant materials from France and
Holland?"

"Yes, I—"

"I checked the local library and Historical Society," Emily ram-
bled on. "I hoped they might have journals or letters written by
the Fairweathers—they were the ones who built the house. The
family died out years ago, unfortunately, so there are no descendants that I know of. The house has passed through several other
hands since."

The path led uphill again, away from the river; Emily led the
way, trotting briskly and chattering about herb gardens and bog
gardens and espaliered fruit trees. Diana's spirits, which had risen
when Emily seemed to accept her pronouncement on roses as the
word of the prophet, sank again. How was she going to keep up
with this miniature encyclopedia of garden information?

All at once Emily let out a yelp and plunged into a tangle of
honeysuckle. "George!" she cried. "He's fallen over! Damn it, I
knew he was unstable!"

In some alarm Diana ran after her and found her struggling to
raise, not the fallen body of a man, but a slab of gray stone, shaped
and smoothed by human hands.

A tombstone. Emily was squatting, trying to lift it. "Wait,"
Diana exclaimed. "You'll hurt your back. Let me help you."

They raised the stone, which had fallen face-down, and propped
it against a tree. Murmuring distressfully, Emily pulled off her
scarf and wiped mud and wet grass from the smeared surface.

"Thank goodness, he appears to be undamaged. Luckily the ground is soft. I'd feel terrible if anything happened to George. I have a feeling he's the one who laid out the gardens. You see the dates—born 1744, died 1806."

Another stone leaned against the next tree, its weathered gray surface dappled with sunlight and shadow. "That's his wife," Emily said. "Amaranth. Isn't it a pretty name? These must have come from a family cemetery, but we only found three stones."

Diana hadn't noticed the third stone. It was smaller and less ornate than the others, and it stood some distance away. At some time in the past a strand of honeysuckle, that most delicately destructive of plants, had bitten deeply into the surface, obliterating part of the inscription. All the letters were badly worn. The material was not marble, but a softer variety, like shale or sandstone. Curiously Diana bent to examine the inscription. She could make out only the dates: "Died April 24, 1789. Aged nineteen years, three months, seventeen days . . ."

Emily's hard little hands bit painfully into her arms. "Diana! Are you all right? What happened?"

The green and gold and shadow of the landscape stopped spinning, steadied into the shapes of foliage and sunlight. She was still on her feet. Emily's face, wrinkled with worry, peered into hers.

"Nothing happened," she said. "I'm fine."

"You made the strangest sound! Like . . . I'm sorry, I should have warned you. There are no graves here, my dear, only the stones; they were moved years ago, when the county put a road through and destroyed the old family cemetery."

She didn't want to admit she had no memory of making a sound of any kind. "I bit my tongue," she said shortly. "Sorry I startled you."

"Oh." Emily released her grip. "Some people are superstitious about graves."

"I'm not." Deliberately she knelt and peered closely at the face of the stone. "How fascinating. We ought to design a proper setting for the stones, don't you think? Something simple and dignified."

"I'd put them back if I could," Emily said defensively. "But I'm not even sure where the cemetery was. The road went through almost fifty years ago. They found only these three stones, and I doubt they looked very hard for other remains. People weren't concerned about historic preservation then. It's a pity. Every estate had its own graveyard in Colonial times, the houses were isolated, and the roads were bad and there were no means of . . . Goodness, how gruesome this conversation has become! Let's go back to the house, we've seen enough for one morning."

She was uncharacteristically silent for a time; perhaps the steepness of the slope robbed her of breath. As they crossed the meadow the grass rustled violently and Emily cried out, not in alarm but in annoyance. "Dammit! No, William! Don't bring it here, I don't want it!"

A large tabby cat—William, without a doubt—emerged from the grass with tail erect. In his jaws he held a small brown object. He pursued his mistress as she backed away and dropped the pathetic, motionless bundle at her feet.

"Well, at least it's dead," Emily said resignedly. "I have to give William credit, he usually does kill them. Some of the others aren't so efficient and I despise having to finish the job. One can't let the poor things linger in pain, of course. Nice kitty. Good William. Thank you very much."

Having made the proper gesture and received the proper acknowledgment, William retrieved his prey and sauntered off.

"Shouldn't I take it away from him?" Diana asked. "Mice have parasites, don't they? I had a cat once . . ."

"It's not worth the effort, my dear. We'd have to chase him clear across the field and then he'd just go get another one. I worm everybody, without prejudice, several times a year, and that seems . . . Gracious, this subject is even more disgusting than the last! I like your idea about a little shelter for the tombstones. Nothing sentimental, mind you."

"Oh? I was thinking of a grotto, like the one at Lourdes."

Emily let out a shout of laughter. "That's the first time I've heard you make a joke, Diana. No grottoes, no shrines. At least not for George and his family. A grotto would be fun, though . . ."

"The third stone," Diana said, as her employer fell silent—contemplating, she felt sure, some particularly hideous architectural fantasy. "Was he, or she, a member of the family? I couldn't make out the name."

"Nor can I. However, the dates suggest he or she was a child of Amaranth and George. Leave your boots here by the steps. What we need is a mud room. And a garden room, where I can grow seeds and transplant things. I hate the idea of building an annex, though; contractors make such a mess."

"What about turning one of those buildings into a garden shed?"

She indicated a group of structures whose tumbledown walls and roofs could be seen through the lilac bushes. One was considerably larger than the others, and in even more ruinous condition. Much of the roof was missing, and the blackened timbers looked like evidence of a fire. When the lilacs were fully leafed they would hide the unseemly sight; even so, she could not understand why the barn, if that was what it was, had not been repaired or torn down.

"They're all going to be demolished," Emily said, standing on one leg and tugging at her boot. "Nothing historic there, just modern sheds and barns. One of them has been fitted up as a cottage; old Miss Musser had someone living there, to do chores and keep a watchful eye on her in her declining years, but it's riddled with rot and termites. The barn used to be a rather handsome structure before the fire."

"Lightning?"

"No, just the local firebug," Emily said calmly, and then burst out laughing at the look on Diana's face. "He didn't torch houses, just barns—abandoned ones at that. Nobody was ever hurt."

The sun had reached the back steps and there were several cats sprawled in attitudes of abandonment on the warm wood. Two dogs, one small and brown, one large, white, and extremely furry, came gamboling toward them; Emily put on a burst of speed, pushing Diana ahead of her, and closed the door on a pair of disappointed muddy faces.

They found Andy, two dogs and three cats, in the kitchen. The man was cooking; the animals were gulping the scraps he tossed over his shoulder.

"Out! Out!" Emily shouted, flapping her shirttails at the menagerie. The dogs scuttled for cover. The cats went under the table. "I asked you not to feed them scraps, Andy. What a mess you're making!"

"This is not a mess, it's my special Western omelet. Don't worry, Ma, I'll clean up the dishes. I always do, don't I?"

"No," said his mother, turning up her face for his kiss as she passed him on her way to the coffee maker. "Say good morning to Diana."

"Good morning to Diana. Did you have a nice time wallowing around in the mud and the weeds?"

"It's a fascinating project," Diana said, accepting the cup Emily handed her and sitting down at the table.

Andy flipped the omelet with more panache than skill. "Where's Charlie? I made enough for everybody."

"You know how Charlie is about cholesterol—and your impromptu meals. It's almost lunchtime."

She took a tray of raw vegetables from the refrigerator and began cutting them into a bowl. Andy scowled. "Why don't you let him make his own salad if he's so fussy?"

"Because I feel like making it for him," his mother replied equably. "Goodness, you're grumpy today. Didn't you sleep well?"

"No. This house makes more damned noise than any place I've ever lived in. Cracks, thuds, things going bump in the night . . ." He hacked the omelet roughly in two, dumped half of it onto a plate, and presented it to Diana.

It looked better than she had expected, and smelled delectable. She realized she was starved—all that unaccustomed fresh air and exercise. Andy rummaged in a drawer and took out two forks. Handing her one, he filled his own plate and sat down next to her.

"Thank you. It looks delicious," she said.

His frown smoothed away and his lips parted in a sunny smile. He was wearing the same clothes he had worn when she first met him; they had been washed but not pressed, and the limp collar of his shirt looked as if something had been chewing on it.

"Did the family ghost keep you awake too?" he asked.

"I slept like a baby. Is there really a—"

"Bound to be. All these old houses are haunted."

His stepfather entered in time to hear the statement. "The only thing haunting this house is a menagerie of restless animals," he said severely. "The cats are the worst; they are nocturnal by nature and extremely hard to locate. Confound it, Andy"—as one of the cats came out from under the table and twined itself around his ankles—"I told you not to let them in the kitchen. Good morning, Ms. Reed. I hope you slept well. What on earth is that?"

He glowered at the remains of the omelet on Diana's plate.

"Never mind, darling, you don't have to eat it," his wife crooned. "Sit down. I made you a nice salad."

Charles waved the newspaper he was holding at her. "Have you seen the latest issue of *Antique News?*"

"I glanced at it. You've found something I missed?"

Charles drew himself up and shouted the word like a battle cry. "Gates!"

"No! Really? Charlie darling, you are a wonder. Where? When?"

"Saturday. Mount Pleasant. I thought," he explained, as she bent over the newspaper, "we could attend the viewing on Friday night on our way to the auction in Lynchburg. If they are what we want, we can leave a bid or stay over, whichever seems most appropriate."

Diana caught Andy's eye. He shrugged, rolled his eyes, and returned to his omelet. "Gates?" she said tentatively.

"Yes, for the front entrance. You remember, we talked about it earlier. We could have them made, but I'd much rather have antiques. Something ornate and lordly . . . Is there any description of them in the paper, Charlie?"

"The word 'ornate' appears." He smiled fondly at her. "What do you say, Emmie? We'll have to leave earlier than we had planned."

"No problem, dearest. Andy said he'd house-sit this weekend . . . Andy? Andy!"

Her son's mouth had fallen open. He closed it and cleared his throat. "Uh—Ma—"

"You promised!"

"I said I'd try. Something's come up."

"Something in skirts, no doubt," Charles said.

"Most of them wear jeans," Emily murmured, cutting short her son's indignant protest. "Can't you bring her here, Andy?"

"Dammit, Ma, this is a business matter! I have to go to Richmond. Why don't you ask Mary Jo?"

"I suppose we could try. It's awfully short notice, though, and she doesn't like staying out here alone."

"This is most inconsiderate of you, Andrew," Charles said severely. "The animals can't go unattended for three days, even if we were willing to leave the house empty so long."

The only thing that made Diana hesitate was the miraculous serendipity of the opening. She cleared her throat. "I'd be more than happy to stay. Of course you don't know me—"

"We do now," Emily said, smiling at her. "It's a perfect solution; you'll be spending all the daylight hours here anyway, and it's silly for you to drive back and forth every day and sit alone in a motel all evening. But are you sure you wouldn't be nervous? They caught the firebug last year—it was rather embarrassing, he turned out to be the son of a local minister—but the house is isolated, and—and—"

"And haunted," said Andy in sepulchral tones.

"Andrew!"

"Stop that, Andy!"

"Oh, I don't mind silly jokes," Diana said, giving Andy a look of kindly tolerance that wiped the smile off his face. "And I'm not at all afraid of firebugs. Or ghosts."

Except one—the elusive young spirit that had brought her here.

CHAPTER THREE

What greater delight is there than to behold the earth apparalled with plants, as with a robe of embroidered work . . .

—GERARD'S HERBALL (1597)

She stood by the window, looking out into the night and straining to see what was not there—the tiny pinprick of light that would announce his presence and summon her to him. Had he received her message? Such opportunities came only too rarely. She had pleaded illness as an excuse for not attending the ball; it was an excuse that could not serve soon again, and it was so seldom that they left her alone . . . Was that a light, or only a firefly, born before its time and doomed to early extinction in the cool spring night? Her eyes ached with staring.

Standing at the tall French windows in the library, Diana blinked and shook her head. She was seeing things again. It was too early in the year for fireflies and there could be no other source of light—nothing but woods and pastures in all directions. She must have glimpsed a low-hanging star through a gap in the trees.

She had lived in cities and suburbs all her life; she had never realized how unrelieved the darkness of a country night could be. The moon was a silver sliver, giving little illumination. The humped, amorphous shapes of trees along the high ground were only a shade blacker than the night sky. It was a good thing she wasn't a nervous type. Imagination could turn that ominous outline into the ridged back of a crouching monster and people the dark woods with ghouls.

She was alone in the house—at last. People had been going and coming all day. Even the Nicholsons had delayed their planned departure for several hours. It was Charles who was responsible for that; he had obviously been having second thoughts about leaving her in charge, and he came up with one objection after another. Diana couldn't decide whether he was worried about her safety or that of the house. The list of emergency numbers he had left by each telephone included the numbers of the state police, the emergency squad, the plumber, and the company that supplied heating oil. He had shown her, not once but three times, how to shut off the water and how to restart the well pump; he had demonstrated the workings of the locks on windows and doors; he had gone into painstaking detail about the operation of washer and dryer, dishwasher and garbage disposal.

Reassured on all these counts and several others, he had finally questioned her ability to deal with the menagerie. Emily, who had watched with visible amusement, chirped, "She knows about not letting them eat mice and moles, Charlie."

Charles threw up his hands. "My dear Emily, you have a positive gift for the inconsequential. They always eat mice and moles and other objects even more disgusting, Ms. Reed can't prevent them from doing so any more than we can. How much experience has she had in dealing with major difficulties?"

Behind his back Emily winked and grinned. Diana managed to keep her face straight; with a solemnity equal to his, she answered, "I had a cat once. It was a long time ago, but I'm in great demand as a cat-sitter for my friends. My father prefers dogs. Purebreds—the larger breeds. But I was the one who took care of them. Once you've learned to poke pills down the throat of a Doberman and hold the jaws of a German shepherd while he gets his shots, you can handle anything."

She glanced at Emily to see how she was doing, and was disconcerted to see that Emily's smile was gone. She looked . . . regretful? Pitying? *What did I say wrong?* Diana wondered.

As far as Charles was concerned, it was the right answer. His solemn face relaxed. "Very well, Ms. Reed. So long as you know what you're letting yourself in for . . . These wretched strays of Andrew's always need some sort of medication. You'd better make out a list, Emily."

"I already have, Charlie darling."

Andy had taken his departure earlier, with a friend who had

come to help him resurrect his overturned vehicle. Investigation proved its condition to be beyond their skills, but they managed to right it and tow it to the barn. Andy's disposition was not improved by the discovery or by his stepfather's sarcastic remarks, but he at least had no qualms about leaving Diana in charge; taking her aside he thanked her for getting him off the hook, as he put it, and gave her his telephone number—in case of an emergency.

"I thought you were going to be in Richmond," Diana said, suspicious of this sudden burst of goodwill.

"I'll be in and out," was the vague reply. "Leave a message if I'm not there."

Finally they were all gone and she was alone. She sat at the kitchen table, watching the clock. Better wait awhile; Charles just might decide he ought to come back and show her how to turn on the stove, or something equally absurd. Had his behavior been caused by suspicion rather than concern? Nonsense, she told herself. She had done nothing to arouse suspicion, and if he had planned to set her up he wouldn't have displayed his reservations so openly.

But the minute hand of the clock had glided past another twenty lines before she went to the kitchen door. It wasn't fear of being caught in the act that had delayed her; she had a plausible, if mendacious, excuse for doing what she planned to do. It was fear of the act itself—of what she would find, or worse, not find.

The outbuildings were scheduled for demolition the following week. They were situated to the southwest, approximately a hundred yards from the house, and half hidden from it by trees and bushes. As Diana picked her way across the uneven ground she could see why the Nicholsons had decided not to preserve any of the structures. Some had distintegrated into piles of rotting wood and rusted metal. Others, constructed of modern cinder block, were in better condition, but they were hardly worth repairing.

At first glance the barn appeared to be equally ruinous, but as Diana circled it, she realized that only one end had been destroyed by the fire. One of the men at the firm was an admirer of old barns; he and his wife spent their weekends driving back roads in search of unknown specimens and taking pictures that he inflicted on his friends. Tod would have appreciated this barn, Diana thought. The beams were hand-hewn and massive, the siding had faded to an attractive silvery gray. On one side scorched timbers marked the farthest extent of the flames; the doors had never been replaced, so that one end stood open to the elements.

The only building that could be considered habitable by man or beast was the one closest to the house. Roof and windows were intact. There was even a small flower bed beside the front door. The knob turned rustily and reluctantly in her hand. The door had sagged on its hinges; it scraped along the floor as she pushed against its weight.

The windows were unshuttered and uncurtained except by cobwebs, and so filthy the sunlight was dimmed to a pale glimmer. There was only one room, plus a small bathroom and kitchenette, the latter barely large enough to contain a single sink, a small refrigerator, and a two-burner gas stove. The surfaces were all dusty but unstained; when she opened the refrigerator she saw bare shelves, without so much as a rotted lettuce leaf or smear of catsup.

It might not have looked so cheerless and cold when it was occupied, with curtains at the windows, books on the shelves, clothing hanging from the pegs behind a curtain in the corner . . . But she couldn't picture it that way, couldn't conjure up the image she sought. The reality was too depressing. I've got to get out of this awful place, she thought wildly; it's a waste of time, and worse than I expected; it's dead, decaying, just as . . .

She forced herself to return to the kitchen. Might as well do the job thoroughly, she'd never have the courage to come back. One by one she opened the cupboard doors, climbing on a chair to investigate the farthest corners. Nothing. Not even an empty match packet, or a fragment of torn label. The medicine chest in the bathroom was equally unproductive. The shelves were solid with rust.

She was on her hands and knees looking under the bed, when she heard a sound. Guilt and superstitious terror curdled her stomach. Scrabbling backward like a cornered mouse, she turned her head, and didn't know whether to be relieved or even more afraid.

"You!"

He clapped one hand to his chest, fingers spread, and opened his eyes till the whites showed all around the pupils. "Yes! 'Tis I, Sir Rupert Murgatroyd, vile seducer of innocent maidens! Sorry I don't have a mustache to twirl. At that," he added, sobering, "you're damned lucky it is me. Anyone else might wonder what you're doing under the bed."

Diana got to her feet, brushing locks of tumbled hair away from her face. He didn't offer to help her; arms folded, lean body relaxed, he remained where he was, half in and half out of the open doorway.

"I wasn't expecting anyone." It cost her quite an effort to keep her voice steady, but she managed it. "What are you doing here?"

"Looking for you. Why didn't you tell me you were staying at the house? I didn't find out till last night."

"From whom?"

"There's not much to talk about in a small town—and very little privacy."

He hadn't answered her question. But then, she thought wryly, she hadn't answered his either.

He didn't pursue it. "I could have told you this was a waste of time," he said. "We cleaned the place last fall, Mary Jo and I. Not that there was much left."

"You didn't find . . ."

"Not even a note pinned to the pillow. I told you." He shifted his weight and moved back a step. "Are you satisfied? Come on, then. Mary Jo will be here pretty soon. It's her day to clean, did they tell you?"

"Afternoon, they said."

"Sometimes she's early." He motioned impatiently and she edged past him, out into the sunshine. With a single heave of his shoulders he lifted the sagging door and slammed it shut.

Diana was uncomfortably conscious of the height and breadth of him as he towered over her, and the strength of the shoulders that had lifted the heavy door so easily. His shirt collar was open under his shabby windbreaker; a pulse beat, strong and steady, in his throat.

"It wouldn't have mattered if anyone had found me," she argued. "I'm supposed to be making plans for landscaping—"

"The inside of the cottage?"

"Curiosity—"

"Look, lady, I'm going to be in deep trouble when they discover you aren't what you claimed to be. Try not to give yourself away before you have to, okay?"

"There was no reason why you should have questioned my references—"

"Maybe not. But I'd have to be a damned fool to fail to notice your lack of experience."

"Will you kindly let me finish a sentence?" Diana demanded. Her anger was directed as much at herself as at Walt, and he knew it. His smile infuriated her; she went on, with increasing heat, "I've gotten away with it so far. I can stall for another week or so. The Nicholsons can't blame you if they were deceived too. They haven't asked me for references or for a license."

"They wouldn't." Walt's face hardened. "They trust people. People like me."

"Just keep your distance, have as little to do with me as possible—"

"Suppose you let me be the judge of what I can and can't do."

His voice was very quiet, but it held a note that made her take a step backward. A spark of what might have been amusement brightened his eyes at her retreat, but he did not, as another man might have done, reach out in a gesture of reassurance.

"Okay, it's your party," he said coolly. "I'll cover for you as much as I can, but if you really do want to protect my reputation, such as it is, you'll finish what you came here to do as fast as you can. The longer you stick around, the greater the risk—to both of us."

"I know."

"What are your plans?"

"Talking to people . . ."

Her voice trailed off, and Walt gave a grunt of exasperation. "How can you ask meaningful questions without telling them who you are and why you're interested? It's all or nothing; if you told even one person, in strictest confidence, the whole town would know within twenty-four hours."

"I told *you*."

"I'm the exception that proves the rule. Anyhow, you've made me a co-conspirator. Accessory after the fact, isn't that what you shysters call it? Point is, I'm no more anxious than you seem to be to have Charlie and Emily find out I lied to them. You don't know much about small towns, do you?"

She didn't. She hadn't even thought clearly about how she meant to proceed. She had come here hoping to find a clue, something simple and obvious, overlooked by everyone else, that would answer her questions and end her quest. Could she really have been so childish?

He stood watching her as she struggled to compose her face. One eyebrow tilted quizzically. "Tell you what. If you can bring yourself to endure my company for a few hours, I'll take you to the Fox's Den tonight. You want talk, that's the place to go."

She knew the name. It was one of the places she had meant to visit. Before she could answer him he went on, "You can't go there alone. I mean, you could, but you might run into some problems. It would be natural for me to take you out for a drink, considering our professional relationship and your—ah—personal attractions."

His last words, and the movement of his eyes from her face to the open neck of her shirt, were accompanied by an exaggerated leer. He was trying to annoy her—and she was damned if she would show he had succeeded. Besides, Diana told herself, she couldn't afford to antagonize him. He could pull the props from under her shaky masquerade anytime he chose, and he was the only one to whom she could speak candidly, the only one who knew . . . part of the truth.

"I appreciate the offer," she said. "And I'll take you up on it. But not tonight. I'm not ready."

Walt shrugged. "Okay. Maybe it is a little too soon. I'm known around here as a fast worker, but not this fast."

The only way to deal with comments like that was to ignore them. Diana changed the subject. "So it's coming down," she said, indicating the cottage. "When?"

"I was hoping to start Monday."

"So soon?"

"There's nothing there. You looked."

"Yes." Daffodils and scattered red tulips had struggled through the matted weeds in the miniature flower bed. Moved by an impulse she could not have explained, Diana knelt and pulled out a handful of weeds. Under them lay a cluster of bright green leaves, curled like hibernating mice.

"What's that?" she asked.

Her companion groaned feelingly. "If you ask dumb questions like that, you will give yourself away. Don't you even know a hollyhock when you see one?"

"I don't think I've ever seen them in embryo," Diana admitted. She pulled out another handful of weeds. The activity was peculiarly soothing. "Did you plant them?"

"No." The word fell like a stone. Diana hunched her shoulders and didn't look up. After a moment Walt said, "You'd better get a trowel if you mean to go on weeding. It's a waste of time, though. The flowers come out on Monday too."

He left without further comment. Diana continued pulling up weeds until she heard the pickup's engine start. It died into the distance as she made her way back to the house.

No one was there. The Nicholsons had been imprecise about the hour when the cleaning woman was expected; though she was anxious to meet Mary Jo, Diana decided she needed to get away from the house for a while. The desolation of the abandoned cottage, and . . . and other things . . . had shaken and confused her.

The papers on the kitchen table provided an excuse for a walk. They were tentative plans for landscaping, drawn up by the Nicholsons and by people whom they had consulted over the past months. Emily had gone over them with her, but the plans themselves were a formidable hodgepodge of changing ideas, and Emily's method of exposition had not made them any clearer. Selecting the one that appeared to be the most recent, Diana headed out across the pasture.

Wire stakes supporting small red and yellow and blue plastic pennons gave her some help in locating sites marked on the plan. A series of terraces had been planned behind the house, some supported by stone walls, one marked with a triumphant "Haha!" in a hand that had to be Emily's. Making her way down a hill slippery with damp grass, Diana realized the terraces were a necessity as well as an architectural attraction; the hill was quite steep. Unless . . . she remembered a photograph she had seen in one of the big coffee-table books of a hillside blue with creeping phlox. That would work here, with stones, individual or in naturalistic-looking piles, and paths winding back and forth. Wildflowers and bulbs in the spring, clumps of grasses and lilies in summer . . . Emily might go for that idea. And so long as the Nicholsons debated alternatives with their characteristic loquacity, the moment for action on her part would be delayed.

Diana's mouth twisted. It was too nice a day for plotting and planning. The sun was high and bright, the breeze warmed her cheeks. She took off her sweater and tied the sleeves around her neck. Through the coarse meadow grasses wildflowers had forced their way: purple violets, bright yellow dandelions, delicate little . . . little pink things. If Walt had been with her he would have jeered at this additional display of ignorance. But Diana's smile was a trifle less sour as she stooped to admire the flowers. She must remember to look them up, along with a number of other names and facts Emily had obviously expected her to know.

Some of the violets were white, with purple streaks at their hearts. She picked a few and put them in the buttonhole of her shirt. A burst of birdsong made her turn her head in time to see a flash of brilliant blue wing its way across the pasture. It lighted on a tree nearby and then she saw the box, its soft faded wood blending with that of the trunk to which it was attached. The bird vanished inside. A bluebird? She had never seen one. Sprawling suburban growth had invaded their habitat, and they had almost disappeared before concerned individuals had begun putting up boxes and protecting the nests from more aggressive birds. It wouldn't surprise her to find that Emily would support such a project, but the box looked as if it had been there for more than one winter. Perhaps Miss Musser had been responsible for the idea, though the actual installation of the boxes must have been done by . . . someone else.

She wandered on, finding signs of new growth everywhere and gaining renewed confidence whenever she was able to recognize a familiar flower. All that hasty cramming, plus the hours she had spent helping her mother with the garden, had paid off. Even in the rough meadow there were cultivated plants—the green blades of iris, the curled crimson sprouts of peonies, and everywhere, in unexpected clumps or isolated sprays, the nodding gold-and-white heads of daffodils. The quiet, inflexible persistence of things so fragile astonished her. This area was part of the old gardens, but it had been untended for years. How had the flowers survived drought, weeds, neglect? Some philosopher could find—perhaps had found—a moral there.

She followed a path to the stream, finding unexpected treasures—a carpet of violets along a bank, a hollow filled with the pink blossoms, swaying on their delicate stems like a pool of rose-tinted water—and a rustic bench, rough but comfortable, at the edge of the stream. The water had risen over the banks during the storm and then subsided, leaving a coating of smooth sand. It was crossed and recrossed by animal tracks, cleanly imprinted—the paws of dogs and cats, deeply indented hoof marks that could only be those of deer.

The flow of the sun-dappled water over submerged stones and branches was gently hypnotic. Diana let herself relax, mentally and physically. She felt more peaceful than she had for days.

A howl and a splash made her start. One of the dogs must have followed her; seeing the water he had decided to take a dip and was floundering enthusiastically in the shallows. When she glanced at her watch she was astonished to see that it was almost four o'clock. How long had she been sitting there in a half-doze? It hadn't been wasted time, though. The peaceful interval had settled her nerves. She knew what she had to do.

When she rose, the dog climbed up onto the bank and trotted toward her, dripping and grinning. Knowing full well what it intended, Diana took to her heels. However, it was a big, agile dog, with a thick coat—the kind that can absorb a lot of liquid—and a loving disposition—the kind that is determined to share its pleasures with a friend. It did not abandon her until she was liberally spattered with muddy water.

Laughing and swearing, Diana returned to the house. When she opened the back door she heard the buzz of a vacuum cleaner and followed the sound to the dining room.

Her footsteps must not have been audible over the roar of the machine, for the other woman did not stop or turn around. Her faded pink T-shirt bared thin wiry arms and her jeans sagged around her hips, as if she had lost weight since she bought them. Her taffy-brown hair looked as if it had been styled by a friend trimming around a bowl. The edges bared her ears and the nape of her neck. The muscles in her back moved rhythmically as she manipulated the vacuum with quick, vigorous strokes.

When she turned, with the same brisk movement, Diana started, but Mary Jo's reaction was even more extreme. Her eyes widened until they seemed to fill half her thin tanned face, and she let out a yell. "Jee-sus Christ!"

After a moment, shared embarrassment gripped them and they exchanged self-conscious smiles. Mary Jo switched off the vacuum.

"Sorry," she said primly. "I didn't mean to swear. Only you scared the—the dickens out of me."

"You startled me too," Diana said. "You did know I was going to be here, didn't you?"

"Yeah, sure, the Nicholsons told me. You weren't around when I got here, so I figured you must be outside doing your landscaping thing. I'm Mary Jo Heiser."

She held out her hand. The gesture caught Diana off-guard; she hadn't expected such formality. The other woman's hand was hard and strong. "Diana Reed," she said. "I was doing my thing, or trying to; one of the dogs followed me down to the stream and shook himself all over me. I'm sorry if I dripped on your clean floor."

"It's a hopeless cause around here anyhow," Mary Jo said ruefully. "The damn—excuse me—the dogs track mud in all the time, and the cats shed like fury."

"You don't have to apologize for a little damn."

"I'm trying to clean up my mouth. You get in the habit of cussing everything if you have a family like mine, but it doesn't make a good impression."

Her hand moved tentatively toward the switch. "I'm interfering with your work," Diana said. "I'm going to get out of these muddy pants and then have a snack. I forgot to eat lunch."

The other woman's polite smile widened into a grin that rounded her thin cheeks and warmed her cool gray eyes. "You don't have to warn me of your every move. I'm not going to scream out loud every time I set eyes on you."

"I was just going to ask if you'd had lunch. Can I make you a sandwich or something?"

"Thanks, but I don't have time. I have a night job, so I have to be through here by six."

"Such energy. When do you find time to study?"

Mary Jo stared at her. "How did you know I . . . Oh, of course— Mrs. Nicholson. She's quite a talker. What else did she tell you?"

It was not from Emily that Diana had heard of Mary Jo's academic aspirations; she cursed her loose tongue and thanked God for being, in this case at least, on the side of the wicked. "She admires you very much. It can't be easy working your way, with tuition as high as it is these days."

"She's been very supportive," Mary Jo said. "Mr. Nicholson too. They offered to lend me the money. I couldn't do that, of course." Her chin, naturally protuberant, jutted out still farther.

"Could you let me make you a sandwich?"

Mary Jo laughed. "Well—I guess I could take five minutes."

"Especially if I get the hell out of your way. Give me a quarter of an hour."

After she had changed and washed—the dog's shower bath had left freckles of mud even on her face—she went to the kitchen, accompanied by a hopeful entourage of cats. They sat in front of the refrigerator meowing imperatively; several of the bolder ones jumped onto the counter and tried to take pieces of chicken breast out of her hand as she put them between pieces of bread. "Mayo or mustard?" she asked, as Mary Jo entered.

"Mayo, please. Hold the cat hairs." She cleared the counter of cats with a sweep of her arm, scooped up a double handful of offenders, thrust them out the door and slammed it in their outraged faces.

"How did you do that?" Diana asked in amused respect.

"Takes practice. And a firm hand. I like cats, but not in my food." She went to the refrigerator and got out a bottle of milk, moving with the brisk efficiency of a woman who has no time to waste. Nor does she, Diana thought. Holding down God knows how many jobs, trying to keep up with classwork . . .

A thought occurred to her, and she voiced it aloud. "I hope I didn't do you out of a job by house-sitting this weekend."

Bluntness obviously suited Mary Jo. "I could use the money, sure. But I wouldn't stay here alone at night for . . . well, a whole semester's tuition might do it."

"Why? You don't strike me as a timid woman."

Mary Jo waved the milk carton at her; Diana nodded, and Mary Jo poured a second glass. They sat down. Mary Jo took a bite of her sandwich. At first Diana thought she was trying to avoid answering the question. As she was to learn, Mary Jo didn't avoid issues. If she chose not to answer a question, she would say so. After chewing in thoughtful silence she swallowed, and then said, "It's hard to put it in words. You'd think I was nuts."

"I doubt it."

"I'm not scared of much," Mary Jo said. "Bats or mice or snakes or burglars—or rapists. A guy tried once. They had to take him to the emergency room."

"What did you do to him?"

Mary Jo told her. Diana winced and grinned. "Congratulations."

"He had it coming. There's not much of that kind of thing around here," Mary Jo added calmly. "You'd be pretty safe anywhere, even in the Fox's Den on Saturday night." She laughed. "Embarrassed, uncomfortable, mad as hell, but safe."

"Oh?"

But Mary Jo did not pursue the subject. She was eating quickly and neatly and, Diana realized, trying to find a way to answer the original question. Finally she said, "I couldn't sleep. I kept seeing things out of the corner of my eye and—and not quite hearing sounds, if that makes sense."

"It may not make sense, but it certainly makes a strong impression."

Mary Jo's lips tightened. "Now you're going to think I want to scare you."

"No. If you were trying to scare me, you'd be more explicit. Levitating furniture and ghostly forms—"

"Clanking chains and moaning in the dark," Mary Jo finished. Her lips relaxed into a smile. "Nothing like that. I could have handled traditional spooks more easily than . . . Hell, there I go again. Pay no attention. The last thing I want to do is discourage you, because I'd have been stuck with the job if you hadn't been here. I wouldn't refuse the Nicholsons anything they asked, they've been so nice to me. I didn't tell them what I told you. Can't imagine why I did tell you. You must think I'm a neurotic nitwit."

"There are a number of rational explanations for your experience," Diana said.

"Yeah, yeah, I know." Mary Jo glanced at the clock and jumped up. "I'd better get cracking. Just forget what I said, okay?"

It wasn't possible for Diana to forget it, or to think Mary Jo had invented the story. Its very vagueness testified to its having been a genuinely disturbing personal experience, of the sort that is impossible to communicate in words. Watching from a discreet distance as Mary Jo dashed around finishing her chores, Diana realized the other woman was uncomfortable in the house even in daylight.

They didn't speak again except for an exchange of good-byes when Mary Jo left. Diana stood at the open door watching as Mary Jo got into her car. It was almost as old and decrepit as the one Andy had wrecked, but not even that uncritical collector would have used the word "vintage" to describe it. It was just old—and undoubtedly the only kind Mary Jo could afford. It was not a luxury for her, it was a necessity; she couldn't get to her innumerable jobs or to class without it.

As Diana moved around the house locking doors and windows, feeding animals, and doing other necessary chores, the darkness outside deepened and she waited, with almost clinical curiosity, for an outbreak of haunted-house syndrome. The phenomenon occurred among medical students, she had been told, when they suddenly developed all the symptoms of the disease they had been studying. But though she delayed turning on lights and deliberately tried to remember the plots of all the ghost stories she had ever read—like poking at a tooth to see if it still hurt—there was not the slightest twinge of uneasiness in her mind. The house seemed to close welcoming arms around her. She lingered by the French windows until darkness was complete, and failed utterly to conjure up the demons she had half-expected. The air was sweet and cool, the velvet sky held more stars than she had ever seen. The trees on the ridge didn't look anything like a dragon. Even the (imagined?) twinkle of light had seemed friendly—like something sparking a brief greeting.

She closed the windows and shot the heavy bolts into place, but she did not draw the draperies. Nothing out there but cute little bunny rabbits and harmless deer, Emily had said—if not quite in those words.

Turning from the window, she stumbled over a fat furry form and had to catch at the back of a chair to keep from falling. The dog—one of Andy's strays, she supposed, since no one else could have been moved to adopt a creature that looked like a mixture of Airedale and dachshund—let out a high-pitched pitiful yip. "Sorry," Diana said automatically.

Picking her way around and past recumbent animals she acknowledged that, strictly speaking, she was not alone. They were all over the place. On the floor, on the couch, on the chairs—and on the kitchen table, where they were not supposed to be. William had the grace to jump down when she made her appearance, but the Siamese only yawned insolently. She picked it up and put it on a chair, then made a simple salad and scrambled a couple of eggs. The Nicholsons had stocked fridge and freezer with enough gourmet goodies to feed a regiment for the weekend, but she didn't feel like cooking an elaborate meal.

Taking a pot of coffee with her, she returned to the library and settled in a comfortable chair with a pile of garden books.

Three cups of coffee later, she yawned and stretched and considered the pile with satisfaction. The books bristled with slips of paper marking ideas she meant to discuss with the Nicholsons. More sources of distraction—and with any luck she might find an even more helpful distraction next day. She glanced at the clock. It was later than she had thought.

An odd little shiver ran through her. She had been looking at pictures of sundials (Emily would undoubtedly want one). "It is later than you think." That was a popular motto for sundials— why, she could not imagine; who wanted to be reminded, when he strolled through a beautiful garden, that his own existence was scarcely less ephemeral? "Tempus fugit" wasn't much better, especially for people who were probably only too well aware of the rapid passing of time. Fortunately there were a few cheerful mottoes. "I count only the sunny hours," for instance. Emily might like that one.

A weird creaking sound made her turn her head. One of the dogs was whining in its sleep. Dreaming—of what? What did dogs dream about, if they dreamed? Bones, or rabbits, or nice smelly puddles to splash in?

If she had been nervous, that noise would have sent her through the roof. Strange that the house should affect a sensible, intelligent woman like Mary Jo as it did. Leaning back in her chair, Diana looked around the room.

Outside the bright pool of light from the lamp beside her, shadows clustered. There *were* sounds almost beyond the range of hearing, like the ones Mary Jo had described. There always were in old houses—and new ones. Wind in the branches outside, the mutter of the furnace in the basement, a faint musical *ping* that had probably been produced by a piece of crystal brushed by a passing cat or responding to the drop in temperature. Diana grinned as she contemplated the bodies littering the floor and sprawled across the chairs. How could anyone be nervous in a house like this?

But there was a crack in the cocoon of comfort—nothing supernatural, only the knowledge she didn't want to face. The slips of paper bristling from the books would show the Nicholsons she had been a busy little bee, but the evening had been a waste of time, an excuse to postpone the more important task. Like scrubbing the kitchen floor when you should be writing a long letter to your aged aunt.

She ought to have accepted Walt's invitation. The Fox's Den sounded like a typical small-town tavern—nothing trendy or elegant, just a place where people went to drink a lot of beer and enjoy what passed for entertainment. Blue-grass and country music, gossip, sexual foreplay of varying degrees, and an occasional fight (often resulting from unguarded demonstrations of the last). It wasn't the sort of place in which she would choose to spend an evening, but it was certainly the best possible source of information. If there was veritas in vino, there was also truth in beer.

Next time he asked her she would accept. Or she'd go alone. She could handle an amorous drunk, she wasn't the wide-eyed innocent Mary Jo and Walt obviously believed she was. It was going to be hard pumping people without giving herself away. If she could come out into the open with even one person, the job would be so much easier. Mary Jo was the obvious candidate, not just because she was a woman, though that was definitely a consideration. She had courage, intelligence, and integrity.

She also had quite an imagination. One way to get rid of an unwanted visitor was to frighten her with vague hints of danger.

Sighing, Diana gathered her books and began the animals' bedtime routine. Tomorrow she would get back to her real work. She couldn't sit here like a mole curled up in the safety of its burrow.

As she started up the stairs the house muttered in myriad voices. The treads creaked under her feet. Branches tapped at the window like bony fingers. The thud of heavy steps across the uncarpeted floor of the hall heralded the arrival of a cat—a brown tabby Maine Coon with a huge plume of a tail—who had decided to accompany her. His outsized paws had sounded like those of a tiger.

Diana read for a while and then turned out the light, squirming to make a place for her body between heaped-up cats. Drowsily she reviewed Charles's list of "Things to Do Before Retiring: appliances turned off, lights out, doors and windows locked, dogs in the back kitchen, cats in . . ." She was almost asleep when a thud and a howl from downstairs brought her to a sitting position.

It wasn't the first time a cat had gotten bored and picked a fight, just for the hell of it. The ones that had been sleeping on her bed jumped down and bolted for the door, to join the fray or to see what was going on. Cursing, Diana followed them to the head of the stairs. "Knock it off, you guys!" she shouted.

She almost dropped in her tracks when a human voice answered her.

CHAPTER FOUR

Some peoples can grow things and some peoples can't.

—ANON.

"Guy," it said. "Not guys. One guy. It's only me. Sorry. Hope I didn't scare you."

Diana recognized the voice. Instead of relief she felt a fury so intense she was incapable of speaking. Retreating to her room she slipped into her robe and returned to the top of the stairs.

Andy was sitting on the floor of the hall below. "It's your own damn fault," he remarked.

A rude reply was on the tip of Diana's tongue when she realized he wasn't talking to her, but to the cat that glowered at him from under a nearby chair. "I didn't see you, or your tail," he went on. "Why can't you sleep on a bed or a couch instead of sprawling all over the floor?"

As he stood up, something crunched under his foot. With a pained expression Andy bent over and picked up his ruined glasses. "Damn," he said mildly. "Oh, well. I don't need them anyhow."

"If you don't need them, why do you . . ." Diana stopped. The Nicholsons' habit of wandering off into intriguing sidetracks of conversation was beginning to infect her. "Never mind. What the *hell* are you doing here?"

"It's my mother's house—"

"Not yours."

"Technically that is correct, but home is where—"

"You hang your hat."

An interested gleam brightened Andy's eyes. I've got to stop this, Diana thought; next thing, he'll tell me he doesn't own a hat and then I'll start talking about figures of speech, and then . . . She snapped, "You said you were going to be in Richmond."

"I did. I was. Only I got stood . . . I mean, my plans fell through."

"So why didn't you go home? Your own home."

Andy sighed theatrically. "I felt the need of comfort from friends who love me. See, I used to work around here, when I was in real estate, and I made a few buddies, and the good old Fox's Den was one of my—"

"You're drunk."

"I am not! But it's a long way to Warrenton (sounds like a song title, doesn't it?) and the official definition of 'impaired' is decidedly illiberal. I figured I could sneak in and out without disturbing you."

"Of all the stupid, inconsiderate—"

"I didn't think you'd be asleep," Andy said, shifting his line of defense. "It's not even midnight."

"I worked today," Diana said coldly. "I was . . . Oh, for heaven's sake, why am I standing here carrying on a conversation with a man who talks to animals and breaks into houses?"

"I didn't break in. I have a key."

"Good night."

"Want a cup of coffee? It's only—"

Diana spun on her heel and stalked off.

She started to slam her door and decided she had better leave it open. The little deaf cat had not been disturbed by the noise; it was still on her bed, curled into a featureless ball, but it would probably want out before morning—or some other cat would want in.

Though she was now wide awake, she didn't want to turn on the light and read for fear Andy would view it as an invitation to conversation. Lying stiff and sleepless in the dark, she found her anger rising again. How could he have been so thoughtless? For all he knew, she might have a gun. A lot of women carried them these days. And any woman hearing footsteps in a supposedly empty house would have been justified in committing assault with whatever weapon came to hand.

Could he be that ingenuous? Or was he checking up on her, thinking he might catch her in the act of stealing the silver or entertaining a fellow burglar?

There was another possibility. Andy had lived in Faberville last year, working for a local realtor. It was through him that his mother had found the house. Did he know her real identity and her purpose for being here?

He certainly wasn't making any attempt to keep quiet now. She heard a cacophony of joyful barks as he greeted the dogs, the rattle of pots and pans from the kitchen—and finally, after what seemed like hours, the expected footsteps on the stairs. He was not tiptoeing. Her muscles tightened, but instead of turning down the corridor on which her room was located, they went in the opposite direction. A door opened. It did not close.

Eventually Diana's eyes did.

The next sound that woke her was not loud or startling. It insinuated itself gently into her dream, like a lengthening ray of moonlight or a green tendril of honeysuckle. She opened her eyes— or did she dream she had opened them? The sound had not stopped. It was a sweet sound, lilting and gay and silvery clear. Music for dancing, she thought drowsily . . .

Fur trickled her nose and she sneezed violently and pushed a cat away from her face. The music was louder, and she was definitely, unquestionably awake. Diana shot out of bed. She didn't stop to put on her robe or slippers. Andy had left the light burning at the head of the stairs; she could see her way well enough.

There was only one open door on the other section of corridor. The room inside was dark, which enraged Diana even more. He had to be drunk, even though he hadn't seemed so, to sleep through that racket. He must have turned on the radio or CD before he dropped off and then something had gone wrong with the volume control. The music was now so loud it echoed inside her head, as if a miniature musician were pounding away at a tiny instrument located in some recess of her brain.

She groped for the light switch. An antique overhead fixture bristling with bulbs blazed into life. The long lump on the bed, rolled in blankets like a pupa in a cocoon, groped blindly for a pillow and put it over his head.

"Wake up!" Diana shouted. "How dare you! Turn that thing . . ."

Her voice trailed away. The music had stopped, as abruptly as if a hand had flicked a switch.

An arm emerged from the cocoon and lifted the pillow. Holding it over his head to shield his eyes from the light, Andy blinked at her. "My God," he said, in a voice that held more awe than anger. "You really know how to hold a grudge, don't you? I said I was sorry. You didn't have to . . . Turn what off?"

Diana's eyes swept the room. It was even emptier of furniture than hers had been before she and Charlie looted other bedchambers for furniture to make hers more comfortable. The chest of drawers she was using had come from this room. There was nothing left in it except the bed and a single straight chair, which held a pile of discarded garments. No radio, no tape player, no hi-fi equipment.

Diana knelt and looked under the bed. Not even dust. She stood up. Andy recoiled, his eyes widening, as she reached purposefully for the bedclothes. "Hey! What's the idea?"

"It's got to be here somewhere," she muttered. She pulled the blankets aside, exposing a pair of long bony legs.

"There's nothing here but me," said Andy with a gasp of laughter. He wrestled the blanket away from her and modestly veiled his lower limbs.

Diana took a deep breath and tried to think calmly. Unless he was literally sitting on it, there was no sound-producing mechanism under the covers. Anyhow, the music she had heard had been crystal-clear and free of distortion. No cheap portable radio or tape player could produce such sounds. Only a CD, like the one in the library downstairs.

Andy was no longer laughing. He watched her as a cat watches a stranger—ready to right, retreat, or purr as future developments demanded. Diana turned and ran toward the stairs.

Starlight filled the library with a dim radiance. Something else filled it—a faint, elusive perfume that was gone after her first inhalation.

The absence of the spots of light, red, orange, and green, had already told her the hi-fi equipment was not turned on. She ran her fingers over the surfaces of the components. They were cool. The French windows opening onto the terrace were closed and bolted as she had left them.

She had an audience now—several cats, and Andy, who stood in the doorway eyeing her warily. He had pulled on a pair of jeans, but his feet and the rest of his body were bare; ruffled tufts of hair rose from his scalp like a ragged halo. He jumped nervously out of her way as she stamped past him, and then followed her to the front door. She turned the knob and threw the door open.

"It's unlocked!" she exclaimed.

"Sure looks that way," Andy agreed soothingly.

"Did you forget to lock up again?"

"No! Well . . ."

"Careless, weren't you?"

"I was distracted! First I fell over the cat and then you started yelling at me. What's the difference?"

"Anybody could have walked in."

"But nobody did." His expression changed. "Did they? Was there someone in the room? Honest to God, it wasn't me. You saw—I was dead to the world, out like a light."

Or feigning sleep. It didn't require that much dramatic ability. Leaving the door unlocked might have been carelessness, or a carefully planned alibi to convince her he wasn't the only one who could have engineered that outburst of music. An intruder had had ample time to steal away, taking his equipment with him, before she came downstairs.

Diana closed the door and locked it. She was calm enough now to realize that she had been on the verge of making a bad mistake— several mistakes, in fact. If Andy was the culprit he wasn't going to admit it, and unless she could figure out how he could have managed the trick she had no right to accuse him. If he believed she had imagined the sound he would write her off as another superstitious female who was too nervous to stay in the house alone. Thank God she hadn't started babbling about music for dancing and delicate, elusive scents. (What could it have been? Sweet but not cloying, unfamiliar yet evocative . . .)

She turned. Andy's expression of mild apprehension was now mingled with another emotion with which she was only too familiar. His eyes wandered interestedly from her face to her feet and back again. She straightened the straps of her nightgown and tried to look calm and aloof. "I must have been dreaming," she said. "Don't tell your mother; she'd think I was afraid to stay alone. I'm not."

"Obviously not. A womanly woman would have pulled the bedclothes over her head and screamed for help instead of chasing the nightmare down the hall." Andy smiled. "I had thought of telling her you burst into my room and tried to seduce me, but she'd be more inclined to suspect it was the other way around."

"I won't say anything if you don't."

"Deal." He wrapped his arms around his bare chest. "Geez, it's cold. Could I interest you in a cup of—"

"No, thanks. Good night."

There was no way she could get up the stairs without letting the light silhouette her body through the flimsy fabric of her nightgown. She moved quickly, with as much dignity as she could muster, but she knew Andy's eyes followed her every foot of the way.

He was gone when she got up next morning after a quiet, dreamless sleep. Lingering aromas haunted the kitchen—nothing elusive this time, only the homely smells of bacon, coffee, and burned toast. He had washed his dishes and pans, but the stove was spattered with grease. On the table, held down by a sugar bowl, was a note. "I won't say anything if you don't," it read.

The dogs had been let out. The cats insisted they had not been fed and she felt too insecure to argue with them, so she opened cans and refilled the containers of dry food. She was drinking coffee and wiping the stove when the phone rang.

"Oh, you're there!" Emily exclaimed.

"Of course. Where are you?"

"Lynchburg. It's a divine auction! There's a heap of Oriental rugs—one Chinese silk that would look heavenly in the drawing room—and a library table, and an eighteenth-century desk, and—Charlie, darling, I can't listen to you and talk at the same time . . ." She giggled. "Charlie says that's the point. Is everything all right? No problems?"

"Absolutely none. Mary Jo cleaned yesterday, and Walt came by to—uh—to have a look at the sheds." Diana hesitated. Should she mention Andy's visit? I won't tell if you won't . . . She went on, "He says he's going to start demolishing them Monday, if it doesn't rain."

"Oh, good. And you're comfortable? Sleeping soundly?"

Now that she had talked with Mary Jo, Diana knew what the older woman was afraid to ask outright. "Except for all the cats on the bed. I have to scoop out a trench between the bodies before I can lie down."

A relieved sigh echoed along the wires. "I'm so glad. Then you won't mind if we stay over till Monday? The auction is going to run late and it's a long drive."

"Not at all. Any orders you want me to pass on to Walt?"

"No, he knows what to do—and so do you."

Guiltily Diana said, "I'll check out that architectural antiques place you mentioned. It was the birdbath you were interested in, you said?"

"Yes, I adore it. Charlie hates it. So the decision is up to you. And of course if you see anything else . . . Oh, all right, Charlie! We'll see you Monday. I can't thank you enough for—"

A decisive click ended the conversation. It was not difficult to deduce that Charles had wrenched the phone from his wife and hung it up. Diana smiled as she finished wiping the stove. What a good time they were having! Old age might not be so bad after all, if you had the capacity for enjoyment those two displayed.

The stainless-steel surface of the stove top shone like silver. Angrily Diana threw the paper towel into the trash. She was doing it again—scrubbing Grandma's kitchen floor to postpone another, more difficult job. This one wasn't as difficult as the other, but it filled her with sour distaste.

She made sure the doors were locked and bolted before she began. Some of the things she meant to do wouldn't be easy to explain away if she should be caught in the act.

The bedrooms first, because that was the most dangerous part and the most distasteful. Charles and Emily had the master suite at the end of the south corridor, where Andy had slept the night before. It was not part of the original central block, but occupied the entire second floor of the added wing. There was no sitting room, but the bedroom was huge, and one end of it had been furnished with sofas and chairs, bookcases and low tables, and a little drop-front desk inlaid with mother-of-pearl. The other end of the room was completely filled by the bed. Forgetting her unpleasant task for a moment, Diana stared at it in disbelief.

The word "majestic" came to mind, as well as words like "monstrous" and "grotesque." There were crowns, and Tudor roses (she was familiar with that kind of rose, at least) and dragons—something with scales, anyhow—coiled around posts as thick as her waist. The hangings had been looped back; the opulence of the brocade dazzled the eyes and gold glimmered over all, not only from interwoven threads but from dangling fringe and the twisted gilt ropes holding the curtains in place. Images of Henry the Eighth and Charles the Second floated through Diana's mind. There was room in that bed for an entire pride of royal mistresses.

It was horribly out of period for the house and the room, but somehow it seemed just right for Emily. How she had persuaded Charles to occupy it Diana could not imagine—until she recalled the glances he gave his wife when he thought no one was looking. Perhaps he had fantasies about Henry the Eighth too . . .

Feeling like a Peeping Tom as well as a sneak, she began searching. None of the drawers in the desk or the built-in bureaus in the dressing room were locked. When she let down the front of the desk, papers cascaded onto the floor. Hastily Diana looked through them as she put them back. Bills, receipts, personal letters . . . It was unlikely that Emily would notice anyone had disturbed them. The contents of the desk drawers were in the same state of confusion.

Diana couldn't force herself to touch the neatly folded piles of clothing in Charles's bureau or the characteristic jumble of fabric in Emily's. She caught a glimpse of herself in the mirror over the dressing table and saw that her nostrils were pinched and her lips drawn down, as if in reaction to a bad smell. After a hasty perusal of the medicine chest, which contained nothing out of the ordinary, she fled from the room.

The rest of the bedooms were easier, not only because they were less personal but because they were virtually empty. One contained a rag rug and a mahogany commode built like a throne; another housed only a huge wardrobe.

One door on the north corridor led, not to a bedroom but to a flight of stairs. The air was dusty and stale; as she hesitated she heard an agitated scrabbling sound from above. Mice—or something worse? If a bat flew at her she would die. Diana looked for a light switch. She wasn't going up those stairs in dusky darkness.

She found the switch and didn't know whether to be glad or sorry. Slowly she ascended the steep, narrow stairs.

The space above was large, occupying the entire area of the central block. Expecting to find a typically Gothic-style attic, filled with mysterious boxes and bundles and a bizarre assortment of cast-offs, Diana was surprised to see that the room was almost empty. The executors of Miss Musser's estate must have disposed of the contents, for it was hard to believe that anyone could have lived for ninety years in a house without accumulating the usual collection of objects too good to throw away but not good enough to use.

A cursory examination proved that everything in the attic belonged to the Nicholsons or Andy—empty suitcases, a few cartons of china and glassware, plastic bags filled with cast-off clothing, and the like.

The search required less time than the process of evicting the cats who had followed her upstairs. They too suspected the attic contained mice and they refused to leave such a happy hunting ground. Diana chased three of them down the stairs, but she had a feeling she had overlooked a few. As she followed the frustrated felines she noticed that they and she had left footprints in the dust on the steps. She considered sweeping them, and then dismissed the idea. Clean floors and steps would betray the presence of an intruder as clearly as prints. The hell with it, she thought wearily. If anyone noticed, she would admit she had been in the attic. Curiosity was rude but it wasn't criminal.

A quick shower washed off external dust but did not remove the sense of internal contamination. It was a relief to abandon snooping and prying for a less contemptible activity.

Faberville wasn't big enough to rate a library of its own. A helpful voice at the number she called informed her that the bookmobile made stops on Mondays and Fridays, and, when Diana explained what she wanted, told her she would have to visit the central library in the county seat.

The road to the highway looked so different she could hardly believe it was the same slippery track she had traversed only a few days earlier under ominous skies and the threat of storm. Now the heavens were blue and serene. Wild blackberry vines had put out clusters of small white blossoms. The stream had shrunk to a modest murmuring brook and the humpback bridge looked picturesque instead of perilous. A haze of fresh green, like a watercolor wash, covered the trees leaning over the road like spectators at a parade.

It took forty-five minutes to reach her destination and locate the library, a modern brick building on the main street. The reading room was relatively deserted; some of the elderly occupants of the comfortable sofas appeared to be napping.

The Historical Documents Collection was on the second floor. Diana climbed the stairs and opened the designated door.

The room was completely deserted—not even a librarian behind the desk to the right of the door. Except for a long table and a few straight chairs beside it, the space was entirely filled with metal bookshelves lining the walls and forming a barrier that cut off her view of the back part of the room. After waiting a few moments, Diana called out. "Excuse me? Is anyone here?"

A thud and a scuffling sound from the maze of bookshelves beyond answered her. After a few more moments a figure emerged. It was tall and lean and stooped and appeared to be gray-haired. A second look told Diana that the gray was dust. The hair under the dust was, in fact, brown, and the face was that of a young man. He blinked myopically at her through thick glasses and then a look of pleased surprise spread over his face. Hurrying toward her he kicked over a pile of pamphlets standing in the aisle, tripped and staggered forward, fetching up against his desk with a force that sent another heap of papers toppling to the floor.

"Can I help you?" he asked. His tone implied that he wished he could, but had serious doubts.

"I hope so." Diana saw that he was blushing furiously. He was younger than she had thought—in his early twenties, perhaps— an age when exhibitions of clumsiness before a member of the opposite sex induce agonies of embarrassment. Without conscious premeditation she heard herself say, "You aren't a friend of Andy Davis, are you?"

"I don't think so. I mean—no. Did he say I was? I mean, did he send you? I mean . . ."

She could hardly explain why she had asked. The poor man was almost a caricature of Andy—skinnier, homelier, even clumsier. "Not exactly," she said. "I'm working for his mother, Mrs. Nicholson. She and her husband bought an old house near Faberville last year."

"Oh, sure. The old Musser house." In his interest the young man forgot to be embarrassed. "Mrs. Nicholson and her husband came in once in February, looking for information about the house. But her son never stopped by, at least not when I was here. I'm only part-time, you see. The county can't afford a full-time librarian for this collection. It's a crime, really. I can't begin to keep up with the job. The storeroom is piled with unopened cartons, some of them have been there for years, and people keep sending us more stuff. Most of it isn't worth preserving, but you never know till you look at it, and it takes a trained historian to—" He broke off, blushing again. "I talk too much," he said apologetically.

Diana laughed. "I'm used to that."

Her new friend grinned. "The Nicholsons? They're great, aren't they? They said they'd come back, but they never did." He looked wistful.

"They've been busy."

"Yeah, I guess. They said they were restoring the house and gardens, and wondered if we had anything about the family that built the house. I wasn't able to . . . Hey, but I'm forgetting my manners. Please sit down, won't you?"

He moved one of the chairs to the side of the desk, and after looking helplessly around in search of a dust cloth, used his sleeve for the purpose. Suppressing a smile, Diana sat down.

He knew his subject, though, and once he started talking about it he forgot his self-consciousness. From a cardboard file box he produced the only material in the collection that concerned the Fairweathers—a handwritten genealogy compiled in the middle of the nineteenth century by one of the last descendants of that family. "She was an old maid," explained the young man, who had finally gotten around to introducing himself as Louis Chaney. "And an only child."

"Like Miss Musser."

"Yes. I've never been able to locate any papers or diaries or such from the Fairweathers. It's not surprising. There are some famous collections of family papers from that period, but the great majority have been lost or destroyed over the natural course of time. And not all the country gentry were intellectuals, like Jefferson and his friends. According to one study, over half the men could read and write but less than a third of the women—" Seeing Diana's look of politely concealed impatience, he broke off. "Sorry. You're not interested in that sort of thing."

"I am interested, but I'm afraid none of it has any bearing on my present job. There's nothing about the gardens, then?"

At considerable length Louis indicated there was not. "I told the Nicholsons I'd keep looking, and I have, but so far I haven't come up with anything. There are some musty files in the basement I meant to check through, but . . ."

"I mustn't take up any more of your time, then," Diana said, rising.

"Oh, it's no trouble. I mean, I've enjoyed talking with you. I don't suppose . . ." He was obviously groping for some means of detaining her. "I don't suppose you'd be interested in Miss Musser's papers?"

Finally! She had thought she'd have to introduce the subject herself.

"What sort of papers?" she asked.

"I don't know, I haven't had time to sort through them. She left everything to the Historical Society, but they're even more short-handed than we are, so they sent them to us. Temporary loan, it's not violating the terms of her will or anything . . ."

"Of course not. I don't suppose . . . No, I couldn't ask you to do that."

"Sort them, you mean? Sure! Why not? I mean, I can work on anything I want."

That wasn't what she had meant, but she was afraid to push him. Allowing a stranger access to the papers would certainly be improper, if not actually illegal. She didn't want to appear too eager.

By the time she left, the hands of the clock were approaching five—closing time—and she had the poor dazzled young librarian committed to spending the next few days with Miss Musser's papers. He promised to call her as soon as he had a tentative index compiled, and she agreed that they should "get together" when it was done.

He escorted her to the head of the stairs and stood staring after her as she descended. At the bottom of the flight she turned and wriggled her fingers at him. He wriggled his back.

"What a loathsome creature you are," Diana muttered, as she left the building. She wasn't referring to Louis the librarian.

She drove too fast on the way home, not so much retreating as seeking sanctuary. When she saw the car parked in front of the house she was unreasonably furious against the invader of her hoped-for privacy. Then she saw that it was a dark-blue Mercedes and her heart leapt up into her throat. How in God's name had he tracked her down so quickly? However, as she drew nearer, she realized that the car had Virginia tags. Her relief and self contempt were so enormous she felt slightly sick.

She came to a stop behind the other vehicle and got out of hers. There was no one in the Mercedes. The thought of someone prowling around the grounds or, even worse, inside the house didn't worry her, it made her furious. The Nicholsons surely would have warned her if they expected a visitor. It couldn't be Andy this time, the car was new and sleek and shining.

He came around the corner of the house—not Andy, a short, stocky man walking with brisk, decisive strides. His feet didn't contact the ground, they punished it. He was dressed with a formality she had seen little of in this area—coat and tie, even a vest. A neatly folded handkerchief peeped demurely out of his coat pocket.

He hailed her from some distance away, seizing the initiative before she could do so. "Ms. Reed? So there you are. I have been waiting for some time."

Diana waited till he was within normal speaking range before she answered. She was too familiar with his technique to be intimidated by it. "Since I wasn't expecting a visitor, I won't apologize," she said coldly. "Who are you?"

"Frank Sweet." The tone implied that she ought to recognize his name. She stared back at him, unresponsive, and after a moment he produced a card. Diana took it between her fingertips.

"Counselor-at-law," she read aloud. "The Nicholsons aren't here. You ought to have called before coming."

"I told them I might drop by today. They didn't inform you?"

"No. They didn't inform you they would not be here?"

His thin-lipped mouth parted in a sudden, unexpected smile. "Touché, Ms. Reed. You're very good at this sort of thing, aren't you?"

The smile improved his appearance considerably, and Diana revised her first impression of his age. Late thirties, perhaps. He wore his fair hair a trifle long; it was thick and wavy, but he shouldn't have bothered with a mustache, she thought critically. It was too pale and too narrow to make an impression, much less a statement.

"I don't know what you mean, Mr.—" She made a show of consulting the card. "Sweet. You'll have to excuse me now. Since I'm not empowered to act for the Nicholsons in any way, there's no point in my talking to you."

His eyes narrowed. "You've got the wrong impression, Ms. Reed. I'm not Mr. and Mrs. Nicholson's attorney—more's the pity. I represent the late Miss Musser."

"I see." She studied him with renewed interest, and then remembered that she had no reason to be interested in Miss Musser's lawyer. "Or rather—I still don't see. What is it you want?"

"May I come in for a moment?"

"No." She added, in a less hostile tone, "The Nicholsons left me in charge, Mr. Sweet, and frankly, I don't know you from Adam. I'd be a damned fool to invite you in, now wouldn't I?"

He let out a short bark of laughter, his blue eyes dancing. "Yes, you would. But I doubt, Ms. Reed, that anyone would take you for a fool. Let me explain."

"Please do." Diana folded her arms.

"The Nicholsons asked me about certain items of Miss Musser's property," Sweet explained easily. "She left the entire estate to various charities, so it was necessary to consult the boards of those charities before disposing of individual items."

"What items?"

The answer suprised her. "Photographs. The Nicholsons have a fancy to collect pictures of the former owners of the house, and of the house itself, in its various stages of development. It was only this week that I was able to obtain them. I fear I may have inadvertently misled you when I implied I had a specific appointment with the Nicholsons; we country folk are casual about such things, we feel free to drop in on one another without warning."

He was about as casual as a barracuda, Diana thought—and that suit hadn't come from a country store. "It was kind of you to bring the pictures," she said. "You can leave them with me, unless you'd rather do it by the book."

"No problem," Sweet said. He opened his car door and took out a thick manila envelope. "Here you are. If you'd care to sign a receipt . . ."

"Certainly." She scribbled her name on the paper he handed her. "Thank you. It was nice to have met you."

"Likewise, I'm sure." Instead of offering to shake hands he nodded—country to the point of caricature—got in his car and drove away.

Diana let out an unconscious sigh of relief as she closed the door behind her. Sanctuary at last. She wondered what the devil the lawyer had really wanted. Even in a small town a professional man surely wouldn't make a business call without telephoning first. In any case, he had no right to prowl around the outside of the house. He hadn't even offered a specious excuse to explain what he had been doing in the backyard.

The cats collected, scolding her for keeping them waiting for dinner. She went to the kitchen, opened cans, and arranged the bowls in the places Charles had shown her; they couldn't be too close to one another or vulgar squabbles would ensue. The dogs' bowls were lined up on the back step. So were the dogs. They always turned up at meal time, no matter how far afield they had wandered. Diana wondered how long they had been waiting—it was an hour past the usual time—and what they had been doing while Sweet snooped around the house. They weren't worth a damn as guard dogs, but they usually greeted a visitor with a chorus of barks and trailed him carrying balls, sticks and bones, hoping to induce him to play with them.

She poured a glass of wine and stood by the back door, admiring the golden light and soft shadows across the pasture. Animals came and went; some of the ones who had been in wanted out, and vice versa. As the big Maine Coon pushed past her, she realized she hadn't seen Miss Matilda. The little white cat seldom went out. No doubt she was handicapped as a hunter because of her hearing deficiency. She had never missed a meal, though.

The cat wasn't in the library or on her bed. With mounting uneasiness Diana searched the rest of the bedrooms. Emily would never forgive her if anything happened to Miss Matilda. She was an engaging little creature, whose very vulnerability added to her appeal, and Emily had made a point of warning Diana not to let Matilda outside unsupervised.

The sound was so faint she wasn't sure she had heard it at first, but it triggered a lost memory. The attic! Hurrying to the door, she threw it open. With one of the piercing squeaks that passed for a meow, Miss Matilda rolled out. She must have been standing up with her front paws against the door.

She appeared to bear no grudge. When Diana scooped her up she started purring. "Bad kitty," Diana crooned. "Stupid kitty. Does she want her dinner now? Is she thirsty? Is she glad to see her friend?"

Miss Matilda squeaked. Diana smiled self-consciously. Even Andy hadn't sounded so inane when he talked to the animals.

By the time she had supervised Miss Matilda's dinner and fed herself, the darkness was deepening. Too late, Diana thought, with guilty satisfaction, to do anything outside. With Miss Matilda draped over her shoulder and trailed by the rest of the entourage, she went to the library for a quiet evening of reading and research.

Several hours later she had identified the little pink flowers—*Claytonia virginica,* or "spring beauty"—and discovered who Lady Skipwith was. The name was bound to come up again, for the lady, wife of Sir Peyton Skipwith of Prestwould on the Dan River, had been one of the most ardent of Colonial gardeners, and her gardening notes were among the few that had survived. The most famous and dedicated early gardener, of course, was Thomas Jefferson. Not only was he constantly improving the gardens at Monticello, but he filled the window recesses of his private quarters at the White House with roses and geraniums, which "it was his delight to attend." It was lovely to think of Jefferson puttering around the White House with his watering can and clipping shears, accompanied by the tame mockingbird that would hop up the stairs with him and sit on his couch, singing while he took his afternoon nap.

Charming, Diana thought, but probably inconsequential. Though with Emily one never knew what subjects might arise. She had better check the other things of which she had made a mental list during that bewildering visit to the rose garden Abigail Adams's roses, that New Zealand rose . . . Anaïs Nin? Something like that. Luckily for her, the Nicholsons appeared to have every book ever written on the subject of roses.

They were scattered around the room, some on the tables, some on the shelves. Diana collected all she could find. She had already consulted several of them—the standard works, as she had believed. Obviously she hadn't gone far enough or she would have recognized Abigail and Anaïs. One name Emily had dropped gave her a useful clue and she was pleased to find that Nancy Steen was not a rose but a writer, and that of course Emily had her book. Sure enough, there was Anaïs—Ségales, not Nin—on the first page. Growing wild along the roadsides of New Zealand, blanketing the graves of early settlers.

Roses weren't indigenous to New Zealand, or, with the exception of a few wild species, to America. Diana had known that; what she had not stopped to consider in her hurried cramming was the appeal these flowers must have held for settlers braving the wilderness of remote colonies in search of a better life. Able to carry with them only the scantiest of possessions, many had found room for a few precious cuttings from the flowers of home, had tended and nurtured them through the long journey. Almost as incredible as the survival of the delicate plants was the desire—the driving need, in fact—of pioneers for something beyond the basic necessities of life. Something beautiful, something to remind them of home.

Finally the "green dog," as she still thought of it, stood up and stretched. With a guilty start, Diana realized it was almost midnight. She still hadn't found Abigail Adams's roses or tracked down Emily's reference to rose rustlers. Graham Thomas at least she knew; he was the acknowledged authority on old roses, and she had skimmed his books.

The animals were beginning to make suggestive noises and move toward the door, but she sat for a few moments with *The Charm of Old Roses* on her lap. She had seen it before. She had glanced through it, along with many others, when selecting the books she intended to study; and then she had discarded it because it was not written in textbook style. Those textbooks she had practically memorized. She could reel off the various classifications—gallicas, bourbons, musk, moss, and Portlands; she could describe the ancestry of the modern tea rose, and glibly discuss the origin of the rugosas. What she hadn't bothered to read were the legends and the stories.

That same unconscious habit of abstraction. Emily didn't think of roses that way, she thought of them as individuals, heroes and heroines of history and fiction. She even used personal pronouns when she referred to them. "I'd love to have Charles de Mills, don't you think his coloring is gorgeous? And Frau Karl Druschki—she's the loveliest of all the white roses."

William, the pushiest of the cats, dug an entire set of front claws into her leg, to remind her of her duties. It was time for the nighttime treat, time to let the dogs out and dose the animals that required medication. Heartworm pills for all the dogs, as a preventive measure; eyedrops for one cat, antibiotics for another . . . They were more trouble than babies, Diana thought, as she went down Emily's list and cornered the Siamese, who did not like to have pills rammed down his throat. After she had passed out the treats she went around the house checking the doors and windows, and then headed up the stairs with Thomas Christopher's *In Search of Lost Roses*—another of the anecdotal books she had not bothered to read before—under her arm. Her room was cool and quiet. Propped up by pillows and surrounded by sleeping cats, she read on.

American pioneers had been as devoted to roses as their New Zealand counterparts; they had carried them across the continent and written home for cuttings. In different environments some of the old favorites carried on in an astonishing manner; one white rose, planted in Arizona in 1885, had made *The Guinness Book of World Records*. By 1968 it had spread over eight thousand square feet and its trunk measured ninety-five inches in girth. Almost eight feet? It sounded incredible, but if you couldn't trust *The Guinness Book of World Records,* whom could you trust? Smiling, Diana turned off the light and was asleep as soon as her head touched the pillow.

In the middle of the night she woke sweating and shaking. She must have cried out in her sleep; the cats were stirring irritably, and Miss Matilda crouched on the pillow, poking a cold nose into her face. The details of the nightmare were still vivid in her mind.

It had begun prosaically enough, recapping the actual event— seeing the blue Mercedes parked in front of the house, feeling the same spurt of panic . . . but this time there was someone in the car. He got out and stood waiting for her. A compulsion she was unable to resist made her follow suit; and as she approached it the stocky, fair-haired figure blurred, like something in a horror film. Its outlines shifted and solidified. He was dressed as she had seen him many times—Brooks Brothers suit, discreet dark tie, Phi Beta Kappa key prominently displayed. The face was equally familiar, undistorted, normal in its features and expression. It was when she recognized him that she started to scream.

CHAPTER FIVE

Oh, no man knows
Through what wild centuries
Roves back the rose.

—Walter de la Mare

*S*unlight sparkled on the brook and made the new leaves glow like emeralds. Diana took her foot off the gas as she neared the bridge. There was no need to hurry, even though she was later than she had planned.

She had had to read for several hours before the chilling memory of her dream faded. Now she knew about rose rustling, at any rate. She ought to have realized the rustlers must be Texans. Incredible to think that such fragile-seeming flowers could not only survive but flourish in the heat and drought of the Lone Star State; but the climate that destroyed hybrid teas in a season or two was perfect for the more delicate China varieties that could not survive northern winters. Cruising the back roads and neglected cemeteries of Texas, the dedicated rose hunters had found antique gallicas and centifolias and even flowers like Souvenir de la Malmaison, a bourbon rose from 1843 named after the famous garden of Napoleon's empress. It was thanks to them and the other "rustlers," taking cuttings from these survivors, that the old roses had endured.

The interest of the subject and the author's delightful style had lessened the effect of her nightmare. It was a variant of one she had dreamed before, and it always ended the same way—with shock and horror when she recognized the face as that of her father. She knew that their relationship wasn't ideal, but a psychiatrist would undoubtedly claim that nightmare indicated there was something particularly nasty in the woodpile of her subconscious. Maybe I should take up rose rustling, Diana thought, remembering how the book had calmed her tattered nerves. Cheaper than psychiatry, and a lot more fun . . .

She stopped at a gas station to fill up and ask directions. The young man—to give him the benefit of a doubt, for he looked no more than fifteen—in charge insisted on helping her fill the tank, though she had stopped at the self-service pump. She decided to regard this as an example of small-town courtesy rather than an expression of small-town male chauvinism. When she asked for directions, the youth's smile broadened. "Overpriced Pearl's?"

"The name I was given was Pearls of Great . . . Oh." Diana laughed. "I suppose the nickname was inevitable."

"Don't know about inevitable. 'Truthful' is more like it. Place was called Joe's Junkyard before ol' Pearl took it over and tacked on some fancy name she got out of a book. Same junk as before, but she soaks the city slickers all right. You make sure and bargain with her, ma'am. You buying for yourself, or for the Nicholsons?"

Walt had not exaggerated; apparently everyone in town already knew who she (ostensibly) was and why (ostensibly) she was there. Diana fended off more curious questions with as much courtesy as she could command, and finally managed to extract the requested directions.

Entranced by a cluster of dogwood whose blossoms hung like a snow shower against a backdrop of deep-green yews, she missed the second turn and had to go back. At first glance, "junkyard" appeared to be a more accurate description than "pearls of great price." There were certainly no pearls in evidence. Everything that wasn't rusty was broken, and most of the objects were both. A claw-footed bathtub stood next to a pedestal sink; the original enamel of both had long since vanished into the mists of time. Pieces of ornamental fencing leaned up against the walls of the barnlike structure that housed the more expensive wares—antique lighting fixtures, stained-glass windows, doors, windows, and moldings, among countless other items.

The name didn't suit the proprietor any more than it suited the merchandise. She was unmistakable—a huge woman, not fat but tall and heavily built, with biceps as burly as those of a weight lifter. They were displayed to the world by a sleeveless tank top that also failed entirely to conceal Pearl's spectacular breasts and a belly that swelled over the top of her tight jeans. She gave Diana a keen look before continuing her discussion with a young couple desirous of acquiring—heaven knew why—a pull-chain toilet, sans seat.

Diana had no difficulty finding the birdbath. It practically yelled at her—exactly the sort of baroque monstrosity Emily would adore. The pedestal had been inexpertly carved with twining vines and huge lumpy flowers. The basin, which was chipped and cracked, had a row of carved birds perched at random around the rim. They were the ugliest birds Diana had ever seen—shapeless and ungainly, with beaks like punches and legs like stumps. After she had stopped laughing she looked again. It was no wonder Charles hated it . . . but it did have a certain primitive charm. And compared to that bed, it was positively restrained.

She found a few other items she thought Emily might like, including a hideous gargoyle head and a beautiful carved column that might serve as a base for a sundial—if she could find a sundial. She was sorting through a heap of stained-glass panels when a voice boomed out. "Hi, there, stranger! Welcome to Pearl's."

Diana straightened and turned, to find Pearl's bosom practically in her face. The woman was enormous, at least six inches taller than Diana, and twice her width. She loomed—deliberately, Diana suspected. Since the view was not one she could appreciate, she stepped back and looked up.

Pearl's teeth had to have been capped. They were too even and too white to be original. Her cheeks were round and pink, her chin had a dimple. It would have been an amiably attractive face had it not been for her eyes—cold as muddy-brown ice and piercing as twin gimlets.

"You looking for stained glass? Got some great pieces. Come from a mansion over by Richmond that was tore down."

"They are lovely, but I'm not interested in stained glass."

Pearl nodded. "Wrong period," she said knowledgeably. " 'Course with Miz Nicholson a person can never tell what she wants. Electric is the word for her."

It certainly was one word for Emily, but Diana felt sure it wasn't the one Pearl thought it was. "Her tastes are—uh—broad," she agreed, diplomatically refraining from correcting the other woman and accepting the fact that Pearl, like everyone else in town, knew who she was.

"You come to pick up that birdbath? I saved it for Miz Nicholson like she asked."

Diana recognized this transparent gambit and ignored it. "No, I'm not picking it up. I told Mrs. Nicholson I'd have a look and let her know what I thought. How much are you asking for that carved pedestal?"

Pearl named a price. Diana raised her eyebrows and curled her lip. Pearl lowered the price. They continued the game for a few more rounds, repeated the process with the gargoyle and several other pieces, and then Diana said, "Thank you. I'll tell Mrs. Nicholson."

"Might be I could knock off another ten percent if you took 'em today," Pearl said. "There's a judge from D.C. interested in that pedestal."

"We'll just have to take that chance." Diana smiled sweetly. "I'm not empowered to act for Mrs. Nicholson, only to advise."

Pearl accepted defeat with relatively good grace. She followed Diana to her car. "Stop by my store sometime. It's on Router's Mill Road, couple miles north of town—regular antique shop, got some good stuff. Furniture, china, glass—"

"Thanks, I will." She had to endure Pearl's bone-bruising hand-clasp before she made good her escape.

On her way back she stopped at the convenience store for milk and instant coffee and, as hunger gripped her unexpectedly, a packaged sandwich and a bag of chocolate drops. She had a silly reluctance to use the food the Nicholsons had left—that old superstition about not eating the bread and salt of those you meant to betray, perhaps? She knew she was being morbidly self-conscious; her lack of candor with the Nicholsons could hardly be called anything so melodramatic as betrayal.

It was still early when she reached the house; plenty of time to accomplish both the tasks she had set herself. After she had eaten her sandwich (which was as stale, flat, and uninteresting as it had looked) she went out the back door. The golden sunlight and the view across the meadow drew her like a magnet, but she set her teeth and shook her head and crossed the yard toward the row of outbuildings. They were coming down tomorrow. This was her last chance to finish the inspection Walt had interrupted.

She went over every square inch of the little cottage, even shoving the refrigerator out from the wall to look behind it. Mary Jo had to be the world's most thorough cleaning woman. The dust and scatter of mouse droppings had obviously accumulated since the previous fall. It was with relief and a sense of completion that Diana pulled the sagging door closed. She hadn't expected to find anything. Now she could forget it.

The other structures had been tool and storage sheds. They were empty except for pieces of rusty broken equipment. Climbing over a pile of rubbish, she entered the barn.

One end, where Andy's horrible collection of "vintage" cars was stored, had retained its roof and solid walls. Next to the cars were piles of cartons. As she read the labels, Diana's tight mouth relaxed into a smile. Emily must have spent the winter reading catalogs and ordering everything that struck her fancy. The boxes, of all sizes and shapes, had come from the most expensive of the establishments catering to garden buffs. Some labels identified the contents: trellises, tools, a potting bench (some easy assembly required), a birdbath . . . two birdbaths . . . What the other boxes contained was anybody's guess. Some were big enough to contain benches and tables, no assembly required.

Something rustled and scuttled behind a pile of stacked firewood. Diana jumped back and staggered, barely maintaining her balance, as a rotten plank gave under her foot. High time the place was torn down, she thought, it was full of hazards. If she had fallen, she'd have landed on top of a tumble of fallen timbers bristling with rusty nails. And that nasty scrabbling sound had been too loud to have been made by a mouse. Rats? One of the dogs was sniffing curiously at the woodpile. Diana called it away. She wasn't keen on finding a dead rat on the doorstep, or having to call the vet to deal with a bite from a notoriously dirty rodent.

Duty done, she started off across the pasture, accompanied by various animals. Most of them wandered off as she proceeded; only a fat black cat and the dog Andy had brought with him on Wednesday stayed with her. The "green" dog was a quiet sort of creature; it ambled placidly along beside her and accepted the candy she tossed it with humble gratitude.

The cat did not care for chocolate; it sniffed disdainfully at the piece she offered it and stalked away. Just as well, Diana thought, remembering—belatedly—that chocolate wasn't good for dogs and cats. "No more for you," she told the green dog, twisting the top of the bag shut and putting it in her pocket. The dog understood the gesture if not the words; it collapsed, head on its paws, in a posture of despair.

Diana had brought with her several of the books on old roses, with some forlorn hope of identifying something—anything—in order to impress Emily; but instead of going directly to the rose garden she turned aside, following the path toward the glade where the tombstones stood.

Only two of them were standing. "George" had fallen again. His stone lay face-down on the brown carpet of pine needles.

Diana raised it, noting thankfully that it had taken no damage. The pine needles lying thick upon the ground had cushioned its fall. It was odd, though; she could have sworn she and Emily had been careful to rest it securely against the tree trunk. The ground under its base must be undermined by mole or groundhog tunnels.

A ray of sunlight fell across the damaged stone that stood apart from the other two, casting a slanted shadow that made the word "nineteen" stand out as if outlined in black marking pen.

Diana turned away.

She pushed her way through the gap in the hedge surrounding the rose garden, wondering what a real gardener would advise with regard to the boxwood. Even an amateur like her could see that the hedge was rank and overgrown. Could it be saved? It would have to be cut back drastically, for it was not only unshapely but far too high, shading the bushes from one side or the other at different times of day.

She wandered from bush to bush, seeking clues. Not even buds had formed, much less full-blown flowers, but experts depended as well on the shapes of leaves and thorns, and the "habit," or shape, of the plant.

Unfortunately she was no expert. Her initial optimism faded fast. The damned things all looked alike to her. They all had branches and thorns and green leaves.

She sat down cross-legged on the ground and opened one of the books. Even if all the roses in the garden dated to the eighteenth and early-nineteenth centuries, which was unlikely, there were a surprising number of varieties known at the time. Jefferson and Lady Skipwith had grown damasks and gallicas, musk roses and centifolias. Surely they must have planted the common moss rose: ". . . sparse young growth, a stem thickly encrusted with tiny thorns or prickles, a moss-like growth on some of the leaflets . . ." Diana squinted doubtfully at a nearby bush. It was sparse enough, Lord knew, and had lots of thorns. Was that a "moss-like growth?"

The hell with the experts, Diana thought. She'd be willing to bet none of them could identify a rose without a flower either. This was a waste of time. But the sun was warm on her bare head and she read on, increasingly entranced, as Emily had been, by the sheer romance of the old roses. Surely no other flower had accumulated such a rich and ancient tradition.

Some of them could trace their histories back, not for centuries but for millennia. The night before she had read of the wreaths found in Egyptian tombs. Those withered blossoms had been plucked four thousand years ago, but when they were put into warm water the buds opened rose-pink petals. Someone had even identified the variety: *Rosa richardii,* called "the Rose of the Tombs" or the "Holy Rose of Abyssinia" because it had flourished in the Christian cemeteries of Ethiopia for countless ages. (Emily would certainly want that one.) The Persian musk rose, cultivated for its perfume, had arrived in England in 1513; Shakespeare mentioned it in *A Midsummer Night's Dream,* and it was a favorite scent of Elizabethan dandies—because, one authority had suggested, it was reminiscent of the smell of the rutting musk stag. One could well believe that, knowing the Elizabethans.

Emily's Autumn Damask, whose double spring had been memorialized by the Romans, was another rose cherished for its scent as well as its prolonged blooming season. Like many of the ancient roses, it had a number of names: Damascena bifera, the Rose of Paestum, "Quatre Saisons," called the Rose of Castile by the Spaniards who carried it to America. "Richly fragrant," said one authority, "with the overpowering, elemental rose perfume . . ."

The book closed as her fingers relaxed their hold. That was the elusive aroma she had caught in the dark library, when she sought the source of the music. The elemental perfume of roses.

"I went to the main library on Saturday," Diana yelled.

She had to yell—scream, rather—in order to be heard. The roar of heavy machinery and the crash of collapsing walls drowned out ordinary speech, even though the doors and windows were closed.

"What?" Emily clapped her hands over her ears and shook her head. "I can't stand this," she shrieked. "Let's go to the library."

They were in the kitchen, eating lunch, or trying to. The Nicholsons had returned a short time earlier, bright-eyed and giddy with the euphoria of successful shoppers. The crew had been on its lunch break at the time, but now the racket had begun again.

Diana had been listening to it since seven that morning, when the arrival of the machines had thundered into her sleep. She didn't like it—who would?—but the noise seemed to affect Emily as painfully as a physical attack. She fled from the kitchen, leaving her half-eaten sandwich on her plate.

The others followed her to the library. With an anxious glance at his wife, Charles went to the windows and closed them. "That's better," Emily gasped. "Now then, my dear, what were you trying to say?"

"I said, I went to the library."

"Why on earth would you do that?" Charles demanded. "Aren't there enough books here?"

"Now, Charlie, don't be rude." Emily's hands fluttered, as if she were trying not to clap them over her ears. "She has a perfect right to go anywhere she likes. We didn't expect her to stay here every instant minute."

"I did not mean to imply anything of the sort," Charles said. "Nor question her activities."

"Then why did you ask?"

Diana felt like an enfeebled salmon trying to swim upstream against the current of the Nicholsons' speech. She began, "I was looking—"

"I expect she was looking for documents relating to the house and gardens," Emily explained. "She'd be interested in the family, after seeing the tombstones. And it would be lovely if we could find something like Lady Skipwith's diary, or Jefferson's letters and notes."

"We've already looked," Charles said. "Asked, I should say. The young man in charge of the archives told us—"

"Do be quiet, Charlie darling." Emily's tone was unusually sharp. "I don't know how you expect the poor girl to get a word in edgewise. You keep interrupting and asking questions, but you don't let her answer."

Charles looked as if he were choking, but he closed his mouth and remained silent. Both of them looked expectantly at Diana.

"Uh," she said.

"There, you see?" Emily exclaimed. "She's forgotten what she wanted to say. You went to the library, Diana . . . and?"

It was now or never, before they started up again. Diana said quickly, "The librarian was very pleasant. He remembered you and said he'd looked for the information you wanted, but so far he hadn't found anything. There is a genealogy—"

"Yes, we have a copy of that," Charles said impatiently. "For what it's worth. I didn't expect he would bother to look further."

"Now, Charlie, that's unfair. You know that funding for historical and cultural research is totally inadequate. He seemed most conscientious." Emily tilted her head and studied Diana with amused curiosity. "I have a feeling he may be even more conscientious now. He was very pleasant, was he, my dear?"

"You're embarrassing her," Charles grunted.

"No, I'm not. Am I, Diana?"

"He's promised to look through Miss Musser's papers," Diana said. "The library has just now gotten possession of them."

"What's the point of that?" Charles demanded. "It's the earlier occupants of the house we—"

"You never know," Emily said hopefully. "The old lady was a quintessential pack rat; Andy said the house was absolutely crammed with things when he first inspected it. They had to haul away truckloads of old newspapers and miscellaneous junk before they could put it on the market, and when they auctioned off the rest of the things, it took two whole weekends."

"That's true," Charles admitted. "It's possible that she had acquired or inherited material that belonged to earlier owners. I retract my implied criticism, Diana, but it seems to me unlikely that the young man will keep his promise if he's as overworked as he claims."

"I had thought of offering to help him," Diana said. "I don't imagine he'd object to a willing volunteer."

"No, I don't imagine he would," Emily murmured with a knowing smile.

"On my own time, of course," Diana added, as Charles fixed her with a considering gaze.

"What you do with your own time is your business," he said.

"But Charlie, we can't let her—" A particularly reverberant crash made Emily cringe. "What in heaven's name was that? This is worse than I anticipated. I wish I could go away and not come back till it's over."

The French doors rattled and a face could be seen pressed against the glass. Its broad grin and flattened nose gave it a clownlike expression. Charles gestured; Walt opened the door and came in, whipping off his cap, as he always did in Emily's presence.

"I didn't realize you were back," he said. "Figured you'd be driving a rental van filled with junk and ask the boys to help you unload."

"The junk is on the way." Emily brightened; the noise had diminished, with only the growl of a bulldozer to be heard. "We got the gates, Walt; wait till you see them, they're wonderful! Now you and Diana can start on the stone wall."

Walt pushed his cap to the back of his head. "You mean you want me to stop what I'm doing out back and—"

"No, of course not! Goodness, Walt, we've been over this a dozen times."

"Yes, ma'am," Walt said meekly. "Only you do keep changing your mind."

"She isn't going to change her mind this time," Charles announced. "We'll stick to the plans we drew up last month. The terraces at the back, the pond and waterfall, the pergola and the gazebo. Speed is of the essence, young man. Put off your other clients, hire all the men you need, but get this job done!"

"I don't have that many other clients," Walt admitted. "Times are tough. Plenty of guys out of work . . . Okay, Charles. I'll hire a second crew. It'll cost you, though."

"Fair enough. Now, then. Did you want to ask something or did you just drop by for a chat?"

His brusque voice didn't intimidate Walt. "I've got all the buildings down except the barn. You never did decide whether to demolish it or repair what's left of it."

"I'll come out and have a look," Charles said. "Diana?"

It wasn't a question, despite the rising inflection; it was an order. Diana went.

Four hours had produced a drastic and demoralizing change. The old sheds were shapeless heaps of rubble, and the bulldozers had cut wide swaths through the yard.

"What do you think?" Walt asked, as they contemplated the chaos.

He avoided looking at Diana, but Charles had no reason to suppose she would not have an informed opinion, and he promptly requested one. Feeling like a tightrope walker with two sprained ankles, Diana mentioned an idea she had seen in one of the books in the library and, as she had hoped, Charles took it up and ran off with it, in typical style. "You're right, what's left of the barn would be easier to repair than replace. It's very solidly built. Tart it up a bit, with weather vanes and doodads of the sort my wife unfortunately cherishes, and it could serve as a toolshed. A covered walkway—Emmie's pergola, perhaps?—leading to it from the terrace. Roses or wisteria . . . Hmm. Yes, I like it. Give us a sketch, Diana. Make it desperately quaint," he added with a smile.

Walt gave her a smile too. It was quite a different kind of smile.

On their way back to the house Charles stopped. "I'd like to talk to you, Diana. Privately."

Diana's stomach lurched. She hadn't been aware of saying anything particularly stupid. That was the trouble, though. If she knew it would sound stupid she wouldn't say it. "Of course. Where?"

"This will do." Charles indicated the front steps. "I don't want Emily to overhear. You saw how upset she was."

Diana forgot her guilty conscience in concern. "Is she all right?"

"Yes, yes." Diana sat down beside her. "Physically she's fine. But hell's bells, girl, neither of us is in the springtime of youth. We want to spend our autumn years smelling roses, not exhaust fumes from trucks and bulldozers. Emily really does have a problem with noise and confusion; it may be psychological in origin, but it affects her physically. I want to get her out of this."

"I understand." Relief raised a cautious head. Was it possible . . .

"You may have wondered why we selected you for this job, instead of someone with more experience."

"I thought Walt—"

"His recommendation was important, of course. But what I really wanted—to put it bluntly—was someone young and unemployed. You could, I believed, give us your full attention instead of running in and out, putting off appointments, fitting us in between other commitments."

"I do have . . . other commitments."

"All I'm asking is a few weeks," Charles said. "If I could leave you in charge, not only of the landscaping but of the house—there are fixtures to be installed, the fireplace, a dozen other minor jobs—then I could take Emily away."

"I don't know," Diana began.

"I did rather spring it on you," Charles said, smiling. "I should have been honest with you right from the start. You have every reason to resent being misled . . . I'm sorry, were you about to say something?"

"No."

"Oh. I didn't want to commit myself, or ask you to do so, until I was certain you were the right person for the job. I felt that we were on trial, as well as you, and I can only hope we have passed the test."

His tone and manner made it clear that she had. She had thought him stiff and gruff at first; now charm radiated from every feature, and his blue eyes were as warm as they had been chilly before.

It was an opportunity she had never dared dream of. If only she didn't feel like a low, crawling worm!

"I can give you till next Saturday," she said. "I have another job, you see."

He looked disappointed, but his reply was gracious. "More than I had any right to expect. Thank you."

Emily received the news with a gush of grateful delight that made Diana feel like an even lower form of insect life. The prospect of escape enabled the older woman to accept the racket with relative equanimity, and Charles's determination to leave on Wednesday morning left no time for Diana to betray her ignorance of her profession by practicing it. It couldn't have worked out better, she told herself—as if some unseen force were on her side, arranging matters to her advantage. Two weeks was the outside limit of the time she had allowed herself anyway. She couldn't stretch her leave time farther than that.

It was also as far as she could stretch the deception she was practicing. She could fake other things, but Charles would expect, at the least, a scale drawing—plan and elevation—of the structure she had suggested. That was totally beyond her powers, and even if it were within Walt's she couldn't ask him to do it. Nor was there any reason why he should.

Charles kept her so busy for the remainder of the day and most of the next that she was able to avoid Walt. He made no attempt to speak with her alone. There would be time for him to say what he wanted to say after the Nicholsons were gone. That he would have plenty to say she didn't doubt.

Charles was a compulsive list-maker. When Diana saw the length of the list she knew he must have been planning this for some time. The electrician was due on Wednesday, to hang the chandeliers in the dining room and library; if he didn't show up by noon, she was to call. The furniture they had bought over the weekend would be delivered Wednesday or Thursday; he had even drawn plans of the rooms to show where the furniture was to be placed. The mantel in the library was promised for Monday. That meant, Charles explained, that the old one would have to be out by the end of the week.

"What's wrong with it?" Diana asked. The structure in question was of black marble, with various excrescences.

"How can you ask?" Charles sneered at the mantel. "It exhibits the worst excesses of Victorianism and none of the charm. The one we found at an auction this winter is a magnificent example of the proper period. You'll see; it has been in the hands of a restorer. Some vandal had painted it—can you imagine painting Carrera marble?"

Diana didn't answer; like most of Charles's questions, this one was purely rhetorical. He went on, "You will have observed that the present mantel is not only stylistically appalling, but completely out of proportion. It's too small. The opening will have to be widened to accommodate the new mantel, but fortunately that will simply be a matter of removing the facing that was applied to accommodate the present atrocity." Seeing Diana's stricken expression, he added consolingly, "You needn't worry about the details, Mr. Plankenhorn is an expert on this sort of thing. He knows what to do. Your only responsibility is to make certain he does it—on schedule."

"Right." Diana tried to look confident. "Anything else to be done in this room?"

"Only the drapes."

"What?"

"For the library," Charles said. He consulted his list. "Jenkins is coming a week from tomorrow. He knows what to do. Your only responsibility . . ."

"Right."

"I think that's all." Charles's eyes moved over the room. "Here—what's this?"

How he had spotted the envelope Diana could not imagine; she had forgotten about it, and it had been buried under the casual accumulation of books and papers the Nicholsons trailed in their wake as they moved from room to room.

"Mr. Sweet left it for you. He was here Saturday afternoon. I'm so sorry, I forgot to tell you."

Charles smiled at her. "Small wonder. I haven't let you finish a sentence or initiate a conversation since we got back. What was he doing here?"

Diana explained. She had barely begun when Emily wandered in; Charles shushed his wife with a peremptory gesture and asked Diana to go on. For once neither of the Nicholsons interrupted.

"Huh," said Charles, when she had finished. "Damned impertinence . . . I hope you didn't let him in the house?"

"No, I didn't."

"Good girl. The fellow's been pursuing us for months. Hopes to acquire us as clients, I suppose. I'd as soon hire Torquemada."

"Now, Charlie darling," Emily murmured. She reached for the envelope. "These must be the photographs he promised us. It was nice of him to drop them off."

"No, it wasn't," said Charles. "If you catch him snooping around again, Diana, call the police."

"That seems a bit extreme," Diana said with a smile. "But don't worry, I can handle Mr. Sweet."

"Fellow's a crook," Charles grumbled.

"He's supplied what we asked for," his wife said. "Look, Charlie. Isn't she divine?"

The eight-by-ten photograph was not a formal portrait; its grainy texture and informal composition suggested it had been enlarged from a snapshot. "Divine" was hardly the word Diana would have chosen. Even the blossoming branches that framed the old woman's figure could not soften its outlines or flatter the grim, unsmiling face. Miss Musser must have been a tall woman before age had bowed her shoulders and curved her back. She was leaning on a stick and scowling at the camera as if she detested it or the person taking the photograph. A few wisps of sparse white hair had pulled away from her slicked-back coiffure; they stuck out at odd angles around the wizened, witchlike features.

"All she needs is a black cat and a pointed hat," Charles muttered. "And a broom on the end of that stick."

"Don't be unkind, Charlie darling. She was old."

"Old age has nothing to do with it. A permanently soured disposition does. You won't look like that when you're ninety."

"I hope not. Poor thing . . . These snapshots of the house are interesting. Look, Charlie."

"Later, my dear. I want to finish my lists. May I suggest that you do the same? There is still a great deal to do before we can leave."

He stalked out of the room. Emily calmly continued to examine the photos.

"What can I do to help you?" Diana asked.

"Just relax, my dear. Don't let Charlie get you all hot and bothered; he loves organizing things. And don't worry about those silly lists of his. I never do. Charlie and I make a perfect pair, you know. I come up with a brilliant idea and then he says it can't be done and then he does it. Wasn't I lucky to find him?"

"Luck had nothing to do with it," Diana said with a smile.

"My dear, what a charming compliment! But luck had every-thing to do with finding you—sheer, blissful serendipity! What you're doing for us is above and beyond the call of duty. I can't tell you how much I appreciate your kindness."

Diana crawled away. Her guilt level soared when a series of deliverymen appeared with items the extravagant pair had bought at the auctions and at various shops along the way—all of them meant for "her" room. Charles hung curtains, Emily draped the bed with antique hangings and embroidered sheets; deliverymen carried in tables and lamps, a mahogany wardrobe, a braided rug. When the work was done Emily stood back and considered it thoughtfully. "It isn't too fluffy, is it?"

Privately Diana thought "fluffy" was too mild a word, but she would not have said so under torture. "You shouldn't have gone to so much trouble. I'll only be here another ten days."

"Oh, but you'll be back," Emily said confidently. "Even after we finish the terracing and the lily pond—and I'm not optimistic enough to suppose it can be done in less than two weeks—there's the rose garden and the walled garden to be designed before fall. That's the best time to plant roses, in autumn, and we need to order—"

"All right, Emily, all right," her husband interrupted. "Diana is a professional, she understands. The tumult and the shouting seem to have died; why don't you two take a stroll while I finish my lists?"

They left the house by the front door. Emily flatly refused to look at what was going on at the back of the house. The old apple tree had fallen that afternoon. Diana had cut armfuls of flowering branches and put them in vases all over the house, but Emily was not consoled. "It's like murder," she mourned. "That tree must have been fifty years old."

"It couldn't have lasted much longer," Diana assured her for the tenth time.

"I know, I'm being silly. But I don't want to see what's left of it."

She cheered up, though, as she began talking about the trip Charles had planned. They were to visit many of the famous gardens of the South, where blossoming was now much farther advanced. Emily was particularly excited about one private collection of old roses. "You've heard of Mrs. Bachelder, of course; I've never met her, but I've corresponded with her. It's a pity you can't come along, you two would have so much to talk about."

"Isn't it," said Diana.

Thanks to strenuous efforts on Charles's part, the Nicholsons were almost ready to leave next morning when Walt and his crew arrived. Emily kept darting back into the house for objects she felt certain they would need and Charles kept shouting, "There are stores all over the country, Emmie! Thousands upon thousands of stores, stocked with millions upon millions of items, including aspirin! Get in the car!"

Walt gave Charles a sympathetic man-to-man grin. "Want me to pick her up and put her in?"

"Not a bad idea," Charles said. "Emmie!"

"But Charlie, darling, I have to tell Walt about the gazebo."

"Diana knows all about it." Charles took his wife's arm in a firm grip.

She pulled away. Before Diana realized what she meant to do, Emily threw both arms around her and gave her a hearty hug. "Of course she does. Walt, you take good care of her. Don't let her work too hard. We'll call every other day—"

"Don't worry about a thing," Walt said, showing all his teeth.

Emily waved vigorously until the car was out of sight. Then Walt turned to Diana. "So you know all about the gazebo, do you?"

The other men stood by the trucks waiting for instructions and listening interestedly. Diana said, "I'll get the new plans we drew up last night."

"I'll come with you."

"I knew it," said one of the other men, grinning. "He's gonna sit around drinking coffee all morning while we work."

"I don't see anybody working," Walt said pointedly. "Get the rest of the apple tree cut up and loaded, Jack. I'll be out before you finish."

"Don't mind him," Jack addressed Diana. "Miz Nicholson drives him crazy changing her mind all the time and he can't yell at her, so he yells at everybody else."

Diana led the way to the kitchen. The plans were still on the table, for Emily had been revising them—or trying to, over Charles's violent objections—during breakfast. The stamp of Walt's feet following her reminded Diana of a horror story she had once read about a man with an invisible but audible monster close on his heels.

He closed the door before he spoke. "Congratulations. How did you manage that?"

"I didn't manage anything. It just happened." His brows drew together and his eyes narrowed. Diana decided to go on the offensive. "What's put you in such a rage? You knew—"

"I thought you'd be in and out, keeping your distance. Now she—they—they like you!"

"I couldn't help it."

"No?" He tossed his cap onto the table and dropped into a chair. "It's not all your fault, I guess. That's the kind of people they are. Charles puts on a big act of being tough and gruff but he's as big a sucker as she is. So now what are you going to do? Leave a farewell note on the pillow or just walk off into the night?" He saw her wince and added, with a certain satisfaction, "You're not too pleased with yourself either, are you? Good."

"I had to do it."

"I'm damned if I know why. When you conned me into this goofy scheme, I thought I knew where you were coming from. I figured this was a—a forlorn pilgrimage that you'd abandon as soon as you realized its futility. Now . . . you wouldn't be so persistent if you didn't know more than you told me. You're holding out on me, aren't you?"

That was a question she had no intention of answering, although, as the silence lengthened, she realized that her failure to reply was an admission in itself. Lowering her eyes, she saw that his big scarred hands had twisted the fabric of his cap into ugly folds.

"I'm not pleased with myself," she said. "I'm doing what I have to do, and my reasons for doing it are none of your business. And don't tell me that's not fair. Life isn't fair. In two weeks I'll be gone, and you'll never see me or hear from me again. I'll do as much as I can before I go, and when I do I'll—I'll try to let them down easily. I can always invent a reasonable excuse for pulling out of the job."

His hands relaxed. He began smoothing out the crumpled fabric, his long blunt fingers moving with the same delicacy he would have used on a fragile seedling.

"Okay," he said. "I'll go along with that. Not much else I can do now, is there? You'll have to put on a show of consulting with me. Otherwise the boys will think it's a trifle odd that a landscape designer isn't helping design a landscape, and when the truth about you comes out—as it will, sooner or later—it will make me look damned stupid or damned dishonest. I'll cover for you the best I can. It would be a big help if you could have a plan of your barn-walkway structure ready by the time the Nicholsons get back. They're both keen on the idea."

"I haven't the skill for that."

"Then find someone who has." His voice was very quiet but he snapped the words off as he would have snapped a twig between his fingers. "You'll also have to put up with some—shall we say nonprofessional?—attentions from me. That will provide an explanation, if not an excuse, for my failure to notice you're a fraud. I'll take you to the Fox's Den Friday, introduce you to the right people. We play it my way or I don't play. If you have any objections, now's the time to make them."

He had risen to his feet. One long stride brought them face-to-face, so close his breath stirred the tendrils of hair on her forehead. Diana fought the impulse to back away and forced herself to say coolly, "That depends on precisely how unprofessional you want to get."

He didn't move, but she was conscious of the sudden tensing of the muscles of his arms and shoulders. For a moment she held her breath, recalling, with insane and incongruous amusement, all the noble heroines of opera and drama who had sacrificed their virtue to gain the release of husband or lover or brother from the villain's clutches . . . Not that her case was exactly parallel.

Then Walt reached for his cap and slapped it on his head. "No more than is absolutely necessary, lady. You're not my type. We rednecks like 'em cute and cuddly and illiterate—didn't you know?"

Later, she thought of several brilliantly sarcastic replies she might have made. Watching her, Walt's thin lips twitched into a fair imitation of a smile. "That's settled then. I'm going to bust my butt doing the impossible by finishing out there before Emily gets back, though I doubt if a gazebo will console her for the loss of a friend. Where does she want the damned thing?"

As Diana washed the breakfast dishes she occupied her mind by composing cutting comments; yet in a way she was glad that she hadn't responded in kind. The words he had used—redneck, illiterate—betrayed a vulnerability it would have been cruel to attack. He was neither; and she was all the things he had accused her of being. Was it possible that his motives were as simple and honorable as they seemed? He didn't know her; he did know and like the Nicholsons. Any decent man would resent being put into a position where he had to lie to his friends.

The arrival of a truck with the famous gates forced her to stop fooling around with housework. She directed the driver around to the back, squared her shoulders, and went out.

She found Walt and some of the other men gathered around the truck, staring in consternation at the gates. They were a pair; each section was eight feet wide and six or seven feet high. The heavy iron bars were topped with a construction that included rampant lions and unicorns and other heraldic devices. They were extremely rusty.

Walt turned to her with a bemused smile. "Did you ever see anything like that?"

He was living up to his part of the bargain; she could do no less. Laughing, she said, "They look as if they came from Buckingham Palace. What on earth are we going to do with them?"

"They'll have to go in the barn for now, I guess." Walt took off his cap and scratched his head. "Show him, Jack. You'd better give him a hand unloading."

"Damn right," said the driver. "Took four of us to get 'em on the truck."

"Be careful," Walt warned. "The floor's still bad in some places."

The men dispersed, shaking their heads and grinning over this latest evidence of the Nicholsons' peculiar tastes, and Walt said pleasantly, "You want to come back and make sure I've got the right place for the gazebo?"

She spent the rest of the morning with him and never once, even when they were alone together, did he say or do anything that conflicted with the role he had agreed to play. When Diana returned to the house and Walt joined the men gathered in the shade with their lunch boxes, the answering machine was blinking furiously. She turned the switch and listened to the messages.

Mary Jo had called to ask if it would be all right if she came tomorrow instead of today. The electrician had called to say he couldn't make it this afternoon but would be there without fail the following morning. Andy had called. He was as loquacious with the answering machine as with people. "Ma? Are you there? I guess you must have left. I just wanted to say have a good time. Well, I guess you aren't there. Diana? You aren't there either? Well. I wanted to warn you I'll be dropping by this evening—I won't stay—I figured I'd pick up my dog, since I got so much flak about dumping animals on certain people. So I thought I'd let you know. It will probably be later in the evening, but not that late. It will probably be . . ."

Diana's lips curved in an unwilling smile as she listened to the prolonged monologue. He certainly loved the sound of his own voice. She wondered which dog it was he meant to take—and whether that was only an excuse for another visit.

Since the electrician had canceled and no other workmen were scheduled for that day, she had the afternoon free. She tried to think of a project that would get her away from the house and still convey an impression of professional zeal. Being around Walt made her nervous, and she was honest enough to admit it wasn't only his well-deserved contempt that kept her on edge.

Taking a clipboard and tape measure, she went out the back door. A chain saw buzzed as one of the men finished cutting up the remains of the apple tree. She paused to watch him throw the withering branches into the back of the pickup. "What are you going to do with the wood?" she asked, thinking it was time to demonstrate some authority.

Walt materialized at her elbow "The part that isn't rotted we'll cut up for firewood. Applewood makes a nice fire."

Diana nodded. "Can I borrow a shovel?"

"Be my guest."

He didn't ask why she wanted it or where she was going. She selected the lightest of the spades, hoisted it over her shoulder, and marched off.

It took her a while to locate the scattered stones Emily had shown her; they were so dispersed and so hidden by weeds that she began to wonder if Emily was correct in believing they had once enclosed a walled garden. But if they had, and if she could trace the line of the walls, she would have something to show the Nicholsons when they returned. With a ruler and graph paper, even she could produce a professional-looking plan.

She had known she would have to do some digging to locate partially buried stones, but she hadn't realized how much hard physical labor it would require. The roots of the coarse grass formed a mat as tough as braided leather; honeysuckle and brambles were knotted around the stones. Yet the work had to be done by hand, for the bulldozer would shift the stones as it removed the weeds. She hacked and dug and perspired, and gradually a pattern began to emerge. By the time she stopped she had located one of the corners. The sense of achievement this produced was remarkable.

The sun was far down the sky when she reached the house. Walt was nowhere in sight, but the other men greeted her with waves and smiles and a few joking comments about her disheveled state. There was respect as well as amusement in their voices; at least none of them could say—afterward—that she had been afraid of hard work.

Aches and pains in various muscles warned her she'd be stiff the next day unless she soaked in a hot tub, but she settled for a quick shower, not wanting to be caught in dishabille if Walt came looking for her. He didn't. It was dusk before the gang packed up and the trucks drove away.

After the sound of the engines had faded away, Diana went out the front door and sat down on the step, watching the stars winking on and enjoying the silence. One didn't realize how appalling the din was until it stopped; there was something particularly outrageous about the mechanical roar of civilization in a setting where the normal sounds were so gentle—leaves rustling in the breeze, birds calling sleepily as they settled in their nests . . .

A sharp echoing crack violated the stillness and brought Diana to her feet. She looked along the driveway. Several long seconds passed before she was forced to acknowledge the truth. It couldn't have been a backfire, there was no vehicle in sight. The crew had been gone for some time.

She had no idea whether hunting was legal at this time of year, but she would have been willing to bet the Nicholsons wouldn't allow it on their land at any time of year. And whether he was trespassing or not—it was difficult to assess from how far away the sound had come—the hunter was behaving irresponsibly. It was almost dark. How could he possibly see what he was shooting at?

She waited for a while, listening, but no other shots followed the first. Maybe it *had* been a car backfiring. Diana dismissed the subject from her mind. Now for that nice hot bath. Then she swore. She had forgotten Andy's message. With his gift for being in the wrong place at the wrong time, he would probably show up while she was naked and submerged.

At ten o'clock he still hadn't appeared, and Diana was regretting the money she had spent on fitness programs. Why hadn't one of them mentioned those muscles on the insides of the thighs? She had never known she had them till today.

She limped upstairs and started to fill the tub. Steam rose enticingly; she sprinkled bath salts with a lavish hand and stripped off her clothes.

It was with a sense of resigned inevitability that she heard the burst of exciting barking from below. Of course. She shut off the water and listened. No doubt about it; now she could hear the rattling of the chain she had put in place, and a cheerful voice calling her name.

She took her time about getting dressed. Let him wait, damn him. If she had had any doubts about the identity of her visitor they would have been dispelled by the behavior of the green dog. His howls were those of delight and welcome and he kept trying to push his muzzle out the door, which had been opened as far as the chain would allow. A hand was visible, administering pats and scratches.

Diana was tempted to give the door a hard shove, but her better nature prevailed. "Get your hand out of the way," she called. "I'll have to close the door to take off the chain."

After this procedure had been performed, she opened the door and then stood frozen. Not at the sight of Andy, though he looked so unnatural in a suit and tie she hardly recognized him. Beside him stood . . . It couldn't be a bear. It was the wrong color.

"Did you forget I was coming?" Andy inquired. "I told you it would be late evening."

It was a Saint Bernard. Or possibly a Great Pyrenees. One of what is euphemistically called "the larger breeds," at any rate. Its eyes were half closed and it looked as if it were about to topple over onto its side and start snoring.

" 'Man's best friend,' " Diana said involuntarily. " 'And a dog.' "

Andy gaped at her and then burst into a shout of laughter. "W. C. Fields? Sorry, no brandy on this one."

"I thought you were going to *take* a dog," Diana said.

"I am, I am. Can we come in?"

"I don't see how I can stop you."

The Saint Bernard stood still, blinking sleepily, until Andy grabbed its collar and dragged it into the house.

"I'm taking this one," Andy said, indicating the "green" dog, which had sensibly retreated and was regarding the newcomer with disbelief.

"And leaving that one, I presume. Your mother will murder you. If I don't do it first."

"Baby is no trouble. She never moves unless—"

"Baby?" The Saint Bernard opened an enormous mouth and emitted a deep bass bark.

"See, she knows her name," Andy said proudly. "Her former owner is a friend of a friend. A female—"

"Who?"

Andy thought. "All of them," he said finally. "Dog, friend, friend of friend. Point is, Baby is used to women. She likes women. She's been trained to defend and protect the weaker . . . Sorry. The stronger sex. So when Marcy's landlord said she had to get rid of the dog, I thought, There's Diana all alone out there, and Baby needing a good home; what could be more suitable?"

Diana looked at Baby, who stared off into space. "That dog," she said, "is in a coma. She wouldn't move if you set her on fire."

"You're wrong. Look, I'll show you. Lie down."

"What?"

"I'd do it, only this is my good suit. Besides, like I said, she's used to women. Come on, be a sport. That's a nice soft rug there—"

"Oh, all right! I must be crazy," Diana added, assuming a prone position.

With a single bound Baby was upon her. Before Diana had time to react, the dog had dropped to the floor beside her, its body pressed against hers and its massive head squashing her breast.

"See?" Andy said. "Now watch this." He advanced, lips drawn back in a menacing snarl, hands clenched into fists.

Baby yawned and draped a paw over Diana's hip. "Oh, well," Andy said. "She knows I'm not going to do anything. But if a stranger tried to get at you, she'd tear him to pieces."

"Can I get up now?"

"Why not?"

"She's got me pinned down. I can hardly breathe."

"Just squirm out from under her."

The process wasn't as simple as his impatient tone implied. Baby made no move to assist or prevent Diana's escape, and after she had wriggled free, the dog stayed where she was, flat on the floor, looking like a three-dimensional rug.

"I don't think your mother is going to like this," Diana said, brushing herself off.

"But I'm going to take—"

"So you said."

They studied one another appraisingly. Diana was wondering what excuse he would offer for remaining, since it was obvious he had every intention of doing so. Finally he said humbly, "Do you mind if I have a cup of coffee before I go? I didn't get much sleep last night and I don't want—"

"Help yourself."

Before he could ask her to join him she beat a hasty retreat, not upstairs—resuming her interrupted bath didn't strike her as a good idea—but into the library. Picking up a book at random, she sat down. Perhaps he would go away if she ignored him, pretended she was working.

A flurry of cats made her look up from the book to see the great dog pace slowly into the room. It came straight to Diana and collapsed heavily at her feet. Diana couldn't help but be flattered; most dogs would have followed the person heading for the source of food. She had no great confidence in its abilities as a guard dog, though. If it weren't for its heavy breathing she would have taken it for a stuffed Saint Bernard.

The cats settled down again, waching the dog with fixed stares. Instead of returning to her book, Diana glanced uneasily around the room. It felt . . . different. As if something else had entered with the dog—a presence that watched her with the same air of expectation as a curious cat. Watching, waiting . . . A pool of silence spread out, like ripples on water, with her as the focus. Even the dog's stentorian breathing faded.

Into the stillness the notes fell like drops of water, with the faintest of crystalline echoes. At first they were on the farthest edge of hearing, barely audible. Gradually they strengthened and shaped themselves, but still she had to strain to hear, to discern the melody whose slow beat gradually increased until it became . . . Music for dancing, light and merry.

Someone *was* watching her. Andy stood in the doorway, a cup in either hand. He had taken off his coat; the white fabric of his shirt looked faintly luminescent in the dim light, and shadows veiled his eyes.

CHAPTER SIX

Ask not why of the rose; she flowers because she flowers.

—ANGELUS SILESIUS

The music had stopped—not suddenly as before, but fading gently into the normal background noises that returned to replace it. Diana sat frozen, her eyes fixed on Andy's face, waiting for him to speak. If he denied having heard it . . .

"That's nice," he said casually. "What—"

He stopped speaking and a puzzled frown replaced his ingratiating smile. He was looking at the sound system. It was the latest state-of-the-art electronic device and when it was on, the batteries of lights made it look like the instrument panel of a jet plane.

His wits were as quick as his face was expressive. As his eyes moved from the unlit machine, scanning the room for another source of the music, she could see him calculating the probabilities. After a long moment he said, "I brought you some coffee. Hope you like it black." Depositing the cups on the table beside her, he took a chair and looked at her expectantly. "Another of your little jokes? Okay, I give up. How did you do it?"

"I didn't."

Her voice sounded unconvincing even to her.

"You're kidding. No. If you were lying you'd be louder and more indignant. Anyhow, I can't see how . . . Unless you're sitting on . . . Hey. Wait a minute. The other night—was that what you were looking for? You heard it then too?"

"I thought I did."

"Both of us thought we heard it tonight. Well, well." Andy went to the hi-fi and felt the surfaces of the various components.

"I did that before," Diana said. "They were cool then too."

"Was it the same melody the other time?"

"I think so. The same kind of melody, at any rate. I didn't recognize it."

"I couldn't put a name to it either. But it sounded familiar." Andy went to the piano. His fingers fumbled at first, sounding notes at random, and then a melody emerged. "Something like this?"

"Something like. Are you a musician?"

"I play a lot of things badly—the way I do everything." His left hand added tentative chords. "That wasn't a piano we heard, though. Those strings were plucked, not struck. Clavichord, harpsichord . . . maybe even a guitar. And yes, before you ask—I do play guitar, a little. If you can explain to me how I could hold a cup of coffee in either hand and play at the same time, I'll confess on the spot."

"It had to be a recording."

Andy went on playing. "That's the melody. More or less. The harmony's wrong. Post-Bach but pre-Romantic, wouldn't you say?"

"I wouldn't. I don't know enough about music."

"I'll see if I can track it down." Andy closed the piano and swung around. "A buddy of mine is a fan of early classical music."

"Why are you so concerned about the tune?" Diana demanded. "I'm more concerned with where it came from."

"There are several possibilities."

"Such as?" Before he could answer she snapped, "If you so much as breathe the word 'haunted,' I'll throw something at you."

"It's one possibility." He threw up his arms, cowering in mock terror. "Don't hit me, lady, let me finish. The trouble with that hypothesis is that the evidence doesn't support it. You haven't seen or heard anything else out of the ordinary, have you? Nothing gibbering at you in the dark, or throwing furniture around in classic poltergeist style? You needn't answer; you have a very expressive sneer, did you know that? Point is, the ambience is all wrong. No blast of frigid air, no sense of nameless horror—and look at the animals. They're supposed to be sensitive to visitors from the other side."

Baby's breathing had deepened into snores. The cats lay in curled contentment.

Andy shook his head. "It won't wash," he said sadly. "Pity. I've always wanted to see a spook. Offhand I can think of two other explanations. First, some peculiar acoustical phenomenon—an outside broadcast that's being picked up by the speakers in this room."

"How?"

"Damned if I know. I'll consult some of my buddies who are electronics buffs."

"You have a lot of buddies, don't you? What's your second hypothesis?"

"Yes, I do have a lot of buddies. You better hope one of them can come up with a theory because the second hypothesis isn't so innocuous."

"I'd thought of it, of course."

"And you immediately suspected me."

"I haven't completely abandoned that idea."

Andy promptly "assumed the position," bracing his hands on the piano and spreading his legs. "Search me."

"You are hopelessly frivolous," Diana said in disgust. "Thanks, but no thanks. Anything small enough to be hidden on your devastatingly attractive person couldn't produce sound of that quality."

"It could be hidden someplace else, though. Have you looked?"

"No. I convinced myself I must have been dreaming."

"That hypothesis is definitely out. We'll have a look now."

As the search proceeded, Diana decided that if Andy wasn't innocent he ought to have majored in theater. He was far more thorough than she would have been, overturning furniture to look under it, taking books from the shelves to look behind them. He traced the wires from the speakers and eliminated any possibility of additional connections. He thumped the walls. He climbed on chairs to examine the tops of bookcases.

Finally Diana collapsed into her chair and reached for her coffee. It was cold and tasted disgusting. She replaced the cup in the saucer.

"It's no use," she said wearily. "There's nothing. What are you doing?"

"Wasting time, I guess." Andy was at the fireplace. "I thought maybe a secret panel . . ."

"You've been reading too many thrillers."

"No, no. Secret hiding places are out of fashion in modern thrillers, but they weren't uncommon in houses of this period."

"That sound couldn't have come from behind a wooden panel. It would have been muffled, echoing."

"Yeah."

"It's after midnight," Diana pointed out.

"Yeah."

"I'm exhausted."

"Is that a hint?" Andy looked down at the ruin of his once-white shirt, shrugged, and wiped his dusty hands on it. Cobwebs covered his hair like the remains of a tattered lace cap, and there was a streak of soot across the bridge of his nose. "This place is filthy," he remarked. "Didn't Mary Jo come today?"

"No, she's coming tomorrow. I have to be up early—"

"So go to bed."

"I have to lock up. After you leave."

"Oh. Yeah. You sure you don't want me to stay?"

"I'm sure."

"I wasn't suggesting—"

"I don't question your intentions," Diana said. "But I'm not nervous about staying alone."

Andy brushed the tangled hair from his forehead and looked mournfully at her. "That's the trouble with this modern skeptical age. Nobody believes in ghosts anymore."

After he had gone, taking the "green" dog with him, Diana locked up and trudged up the stairs. The Saint Bernard followed her into her room. It would have accompanied her into the bathroom as well if she hadn't closed the door in its reproachful face. When she came out it was lying by the bed. She decided to let it stay, primarily because she couldn't think of a way of making it go away.

A thump and a squeak announced the arrival of Miss Matilda. She seemed to be the only cat who was not intimidated by the Saint Bernard, for none of the others joined her. Her purr blended with the dog's snores. The duet was rather soothing, but despite her physical exhaustion Diana did not fall asleep at once.

Her face must not betray her feelings as clearly as did Andy's. He had apparently noticed no change in her expression when he asked whether she had heard or seen anything else out of the ordinary.

But, she argued with herself, those quick flashes of déjà vu were not paranormal. A lot of people had them. There were several accepted, scientific explanations for the phenomenon. Andy's anti-occult argument applied to them as well; she had never found them frightening, nor had the animals exhibited abnormal behavior. Nothing in the house or out of it held any terror for her—except the fear that she would find what she sought, and prayed she would not find.

A haunted house filled from cellar to attic with evil spirits would have been preferable to that.

The rumble of arriving trucks woke her and for a few minutes she lay still, trying to remember the dream from which she had been so rudely wrenched. Something about roses, and a storm-blackened sky laced by streaks of lightning.

Her muscles had stiffened, and getting into her jeans was a painful process. Ignoring the suggestive meows of the cats, the barking of the dogs, and the shouts from outside, she concentrated on making coffee. Her head felt as if it were stuffed with cotton, and she had a deep, sincere hatred of the entire male sex. Between Andy keeping her up till all hours and Walt waking her at dawn, she had had less than five hours sleep.

Cup in hand, she went to the door, at which someone had been knocking for several minutes.

Walt, of course. "Morning," he said with hideous good cheer. "Hope we didn't disturb you."

She was in no mood to be conciliatory. "The sun's barely up. What are you doing here so early?"

"I told you I'm going all out on this job. Besides," he added, glancing at the brilliant-blue sky, "I think we're going to have a thunderstorm."

"The weather forecast said no rain in sight." Diana yawned.

"What do they know? I want to get the pond excavated before the rain starts. Got a second crew coming to work on that. Want to have a last look before they start, make sure the dimensions are correct?"

Several of the other men were within earshot. "As soon as I finish my coffee," Diana said.

When she went out, she had to dodge a bulldozer driving across the upper terrace, and a dump truck unloading top soil. She found Walt down below, at the site that had been designated for the pond. Pennoned stakes outlined its perimeter.

A massive front-loader was already in position, its engine growling, while Walt talked to the driver. "Here she is," he said. "Ms. Reed, meet Joe White. He's all set to go as soon as you tell him what to do."

"You mean you haven't already told him?" Diana inquired.

White let out an appreciative guffaw. Leaning against the giant wheel, he lit a cigarette and prepared to chat. "I see you've got him figured, ma'am. He'll tell you how to brush your teeth if you let him."

"I didn't mean that," Diana said. Much as she would have enjoyed needling Walt, she couldn't afford to antagonize him, or, in fairness, undermine his position any more than she had to. "This part of the plan was done before I arrived. You just go right ahead, Mr. White."

"Okay," said Mr. White, showing no signs of doing so. "This is really gonna be something, isn't it? Poor old Aunt Matilda wouldn't recognize the place. She'd be pleased, though, I reckon. Sure loved her garden."

"Miss Musser was your aunt?" Diana asked. "I thought she was an only child."

"You got that right. She was some kind of cousin, matter of fact. Through my mother. Courtesy aunt, you might say. Not that she appreciated me calling her that. Thought all her relatives was waiting for her to die and leave them—" He broke off, staring. "Jee-sus! What the hell is that?"

Ambling toward them came Baby, her mouth ajar and her long red tongue hanging out. Her pace was as brisk as Diana had ever seen, and both men retreated as the dog headed purposefully for her new mistress.

"It's a Saint Bernard, you jackass," Walt said. "Where did it— Oh. Sure. Andy, who else? When? Last night?"

His voice lacked any suggestion of innuendo, but the look Mr. White gave Diana convinced her it would be a good idea to squelch speculation before it turned to gossip. "He dropped by for a few minutes to pick up one of the other dogs," she said.

"And leave another one." Walt grinned and shook his head. "Charles is going to have a fit when he sees this monster."

"She's very gentle," Diana said, resting a hand on the massive head. Baby panted appreciatively.

"Yeah?" White backed off another step. "Well, maybe, but I bet nobody's gonna bother you while it's around."

"That's right," Walt said thoughtfully. "Okay, let's get at it. Watch out for the damn dogs, Joe."

"And the cats," Diana added.

"You don't need to worry about them, they have sense enough to get out of the way. Okay, Joe." Walt started to take Diana's arm, met Baby's considering eye, and thought better of it. The machine clattered into motion as they moved away. "We should have built a pen for those damned dogs," Walt muttered. "They're always underfoot. I don't suppose you could keep them in?"

"I have to let them out sometimes. And once out, they're gone."

"True. Oh, that reminds me—I'm trying to keep them, and the cats, out of the barn. Don't you go in there either. Place is full of mice and rats."

"I'm not afraid of mice."

"You're afraid of rats, I hope. I mean it, Diana—you could get hurt poking around those piles of junk. There's nothing in there that concerns you."

Without waiting for an answer he trotted off, yelling at Jack, who was doing something inappropriate with the topsoil.

The topmost terrace was now a flat surface of dirt. Diana decided to go in the front door. She was just in time to greet the electrician, who had not one but three chandeliers to install. From then on she was too busy to check on the landscapers. The electrician was a type she had encountered before; he liked company and expected sympathy for the difficulties he encountered and admiration for his brilliance in solving them.

His truck had just pulled away when another one arrived, with the men who were supposed to remove the mantel. Diana hoped to heaven the foreman knew what he was doing, for she certainly did not. A series of reverberating crashes from the library did nothing to increase her confidence.

Her empty stomach reminded her she had had only coffee for breakfast, but she hadn't realized how late it was until she looked at the clock in the kitchen. After two. What had happened to Mary Jo?

The answering machine held several messages, including one

from Andy, informing her at considerable length that he couldn't find his glasses and asking her to let him know if she ran across them. There was no word from Mary Jo. Diana was finishing her sandwich when she heard a car come to a crunching stop in front of the house. The engine sounded like Mary Jo's old clunker, and she was obviously in a hurry.

She didn't come to the kitchen. When Diana went in search of her she was stripping the bed in the master bedroom, her wiry arms whirling like the sails of a windmill. She glanced at Diana but did not stop. "Sorry I'm late."

"It doesn't matter to me."

Mary Jo unfolded a clean sheet with a vigor that made it flap like a sail in the wind. Diana went to the other side of the bed and tucked one of the fitted corners over the end of the mattress.

"You don't have to do that," Mary Jo said, finishing the other side and unfolding the top sheet.

"I'm not going to ask you to split your pay with me," Diana said dryly. "Hand me that pillow, will you?"

The other woman gave her a slight, self-conscious smile. "I didn't mean to sound rude. It's just that I get so damned tired of rushing all the time. Seems as if every time I start to get things under control, some ass . . . some jerk crosses me up."

"I know what you mean."

"Yeah, it must happen a lot in your business. Always waiting for somebody to finish their job before you can start yours. I had a paper due today and I was all set to print it out when the whole damned computer system at school went down. I had to wait two hours before they fixed it."

"It is maddening," Diana said. She stooped to gather up the bundle of discarded bedding, and Mary Jo said sharply, "I wish you wouldn't do that. It's my job, not yours."

Her face had closed down, like the balky computer. "All right," Diana said. "I'd better go down and see what havoc those characters have wreaked in the library."

It was even worse than she had expected. They had covered the furniture, but bits of debris spread out far and wide.

Her exclamation of dismay was received with a sort of morose triumph by the foreman. "I told Miz Nicholson this wasn't going to be as simple as she thought. Ran into a few problems . . ."

"I've never seen a job that didn't," Diana snapped. "What's the matter now?"

"The chimney—"

"Don't tell me the chimney needs repairs. Mr. Nicholson had them all done last fall."

"That's what I was gonna say." The foreman looked hurt. "The chimney seems to be okay. We got the mantel off all right, had to smash it up, but it wasn't worth much anyhow. See, the new fireplace opening is a couple feet wider than the old one. I thought we could tear out them old bricks, but—"

Diana's patience cracked. "I don't want to hear about what's wrong, I want to know what you're going to do about it."

What they were going to do was come back tomorrow. They didn't have the right tools, or the time to finish the job that evening. Diana finally forced her adversary—as she had come to think of him—to admit that, yeah, he figured they could get it done tomorrow, providing nothing else turned up.

In the hall she met Mary Jo coming downstairs with the vacuum in her hand. "There's no point in cleaning the library," Diana said. "It's a god-awful mess, but the men won't be through until tomorrow."

"Right." Without stopping, Mary Jo headed for the kitchen.

Diana followed. Maybe Mary Jo would let her help now. Otherwise she'd never finish before dark. It must be later than she had thought; the hall was dusky with shadows.

She found Mary Jo bending over Baby, who was flat on the floor in her usual position.

"I see you two have met," Diana said.

"Uh-huh." Mary Jo straightened, smiling. "Andy must have been here. Where'd he get this one?"

"A friend of a friend. I'm sorry, I meant to warn you about her."

"That's okay. Dogs don't bother me." Mary Jo went to the sink and turned on the water. "Would you mind opening the door? I think one of the cats wants in."

There was no question about it. Claws attacked the door, and a yowl rose piercingly over another sound, like the rumble of a heavy motor.

When Diana opened the door a streak of vibrating calico whizzed in. She stood transfixed. Hanging low over the meadow was the sky of her dream—dull-brown and black and sickly gray clouds laced with ribbons of lightning. Thunder growled in the distance. And another sound . . . What was it? Suspended between nightmare and reality, she struggled to remember.

The men were getting into the trucks. Seeing her at the door, Walt came running. "We're leaving. It's going to rain like hell in a few minutes. Make sure all the windows are closed and run some water in case the power goes out . . . Oh, hi, Mary Jo. You still here?"

Unheard by Diana, the other woman had come to stand behind her. "Obviously. You don't have to tell me what to do, Walt. Get moving, if you're so scared of a little thunderstorm."

"As always, you are the soul of grace and charm," said Walt. "Good luck, girls. If the phone and electric both fail, you can always tie an SOS to the dog's collar."

He went loping off. "Son of a bitch," said Mary Jo calmly. "He's right, though, this looks like a bad one. I'll check the windows. See if you can get the animals in."

Diana tried to collect herself. There was no need for her to do anything about the dogs; when it came to thunderstorms, they had better sense than their feline counterparts. Another roll of thunder brought the rest of them bolting toward the house. Distractedly Diana tried to count cats. It was a hopeless task. There were so many of them, and some might be inside already. She hadn't seen Miss Matilda . . .

A blast of wind lifted her hair. The darkening sky split into multiple cracks of brightness. Dream or reality? She could not tell, but she heard it again, or remembered that she had heard it—a sharp, shrill cry that must have come from a living throat. The sound of a creature in pain or fear.

She was awake, not dreaming. The wind, chill with pent moisture, touched her face. She strained to see and hear. Where had the sound come from? Somewhere near at hand . . . Then she thought: the barn. Despite Walt's efforts, the cats continually prowled the place, looking for mice. Miss Matilda couldn't hear the thunder. If she had been trapped by a fallen piece of wood, or . . . A jagged bolt of lightning crossed the sky. Automatically Diana counted. One thousand, two thousand . . . It was still some distance away. As the thunder faded she thought she heard a repetition of that pitiful cry.

Diana bolted out the door. Mary Jo shouted her name, and she called back. "I'll only be a minute."

The gathering darkness was not the clean dark of evening but a sickly brown-green. Even the air was mud-colored. She reached the open end of the barn and stood peering in. Involuntarily she ducked her head as thunder sounded again, closer, louder. As it died away, she could hear faint ringing echoes as metal surfaces responded to the vibration. The ring of metal or a weak cry? She started forward.

A hand closed over her arm. It was warm and solid and it gripped with a strength sufficient to stop her in her tracks. There was a groaning sound and a stir of movement in the darkness to her right. It came with a rush, like a black avalanche. The grasping fingers tightened and jerked, pulling her off-balance. She fell flat on her back, and the gate, forty-eight square feet of twisted iron, smashed onto the barn floor, skimming the soles of her sneakers.

When she opened her eyes she saw a face, so close to hers that the features were distorted into caricature. It seemed to have four eyes and two mouths. She blinked. The features reduced themselves to the normal number.

"Are you all right?" Mary Jo . . . that was her name . . . Mary Jo touched Diana's face. Her fingers were ice-cold. "My God! That damned gate missed you by less than an inch! I heard the crash and came running . . . You shouldn't have tried to move it. What were you looking for?"

"I thought . . ." Diana raised a shaking hand to her head. "I heard one of the cats . . . crying."

"They're all inside. Can you walk?"

"Yes . . ."

But when she stood up, her knees buckled, and only Mary Jo's thin muscular arms kept her from falling. Through the ringing in her ears the other woman's voice sounded like the buzz of an angry insect.

"God damn it!" Mary Jo sounded more furious than sympathetic, but Diana sensed the anger wasn't directed against her. "You must have hit your head hard. Maybe I shouldn't . . . But we can't stay here. Come on, lean on me."

Without Mary Jo's arm around her waist, and the support of

the other woman's wiry shoulder under her own arm, Diana couldn't have made it. In the garish, ghastly flashes of the lightning they stumbled on as fast as they could. The trees bent under the lash of the rising wind. The thunder was almost overhead. In one lull between claps Diana murmured, "Thanks."

"Don't thank me yet," was the grim reply. "I'm not sure I did the right thing. Moving you could aggravate some injury you . . . watch it!"

They managed to avoid the tree branch that lashed out at them. Diana persisted. "No, I mean—for stopping me. If you hadn't grabbed my arm, I'd have been under the gate when it fell."

Mary Jo grunted. "I don't know what you're talking about."

"You took hold of my arm—"

"You were flat on your back, out cold, when I got there. Oh, shit—here it comes. Run. If you can."

"How many fingers?" Mary Jo held up her hand.

"Three. I'm all right, I tell you. I'm not going to stay in bed—"

"Oh, yes, you are." Mary Jo pushed her back against the pillows. "You've got a lump the size of a goose egg on the back of your head and your backside is turning purple."

She was in a position to know. They had been only a few feet from the house when the rain began, but before they reached the door they were both drenched to the skin. Mary Jo had dragged Diana upstairs, stripped her with ruthless efficiency and rubbed her dry before shoving her into bed. Now she opened a bureau drawer and began rummaging through the contents. "Haven't you got any flannel nightgowns? It's turned cold, and if the power goes off . . ."

The lights flickered. "Stop fussing over me and get out of those wet clothes," Diana ordered. "There's a robe over the back of the chair."

Mary Jo stiffened. Diana wondered whether she was offended or simply surprised that anyone should be concerned with her comfort. "I mean it," she insisted. "You're shivering. And you're dripping all over the floor."

Mary Jo turned from the bureau and tossed Diana a nightgown. Without speaking she picked up the robe and went into the bathroom. When she came out, Diana was sitting on the edge of the bed buttoning the nightgown. Mary Jo eyed her critically.

"Get back in bed."

Diana suppressed a smile. Mary Jo was trying to reassert her authority, but she was at a disadvantage; the robe was simply cut, without ruffles or frills, but the rich crimson color and opulent fabric made her look younger and more feminine, and the skirt trailed like a train.

"You ought to wear red more often," Diana said cheerfully. "The color is becoming to you. The storm will probably be over by the time your clothes are dry, but if you're in a hurry to leave, you can borrow my raincoat too."

"I'm not leaving you here alone, with a possible concussion and no way of getting help if the phone goes out. Get back in bed."

"But you—"

"Get back in bed."

She stalked out of the room, holding up the skirts of the robe like a medieval lady.

Diana looked at the cats, who were sprawled across the bed. "I lost that round," she remarked.

The cats had no comment. Diana shifted one of them—the little fluffy white one who had been the unwitting cause of her near demise—and got into bed, pushing both pillows behind her so she could sit up.

Pride as well as common decency had forced her to offer the other woman an excuse to go, but she was glad she had lost that particular argument. Her head was throbbing and she felt wobbly and disoriented. The weakness was more emotional than physical. There was no reason why Mary Jo should not have spoken the literal truth when she denied having reached the barn until after Diana fell—but then whose hand had held her back from a crippling, possibly fatal, accident?

She couldn't have imagined it, or mistaken the touch of some other object for the grasp of fingers and palm. Any more than she could have been mistaken about the sudden overpowering scent of roses.

At that particularly inappropriate moment the lights went out. The darkness was so intense she could almost feel it, like dusty black velvet against her face. Then the mattress heaved under her body, and the heavy frame of the bed shook as if in an earthquake.

Every ghost story Diana had ever read invaded her mind like ugly unwelcome guests. There were dozens of reports of poltergeists, the "racketing spirits" who banged on walls and moved furniture and pulled blankets off sleepers . . . Frantically she groped for the bedside table and opened the drawer. Her fingers closed around a cold metal cylinder and she thanked God for Emily's thoughtful, thorough hospitality. After some fumbling she found the switch.

The cats' eyes reflected the flashlight beam in eerie circles of red and yellow. Beyond the limited path of light, darkness hovered. Again the mattress shook and shuddered. Diana decided that nothing on the earth or off it could have induced her to get out of bed; leaning over at a perilous angle, she directed the flashlight beam down at the floor.

A dog's face is capable of only limited displays of emotion, but Baby's showed as much terror as a dog is capable of showing. Her mouth opened and she began to pant heavily. "It's all right," Diana said in a gasp of relieved amusement. "Mama's here. No—no, don't—Baby, stay!"

Baby had responded to the command earlier but her need for comfort overrode acquired instincts. She came out from under the bed and flung herself onto it in a lunging leap that would have collapsed any structure less solidly built.

Cursing, the cats flew in all directions, and Diana tried to push the dog off her face. By the time Baby had settled down beside her she was helpless with laughter. Heaven protect the poor poltergeist who tried to take up residence in this house!

A wavering light heralded the arrival of Mary Jo, carrying a flashlight in one hand and balancing a tray in the other. She had tied a scarf around her waist to kilt up her skirts.

"That dog shouldn't be on the bed," she said disapprovingly.

"You get her off. I tried and lost."

Mary Jo slid the tray onto a table with a neat economical movement. "She's afraid of thunder, I suppose. We had a dog that kept trying to get under the sofa whenever there was a storm. Trouble was, there was only about a two-inch clearance and he was a German shepherd."

Friends again, Diana thought. For the moment. She countered with another story about dogs and storms, and watched Mary Jo kneel in front of the fireplace. The fire had been laid—another of the Nicholsons' graceful gestures of hospitality—and in a few minutes flames were leaping, lending not only light and warmth but the sense of comfort only an open fire can give.

"I had soup heated, and water for coffee simmering," Mary Jo said. "I had a feeling the power would go out. It always does in a bad storm." She handed Diana a plate.

Diana waved it away. "I'll get up. I can't eat in this bed. I always spill things, and these sheets are too beautiful to spoil."

She joined the other woman at the table. They ate in silence for a few minutes. Mary Jo waited until Diana had swallowed a mouthful of soup before dropping her bombshell.

"You're Brad's sister, aren't you?"

PART TWO

Unmasking

CHAPTER SEVEN

Enjoy life while the lamp yet glows,
Pluck the rose before it withers.

—GERMAN UNIVERSITY SONG

*D*iana felt as if an invisible burden had been lifted off her shoulders. "How did you know?"

Mary Jo leaned back in her chair. The firelight softened her angular features and gave her hair a golden sheen. "He showed me a snapshot once. When I first met you, I thought you looked vaguely familiar, but I couldn't think why. Then, when I was looking for your nightgown, I found this."

She took an envelope from her pocket and handed it to Diana.

"Funny, I don't even remember putting it there," Diana said. "Such an obvious hiding place. It's almost as if I—"

"The Nicholsons don't pry in people's drawers," Mary Jo said sharply. "Neither do I. Finding it was an accident."

"I didn't mean—"

"I saw Brad's name and the return address, and then I remembered the photo. But I had no right to take it. I apologize."

"I'm glad you did. You don't know how often I was tempted to confess to you. Now that you've read it you can understand why—"

"I don't read other people's mail."

"You mean you haven't read it?"

"I said so, didn't I? I was so surprised I just grabbed the envelope without thinking what I was doing. The names were so similar—Diana Reed, Diana Randall. Brad talked about you a lot."

"Read it. Really—I want you to."

Mary Jo shied away from the envelope as it were a snake. "All right," Diana said, "I'll read it to you."

The flickering firelight was inadequate but Diana didn't need to see the words. She knew them by heart.

"Dear Sis: I'm still doing the back-to-nature bit. It's been good here but I'm gathering too much moss. There's something funny going on, though, and I don't want to leave the old lady till I've figured out what to do about it. She's been nice to me. I can't believe anyone would do her dirt. Maybe it's my imagination; you always said I had too much. Anyhow, I'll be moving on as soon as I get this business settled, so don't write me here. I'll be in touch.

Love, Brad."

For an interval the only sounds were Baby's snores and the crackle of the flames and the diminishing drumbeat of water outside the window. The storm had moved on, trailing skirts of rain behind it.

" 'Something funny,' " Mary Jo said at last. "What did he mean?"

"I don't know. This is the last letter I ever got from him."

"He left here in August. That's eight months ago. You mean you haven't heard from him since?"

"One postcard, from New York. You can probably guess how the New York City cops respond to a missing-persons report."

"Especially when it's somebody like Brad." There was no criticism in Mary Jo's voice; she had simply stated a fact. "I wouldn't think he'd be much of a correspondent."

"Then you'd be wrong. He wrote me at least twice a month. Not long chatty letters, but he never failed to let me know where he was and how to reach him if the need arose. The police weren't impressed by that," Diana said bitterly. "They assumed the worst—which is, God help us all, the usual explanation: that he got hooked on drugs or booze and fell between the cracks—homeless, irresponsible, incompetent."

"He didn't drink or dope when he was here. People used to kid him about being a health freak."

"Exactly. But the official view was that people are unpredictable, especially when they are only nineteen. It's an unstable age, they said. And heaven knows his past record wasn't reassuring." She hesitated. She had been about to ask Mary Jo how much she knew about Brad's past record, but something told her Mary Jo would deny knowledge of personal matters; she had an instinctive delicacy that was, in this uninhibited day and age, almost Victorian.

Start from the beginning, then; assume Brad had told her nothing.

"Brad was—is—six years younger than I am. I'll never forget the day he was born; when my father came home from the hospital he got me out of bed and opened a bottle of champagne, and made me drink a toast with him. When I sneezed, from the bubbles, he laughed and gave me a hug. I'd never seen him behave that way. I loved it. I didn't even notice, then, that he said, 'To my son.' Not 'To your little brother.'

"If there had been another son . . . But there wasn't. Brad was the one, the only, and Father pushed him hard. I loved him, but I sure as hell didn't make his life any easier. I was Miss Perfect, an impossible act to follow. Straight A's, impeccable conduct, the highest LSAT scores in the state . . ."

"So you're a lawyer? Like your dad?"

The flames had died down. Diana wished she could see Mary Jo's face more clearly. Her voice gave nothing away.

"Yes. Naturally he wanted Brad to follow in his footsteps. It wasn't lack of intelligence that held Brad back. Brad . . . is . . . brilliant—far more than I, he has a streak of originality I lack. But he's stubborn as a mule, and so is Father; they came together like the irresistible force and the immovable object. Brad didn't want to study law, he wanted to be a writer. Father said that was a childish, impractical idea, and that only a person with huge amounts of talent could hope to earn a living by writing. The implication being, of course, that Brad didn't have talent.

"He fought Father by being all the things Father didn't want him to be—unkempt, uncouth, profane, lazy. He was always in trouble. When Father cut off his allowance he'd sneak to Mother and beg money from her. She'd give him anything he wanted, except the support he needed to fight Father for the right to lead his own life. She didn't have the courage for that. And—and neither did I."

Mary Jo cleared her throat. Her comment was the last one Diana had expected to hear.

"He loved you very much."

It was several seconds before Diana could speak evenly. "That's because he was too young to understand how I had failed him.

I'm not trying to excuse myself—I should have interfered, tried to defend Brad when Father abused him—but you can become so accustomed to a particular set of assumptions that you aren't able to analyze them critically. Maybe it takes more courage to break away from mistaken love than from outright cruelty. It certainly takes a maturity of insight and self-analysis that adolescents lack and many adults never attain . . . I'm sorry, were you about to say something?"

"No."

"Father's demands weren't that unreasonable, on the face of it," Diana insisted. "Shape up, study, work hard . . . He did love Brad. But he isn't . . . he isn't a demonstrative person."

"He looks like one of those Puritan judges," Mary Jo said unexpectedly. "All the lines on his face are from frowning."

"You've met him?" Diana asked in surprise.

"He was in that snapshot Brad showed me, that he carried in his wallet. Must have been your graduation picture; you were wearing a cap and gown, and you were standing between your parents. Your mom was smiling, and you were smiling. He wasn't."

"I remember that picture," Diana said slowly. "Brad took it. I can't imagine why he would pick that one to carry in his wallet, though. Well, it doesn't matter. The point is, he never seemed to hold my achievements against me, which a lot of brothers would have done. I was the one he came to when the explosion hit the fan. I was in my last year of law school and he was seventeen—just about to graduate from high school. Only he wasn't going to graduate if he didn't pass one essential course, and he wouldn't turn in the paper, and Father kept nagging him and he kept putting it off, and . . . I don't know exactly what happened. It was bound to happen, it had been building up for a long time—and wasn't that the perfect punishment for a pressuring father, to become a high-school dropout?

"He promised me that night he'd never lose touch with me, and through me, with Mother. He kept his word. He'd borrowed fifty bucks from me—it was all I had; Father paid the bills without question, but he kept me short of cash. Three months later I got a money order from Brad, for fifty-three dollars. The three dollars was interest, he said. I'd heard from him in the meantime. He was having a wonderful time, seeing the country, meeting people, making friends. He never asked me for money again. He never failed to write.

"I was in Europe, on holiday, when he sent that last letter. It was waiting for me when I got back. I was a little surprised to find only one—I'd been gone for three weeks—but he'd said he was about to move on, and I thought perhaps it was taking him a while to get settled. Then the postcard came, and that did strike me as a little strange because it was so uninformative— I'm fine, hope you're the same—but I was busy catching up at work, and . . . Anyhow, it was November before I decided I'd better go to New York and make inquiries. They tried to be kind—but they were so tired. It was just another impossible case to them, I could see they never expected to get results. They did come up with a few bodies that fit his general description. Every now and then I'd take another day off and go and look—look at . . ."

She turned her head away.

"Must have been tough."

"It wasn't seeing the poor, mutilated things that bothered me. It was the hours before I saw them—wondering whether this time it would be Brad." Mary Jo got up to put more wood on the fire, and Diana continued, "Finally, in March, I managed to get in touch with Walt. I knew Brad had worked for him temporarily, before he moved into the cottage as handyman and caretaker for old Miss Musser. I had already tried to call her, but the operator told me the number had been disconnected. Walt was sympathetic at first; he told me about the house being sold and Miss Musser going to the nursing home and dying a few months later. He wasn't so sympathetic when I told him what I planned to do. He tried to talk me out of it, but I've got a streak of the family stubbornness too, and by that time I had come to believe the clue to Brad's disappearance had to be here. It was the last place he was actually seen; the postcard wasn't his usual style, it was typed instead of handwritten, and had no return address. And there was that last letter, with its hints of something underhanded going on. If Brad had thought someone was taking advantage of Miss Musser, he'd have tried to stop it. He was a sucker for children and animals and old or handicapped people. 'The defenseless ones,' he used to call them."

"You keep trying not to use the past tense," Mary Jo said. "You think he's dead, don't you? That's why you came here incognito. You think . . . You believe someone killed him. One of us."

She had not underestimated Mary Jo's intelligence. The conclusions were obvious, but not everyone could have put them together with such quick, inexorable logic.

"I don't suspect you."

"Why not?" Mary Jo got up and put more wood on the fire. The flames flared up, illuming a face as tightly controlled as her voice. "I knew Brad pretty well. We were lovers for a while. Didn't he tell you that?"

"I suspected. But no—he never said so."

"He wouldn't." The quiver of her lips might have been only an effect of the shifting shadows. "It was only a couple of times. I needed . . . reassurance. Comfort. He gave me what I wanted. He was never in love with me, nor I with him. You've no reason to take my word for that, of course."

"Nor any reason to doubt your word."

Mary Jo's expression did not change. It was as distant and contemplative as that of a judge weighing evidence. "Passion is one of the classic motives for murder. Brad dated a couple of other women. Nothing serious—I think. You can't take my word for that, either. He hinted at another motive in that letter. If he knew, or even suspected, that someone was ripping off the old lady he'd . . . He'd confront them, wouldn't he? Give them a chance to explain before he acted?"

"You knew him well," Diana said.

She meant it as a compliment to Mary Jo's intuitive powers, but the other woman gave her a sly, sidelong look, her eyeballs gleaming uncannily in the firelight. She went on, "A lot of people had the opportunity to take advantage of Miss Musser. Including me. I worked for her when I was in high school, before she got senile and miserly. I used to drop in from time to time, to see how she was doing, or to visit Brad. I could have taken things."

"Was there anything worth taking?"

"Depends on how you define worth," Mary Jo said coolly. "You probably wouldn't be tempted by anything less than a diamond necklace. To some people a watch they could hock for fifty bucks would be worth the trouble."

"But—surely—not worth killing for."

"Depends," Mary Jo repeated. "She had a lot of stuff like that. China, crystal, quilts. She did complain the last couple of years about being robbed. But some old people get paranoid. Nobody paid any attention."

Diana shivered. "That's horrible, isn't it? To dismiss someone's fears and accusations just because they're old? Maybe she wasn't paranoid. Maybe she was right."

"Maybe." Mary Jo's voice quickened. She was beginning to enjoy the pure intellectual challenge of the game. "But I'm inclined to agree that pilfered odds and ends wouldn't add up to a motive for murder. Suppose she had something more valuable—bonds, jewelry, money—squirreled away. She didn't trust banks, she said that more than once."

"Did she ever mention losing something of that sort?"

"Not to me. Her lawyer would be the person to ask."

"He's also a prime suspect."

Mary Jo let out a snort of cynical laughter. "You must have met him."

"The lawyer is always a prime suspect," Diana said with matching cynicism. "But I have met him, in fact. He dropped by one day with a very specious excuse. I thought he was just being nosy."

"He's one of the worst busybodies in town," Mary Jo agreed. "And I sure as hell wouldn't put a touch of embezzlement past him. But how could Brad have found out about that?"

"There are all sorts of possibilities. He might have observed signs of undue influence, or caught Sweet snooping in some place where he had no right to be. Don't forget Brad had—has—a sister and a father who are in the legal profession. He'd be more likely to notice something out of the way than the average person."

"Good point. So Sweet goes on your list. So does every antique dealer in town."

"What?"

"Especially good old Pearl," Mary Jo said musingly. "She bought some stuff from the old lady—at least she claimed she paid for it. She's a pushy broad, she was always barging in here without an invitation, making offers Miss Musser couldn't refuse. A couple of other dealers were at the house once or twice, but Pearl's the only one shrewd enough to spot something really valuable, and unscrupulous enough to make off with it."

"I've met Pearl. I agree with your appraisal."

"Then there's Walt," Mary Jo said. "You told him who you were and why you came here—"

"I had to tell him. I could never have gotten this job without a recommendation, or fooled a real expert into thinking I knew anything about landscaping."

"You're a trusting soul, aren't you? Walt should be a prime suspect. He and Brad got to be fairly friendly, and he was in a swell position to rob the old lady."

"I'm not that trusting. I didn't tell him about the letter. You're the only one who knows of it."

"God." It was only a murmur of sound, so soft Diana couldn't be sure she had had heard it. The other woman's body, silhouetted against the fire, sagged a little as if under a heavy weight, and then straightened.

"I'm sorry," Mary Jo said. "It's tough. I wish I could do something to help."

"You can! Now that you know the whole truth—"

"No. I haven't any idea what happened to Brad. And—if you'll excuse a cliché—I don't want to get involved. I've got enough on my plate as it is, I don't need any more trouble."

"But—"

"I'm sorry," Mary Jo repeated. This time the words had the inexorable finality of letters graven on stone.

Diana lay sleepless, staring into the dark. The rain had stopped except for a slow soft drip of water from leaves and branches. Her bruised body ached and a couple of aspirin had had little effect on her headache, but it was not physical pain that kept her awake.

From the next room, where Mary Jo had retired, there was only silence, not even the creak of springs or the rustle of bedding. Was the other woman asleep, or did she too stare open-eyed at the pictures in her mind? She seemed to have forgotten her nervousness about staying in the house. No wonder, Diana thought wryly. I gave her plenty of other things to worry about.

She couldn't blame Mary Jo for refusing to become involved. There was no proof of a crime, and very little hope of ever obtaining any. Mary Jo had no time to waste on vague melodramatic theories. Brad hadn't said much about her, but he had mentioned a nasty divorce and an unsupportive family. I must have struck a nerve with those pompous remarks about mature insight and escaping from mistaken love, Diana thought. How could I have been so stupid and insensitive? It's been a lot harder for her than it was for me. And yet we have a lot in common. Our problems appear very different, but they stem from the same underlying weakness . . .

When the sound came, she realized that that was what she had been waiting for. At first the crystalline notes were scarcely distinguishable from the drip of the rain. Then they strengthened and took form.

Instead of getting up, Diana lay still, listening. Her attempt to localize the sound failed; it pervaded the room. The animals hadn't stirred. She reached for the flashlight and slid cautiously out of bed.

She did not switch on the light. Feeling her way, she crept to the door and turned toward the stairs. The music had quickened, but it was still soft, far below the volume it had attained on the other occasions.

Her groping hand found the frame of the open door next to hers. Then a ray of light caught her full in the face, blinding her. She threw up her hand.

"Sorry." Mary Jo's voice was barely audible. "I didn't want to wake you."

"I had the same idea." Diana switched on her own flashlight.

Light and lilting, the fragile notes surrounded them. Mary Jo tilted her head, listening. "Where's it coming from?"

"I don't know." Diana started toward the stairs.

"Wait a minute, let's not go riding off in all directions." The other woman's hand closed over her arm, and even in her distraction Diana's mind registered the difference between this grip and that other. Mary Jo's fingers were blunt and narrow, her palm hardened by callouses. She went on, in the same soft whisper, "Down this way."

The sound seemed to diminish as they moved away from the stairs, and to rise in volume as they retraced their steps. It was like the child's game—"Hotter, colder, warmer . . ." Who was the player on the other side?

They stopped, my mutual consent, at the head of the stairs. "Can't be the record player," Mary Jo whispered. "Power's still off." Without waiting for an answer, she started down.

The player on the other side seemed to be trying to cooperate. When they reached the door of the library, the music stopped abruptly.

"Don't go in," Diana warned. Like herself, the other woman was barefoot. "There's plaster and chips all over the floor, you'll cut yourself."

"They sure made a mess, didn't they?"

The twin beams surveyed the room, showing the gaping emptiness of the fireplace, the littered floor, the shrouded furniture. Mary Jo's light focused on the hi-fi for a moment, then moved to the piano. "See anything?"

"No. I never have."

"So this isn't the first time."

"Twice before. And you—"

"I think maybe this is what I didn't quite hear before."

"You're taking it very calmly."

"So are you."

"Familiarity breeds contempt, perhaps."

Mary Jo gave a brief derisive laugh. "Or misery loves company."

"I can't deny that. It's odd, though; I've never really been afraid. Angry, because I thought someone was trying to frighten me—but never afraid."

"So you've done all the obvious things—looked for a hidden speaker, wire, that stuff? Yeah. Well, there's no sense looking again, with this mess and no lights. I'll come out tomorrow. Not till later in the evening; I have to work all day."

It took Diana a few seconds to understand. "No. I was lying awake, thinking, and realizing what a selfish bitch I was to ask you for help. I won't—"

"Looks to me as if you could use some help, lady."

"Not from you. We may as well go back to bed, I guess the show's over."

"I was lying awake too," Mary Jo said. "I had already decided before this happened. I think—I hope to God—you're wrong about Brad. But you've got enough of a case to warrant investigation. I know if I were in your shoes I'd do the same thing. The truth, no matter how bad, is better than never knowing."

Diana stopped at the foot of the stairs. "No," she repeated. "I had no right to ask you. It's not only that you have enough problems of your own. If I'm right—and I too hope to God I'm wrong—this could be dangerous."

"Oh, that occurred to you, did it?"

"Right after that gate almost mashed me."

"I don't see how that could have been rigged," Mary Jo muttered. "It must have been an accident. But if you're set on protecting me, nobody has to know I'm involved."

"You aren't going to be involved. You've already done more for me than you realize. You let me talk, and you took me seriously. You can't imagine what a catharsis that was."

"Maybe I can," the other woman murmured. She gave herself a little shake. "Talking is fine, as far as it goes, but action is better."

"I won't allow you to stick your neck out."

"Don't see how you can stop me," Mary Jo said coolly. "Anyhow, my neck's so far out now, it looks like that picture of Alice after she drank out of the magic bottle. What's another inch or two?"

The show was over, for that night at least. How she knew, Diana could not have explained, but she settled into bed with every expectation of sleeping without further disturbance. Sleep did not come easily, though. She should have been rejoicing at acquiring a confidante and ally, especially one so determinedly rational as Mary Jo. She had all the more need of common sense now when her own mind was in turmoil, cracking as the lightning had split the clouds, admitting thoughts she would once have dismissed with contemptuous amusement. The evidence was mounting up. Those eerie instants of déjà vu . . . no, that term was inaccurate, it had not been the classic sense of recognition when beholding a scene or object for the first time, but rather the feeling that she was seeing a different world through the eyes of a dweller in that world. The music—sounds from that same unknown world? The scent of roses. And the final manifestation, which had left her trained lawyer's brain teetering on the brink of superstition—the warm, firm clasp of an unseen hand.

She snatched at the sheet and pulled it over her head, as if that childish gesture could shield her from the thoughts that threatened what she had always defined as sanity. If she allowed herself to believe what she half wanted, half feared to believe, she would topple over the edge.

She slid slowly, gently, out of sleep to waking. The sun was bright against her closed eyelids. For a while she lay still, tasting

*anticipation like a child on Christmas morning. It was going to
be a wonderful day. She was going to see him.*

The sun was bright against her closed eyelids. For a while she lay
still, wondering why she felt so happy—like a child on Christmas
morning. Something wonderful was going to happen. Or had it
already happened?

Something warm and wet poked her cheek, and fur enveloped
her nose. She sneezed and sat up. The little white cat rolled over,
all four feet in the air, and rolled a reproachful blue eye at her.

"You're right, it's time to get up," Diana said. She could hear
the trucks outside. It was no wonder she had overslept; what with
one thing and another, she and Mary Jo had had a busy night.

Mary Jo. That was why she felt so good. She had no right to
rejoice at having involved the girl, but the relief of candor, and of
acquiring an ally—a friend, perhaps—was so great she didn't even
mind the twinges of pain that accompanied her rising. She couldn't
see the bruises, twist and turn as she might, but she could certainly
feel them, and she had to settle for a childish ponytail instead of
her usual French twist. Poking pins into the back of her head wasn't
going to be comfortable for some days. At least none of the damage
was visible.

She had forgotten that most of the damning evidence of what
had happened was highly visible indeed. She had poured the coffee
her thoughtful guest had brewed and was reading the note that
had been left on the table when the back door burst open and
Walt erupted in.

"I told you to stay the hell out of that damned barn!"

"If not in those exact words," Diana agreed. The gate, of course.
He could hardly miss noticing it was not where he had left it. "I
thought I heard one of the animals—"

"So you decided to shift the gate? Jesus Christ! You could have
been killed!"

His face was brick-red and his hands were clenched as if he
were trying to prevent them from doing something he would later
regret. She had never seen him so angry. As he advanced she
retreated, and the back of her head met the open cupboard door.

Her cry of pain stopped Walt in his tracks. He pushed away the
hand she had raised to her head. She cried out again in protest
rather than in pain as his fingers explored the impressive dimen-

sions of the bump. The angry color faded from his face. Cradling her head in both hands, he said quietly, "Have you seen a doctor?"

"It's just a bump. Let go. Please."

"I'm not going to hurt you." His fingers spread, slipping through her hair. His thumbs, resting on her temples, exerted just enough pressure to tilt her head back. His eyes were so close to hers they filled the entire field of her vision. There were little flecks of green in the grey irises.

Then his hands released their hold and he stepped back. "Your eyes look normal. How many fingers—"

"Oh, stop it!" Diana knew her anger was excessive—and she knew why, which made her even angrier. "There's nothing wrong with me. Mary Jo was here, she checked me over from hair to toenails."

"Ah." His nod acknowledged Mary Jo's competence.

"And I didn't touch the damned gate," Diana insisted. "It must have been resting on some support that collapsed. The thunder was rattling everything—"

"Are you accusing me of carelessness?" He didn't wait for an answer. "I wouldn't take chances with anything so potentially dangerous. My guys are in and out of the barn, and so are the animals."

"Now you're accusing me of lying!"

"I wouldn't blame you for being reluctant to admit you'd been so stupid." He studied her thoughtfully. "I suppose some animal could have knocked it down. But it would have to be bear-sized."

"It wasn't Baby. She was under my bed."

"Baby?" His eyebrows lifted and a reluctant smile curled his lips. "Well, forget it. No harm done, thank God. Stay out of there from now on, will you? If I'm taking you out tonight, I want you in good condition. I'll pick you up at eight-thirty."

He was out the door before she could think of an appropriately sarcastic reply. In fact, she couldn't think of one at all.

As she prepared for her appointment—"date" didn't seem quite the right word—Diana had some difficulty deciding what to wear. This was supposed to look like a social occasion, so work clothes would hardly do, but she had no idea what constituted proper attire for a tavern in a small country town. She finally settled on a denim skirt and print blouse; then she realized that the print consisted of sprays of rosebuds, and that she was trying to identify the species. Swearing, she tossed it aside and put on a plain white shirt.

Studying her reflection in the mirror, she made a sour face. The outfit looked like a school uniform and the ponytail took another couple of years off her age. But she was damned if she was going to deck herself out in a tight-fitting tank top with a plunging neckline for the delectation of the good old boys at the Fox's Den—or for Walt.

She hadn't spoken privately with him since that morning. She had gone outside a couple of times, ostensibly to confer with him, and his manner toward her had been gravely courteous, as it always was in the presence of the other men. However, he had made it clear that she was only in the way, and she had been more than glad to retreat to the house.

The crew who had been working on the fireplace had not shown up. When Diana called the first three times, she got an answering machine. When the contractor finally called back, late in the morning, he was apologetic, but not very. Something had come up, he explained vaguely. They'd be there Monday for sure. Bright and early, yes, ma'am. With all the necessary tools, you bet.

"Not more than five cents I wouldn't," Diana muttered, hanging up the phone. There was nothing she could do about it, but after an infuriated survey of the library she decided she was not going to spend the entire weekend looking at and walking on chunks of plaster. The library was her favorite room in the house and she didn't intend to be kept out of it by a worthless lying contractor. An hour's work restored the room to livability, except for the rough hole in the wall where the old fireplace had stood.

After that she went upstairs and remade the bed in which Mary Jo had slept. Mary Jo had simply tossed sheets and blankets onto it the night before. She also raided the other rooms for additional furniture—a dainty miniature chest to serve as a nightstand, a lamp, a few chairs. Mary Jo's note had said she had to work till ten, so she wouldn't be in until late. She wrote the way she spoke, simply and to the point, without unnecessary verbal frills or any pretense of polite consultation. She intended to spend the night, and that was that.

Since she had not been invited out to dinner, Diana prepared a light meal and forced it down. She wasn't hungry, and she didn't intend to drink more than conviviality made necessary, but she knew that even a few beers on an empty stomach could have a dangerously relaxing effect. Tonight of all nights she had to be on the alert for those mental slips.

She took longer than she meant to over dressing, and was still looking for her sandals when Walt arrived, five minutes early, announcing his arrival by a raucous tattoo on the horn. Diana finally located her sandals under the bed, slung her purse over her shoulder, and went downstairs.

Good ol' boy Walt hadn't bothered to get out of the pickup. He graciously condescended to open the door of the truck for her, leaning across the front seat to do so, and then offered her his hand to help her up. When he reached across to close the door, his arm brushed her breast. Diana made no comment. He was overdoing it so thoroughly—the oldest, rustiest of the trucks, the conspicuous absence of basic courtesy—that she felt sure he was deliberately caricaturing the city impression of rustic redneck manners, even to his clothing—plaid shirt, clean but faded jeans, and the cap, which he did not remove.

"How's the head?" he asked.

"Fine."

He didn't speak again until they were almost in town. "Maybe you'd better give me some idea of what you hope to accomplish tonight."

"Talk to people about Brad. You were the one who said the Fox's Den was the place to go."

"I said it was the best of all possible alternatives. That doesn't mean it will be easy to introduce the subject. He wasn't here long and he left months ago. If you'd let me tell people who you are—"

"No."

Walt shrugged.

The Fox's Den was on the outskirts of town. It was located between a used-car dealership and a garage, and its outward appearance did not suggest that it was popular with the haut monde of Faberville. The decor featured booths along one wall, tables in the center of the floor, a small stage at one end, and a bar. Posters and advertising signs covered the walls. The pièce de résistance, behind the bar, was a stuffed fox in a glass case. Presumably it was a female fox, for two stuffed cubs nuzzled its flank. Some

comedian had put minature baby bonnets on the cubs' heads. One
of the mother fox's glass eyes was missing.

Seeing Diana's expression, Walt grinned and guided her to a
booth whose high back hid the tableau. It was occupied by a single
man who was staring at the empty beer glass in front of him. A
fringe of sandy hair circled his bald head like a tonsure and his
drooping jowls gave him the morose look of a basset hound. He
didn't look up, even when Walt took him by the arm and heaved
him to his feet. "Thanks, Bill, the lady appreciates your courtesy."

He steered Bill's unsteady feet to an empty table and deposited
him in a chair. " 'S quite awright," said Bill vaguely. "Pleasure."

Walt gestured at the waitress and called out an order—light beer
for Diana, regular for himself and Bill. "That all right?" he asked,
sliding into the seat across from her.

"You and Bill can drink whatever you want. Obviously my
preferences are irrelevant."

Before he could reply, the waitress arrived with their drinks and
began clearing the table. "Long time no see, Walt. What've you
been up to?"

She gave Diana a knowing grin. "Been busy," Walt said. "Ruby,
meet Diana."

Except for an overenthusiastic use of eye makeup, Ruby looked
like someone's mother (which in fact she probably was, Diana
thought). She wiped her damp hand politely on the ample folds
of her skirt before offering it.

"You're the lady's doing the garden stuff out at the Musser
place?"

"That's right." Diana knew enough about small towns to know
that the house would retain that name for at least another decade.

"Don't know how you keep your hands so nice with all that
digging," Ruby said innocently, inspecting Diana's hand before
she returned it to its owner. Walt choked on his beer.

"I wear gloves," Diana said.

"Well, that makes sense." Ruby lifted her tray, but she seemed
in no hurry to depart. "You're staying out there, I hear, while the
Nicholsons is gone. Gotta hand it to you, honey. I wouldn't stay
in that house alone at night for all the tea in China."

Walt frowned at her. "Now don't start, Ruby. Those stories are
all lies and rumors."

"What stories?" Diana asked.

"Why, honey, the place is haunted. And it ain't all lies," Ruby added, returning Walt's scowl. "Old Miz Musser used to hear 'em singing and dancing half the night."

"Miss Musser was senile," Walt snapped. "She also used to get messages from her dear departed father and the ghost of Thomas Jefferson."

"Well, how about what happened to that boy . . . what was his name . . ."

Diana's heart skipped a beat and then steadied as Ruby went on, "One of the Morgan boys—Billy Bob, I think—he seen a white lady walking through the woods, wringing her hands and groaning like a lost soul."

"He was drunk and poaching," Walt said. "Shut up, Ruby, and go get me another beer."

"You sure are grouchy tonight," said Ruby. "If he gives you a hard time, just call out, honey, and I'll stomp him."

"She could do it too," Walt said, as Ruby moved away. In a lower voice he added, "You don't believe that crap, do you? You look sort of peculiar."

Singing and dancing half the night . . . Diana swallowed. "No, I don't believe that crap."

"Billy Bob may have seen the old lady," Walt said. "She used to wander around at night after her mind started to go. It was worrisome. I was always afraid she'd fall, break a leg or something, and lie helpless till she died of exposure."

"Brad said you used to drop by often."

Walt shrugged. "I used to do errands and chores for her. Couldn't do much, she was too cheap to spend money and too proud to accept what she called charity. Lord knows what she paid Brad, it sure wasn't much, but at least he had a place to stay. It was a relief to have him there keeping an eye on her. I didn't have to go out so often."

Ruby darted back with Walt's beer, cast an expert glance at Diana's untouched glass, and trotted off again. Almost all the tables were occupied now, and a group of musicians was setting up on the little stage.

"Who do you want to talk to?" Walt asked, changing the subject somewhat abruptly. "We'll have to invite them to join us, they're tactfully leaving me alone to work on my new conquest."

Diana ignored the sarcasm. She glanced around the room. "Whom do you suggest?"

"They all knew him. He was a . . . sociable guy."

One of the people standing at the bar turned. He was a huge man, a little overweight but massively muscled, and in spite of his slouching posture she could see he stood several inches over six feet. His face was almost square, and with an angled jawline; his nose looked as if it had been broken and inexpertly reset. His eyes caught hers and lingered on her face with a look of half-puzzled, half-challenging inquiry. Then his gaze moved to Walt. With casual violence, he flung off the girl he had been holding in the curve of one arm and started toward them.

Walt said something under his breath that Diana didn't quite catch. Then the man was upon them, standing so close she instinctively slid farther back along the seat. "Where is she?" he demanded.

"Who?" Walt's voice was even but his brows had drawn together.

"You know who I mean, goddammit! Don't fuck around with me, Walt."

"Watch your mouth. There's a lady present."

"Oh, you got another one, huh? Keeping Mary Jo on the side till you get tired of this—lady, is she? Not your type, then, Walt. Look, lady—" He thrust his face into Diana's. She recoiled. His breath was strong enough to fell an ox.

Walt's arm moved in a deceptively easy movement and the big man staggered back. "Don't breathe on my date, Larry. Why don't you go home? You don't want to start trouble—"

"Who says I don't? I'm telling this . . . lady . . . about you. Stay away from him, lady. He's bad news. He . . . Say. Ain't you the one that's staying out at the Nicholsons'? You know Mary Jo. Where the hell—"

"I told you to watch your mouth."

The room had gone very quiet. The musicians stood watching, ready to begin, but unwilling to interrupt an equally interesting performance. Only the bartender, who was presumably also the owner, showed any signs of wanting to interfere.

"Hey, Larry, come get your beer before Misti finishes it off," he called.

A little snicker of excited laughter rippled through the room, but the feeble attempt at distraction failed. "Soon as this bastard tells me what I wanna know," Larry said. "Where is she, Walt?"

"Oh, well," Walt said. "I guess I haven't any choice."

This time the movement of his arm sent Larry stumbling backward. Walt slid out of the booth. The spectators retreated, clearing the floor. Larry grinned happily. He swung a fist the size of a ham. Walt stepped under it and hit Larry well below the belt with a force that doubled him over. Clasping his hands, Walt chopped down on the back of Larry's neck, stepping agilely to one side in order to avoid the other man's falling body.

Diana let out her breath. She hadn't had to hold it long. The whole business had been as brief as it had been brutally effective.

"Get him out of here," Walt said, studying the motionless form with disgust. "Dump him in the cab of his truck. Better take his keys away from him."

The bartender was happy to cooperate. He managed to enlist the assistance of a couple of disappointed spectators and then turned to Walt. "Thanks. Next round's on me. Sorry, miss, I sure hope you won't think this kind of thing happens often. Larry's a mean son of a—a mean guy."

Diana reassured him, feigning a conviction she certainly did not feel. "Neatly done," she said, facing her companion.

Absently Walt rubbed his knuckles. "I've had a lot of practice. You know who that was?"

"I can guess. Mary Jo's ex-husband?"

"Only he doesn't consider himself an ex. He's driving that poor woman crazy. You know how many times she's had to move? He finds out where she's living, and the first time he gets a load on he goes there and raises hell."

"Can't she get a restraining order?"

Walt gave her a look of blistering contempt. "Yeah, that's just what I'd expect a lawyer to suggest. So they pick him up and shove him in the slammer, and he stays there a couple of days, maybe a week. Then he's out and after her again."

She couldn't resent his anger. She had felt the same frustrated rage herself when reading about such cases. It was even worse when one knew and liked the victim. "Has he ever abused her physically?"

Walt studied her with raised eyebrows. "Why don't you come out with it, instead of beating around the bush? You don't give a damn about Mary Jo. You want to know whether Larry is capable of committing murder. The answer should be obvious."

"I never said anything about—"

"I'm not quite as stupid as I look." Walt kept his voice low and a smile glued to his lips, but his eyes bored into hers. "And I particularly hate having people underestimate my intelligence. If you had come here hoping to find someone to whom Brad might have confided his future plans, you'd have done it openly, using your own name. People would understand and sympathize with a sister's concern. There's only one reason I can think of why you'd insist on anonymity. Well, lady, you just met your number-one suspect. Larry hated Brad's guts. Too bad I had to shut him up before you could question him, wasn't it?"

CHAPTER EIGHT

*T*he party was still going strong when they left the tavern shortly
before midnight, followed by a chorus of friendly farewells and
(for the most part) good-natured jokes about their presumed reason for leaving so early.

"You made quite a hit," said Walt, forgetting himself and helping
Diana into the truck. "Very neatly done."

"It wasn't entirely calculated."

"Oh, yeah? Come off it. That isn't your kind of place and they
aren't your kind of people."

"The stuffed foxes didn't exactly grab me, I admit. And the
looks on their faces when they were watching you and Mary Jo's
husband—those sickly, excited half-smiles . . . They were almost
disappointed when you finished him off so quickly. They wanted
to see blood."

"Yeah, well, people who admire stuffed foxes wearing baby
bonnets aren't the only ones who lick their lips at the sight of
blood."

"I know."

"Not from personal experience, I bet. What kind of law do you
practice? Nice bloodless tax and corporation stuff?"

Stiff with resentment, Diana didn't answer. Giving her a sidelong
glance, Walt went on, "I hope I didn't offend your delicate sense
of fair play."

"Did you have to hit him below the belt?"

"No. I chose to."

145

"He was drunk. He could hardly stand up."

"I don't fight for fun, lady. My aim is to do it only when I have to and get it over with as fast as possible, with minimal damage to me."

In the light from the dashboard Diana saw that his lips were tight and his eyes had narrowed. He was offended as well as angry, and she was forced to admit he had some right to resent her attitude. "I'm sorry if I sounded judgmental. I suppose you handled it in the best possible way."

Walt was willing to change the subject, but he was not entirely appeased. "I never expected to spend the evening listening to ghost stories," he grumbled. "Why did you keep bringing up the subject?"

"Can't you guess?"

"They enjoyed it, of course. Scaring innocent city slickers is a popular hobby."

"And it led them to talk about the house and Miss Musser—and Brad."

In fact, it had been Walt who asked casually if anyone had heard from Brad. No one had, nor, it seemed, had they expected to. They knew too many people like him—wanderers, itinerants, unable or unwilling to settle down to a steady job.

"You're the one would have heard from him, Walt," said one of the group. "You knew him better'n anybody else."

"Except Mary Jo," said another man with a snicker.

Walt had pointedly changed the subject.

Now he said, "All those stories about Brad seeing ghosts were bullshit, you know. He never saw anything out of the way."

"You mean he never said anything to you."

"Touché. He might not have. We weren't close."

It was probably true; Brad had spoken of Walt as a friendly acquaintance rather than an intimate friend. The claim struck her as unnecessarily defensive, however, so she persisted.

"You went out drinking with him."

"I drink with a lot of people."

"Larry implied that you and Mary Jo—"

"Oh, for God's sake! Larry's pathological jealousy was partly responsible for breaking up the marriage. He's accused Mary Jo of sleeping with every guy in town."

But she had slept with Brad. That admitted fact was probably irrelevant insofar as Larry was concerned; he might be driven to violence by his own sick suspicions. Walt was a horse of a different color. Did he care enough about Mary Jo to fly into a murderous rage at finding her in the arms of another man?

"Ridiculous," Diana murmured.

"Damn right," Walt said. "Mary Jo's not like that. Besides, she's taken enough crap from men to hate the lot of us."

"What men?"

"Her old man, for one. He's been beating on her mother for years. On Mary Jo too, for all I know. She ran off with Larry when she was seventeen. From the frying pan into the fire, as it turned out, but she didn't know that. Larry wasn't so bad at first. It was when she went back to school—'getting fancy ideas,' as he put it—that he started . . . Oh, hell, why are we talking about Mary Jo? Her history is none of my business. Or yours."

"We could go back to talking about ghosts," Diana said.

"Even that would be an improvement." After a moment Walt said thoughtfully, "Brad did sort of egg people on to tell him hair-raising stories. He was going to write a book, he said. Local legends and lore—that sort of thing. He asked me once . . ."

"What?"

"Shut up, I'm trying to think," Walt said without rancor. "Something about the gravestones. He was fascinated by them. Wanted to know who the people were, where the stones came from. I couldn't tell him. I've never been interested in that kind of thing."

Diana could believe that. Walt was far more intelligent than he liked to let on, but the past would hold no interest for a man of his practical temperament.

"He was the one that found the stones," Walt went on. "Looking after the old lady didn't take much of his time—he ran errands and drove her places, that kind of thing, but she didn't like him hanging around the house. He spent most of his time wandering around the pasture and down by the stream. That's how he ran across the tombstones. Took me out there one day, to show me. He was excited about them—quoted a poem at me."

"What poem?"

Walt shrugged. "I'm not much on poetry. Some cheerful little item about how the dust was once lords and ladies."

" 'This quiet dust was Gentlemen and Ladies . . .' "

"That's it. Not too appropriate," Walt added. "The graves weren't there, only the stones."

"What else did he say?"

"I don't remember."

A white form glided toward them, dipping and curtsying, waving diaphanous arms—a blossoming tree, given spurious movement by the headlights' glare and shadow.

Not one but two cars were parked in front of the house. One was Mary Jo's. Diana did not recognize the other.

"So she is here," Walt said. "Did you know she would be?"

"Yes, of course."

"Damn." Walt turned off the ignition but did not move.

"What's your problem? I'm glad to have her. Not that I'm nervous—"

"Oh, hell no, not you! You should be. If Larry comes looking for her . . . At least she could park around in back. I'd better have a word with her."

"No, don't! You know how scrupulous she is; she thought she was doing me a favor, but if she believed she would be the cause of unpleasantness she'd leave this instant."

"It wasn't very smart of her to come here, though. Larry knows she works for the Nicholsons and he probably knows they are away. It was bad luck he saw us together tonight, otherwise he might not have made the connection for a while. His IQ's not the highest in town." Walt's fingers drummed impatiently on the steering wheel. "Let's hope he was too drunk to remember. I won't say anything to Mary Jo. Are you hinting that you don't want me to come in?"

"Come ahead. The more the merrier."

It wasn't difficult to deduce who the other visitor must be. Mary Jo wouldn't entertain a friend without permission; she would consider that taking advantage. However, when Diana opened the front door, the sounds that reached her ears brought her to an abrupt halt. Walt, following closely, ran into her and caught her around the waist as she staggered.

Music for dancing. Gay and lilting, conjuring up images of ladies in hoop skirts and gentlemen bowing over their partners' hands . . . The tune was not the one she had heard before, though, and the notes lacked the crystalline delicacy of those others. They came from the piano in the library.

"Let go," she exclaimed, prying at Walt's fingers.

"Nothing personal. Being a swell guy, I usually try not to knock people down. What's the matter with you?"

"Nothing. I wasn't expecting . . . Nothing."

"Who'd you think was here? Whenever I see a strange vehicle," Walt said, ignoring her efforts to free herself, "I know it's Andy. He collects them the way he collects dogs. Speaking of which . . ." He let her go then, and prudently retired a step or two as a large white form came gamboling toward them.

The music stopped and a voice bellowed, "We're in here." With the dog pressing close to her side, Diana headed for the library. Walt followed at a discreet distance.

Andy greeted their entrance with a few strains of *Pomp and Circumstance,* ending with a long inappropriate arpeggio. "Hey, Walt."

"Andy. Hi, Mary Jo."

Mary Jo's cheeks were flushed and her eyes sparkled. "Andy's been doing imitations of famous musicians. You should see his Beethoven."

"That wasn't Beethoven," Walt said.

Diana looked at him in surprise, and then reproached herself for being such a snob. She shouldn't have been surprised to see Walt demonstrate an acquaintance with classical music; once before he had quoted Gilbert and Sullivan.

"Right. Elgar, preceded by Scarlatti." Andy ran his fingers through his hair, struck out his lower lip, frowned portentously, and pounded out the first sonorous chords of the *Pathétique.* "This is Beethoven. Enough already. I was just keeping Mary Jo company till you got here. How about a cup of coffee, Walt?"

"No, thanks. I'm working tomorrow."

"Here?"

"Where else?"

"Speaking of working tomorrow," Andy said, "some character called and said he's delivering a mantel. With the brilliant logic that marks all my mental processes, I deduce it's the mantel that goes around that hole in the wall. He wanted to know if someone would be here. I told him I'd come out if—"

"I'll be here," Diana said brusquely. "I don't know what he's going to do with the darned thing, though. He wasn't supposed to come till Monday. He can't install it, they haven't finished preparing the opening."

"What's wrong with it?" Andy went to the rectangular hole in the wall and poked his head in. "Dark in here," he remarked, his voice echoing eerily.

Mary Jo laughed. "Andy, you'll be covered with soot. You're as curious as a cat."

"It has to be enlarged," Diana said. "They were supposed to come today, but of course they didn't show up."

"That's par for the course," Walt said. "Don't worry about it, Di, I'll have the boys put the new mantel in the . . . I'll have them put it someplace. Well. I'll be running along. Let you girls—excuse me, you ladies—get your sleep."

"Is that hint directed at me?" inquired Andy.

"I have to work tomorrow too," Mary Jo said. "Thanks for the entertainment, Andy. He came by to look for his glasses," she explained, glancing self-consciously at Diana.

"He didn't find them, I see," said Diana, inspecting a face that was bare of those accessories, though liberally streaked with soot. "You're speaking of a second pair, I presume, not the ones you mashed the other night?"

"I don't really need them," Andy said vaguely. "You know, that brickwork along the left side is interesting. Do you have a flashlight handy?"

"No," Diana said in a tone that brought a low growl from the big dog at her feet.

Andy burst out laughing. "Okay, okay, I'm going. Don't let your dog kill me, lady. I told you she was a great watchdog, didn't I?"

He was still babbling when Diana closed the door on him and Walt. She locked and bolted it with more care than usual, and then moved to the window. The two men stood at the foot of the steps, engaged in earnest conversation. For once Andy was not doing the talking.

Mary Jo came along the corridor as she turned from the door. "I put out the lights," she said, gesturing toward the library. "You weren't going to stay up any longer, were you?"

"No. I'll just check the locks."

"I already did. The animals are taken care of too."

"Thanks."

"You didn't think I was going to sit around here and pretend I was a guest, I hope. Anyhow, I owe you—for cleaning the library and making the bed and everything. That's my job."

Diana looked at her in mild exasperation. "Look here, Mary Jo, I know you think I'm a spoiled child of privilege, but I've made a couple of thousand beds in my time, and even scrubbed a toilet or two. Don't be such a snob."

Mary Jo's angular face broke up. My God, Diana thought—she's got a dimple, or the embryonic beginnings of one. No wonder the poor thing hasn't had a chance to develop.

"Snob," Mary Jo repeated wonderingly. "Funny, I never thought of it that way. Okay—you can clean all the toilets you want."

Diana laughed, and Mary Jo gave her a tentative smile. She's as prickly as a hedgehog and as timid as a rabbit, Diana thought. Let me do this right. Don't let me screw up!

It was not one of the most elegantly phrased prayers she had ever breathed, but it was one of the most heartfelt. Mary Jo was important to her. She couldn't have said why, but she knew it was true.

"I work at the bakery till noon tomorrow," Mary Jo went on, "I'll come out after that."

"That's fine. It isn't necessary, but I do appreciate the company."

"You don't have to feel you're under any obligation. The fact is . . ." Mary Jo hesitated. "The fact is, I need a place to stay for a few days. I already asked Mrs. Nicholson if it would be all right. She called tonight."

Diana knew better than to ask why Mary Jo needed a place to stay. After the things Walt had told her, she was fairly certain she knew why. She felt as if she were walking on quicksand, testing every step, for fear of saying the wrong thing. That shell of Mary Jo's had been years building. It wouldn't fall in a moment or a day or a week.

"I'm sorry I wasn't here to talk to her. Is everything going well with them?"

"They're having a wonderful time," Mary Jo said, smiling. "She raved on about some gardens in South Carolina. Azaleas, is that right?"

"Probably. I mean—yes, that's right."

"They must be beautiful. I want to see them someday. There are so many places I want to see . . ."

Gardens were a subject Diana didn't want to discuss. She gestured at the big dog, who had followed them upstairs and now stood panting heavily and looking from one to the other. "You want to toss a coin to see who gets to sleep with Baby?" she asked.

"She's all yours," Mary Jo said. "Oh. That reminds me." She reached into her pocket and produced a handful of fluffy white. "Want some cotton?"

"What for?"

"I'm putting it in my ears. If the National Symphony wants to play in the library tonight, they can go right ahead."

"That's not a bad idea. Thanks."

They parted with brief good-nights. Mary Jo had not been joking; she was stuffing cotton into her right ear as she entered her room. With a smile and a shrug, Diana followed suit. Of all the diehard rationalists she had ever encountered—including her father—Mary Jo topped the list. Her method of explaining the insoluble was to ignore it. Maybe that wasn't such a bad idea.

The earplugs might or might not have been responsible for the fact that Diana slept through the night undisturbed. They didn't shut out the rumble of approaching vehicles, however. When she went downstairs she found that Mary Jo had fed the animals and made the coffee. A note on the table made another reference to cleaning toilets. Diana smiled as she read it. Apparently Mary Jo had decided it was safe to joke about that subject. Maybe they could move on from there to something really daring.

After she had finished breakfast she went out. The men were laying the stones for the wall and waterfall above the pond. Some of the rocks were of massive size, and Walt, nursing a bruised thumb, was in no mood for idle conversation. Her polite inquiries about the injury were received with a dark scowl, so she said briskly, "The men should be here soon with the new mantel for the library. Where shall I tell them to put it?"

Walt's scowl deepened and Jack said, laughing, "I know where he'd like to tell them to put it. I'd better talk to them."

"Go ahead," Walt grunted, with a critical eye on two of his crew who were preparing to lay a huge slab in place. "Watch out for—"

"I know, I know. He doesn't think anybody but him can do anything right," Jack added, as he joined Diana. "What kind of thing is this mantel, anyhow? I mean, does it have to be under cover?"

"I haven't seen it myself, but I imagine it's pretty fancy."

It was. The marble had been cleaned and polished to a creamy sheen; on either side, draped caryatids bowed graceful shoulders under the swags of flowers and leaves lining the mantelshelf.

The barn was obviously not a proper repository for such glory. Diana hadn't been in the place since her near accident; she was horrified to see the amount of damage the fallen gate had caused. It had not been moved. Under its upper section gaped an irregular hole framed by boards that had splintered into sharp fragments.

As her bones would have splintered.

"How about over there?" Jack pointed to a spot on the floor next to the half of the gate that remained upright, leaning against the wall.

"No." Her brusque tone made Jack glance at her in surprise. "It'll have to go in the library. I should have realized that from the first. Sorry to have bothered you, Jack."

After the mantel had been disposed of and the men had left, she went out again. Baby was waiting by the back door; the big dog plodded quietly beside her as she started off across the pasture. The weeds that had been only a few inches high a few days ago now brushed the backs of her calves. The longer, warmer days and frequent rainfall had brought new growth leaping out of the ground. The honeysuckle seemed to have a special relationship with Mother Nature; new tendrils groped blindly toward the worn gray faces of the tombstones.

George had fallen face-down again. The hell with him, Diana thought.

So Brad was the one who had found the tombstones. Odd that he hadn't mentioned them in his letters; it was the sort of discovery that would appeal to his writer's imagination. Unless . . . She frowned, searching her memory. He had said something in one letter about playing archaeologist, finding the remains of old structures—and yes, the word "stones" had occurred—while he was mowing the meadow. She had assumed, if she had given the matter much thought, that he meant building stones.

She should have brought all Brad's letters with her, instead of only the last, but she hadn't been able to think of a way of getting them from her mother without explaining why she wanted them.

Ann was convinced her son was dead. That pathetic little packet of papers, tied with a blue ribbon like letters from a lover and kept in the drawer of her dresser, was sacred to her. Diana had managed to slip one out; she could only hope Ann wouldn't notice its absence. To remove the entire collection would have been unthinkable. Her father had tried, using words like "morbid obsession" and "absurd melodrama." The ensuing scene had resulted in Ann's being hospitalized. She was now seeing her psychiatrist five times a week and consuming tranquilizers like peanuts.

It probably wasn't important, Diana assured herself. None of Brad's letters had been long or discursive. He had told her what he was doing, but never what he was thinking or feeling . . .

The realization, so evident and so long denied, was like a slap in the face. Was he so insecure about his relationship with her that he was afraid to expose his feelings, or express them freely? Those brief, casually friendly notes from a would-be-writer—from Brad, who had spent hours in his room scribbling when he should have been doing homework or trying out for the football team, or any of the other socially acceptable activities his father nagged him about . . . Why hadn't she realized what was missing from them?

The burden of guilt she had carried so long was suddenly overpowering; she wanted to sink to the ground under the weight of it. Impulsively she closed her eyes and held out her hands. "Brad," she whispered. "Where are you? Come back. Tell me you forgive me . . ."

Where are you? Why didn't you come?
Against the darkness of closed eyelids she saw him walking away with slow deliberate steps, diminishing into the distance, never looking back. She hurled her thoughts after him, desire and demand. Come back. Come back. Or, if you can't . . . At least tell me why!

Diana opened her eyes and caught hold of a nearby branch until the sense of vertigo passed. Standing still with closed eyes was a sure way of inviting dizziness. What a fool she was! Had she really hoped to feel a ghostly hand clasp hers in reassurance and love? That was not what she wanted. She wanted him living—angry, resentful, unforgiving, so long as he was alive. If something unseen and protective had reached out to her from the darkness—from the quiet dust—let it be someone—something—other than her brother.

The dog lay still, its big head resting on its paws, its grave brown eyes watching her. Behind its bulk the face of the third stone, with its mutilated inscription, flowed with shifting shadows from the shaken boughs above. Was it a man or a woman whose dust that monument had marked? Nineteen was barely old enough to merit either word. A boy or girl, rather—a lad or lass . . . The words came unbidden, spontaneously, to her lips.

> "This quiet Dust was Gentlemen and Ladies,
> And Lads and Girls—
> "Was laughter and ability and Sighing,
> And Frocks and Curls."

The voice that had finished the verse was a man's. For a moment—of horror or delight, which?—her senses reeled. Only a moment, though.

"Andy," she said, turning. "I didn't hear you."

His cheerful smile faded. "I didn't mean to sneak up on you. Sit down. Your face is kind of a funny color."

"Sit down where?"

Andy indicated the fallen stone. Diana shied back, and he raised an eyebrow. "Superstitious?"

"I guess I am. About some things."

"George wouldn't mind. And if he does, he's in no position to complain. How about this nice dirty rotten log, then?"

Diana joined him on the log. "The last time I was here, it was with a guy who recited that same poem," Andy explained penitently. "I couldn't resist joining in. Sorry if I—"

"That's all right." She didn't want him to wander off the subject. "Who was the guy? A friend of yours?"

"Yes. No . . . He wasn't here long enough to become a friend, I guess. He worked for Walt and then for Miss Musser, as a sort of handyman and caretaker. Interesting dude."

"Not too many people are familiar with Emily Dickinson."

"Including me. All I knew was the tripe they made us memorize in school." He rolled his eyes heavenward and raised his voice to a falsetto. " 'If I can help one fainting Robin Unto his Nest again. . . .' I despised that sickly robin."

Diana laughed. His cheerful irreverence was comforting, but she wanted to get him back on track. She needn't have worried. For once she blessed the family habit of talking interminably about anything, to anyone.

"Brad—that was his name—Brad was the one that got me interested in Emily," Andy went on. "I liked that poem he quoted, so I read some more. Decided I had misjudged the lady. I told Brad, next time I saw him. Yeah, we had some good talks. I was sorry when he left."

"Where did he go?"

Andy didn't appear surprised by the question or her urgent tone. He shrugged. "Dunno. As I said, we weren't buddies. Walt was pissed because he—Brad—just picked up and walked away, without giving notice or warning anybody. It was kind of a dirty trick to play on Miss Musser, but I suppose he figured she didn't really need him anymore. She'd got her room at the nursing home and put the house on the market—that's how I happened to be around so much, I was handling it for her—but she kept stalling. Turned down a couple of offers. I didn't really blame the poor old gal. It's tough to take that step—like ordering your coffin. I always wondered if it wasn't Brad's leaving that nudged her into making her decision."

"You mean he just walked out on the poor old woman, without so much as a word of warning? He must have been a . . ." Diana cleared her throat. "A rotten, irresponsible person."

"He wasn't, though," Andy said. "It was kind of odd, his leaving so suddenly. He may have told the old lady; at that stage she couldn't remember her own name for more than five minutes. He'd been good to her—and she wasn't the easiest person in the world to get along with, believe me. It wasn't just senility or Alzheimer's or whatever. She was always a mean old goat." Seeing Diana's shocked expression, he gave her a broad, unabashed grin. "You have to take people as they are, honey. She was old and feeble and pathetic and also a mean old goat. I kind of liked her. So did Brad, in spite of the fact that she chewed him out and drove him crazy and accused him of robbing her."

"Robbing her?"

"Old people get like that," Andy said casually. "Paranoid. She accused everybody of robbing her, including me. God knows she didn't have anything worth stealing, except the house and the land."

"No buried treasure? No valuable antiques?"

"She collected Avon bottles," said Andy, in a voice that brought a reluctant smile to her lips. "That should give you an idea of what we had to clear out of the house. There were a few good pieces; the antique dealers got those. As for buried treasure . . . it's a lovely thought, but . . ."

A fat bumblebee drunk on honeysuckle blundered into his face. He brushed it gently aside. As Diana tried to think of an innocent-sounding but pointed question, he began to hum. Gradually words emerged. His voice was a resonant, true baritone; though obviously untrained, it suited the quiet glade and the warm spring day.

"What was that?'" she asked after he had fallen silent. "Something about roses?"

"*Heidenröslein*—heath roses. It's a setting of a poem by Goethe. Very sentimental. The guy plucks the poor little wild rose, but she sticks him with her thorns . . . '*Half ihm doch kein Weh und Ach, must es eben leiden . . .*' He must forever suffer."

"Served the bastard right," said Diana.

Andy whooped with laughter. "A proper feminist reaction. Not that I don't agree," he added hastily.

"It's a pretty tune. What made you think of it?"

"Wild roses," Andy said. "They were in full bloom along the fence the first time I ever saw this place. Big fat crumpled pink blooms, weighing down the branches—grown wild and rampant, uncared for but surviving somehow for God knows how many years. I guess I was still thinking about that guy Brad. He was the one who found the old rose garden and cleared out the weeds."

"I thought it was your mother."

"She thinks so too," Andy said with a grin. "You know how Ma is, her enthusiasm tends to blur her memory. She and Charles were looking for a place, and the house was still on the market, so I brought them out here, and Ma insisted on exploring. I was disappointed to find most of the roses gone—they were blooming like crazy when Brad brought me out here in June—but Ma spotted the Autumn Damask and started waving her arms and spouting Latin. That damned rose sold the house, I honestly believe."

"It's a shame you didn't ask your friend Brad to identify the roses. I won't have a clue until they bloom again."

"Oh, he didn't know what they were. He just liked flowers. And," Andy added, after a moment, "rescuing things. That was what he said. He felt as if he'd rescued the roses, and the tombstones and . . . What's the matter, your sinuses acting up?"

"Yes." Diana turned her head away and fumbled for a tissue.

The comment had been unexpected; she had not had time to raise her defenses.

"That's a helluva handicap for a lady in your business," Andy said. "Which reminds me—have you decided what you're going to plant on the upper terrace? Ma was leaning toward the English-cottage style, with lots of perennials and winding paths and general chaos—you know—but I think it ought to be more formal. Ma has a book on historic gardens, with a plan like the one I had in mind. There's a central brick walk, with oval flower beds on either side—outlined in boxwood—and a magnolia in the center of each bed—"

"I'd better go back and take an antihistamine," Diana said, getting to her feet. She did not want to discuss garden plans with Andy.

The distraction might not have worked it not been for the dog. Instead of waiting for Diana to lead the way, she headed purposefully in the opposite direction, toward the stream. She stopped when Andy called her name but instead of coming to them she barked emphatically and stood still, tail wagging.

"Let her go," Diana said. "She's been dogging my footsteps all morning. She deserves some time off—and so do I."

"She's supposed to dog your footsteps. (That's a terrible pun, by the way.)" Andy's brow furrowed. "I wonder what . . . Hey, Baby, come here."

He started after the dog. With another deep-throated bark Baby went on, pausing occasionally to make certain he was following. Andy's increasingly peremptory orders—stop, stay, come back here, you stupid dog—had no effect. When Andy broke into a run, Baby broke into a trot. She had no difficulty keeping ahead of him. Now moving at a gallop, dog and man vanished into the trees lining the stream.

Her curiosity aroused, Diana followed. If Baby was living up to the reputation of her breed, she had found something she thought might interest them. A lost child? A wayfarer in need of rescue? Neither seemed likely. She could hear Andy scolding Baby in a voice breathless with laughter and exasperation.

Then he let out an exclamation. There was no amusement at all in his next order to the dog. "God damn it! Get away—get out of there!" The dog's excited barking mingled with a stream of expletives.

She met them on their way back. Andy had the dog by the collar. He caught Diana's arm in an equally forceful grip and spun her around. "Go back," he ordered curtly.

She had already seen it—white bones and tattered brown-and-white hide jumbled into an indecent pile of rubbish. The muzzled face was relatively intact, except for the ruined eyes, crawling with insects whose greedy movement gave them an obscene appearance of life.

CHAPTER NINE

The rose looks fair, but fairer we it deem
For that sweet odour which doth in it live.

—SHAKESPEARE

Andy kept his grip on the dog and Diana until they had passed through the trees and the carcass of the deer was hidden from sight. "Hold the dog," he ordered. "Baby, stay! Stay with Diana."

Baby did not want to stay. Not until Diana sat down on the ground did the dog give an almost human sigh and take up the defensive position to which she had been trained, curled around Diana's body. Andy vanished again into the trees.

He was gone for several minutes. When he came back his face was darkly flushed—with anger, Diana thought. He held out a hand to help her rise, and then pulled it back. The palm and fingers were crusted with dirt which, she realized, must cover uglier stains.

She got to her feet unassisted and they started toward the house, Andy towing the reluctant dog. "You didn't happen to hear shots recently, did you?" he asked.

"No, I . . . Wait a minute. I did hear something that sounded like a gunshot—but only one. Wednesday night."

"That would be about right."

"But this isn't deer season, is it?"

"No."

"How do you know the poor thing didn't die of disease?"

"It was butchered."

"Oh. That's why you went back."

"It wasn't for the beauty of the view. I hoped to find some indication of whether it was killed by an arrow or a bullet, but it was too . . ."

"I suppose animals had been at it," Diana said, with an involuntary glance at the dog, who was now trotting quietly at her side. "How could you tell it had been cut up, then?"

"I could tell." Andy gave her a faint smile. "Am I treating you like a delicate little city lady?"

"Yes. I'm not that squeamish. But I appreciate your concern. If I'd come on that awful thing without warning . . ."

"That's the point," Andy said. "The carcass was only a few feet from Ma's bench. She had it put there so she could sit by the stream in the evening and watch for the deer. They have a regular path down to the water and back. There's been no hunting on this land for years, so they're comparatively tame."

"Do you think the hunter knew that?"

Andy appeared not to have heard the question. He went on musingly, "The property lines are marked and posted. I put up the signs myself. So he was breaking the law twice over. If he'd disposed of the carcass, we might never have known. Yet he left it there, right by the bench, almost as if he wanted someone to find it."

"Your mother would have been very upset, wouldn't she?"

"She talked about those deer as if she knew each one personally. You heard only one shot?"

"Yes."

"What time of day?"

"Evening. It was almost dark."

"Quite a marksman, our poacher. Though, as I said, the deer are pretty tame."

"I can't believe anyone would deliberately leave it for her to find. That's sick."

Andy shook his head. "I may be crediting the bastard with more imagination than he has, and more skill. It could have been a lucky shot. All hunters claim to be expert marksmen, but few of them are—hence the popularity of assault weapons—and some of them will fire at anything that moves. I'd hate to think anyone around here dislikes my mother enough to leave an ugly souvenir like that for her to find, but I'd hate even more to have her shot by some macho moron."

When they reached the house Andy left her with a brief "I'll see you later," and headed for the barn. Diana didn't ask where he was going. Shortly afterward she saw him walking back across the meadow with a shovel over his shoulder.

Mary Jo was mopping the kitchen floor and scolding a staring assembly of cats for neglecting to wipe their feet. When she saw Diana, she immediately asked what was wrong.

"I thought I had a poker face," Diana murmured. "I wasn't going to tell you, but . . ."

Mary Jo was a country girl; the news of the deer's demise didn't distress her unduly, but she was quick to comprehend the implications. "Mrs. Nicholson would have been sick if she'd found it; she's crazy about animals. And Mr. Nicholson will have a fit when he finds out someone's been trespassing. You should have called the game warden when you heard that shot, Diana."

"I didn't realize. And there was only one shot."

"Yeah, that's unusual. The guy must have . . ." Mary Jo shook her head decisively. "It's stupid to waste time playing guessing games. If it happens again, make that call. I'll look up the number for you. And tell Walt to get rid of the carcass before—"

"Andy's doing it now."

"Good. Although," Mary Jo went on coolly, "there wouldn't be much left by the time Mrs. Nicholson got back. I thought the dogs and cats had been off their feed the last couple of days."

Diana glanced at the little white cat, which was twining around her ankle, and withdrew her foot. "The cats too? That's disgusting."

"It's nature. You can't blame them."

"No . . . Maybe I'm not cut out for country living."

"You get used to it. At least most people do." Mary Jo's face softened. "Poor Andy never has, not really. He covers up well, and he'll do what's necessary, but he hates the whole scene— hunting, trapping, the way some of the people around here neglect and abandon pets. He's always getting into fights about it."

"Andy?" Diana said in surprise.

"Yeah, he's a holy terror when he loses his temper," Mary Jo said, with the rueful pride of a mother discussing a pugnacious little boy. "And he can't keep his mouth shut. He started the worst brawl they've ever had at the Fox's Den one time when he took exception to something Larry—" Her mouth twisted into an ugly shape, as if she had bit into an apple and found half a worm. "I brought Chinese for supper, hope you like it. Maybe we can persuade Andy to stay."

"Oh, I'm sure we can," Diana said.

Mary Jo began pushing the mop with an energy that indicated she was through talking. She didn't object when Diana pitched in to help, which was, the latter considered, a distinct step forward.

As she dusted and waxed and brushed cat hairs off various surfaces, Diana thought about that revealing conversation—even more revealing than Mary Jo had meant it to be. How typical of her to bring carry-out to a house whose shelves, refrigerator, and freezer bulged with food. It was not so much repayment for her temporary lodging as an assertion of independence, and Diana could only respect that attitude, though she thought regretfully of the flounder almondine she had meant to defrost for supper. She didn't particularly care for Chinese.

From the next room, Mary Jo's voice lifted in a brief snatch of melody. *"Röslein, Röslein, Röslein rot . . ."* Diana recognized the little German song Andy had sung that afternoon. Mary Jo must have heard it from him. Had he been serenading her with romantic ballads the night before? The cloth in Diana's hand slowed its rhythmic polishing of a mahogany table as her mind wandered off into sentimental fantasies. Mary Jo's practical good sense would steady Andy's fecklessness, and his affectionate good humor would soften her prickly nature. A perfect match, Diana thought, and then, smiling to herself, I sound like some character out of Jane Austen.

At any rate, she would prefer to believe romance, not suspicion of her, was the reason for Andy's frequent visits. He had known Brad; he had known Miss Musser, and been in a perfect position to take advantage of the old woman. Something shady about the terms of the sale of the house, perhaps. Miss Musser hadn't been competent to watch over her own interests, and her lawyer might have been a party to the scam. Andy had a legitimate excuse to be in and out of the house, with and without prospective buyers. He had jeered at the idea that Miss Musser had anything worth stealing, but Mary Jo had mentioned quilts and china and crystal . . .

Oh, stop it, Diana told herself. You're getting paranoid.

Just because you were paranoid didn't mean somebody wasn't following you, though. One of Mary Jo's casual comments had shed a different light on the deer episode.

The poacher must be a local man. Half the town seemed to know the Nicholsons were away; he might know that, too. And it was probable that predators would eat or carry off the deer's remains before Emily and Charles got back. Andy's concern for his mother was understandable, but the more Diana thought about it, the less likely it seemed that the affair had been deliberately designed to distress Emily. Either the hunter had been indifferent to this aspect of the matter or he had designed it to distress someone else. A squeamish city girl who was known to wander through the woods and pastures?

Proceeding to the library, dust cloth in hand, she saw Andy— or rather, the lower half of him—in the gaping cavity of the fireplace. A floor lamp, divested of its shade and propped precariously against the wall, illumined his long legs and the blackened stones of the hearth. Apparently this was not the effect he had in mind, for he let out a ripe oath, which echoed hollowly in the chimney, and fumbled for the lamp.

Diana, who had anticipated the inevitable result, caught the lamp before it hit the floor. Andy turned and peered out at her. "Oh, it's you. Good, hold that for me, will you?"

"I am holding it."

"Not that way. Point it here." He took her hand and the lamp and adjusted the latter to his satisfaction, if not to Diana's; she had to bend sharply at the waist to keep the beam of light where he wanted it.

"What the hell are you doing?" she demanded.

Andy took a hammer and a chisel from his pocket. "I want to see what's behind these bricks." Before she could object he had positioned the chisel and struck a sharp blow with the hammer. A cloud of sooty dust descended on his head and wafted gently out into the room.

Diana sneezed. "Stop it! You're making a mess."

"I thought they had this chimney cleaned," Andy muttered. "Hmmm. Maybe I can get at it better from the front."

He emerged from the opening like a gnome from a cavern, his eyeballs gleaming whitely in his soot-streaked face.

Diana decided to try another approach. "Andy, give me a break. Your mother left me in charge here, and I promised her I'd have this room in order when she gets back. If you're going to tear it apart—"

"Oh ye of little faith! I'm just trying to help. That crew Ma hired to fix the fireplace are no damned good, I warned her about them, but she wouldn't listen to me. If you're counting on them to finish this job by the end of next week, you're living in a dreamworld."

"So you're going to do it all by your little self?"

Andy struck an attitude, brandishing his hammer like a sword. "Lady, by yonder blessed lamp I swear, that by hook or crook, one way or another, come Friday that new mantel will be in place. But first there's something I want to check out. Look here—" He took the lamp from her hand and poked it back into the cavity. "See how the brickwork on the sides differs from the bricks toward the back? This fireplace has been made smaller, probably when some Victorian vandal ripped out the old mantel so he could 'modernize' the decor."

"Very interesting," Diana remarked. "But is there a practical point to your lecture?"

"Certainly. I'm just filling in the necessary . . . Oh, all right, I'll get to the point. When the fireplace opening was narrowed to fit the fancy new mantel, they had to fill in the frame of the opening. This room was probably paneled originally, with cupboards or shelves on either side of the fireplace. Maybe the wood rotted out, or got chewed by termites, or maybe the owner preferred wallpaper covered with bright-red cabbage roses. There's no accounting for tastes, like the man said, and I . . . Oh. Right. Get to the point. So, when the fireplace was altered, they also removed the paneling, plastered the wall and then painted it, or maybe . . . What's the matter?"

"I have a horrible premonition of what you're going to propose," Diana said. "If you think I am going to allow you to knock the plaster off a twenty-foot-long, twelve-foot-high stretch of wall—"

"No, no! Just the part next to the fireplace."

"Andy!"

"You said yourself the opening has to be widened."

"That's what the foreman told me. And you told me he was no damned good."

"Unreliable, I said, not incompetent. I mean, for God's sake, you can see it yourself—just measure the opening in the wall and the new mantel. They don't fit."

"I don't know why I'm arguing," Diana sighed. "There's no way I can stop you short of physical violence, and I'm too tired for that."

"Good. I hate physical violence." Andy aimed the chisel and gave it a resounding whack. Plaster flew far and wide.

Diana fled into the hall, where she saw Mary Jo running down the stairs. "What on earth is going on?" the other woman demanded. A series of horrible crashes came from the library.

Diana explained. Mary Jo's eyes narrowed with amusement. "Don't feel bad, Mr. Nicholson's the only one who can stop Andy when he's on one of his crusades. You know what he's hoping to find, don't you?"

"I wouldn't dare venture a guess."

Mary Jo grinned broadly. "Secret passages, hidden rooms, priest holes—"

"There aren't any priest holes in American houses," Diana exclaimed. "They're only found in England."

"And they're called priest holes because devout Catholic families practicing their religion in secret after Queen Elizabeth the First forced everybody to turn Protestant needed a hiding place for visiting priests who would have been executed if they had been found." Mary Jo blurted it out in a single breath, and gave Diana a challenging look.

"You know more history than I do," Diana said equably. "Shall we tell Andy?"

"It would take more than cold, hard facts to stop Andy. Old houses like this were remodeled over and over; he might actually find an empty cupboard or a door that goes no place. Let him mess around awhile longer, and then we'll eat. Are you getting hungry?"

"Anytime."

Half an hour later they gathered around the kitchen table, which was spread with an assortment of white cardboard cartons. Andy had washed "the parts that showed," but his hair was prematurely white with plaster dust and his clothes emitted puffs of the same substance whenever he moved. Mary Jo had refused his invitation to join him in a beer; she was drinking coffee. When Andy went to get a second can she said firmly, "That's the last, Andy. The cops have had a checkpoint on the highway the last two Saturday nights."

"I was thinking maybe I could—"

"No, you can't. I have about eight hours studying to do tonight, and I need to use the word processor."

"But I won't—"

"Yes, you will. You can't resist that fireplace any more than a kid can resist a box of cookies, and the computer's in the library." Mary Jo helped herself to another serving of Moo Goo Gai Pan and shoved the carton toward Andy. "Finish it, and then go away. Don't you have a date or something?"

"I thought I had something," Andy muttered, eating from the carton. "I don't suppose there's any use appealing to you." He turned pensive brown eyes on Diana. She shook her head.

"I have to work too."

"Oh, okay. Anybody want the rest of the sweet and sour shrimp?"

Nobody did. After he had emptied the carton Andy pushed his chair back. "I'll just go clean up the mess in—"

"You'll go straight out the front door," Mary Jo said sternly. "I'm not letting you back in that library."

"Can I have my fortune cookie first?"

Diana declined her cookie. "You don't have to eat the damned thing," Andy said. "But you have to open it and read your fortune. I'll go first."

Unfolding the slip of paper, he read aloud, " 'Lucky in love, unlucky in war.' A portent, a definite portent." He looked soulfully at Mary Jo.

"That's not right, is it?" she asked, ignoring the byplay. "I thought it was the other way around."

"Unlucky at cards?" Diana contributed.

"Whatever." Mary Jo unfolded her fortune. " 'A word to the wise is sufficient.' That's not very interesting. What's yours, Diana?"

Diana cleared her throat. " 'Honesty is the best policy.' "

"None of them is exactly dazzling," Andy admitted. "I remember once . . ."

Mary Jo cut short his monologue on "Interesting Fortune Cookies I Have Read," refused his plea for another beer or another cup of coffee and his offer to help with the dishes, and escorted him to the door. She was back sooner than Diana had expected; together they rinsed the dishes and put away the remains of the food.

"I'm going for a walk," Diana announced. "I ate too much. Want to come along?"

Mary Jo looked wistfully at the window, which framed a brilliant sunset and a vista of green boughs. A cool breeze stirred the curtains. "I'd like to, but I've got two papers due Monday and I haven't started either one. I have to ace them both if I want that scholarship."

"Isn't it late in the year to be applying for a scholarship?"

"I applied months ago. I still have a chance to get it if a couple of other people who are ahead of me on the list turn it down. You know how the system works; people submit multiple applications, for colleges and for aid, turn down the ones they aren't keen on if a better offer comes in." Mary Jo's eyes went distant. "I've got to assume I'll get it," she said flatly. "I'm not going to one of your fancy four-year colleges—didn't Brad tell you? This is the local two-year junior college, the only one I could afford. If the scholarship comes through, I can go to the university for my third year. Without it, I'll have to go to work, and save the money . . . somehow. I don't know whether I've got the guts to do that."

It was not an appeal for sympathy; in fact, Diana knew meaningless words of admiration or encouragement or pity would be deeply resented. She remained silent, and after a moment Mary Jo went on in her usual brisk voice, "So I better do a damned good job on these papers. You go ahead and take your walk. Later, I'd like to talk to you about Brad. That's one of the reasons why I kicked Andy out, so we could talk. Not that I've got any new ideas," she added quickly. "I'd have told you right away if I'd remembered anything important. I just think we ought to discuss it some more."

"I appreciate that."

"Let me get in a couple of hours work first, okay?"

"Of course. Will it bother you if I work in the library too? I won't open my mouth, I promise."

"Lady, I've learned to read a book while I flip hamburgers and wash dishes." Mary Jo's smile was not amused. "You won't bother me. Andy's the only one who gets under my skin."

She left the room and Diana went to the back door. The big Saint Bernard heaved itself to its feet and followed.

Instead of going farther, she sat down on the terrace steps, the dog huddled next to her. Sunset was deepening into twilight; a single bright star shone in the west. The dying light washed the quiet meadows and darkening trees with gentle shadows. Yet there was a difference in the peaceful scene that evening—something felt or known rather than something seen. The woods were not empty and peaceful. Death walked between the trees; before morning it would end innumerable small lives. Mice, fallen prey to owl and cat, rabbits cornered by dogs and foxes. She had not thought of it that way until the most vicious of all killers had left the signs of his intrusion. It might not be such a bright idea to stroll romantically in the twilight.

Yet the silence was unbroken except by the chirping of birds— or bats?—whose winged shapes swept across the sky on a last evening flight before they settled into their nests. They were probably killing things too, Diana thought morbidly—getting a little bedtime snack of stray bugs and beetles.

The dog's head lifted alertly. A low growl rumbled in her throat. She was looking out across the meadow toward the trees.

"Stop that!" Diana exclaimed—and cringed at the sound of her own voice, abnormally amplified by the quiet and by her own state of nerves. She was familiar with the infuriating habit dogs have of staring fixedly at some invisible—and, one must assume, nonexistent—object. It didn't mean a thing. However . . .

She locked and bolted the kitchen door as soon as she was inside, shutting out the night like a timid Victorian female or primitive believer in evil spirits. There were worse things in the dark than evil spirits, though. Human beings—the most dangerous of all species.

When the decision had come to her she could not have said, but she acted on it at once before she could change her mind. She charged the call on her credit card. The phone rang for a long time, and she was about to hang up, with a cowardly feeling of relief, when she heard her father's voice. Usually someone else answered the phone for him. When he was forced to do it himself he always sounded as if he were expecting an obscene phone call.

"Yes? Who is it?"

" 'Hello,' is the conventional greeting," Diana said.

"Diana? Is it you? Where are you? I've been trying to reach you."

Her throat tightened. "Mother! Is she—"

"The situation is unchanged," said the dry cool voice. "But it was irresponsible of you to make yourself unavailable. I had no idea until today, when I called your office, that you had decided to take a holiday. Where are you?"

The rush of emotion that filled her wasn't anger or guilt or any single simple sensation. It started in the pit of her stomach and erupted like a geyser, filling every part of her body in a single gush.

"I want you to do something for me," she said calmly. "Is Mother there?"

"She's sleeping." He was furious at her refusal to answer his question, but he wouldn't ask again.

"At this hour? It's only—"

"Sleeping, unconscious, drugged. She had a bad day. They are," said the cool voice, "all bad lately. She took some of her dope and went to bed."

She had planned to keep her mother on the phone while her father did as she asked, but this might work just as well. "You know where she keeps Brad's letters, don't you?"

The silence went on so long she thought he was going to hang up on her. When he said, "Yes," the word snapped like a whip.

"If she's that far gone, she won't hear you. I want copies of those letters, Father. Send them to me Monday morning, overnight express. I'll give you the address. Have you got a pencil?"

His arrogance had one advantage; it forbade demands, pleas, even questions. He repeated the address after he had written it down. "So that's it," he said. "I'm surprised at you, Diana. You are wasting time and effort on a silly, sentimental pilgrimage."

She didn't ask how he knew the significance of the address. He made a point of knowing things, and he could not be wholly indifferent to his son's fate.

"Make sure you put the letters back before Mother looks for them," she said. "Not that she wouldn't be pleased to learn that you had bothered to read them."

His indrawn breath was harsh enough to sound clearly across the miles. Dazed by her own daring, Diana went on, "Did you have some reason for calling my office, or did you just want to chat?"

Perhaps he didn't even recognize it as sarcasm. She had never used it with him before. "Neither. I expect you to communicate at reasonable intervals. When you do not, I . . . I am forced to take action myself."

How had he learned to use his voice as a weapon? She had to bite down hard on her lip to keep from babbling apologies. "Well, you have the address now, Father. I'm staying a little longer, but I'll be back in the office in a week or ten days. Thanks for making those copies. I'll expect them Tuesday. Tell Mother I called and give her my love. Good night."

She hung up before he could ask for the phone number. Her hands were so unsteady she had to try twice before the instrument landed in the cradle.

A warm, heavy weight lay across her feet. Looking down, she saw Baby curled up in her protective posture and reached down to place a reassuring hand on the massive head. "It's okay. I appreciate your sympathy, but you can't defend me from this."

Responsive to voice and touch, the big dog whined in a puzzled way, but she relaxed when Diana let out a breath of shaky laughter. How had she ever had the guts to say those things? It was as if some demon had seized control of her vocal cords. Who knows, she thought sardonically, someday I may get courage enough to say them to his face.

He would do as she had asked, if only to prove that he wasn't afraid of seeing—touching—Brad's letters. He might even read them. It would require inhuman control not to do so, for he did care—deeply, painfully. He had come close to betraying himself when he tried to find a rational, unsentimental reason for calling her. To have a second child vanish into nothingness as the first had done . . . He must have had a few bad moments since he learned she wasn't at the office.

She found she was glad of that, and ashamed of herself for being glad.

Night had gathered around the house when she roused herself from her reverie, and she went to the back door to call the cats in. She doubted they would choose to answer the call; as the lure of warm weather and brightening moonlight strengthened, they preferred prowling to sleeping. Both males and females had been deprived of one popular feline sport, for the Nicholsons were conscientious about not adding to the pitiful numbers of unwanted, abandoned pets, but the operation obviously didn't diminish hunting skills. Almost every morning there were trophies on the doorsteps.

Diana opened the door. The moon hung low above the dark outlines of the trees.

Light from the open doorway stretched across the clipped green grass. The beds by the kitchen door were purple with violets; their heart-shaped leaves looked as if they had been carved from jade.

*The breeze carried a soft, pervasive sweetness. Moonlight silvered
the blossoms of blooming trees. A square of golden lamplight shone
through the leaves, and near the steps leading to the lower terrace
a dark shape moved.*

"Don't yell, for God's sake—it's only me," said Andy, hurrying
up the steps.

Relief and fury gripped her throat and robbed her of the ability
to speak for a moment. "You," she gasped. "You are the
most . . . How dare you frighten me that way? What are you doing
here?"

"My car broke down."

"You left over an hour ago!"

"I've been trying to fix it," Andy said in an injured voice. "I
knew you didn't want me here, so I . . . What's the matter? You
look funny."

"Funny! I don't feel . . ." Funny was one word for it; dizzy,
disoriented, confused . . . He caught her as she swayed and she
clung to him as the ground shifted under her feet and the shapes
of trees and buildings wavered like images painted on windblown
fabric.

Pain gnawed at her arm and as her head cleared she realized his
hand was pressing on the bruises his fingers had left earlier that
day. She drew a deep, steadying breath.

"Let go."

"Are you sure you're all right?"

"Certainly."

"My fault, I suppose," Andy said resignedly. "It's the first time
I've ever scared a woman into a faint, though."

Diana started to speak, but caught herself. Much as she disliked
having him think of her as a timid, swooning female, it was better
than trying to explain that bizarre experience—even to herself.

"I've got jumper cables," she said.

"No good. The battery's had it. I need a new one, but I'm
damned if I'm going to go looking for one tonight."

"Mary Jo will kill you."

"She doesn't have to know I'm here. I'll sneak up the back
stairs—"

"And scare the fits out of her when she encounters you prowling
around in the middle of the night, which she will, because you

will, and that's what you call the general perversity of things."
Diana put both hands against his chest and shoved. He let her go,
grinning, and she went on, "Stay in the kitchen. I'll tell her you're
here, but not till later."

"Yes, ma'am. Whatever you say."

She led him in and closed the door. The big dog raised a lazy
head and gave a sharp bark of greeting. "A helluva watchdog you
are," Diana said, glowering at the animal.

"She knows me," Andy said. "If I'd been a burglar—"

"Lower your voice! Stay here, keep the door closed, and don't
make a noise. Mary Jo needs a few hours of peace and quiet. If
you interrupt her I'll kill you myself and spare her the trouble."

"Sure, right, absolutely. Can I—"

"No."

"Can't I even finish a—"

"No."

Andy's smile was broad and unrepentant. "If I tell you you're
cute when you're mad, will you—"

"Yes. Sit down. There." Arms folded, she watched him tiptoe
to the rocking chair and lower himself into it. "Good," she said.
"Now stay there. Maybe if you behave yourself I'll let you join us
later. Don't call us, we'll call you."

Andy opened his eyes as wide as they would go, pressed his lips
tightly together, and nodded vigorously. Diana kept her face
straight until she had closed the kitchen door. He was a rather
engaging character, but if you gave him an inch, he'd take a mile.

Her amusement didn't endure, however. As she went slowly
along the corridor, absently rubbing her sore arm, she relived the
uncanny shift of viewpoint. The first time it had happened she had
been too busy falling down in the water and trying to rescue Andy
and the dog to worry about it. On the other occasions she had
slipped gently back into reality, hardly conscious of the transition.
But this time Andy's abrupt appearance had shocked her into
awareness, and forced upon her the realization that what she had
seen bore no resemblance to the reality of the present. "Déjà vu"
was a comforting term, but it was beginning to wear a little thin.

CHAPTER TEN

If you want a red rose you must build it out of music by moonlight, and stain it with your own heart's blood.

—OSCAR WILDE

*T*he sight of the mess Andy had made in the library distracted Diana from her uncomfortable cogitations. She let out an emphatic "Damn!" and then looked guiltily at Mary Jo.

She needn't have worried. Mary Jo did not speak or look at her; perched on the edge of the chair like a chessmaster pondering his next move, she stared at the glowing screen of the computer.

It didn't seem possible that all the debris scattered across the floor could have come from the relatively small hole in the wall. Torn between curiosity and outrage, Diana tiptoed toward it, trying to avoid stepping on the plaster. Andy's feet had already ground some of it into powder, but at least he had had the decency to fold back the rug before he began.

The opening was irregular in outline and in depth. Only in the center had Andy managed to penetrate beyond layers of plaster and lath to a rough wooden surface. No doubt a student of historical architecture could have interpreted the meaning of the various layers, but they meant nothing to Diana; after a cursory glance she retreated, wondering if she dared fetch a dustpan and broom. Reluctantly she decided she didn't. Mary Jo would feel compelled to help her, and in order to get cleaning materials she would have to return to the kitchen, where Andy perched like a vulture ready to pounce. She'd never get away from him if he started talking.

She sat down with her back to the chaos and selected a book at random. Two cats joined her; after a mild disagreement as to which had priority, the calico walked off in a huff, tail switching, and Miss Matilda settled onto her lap in a smug, purring ball.

By a not-so-strange coincidence, the book turned out to be about roses. At first her mind wandered, wondering what Andy was doing and how long he would go on doing it, recalling her conversation with her father and fighting to keep from feeling guilty about it, remembering those uncanny moments when she had seemed to be somewhere else—or *someone* else? Gradually, however, the charm of what she was reading quieted her troubled thoughts. She would never be an expert, but she certainly had learned more about roses than she had ever expected to know.

It was no wonder Emily's historian's heart was entranced by the old roses. Modern tea roses had a porcelain perfection, but except for differences in color, they looked very much alike, and they had not been developed until the middle of the nineteenth century A.D. How could such a parvenu hold the romance of a flower that had been found in tombs of nineteen hundred B.C.? Who would prefer an upstart of recent lineage when he could own the same rose that had bloomed in Joséphine's garden at Malmaison, or one that had been plucked from a bush in the Temple courtyard by a medieval knight as symbol of loyalty to his king? That story about the red and white roses, immortalized by Shakespeare, had been questioned by historians; but who cared whether it was true? It *ought* to be true.

The White Rose of York and the Red Rose of Lancaster were Abigail Adams's roses, the ones Emily had mentioned. Abigail had carried shoots of them to her new home in Massachusetts in 1788. The white rose was still alive a century later, but it had stopped blooming; when Abigail's great-grandson, Brooks Adams, transplanted the bush, it burst into blossom. It had marked its bicentennial in 1988. Perhaps Emily's hopes for the antiquity of her rose garden weren't so unreasonable.

We'll have to have that one, Diana thought, studying the photograph of ruffled white petals surrounding a heart of golden stamens. She had seen it listed in modern nursey catalogs—*Rosa alba semi-plena,* the White Rose of York.

But she would never see it—at least not here. Nor anywhere else, in all probability. She would never be able to see a rose, much less one of the lovely old varieties, without being reminded of her perfidy toward people who had trusted her.

The shrill buzz of the telephone made her start. Mary Jo hunched her shoulders irritably and went on typing. Diana shifted the cat and got up, but before she could reach the phone the ringing stopped.

Andy must have picked up the extension in the kitchen. It was time she checked on him; she was surprised to see how late it was. She had been dreaming over old roses for several hours.

She found Andy sprawled on the couch in the kitchen with the telephone in his hand. "Here she is now," he said. "You want to talk to her?"

A sour expression crossed his face as he listened to the reply. Then he said, "Yes, I know that's why you called. Here she is."

There must have been two telephones in the hotel suite, for both Nicholsons were on the other end of the line. They were talking to each other, and Charles was sputtering over Andy's loquacity. "This is long-distance, damn it! Doesn't he realize that if we'd wanted to chat with him we'd have called his number? What's he doing there anyhow?"

"Now, Charlie, darling, don't get excited. We're rich, remember? We can afford to talk as long as we like. Although it is a little silly, darling, for you and me to converse via long distance. Diana, are you there?"

"Yes." She went on without stopping to draw breath, knowing she would never manage to insert a question if she let the Nicholsons get control of the conversation. "Are you having fun? Where are you?"

She heard all about Charleston, and Mrs. Bachelder's rose garden, and all the new flowers Emily had seen and wanted. After some time Charles cleared his throat loudly. "What's going on there? Andy was telling us some cock-and-bull story about the fireplace. Is he tearing the place apart?"

"Uh . . ." Diana glanced at Andy, who was spooning instant coffee into cups and pretending not to listen. If normal human ears could prick like those of a listening cat, his were doing it. They were rather pointed, now that she looked closely.

She launched into an explanation, trying to make Andy sound like a good Samaritan instead of a wanton destroyer of home and hearth—not only because he was listening, but because she didn't want to upset the Nicholsons. In the latter aim she did not succeed; Charles kept making noises like a kettle boiling over, and finally exclaimed, "Your tact does you credit, Diana, but I can read between the lines. Let me talk to that young—"

"Don't you dare," Emily cried. "I will not have Charlie and Andy yelling at each other across the miles. Charlie, you stop picking on Diana."

"I'm not picking on her! I'm not blaming her. That's why I want to talk to—"

"Hang up, Charlie, darling."

After a further interval of huffing and puffing, Charlie darling did as he was told. "Everything is fine, really," Diana said. "Andy's car broke down, that's why he's here."

"That I can believe." Amusement warmed Emily's voice. "Let him play, Diana, if he isn't driving you crazy. I'm sure he'll have everything cleaned up by the time we get back."

Touching confidence, Diana thought—but she didn't say it. She couldn't have done so in any case, for Emily went on, "I didn't tell you the most exciting thing—we got an introduction from Mrs. Bachelder to another old-rose grower. His garden is supposed to be absolutely magnificent, and he never lets people visit unless they're recommended by a friend—of whom, apparently, he only has two . . . Oh, all right, Charlie, I know it's late and this is costing a fortune and so on. The point is, Diana, we can't see it till next Sunday, so we may be a few days late getting back. I know you have other plans, so you just go ahead with them, I've already spoken to Andy about it, and if Mary Jo doesn't want to stay, he will. So that's all right. Oh, I must tell you about the White Rose of York I saw in Mrs. Bachelder's garden—it is so beautiful, we must have one. Some. Lots!"

"That's funny," Diana said slowly. "I was just reading about it and thinking the same thing."

Emily crowed with delight. "Were you really? We are en rapport! I firmly believe in ESP, or whatever they're calling it these days— we used to call it thought transference, and I'm convinced that two minds can communicate if they are in sympathy with one another. Oh, dear, Charlie's yelling at me, I must hang up, but I have to tell you I'm not at all surprised we should be able to touch one another's minds. I knew the minute I saw you we would be friends. Good night—"

"Just a minute," Diana said.

"Yes, my dear?"

"About next weekend." The words emerged as smoothly as if they had long since formed and settled in her mind. "There's no problem. I'll stay till you and Charles get back. Take as much time as you like."

"But your other job—"

"I can postpone it."

"Are you sure? I don't want to impose—"

"I'm sure. Absolutely sure."

After she had hung up she stood staring blankly at the telephone. Her back was turned to Andy; she could hear his footsteps, the splash of water into the cups, the clink of teaspoons.

"What do you take in your coffee?" he asked.

Diana turned. "I'll do it," she said. "Do you want milk or cream in yours?"

"Those are for you and Mary Jo," Andy answered. "I'm so full of coffee I'm sloshing. She takes hers black."

Diana smiled. "Indulgence isn't her style, is it?"

"You've got her pegged." Andy yawned and laughed simultaneously. "I was tempted to dump whipping cream and four teaspoons of sugar into her coffee as a gesture of protest against unnecessary abstemiousness. God knows she's had a tough time, but she's made doing without a personal religion."

"I'll take it in to her. I haven't told her you're here, Andy; she's working so hard I can't bring myself to disturb her. Maybe later."

"Oh. I don't suppose you have time for a little—"

"Chat? No."

To her surprise he didn't insist. Flinging himself down on the couch, he smiled lazily at her. "Okay. Feel free to change your mind at any hour of the day or night."

"Thank you."

She was almost at the door when he added, "I'll sack out here instead of going upstairs. So if you see anybody—or anything— wandering around, it won't be me."

When Diana entered the library, Mary Jo leaned back in her chair with a sigh. "I'm almost through," she said apologetically.

" 'Finished,' you mean," Diana said, studying the other woman's drawn face and shadowed eyes.

"I'm fine. That coffee is just what I need. Thanks. Give me another half hour?"

"Another eight hours, if you want them."

"My brain's going to go down in a few more minutes," Mary Jo said. "But I've got a lot done. It's easy to work here—so nice and quiet, you know."

Her eyes had already strayed back to the notes beside her, so Diana only murmured agreement and retreated to her chair. Compared to the crowded computer room at the college or Mary Jo's own quarters—a single shabby, cramped room in a boarding-house, probably—this must seem a haven indeed.

Diana picked up her book and turned the pages, looking for a picture of the Red Rose of Lancaster. Emily would certainly want a few of those, though she was probably a Yorkist by sympathy. And how about the one called Lancaster and York—a striped blend of the two colors?

The picture on the page blurred as her eyes focused on some other object—something invisible, within her own mind. The import of what she had done had been slow to achieve full realization. The commitment was more than that of a few extra days of time. Implicit in that promise—to her, at any rate—had been full confession.

It had not been the impulse of a moment. She had no inclination to change her mind. This must be how a good Catholic felt after receiving absolution—purged and at peace. She hadn't made her confession yet; it would have to be done in person, face-to-face, not blurted out over a telephone. But the decision to do so had been made; it was irrevocable, and almost as cathartic as the act itself.

Admittedly there was a certain element of selfishness in that decision. Whether the Nicholsons forgave her or not—and she knew she could expect, at the least, a prolonged tongue-lashing from Charles—she had a chance of retaining a friendship that had come to mean a great deal to her. And of seeing the White Rose of York flower in a friend's garden.

It was more than that, however. Something drew her to this house—something that had gradually strengthened its hold on her as slowly and inexorably as honeysuckle coils around a branch. Something to do with Brad.

She must have been crazy to believe she could accomplish anything by coming here incognito, under false pretenses. Literally crazy—temporarily insane. She had had the consummate arrogance to despise her mother—oh, yes, she had—for going off the deep end, but her own state of mind had been equally abnormal. Luckily she had come to her senses before it was too late. There was still a chance of finding a clue to Brad's fate, or exhausting all hope of ever finding one. The Nicholsons would help, she had no doubt of that. Odd, how in such a short time she had come to know them well enough to be absolutely certain of how they would react. Charles would cuss her out, not only for lying to them but for stupidity; Emily would understand and sympathize and throw herself zestfully into the role of little-old-lady detective. Emily's enthusiasm might be a problem. If she started thinking of herself as the Miss Marple of Faberville . . .

The big dog, who had been drowsing at her feet, suddenly rose and began to growl. Several seconds later Diana heard the sound its keener ears had caught—the sound of a car's engine.

Too quickly it rose to a roar. Only a dire emergency or a driver's irresponsibility could account for such speed. Diana jumped up as the vehicle came to a shrieking stop outside. Heavy feet thudded up the steps and an even heavier object struck the door. A voice called out. She knew it was a man's voice, though it sounded more like an animal roar, the words barely intelligible.

Shocked into immobility, Diana realized she ought to have anticipated this. Walt had—and Andy had heeded Walt's warning, that was why he had invented a series of absurd excuses for spending the night. He hadn't wanted to frighten them unnecessarily in case Larry didn't show up, but it was a safe bet that Larry would. This was Saturday night, the traditional time to tie one on, to remember old grievances and go out looking for trouble.

He was pounding on the door and yelling—demands to be let in mixed with unimaginative obscenities. Diana caught Mary Jo by the arm as the other woman started toward the hall. "Where are you going?"

Mary Jo's face was a gray stone mask. "I shouldn't have come here. Let go of me. I'll get rid of him."

"If you try to open that door I'll break your arm." Diana tightened her grip. Under her fingers Mary Jo's muscles were bunched into tight knots. "Don't even answer him. He can't get in. Let him wear himself out yelling and kicking the door. There," she added triumphantly, as the noise stopped. "He's given up."

"He's gone around to the back," Mary Jo said. "You don't know him. He won't give up so easily."

Her seeming calm was only a thin shell; she gasped and flinched when she heard footsteps in the hall. Diana said quickly, "It's only Andy. His car broke down and he came back to spend the night."

Andy had obviously been asleep. His hair stood up in an agitated halo at the back of his head and hung down over his forehead in front. He was clawing it out of his eyes as he came in, accompanied by a furious chorus of distant barking. "Everything all right?" he inquired.

"Of all the stupid questions!" Diana exclaimed.

"He's at the back door," Mary Jo said. "Listen to the dogs. Diana, believe me, he won't give up and go away. Remember I told you about the guy who tried to rape me?"

"Oh, my God. Was it—"

"I was lucky that time," Mary Jo admitted. "Caught him off-guard. But I can handle him. Let go of me, Diana. I'll try to talk some sense into him. If I don't he'll . . . There's hardly anything he won't do. Break the door down, try to set fire to the house."

"We could let the dogs out." Diana looked at the Saint Bernard, who was pressed close to her side.

"He's probably got a gun," Mary Jo said. "He collects the damned things—carries a shotgun in the truck—and he wouldn't hesitate to use it on an animal."

"You have called the cops, haven't you?" Andy asked.

"What?" Diana stared at him.

"Oh, for God's sake!" Andy headed for the phone. "I admire tough ladies, but tackling that bastard yourself wouldn't be courageous, it would be terminally dumb. You notice I'm not offering to take him on."

The suggestion was so obvious Diana was infuriated that she hadn't thought of it. Illogically and inevitably, her anger turned on Andy. "Yes, I did notice."

He gave her an amused smile. "Here, you talk to them. They'll respond more promptly to a woman, and I have my macho image to maintain."

Diana snatched the phone from him and began explaining the situation to a rather bored desk sergeant. She got the impression that Saturday-night brawls, public and domestic, were not uncommon, but one of his questions brought her anger to the boiling point. "No, he's not my goddamned husband," she shouted. "What difference does it make? He's drunk and violent and he's—"

"Breaking and entering," said Andy, with a certain grim satisfaction. "That was window glass shattering. I'd better go see . . . God damn it!"

The sounds that sent him sprinting for the door were not those of breaking glass. The crack of a gunshot mingled with the high-pitched howl of a dog.

"He's just shot one of my dogs," Diana reported. "Is that sufficient, or do you want to try for—"

"On our way, lady. Now you keep calm. Don't confront him, go lock yourself in a closet or the bathroom or—"

"Oh, shut up," Diana snarled, slamming the phone back into the cradle.

The room was empty except for a few confused cats and Baby, who was trying to push her down onto the floor. Diana shoved ineffectually at the big hairy mass. Mary Jo must have followed Andy to the kitchen, she was fool enough to get in the way of a bullet to protect him, and Andy was fool enough to attack a man with a gun to shield the dogs, much less Mary Jo . . . Baby would not get out of her way. The big dog kept shifting and shoving. Diana darted for the door.

Later, she insisted Baby had put out a paw and deliberately tripped her. She stumbled and fell; with a whoop of relief, Baby collapsed across her, pinning her down. Simultaneously, the French windows exploded inward.

He looked larger than life as he stood there, weaving back and forth and squinting through half-closed eyes. He did have a gun— not a shotgun, a hand weapon of some kind. Diana couldn't see it clearly, dog hair fogged her vision. The breath had already been knocked out of her by her fall and by Baby's weight, but if there had been any air left in her lungs it would have been driven out by sheer terror. Nevertheless she struggled to push the dog off, or to squirm out from under it. Her efforts only increased Baby's determination to keep her prostrate and—in Baby's judgment— safe.

Larry stared bemusedly at them. The combination of dog and woman would have confused even a sensible individual, and he was so blind drunk Diana marveled that he could stay on his feet. "Mary Jo?" he said uncertainly.

Diana found her breath. "No! No, it's not Mary Jo, she's not here. Go away! You'd better hurry, the police are coming."

They were, in fact. The scream of a siren undulated and swelled.

The sound penetrated Larry's alcohol-fogged brain; his slack, stupid face took on a look of crafty calculation. He tried to stuff the gun into his pocket. Unfortunately Mary Jo and Andy arrived on the scene before his clumsy hands could complete the job.

Andy jerked to a stop and threw both arms around Mary Jo. Nothing less would have stopped her; she struggled, mindlessly and frantically. The siren cut off, leaving a deafening silence, in which the sound of knocking at the door sounded like bass drumbeats.

The door was chained and bolted; the police couldn't get in that way unless someone let them in. "Go around to the back!" Diana screamed. Larry paid no attention to her or the pounding on the door; the sight of Andy and Mary Jo, locked in a close embrace, had focused his entire attention. He raised the gun, gripping it with both hands in a drunken parody of the approved stance, squinted, and squeezed the trigger.

Andy threw Mary Jo to the floor behind a high-backed Victorian sofa, and followed her down. Ears ringing from the thunder of the shot, Diana couldn't tell whether either of them had been hit. Only Andy's legs were visible; for an eternity—or so it seemed to Diana—they did not move. Then they disappeared and Andy's face rose slowly into view over the top of the sofa. Blood trickled down his chin.

Larry fired again. The bullet slammed into the wall near the empty fireplace. Andy turned his head to follow its path, an expression of idiot curiosity on his face. He stood up. The third shot took a chip off the carved rosewood arm of the sofa, and Larry let out a wordless bellow of frustration. He advanced into the room in a sudden rush and took careful aim. Andy raised one hand to his head and blinked. His mouth hung open.

Where the hell were the police? It was some time later before Diana was calm enough to realize that the entire episode had lasted only a few seconds. She started to scream at Andy, but before she could get the first word out she saw it.

It hovered in the open archway. At first it was only an amorphous shape, pale against the shadows of the hall beyond. As the darkness behind it intensified it took on dimension and detail, glowing with a sickly light of its own making. It stood unmoving, unbreathing, unblinking. The sunken ragged hollows that had once been eyes were fixed on her face.

At first she thought the scream had come from her throat. She wanted to scream . . . but she hadn't, she couldn't utter a sound. It was Larry who was making the horrible high-pitched noise.

Tearing her eyes from that unspeakable vision was like pulling a finger free of hardening glue, but she knew if she couldn't do it she would start screaming too. With a gigantic effort she turned to look at Larry.

Like the crack of a stretched string, time and action snapped back to normalcy. Larry emptied the gun in a stutter of ear-splitting sound, aiming not at Andy but at the thing in the archway. He didn't wait to see what effect the bullets would have. Throwing the weapon blindly aside, he plunged out the window and vanished into the darkness.

When Diana looked again, there was nothing in the archway except shadows. The dog lay quietly beside her. She got slowly to her feet. People were running and shouting and crashing through the shrubs outside.

"Andy?" she said tentatively.

Andy's head swiveled back toward her. He looked as if he were about to be sick. Summoning up a feeble smile, he subsided slowly down behind the sofa.

The police had no sooner bumbled away than Walt arrived. No one had thought to lock the front door; Walt burst through it with the force of a cyclone, and with almost as much noise. He was in the library before any of them had time to react.

His gaze went straight to Andy, who was reclining wanly on the couch while Mary Jo arranged an icebag on his forehead. The wounded warrior got no sympathy from Walt.

"What the hell went on here? Damn it, Andy, I told you you ought to take my rifle!"

"I'd probably have blown my foot off," said Andy. "How did you find out so fast?"

"One of the guys listens to the police broadcasts. He called me." His eyes moved from Andy to Mary Jo to Diana. "You're all okay," he said.

He sounded cool, almost bored, but his face was not so well-controlled. "All they said was there'd been shooting," he went on. "I thought . . . Well."

"I was the only casualty," Andy said smugly. "A little more to the left, Mary Jo. Wounds incurred in the course of a gallant rescue—"

"What'd you do, bump your head when you dived for cover?"

Mary Jo rounded on him like a miniature Fury. "He pushed me out of the way of a bullet, you smart-ass redneck! And fell on top of me to shield me. I think he's got a concussion, but he won't go to the hospital—"

"I haven't got a concussion," Andy broke in. "Just a bump on the bean and a sore lip. I bit it when I fell. It's so damned embarrassing. I was hoping for a nice romantic (and relatively painless) wound, in the arm, say, so I could go around wearing a sling and be waited on hand and foot by adoring females."

"Tough luck, buddy." Walt sat down. "Sorry," he added awkwardly.

" 's okay." Andy waved a gracious hand. "You were worried."

"I'm still worried. They didn't catch him, did they?"

"Not yet. But this time they'll throw the book at him. Breaking and entering, assault with a deadly weapon, assault with intent to kill—"

"He did kill one of the dogs," Diana said soberly. "Emily is going to be so upset."

"No point in telling her till she gets back," Walt said. "In fact . . ."

"Right." Andy sat up, holding the icebag in place. "No point in telling them anything until they get back. With luck the cops will have nailed Larry by then."

Mary Jo shook her head. "He may not be very bright, but he's hunted and trapped all over the area. He knows every cave, every hiding place. They won't find him in a hurry."

She got up from the floor, where she had been kneeling next to Andy, and went to the computer.

"What are you doing?" Diana asked.

Mary Jo's hands moved across the keyboard. "I had almost finished the second paper. I'm going to write the last paragraph, print both of them out, and then leave. It won't take very long."

The other three exchanged glances. Diana expected Walt to expostulate, but for once he had sense enough to think before he spoke. His raised eyebrows asked a silent question of her. She nodded and shrugged. Might as well let him open the ball. It would take all three of them, and a lot of time, to convince Mary Jo. And maybe a locked bedroom door.

"Where are you going?" Walt asked.

"I'll check into a motel somewhere."

"What are you planning to use for money?"

Mary Jo didn't turn. "Get off my back, Walt."

"You can move in with me if you want."

Mary Jo told him what she thought of that idea. "Then I'll move in here," Walt said coolly. "That's probably a better solution. This is where Larry will come if he decides to try again. His skull is pretty thick; once he gets an idea into it, it stays."

There was a muffled sound from Mary Jo. Her head was bent over the keyboard, and her hands were still.

"I resent the implication that I'm not capable of protecting all and sundry," Andy said indignantly. "Just because I fell over my own feet and knocked myself out—"

"Shut up, both of you," Diana said, her eyes on Mary Jo's hunched shoulders. "You can move in and bring all your friends and relatives, I couldn't care less. Mary Jo is staying."

The bowed shoulders stiffened. Diana went on, before Mary Jo could object. She could only hope that Mary Jo's normally quick intelligence would be too fogged by emotion to spot the fallacies in her reasoning. God knows she had learned the techniques of making the most of a specious argument. "I'll tie her up and feed her with a spoon if I have to. I need her as much as she needs me—and I hope she cares as much about me as I do about her. Hasn't it dawned on you, Mary Jo, that Larry might be after me, not you? He killed my brother. And if he knows who I am—"

All three of her listeners spoke at once.

"What came over you all of a sudden?" Walt demanded.

"Brother?" Andy gasped. "What brother?"

Mary Jo had whirled around. Her eyes were bright with unshed tears, but as Diana had hoped, astonishment made her forget her own predicament. "Have you got proof?"

"Not yet. But I'm convinced now that—"

"Wait a minute," Andy shouted. "Everybody seems to know what you're talking about except me. Who the hell are you? Who the hell is your brother? What the hell is going on?"

Diana's brief explanation left him even more bewildered. "The guy who worked here last summer? The one that quoted Emily

Dickinson and . . . He's your . . . And you haven't heard from . . . Excuse me, lady, but I don't follow your logic. If that's what it is. He didn't write you for three months, so you decided he was dead? And then you decided to track him down by coming here under an assumed name, which meant you couldn't ask questions—"

"Leave her alone, Andy." Mary Jo came to Diana and put a protective arm around her. "It's been eight months, not three, and he'd never failed . . . Oh, hell, take my word for it, her reasoning makes very good sense."

"Huh," said Andy. "You were in on this too, Walt?"

"Under duress."

"What duress?"

"The feeling that she might be right," Walt said coldly.

"Oh. Yeah. Okay, I'll buy that part of it. But what she did makes no sense at all. Why not come here openly and ask people about Brad?"

"That crack on the head must have addled your brains," Mary Jo said. "Think about it, Andy."

Andy thought. Diana leaned against Mary Jo's thin shoulder, wondering how she could have been so dim as to miss the obvious. The way to win Mary Jo's friendship, and the fierce loyalty that would accompany it, was to ask for help, not offer it.

"Oh, my God," Andy said after a moment. "You didn't have the infernal gall to suspect my mother, did you?"

The outrage in his voice brought a smile to Walt's lips and made Diana laugh ruefully. "Not after I'd met her. But by then there was no graceful way out of the mess I'd gotten myself into—or so I thought. I was . . . worried sick. That sounds trite, but I guess it's literally true. I wasn't thinking clearly. I had already made up my mind to come clean with Emily and Charles; that's why I told her I'd stay till they got back."

"So you did." Andy's frown relaxed. After a moment he said quietly, "I hope you're wrong, Diana. I liked Brad."

"I hope I'm wrong too. But I'm horribly afraid I'm not wrong. After what happened tonight—"

"Larry certainly demonstrated he is capable of killing somebody," Andy agreed.

"You all knew that," Diana said. "I wasn't thinking of what he did. I was thinking of what—of what he saw. You saw it too, Andy. I know you did. And Mary Jo . . ."

She couldn't go on. The memory caught at her voice, blocked her throat.

"What he saw?" Mary Jo repeated in a puzzled voice. "The cops, you mean?"

"No." Diana tried to clear her throat, without much success. "I didn't . . . I thought you . . ."

Andy's eyes narrowed as he watched her. "Take it easy, Di. A little delayed shock, maybe? I wouldn't try to talk if I were you. How about a nice hot cup of tea? I could use one myself."

"I'll get it." Mary Jo straightened. "You want something, Walt?"

Walt caught the almost imperceptible motion of Andy's head. "I'll come and help you."

The two went out together. "He thinks he's keeping a watchful eye on her," Andy said. "Not a bad idea, actually. But I didn't want him to hear either."

"She didn't see it?"

"She was flat on the floor trying to get her breath back after I fell on her. She probably wouldn't have believed it if she had seen it. She's the ultimate rationalist. Walt's a worse skeptic, and he wasn't even here. Don't try to convince either of them, they'll simply conclude that your trolley's off the rail. I'm not so sure it isn't," Andy added wryly.

"But you saw it! I know you did!"

"I saw . . . something. I'm beginning to suspect it wasn't the same thing you saw."

"What do you mean?"

Andy shifted uneasily. "What I saw was . . . well, it could only have had meaning for me. It couldn't have frightened you—and it did, didn't it? You can't even refer to it except by using a safe impersonal pronoun. And it sure as hell couldn't have scared the bejesus out of Larry."

"What I saw . . . could have." Diana hid her face in her hands.

"Tell me." Andy's voice was very gentle.

"I can't."

"I'll go first," Andy said in the same voice, the one he might have used with a frightened child. "Once, when I was about six, I got lost in the woods. Our house backed up onto a state forest and I wasn't supposed to go off alone, but of course I did all the time. This time I went too far and couldn't find my way back. Night fell. There was no moon. The trees creaked and the branches rustled, and I knew—I knew!—there were monsters in the dark. I ended up crouched at the foot of a tree, and finally I cried myself to sleep. When I woke up it was still pitch-black dark, except for a dim circle of light around me. It came from an old-fashioned oil lantern, and someone was holding it. She was bent over me, her face close to mine. She had ragged white hair sticking out from her head, and a million wrinkles on her face, and only a couple of teeth. I could see them because she was grinning at me."

Andy's laugh sounded a trifle forced. "The whole damned town was out looking for me, of course. She was the one who found me—a confused but kindly little old lady who lived in a shack near the woods. She had tried to call the other searchers, but her voice wasn't very strong; it was my screams that brought my dad and the others running. I thought she was a witch. She sure looked like one, poor woman. She had barely enough money for food, much less dentists and hairstylists. We got to be friends, later. But sometimes I meet her again in nightmares, and it's the same as it was the first time I saw her. Pure, wet-your-pants panic."

"That—she—was what you saw?" Diana asked in disbelief.

"You didn't, did you?"

"No."

Andy said nothing, which was probably the smartest thing he could have said. After a moment Diana whispered, "It was Brad. Looking the way he'd look if he had been dead and buried for eight months. There was . . . there was enough left to be recognizable."

CHAPTER ELEVEN

As this blind rose, no more than a whim of dust
achieved her excellence without intent,
so man, the casual sport of time and lust
plans wealth and war, and loves by accident.

—Humbert Wolfe

*H*er face hidden against the cushions of the couch, Diana was vaguely aware of footsteps approaching, and then, after a pause, retreating. Andy must have waved them away. His hand rested on her shoulder. It was a big hand, broad across the palm, with long fingers. Brad's hands were almost as small as a woman's, delicately shaped . . .

A violent shudder ran through her body. Andy's grip tightened. "It's okay. Cry if you want to. Let it out. There's nobody here but me."

Both hands held her now, fingers curving over the angles where neck and shoulders met, palms firm in the middle of her back. It was not so much the physical touch as what it implied—sympathy, concern, companionship—that helped Diana dispel the memory of those shapeless stumps, with white bone protruding through flesh iridescent with decay.

She turned and sat up. "I'm all right now. Sorry."

Andy leaned back, studying her with a frown. "What the hell for? I admire self-control as much as the next man, but you're overdoing it. Have yourself a nice loud fit of hysterics, why don't you? How long has this been building up—seven, eight months, did you say?"

"Not so long." Diana let her head fall back against the cushions. She felt drained. "I didn't start worrying until—oh, four or five months ago."

Andy let out a grunt of exasperation. "Is that all? Talk to me, will you, and stop being so stoic. I'm still trying to take this in. You haven't heard from him since last August?"

"A postcard from New York, typed, impersonal, with no return address. Always before that he had told me where I could reach him. He always wrote every couple of weeks."

"Uh-huh." Andy thought for a minute. "So this was his last known address. You've reported him missing, I suppose?"

"To the authorities in New York, yes."

"No results?"

"Three—no, four—bodies. None was Brad."

"Jesus," Andy muttered. "That must have been fun."

"A couple of them looked . . . were in pretty much the same shape . . ."

"I get it. So your imagination had material to work on."

"It was Brad," Diana said steadily. "Maybe what I saw was imagination, but it was also my worst nightmare. The thing I dread most in the world."

"Yeah. Think about that."

"I have been thinking about it. We saw different things. So may Larry have done. But if he did kill Brad—"

"Then his worst nightmare could be identical with yours, for different reasons. That's arguing in circles, though—assuming he saw something because you're assuming he had reason to see it."

"Point taken." Diana forced a smile. "I feel better. Why?"

"Because that wasn't your brother's avenging spirit, only an image of a horrible possibility."

Diana winced. "It sounds so stupidly melodramatic. Things like that don't happen in real life."

"They do, though. There are a number of studies on collective hallucination and mass hysteria. Hundreds of people seeing visions of the Virgin, or Elvis's profile on a refrigerator door."

"The cases are hardly parallel."

"Depends on which authority you consult. Far be it from me to be dogmatic about matters that baffle the world's great minds." Andy sighed and rubbed his forehead. "I don't have to tell you what the alternative is. I used to think ghost-hunting would be fun. *That* was not fun. It would be easier for me to dismiss it as a comfortable example of collective hallucination if I hadn't shared another one with you a few hours earlier."

His cool rational discussion of the seemingly irrational had a calming effect. For a moment Diana didn't understand what he was referring to. Then she stiffened and stared. "You too?"

"Me too. We have to talk. But," his voice quickened, as voices were heard, making loud, tactful conversation to herald their approach. "Not now. Not in front of them."

Once aroused, Mary Jo's protective instincts threatened to become overpowering. She had put so much sugar in the tea it was virtually undrinkable. When Diana choked on it, the other woman said firmly, "Drink it down. Sugar is good for shock. Then I'm going to put you to bed."

Diana didn't argue. Better to have Mary Jo think she was a sensitive shrinking violet than explain the real reason for her breakdown.

Mary Jo must have slipped a sleeping pill into the tea. Diana didn't waken until late afternoon, and she was still yawning when she and Andy met for the private meeting he had suggested.

"How romantic," she remarked. "The rose garden at sunset. Couldn't you have picked a more suitable spot?"

"The sun isn't setting and the roses aren't blooming and the place is full of weeds, and if you squat there, as you seem to intend, you'll wake up tomorrow with a flaming case of poison ivy. Try that folding stool. I brought it for you."

Diana did as he suggested. After another ear-splitting yawn she said, "Sorry. Mary Jo doped me last night. I never take sedatives because they leave me lethargic and grumpy for hours afterward."

"I noticed," Andy said. He had brought a trowel; kneeling, he began to attack the weeds. "You needed a good night's sleep, though."

"I've always slept well here."

"Without dreaming," Andy added dryly.

"I haven't had bad dreams, either. Except . . ."

"What?" He turned his head.

"It had nothing to do with this house." She didn't want to get into a discussion of her relationship with her father, so she went on quickly, "Last night I had a beautiful dream. All about roses, and music, and people dancing and laughing."

"What people?"

"I don't remember," Diana said irritably. "Don't start analyzing my dreams, Andy. They have no bearing on—"

"How do you know?" Andy dropped to a sitting position, legs crossed, and brandished the trowel at her. "Music, roses, dancing. Is there a pattern? The music, at least, is a recurrent theme. I've found your tune, by the way."

"You have?"

"Uh-huh. It's Boccherini. A minuet from one of the string quintets. A minuet," Andy said pointedly, "is a kind of dance."

"I know."

"Music, dancing. What about the roses?"

"I thought, once or twice, I caught the scent of roses. But olfactory hallucinations are—"

"God damn it," Andy said without heat. "Do I have to drag every admission out of you? Stop fighting it. We're putting together a theory, not joining the Inner Circle of the Believers in the Occult. There may be a logical explanation for all this, but we won't find it unless we discuss it."

His eyes were narrowed against the sloping sunlight and lines of laughter radiated from the corners of his mouth. One wouldn't call him good-looking; his nose was too broad and his mouth was too big, and his ears were definitely pointed. He didn't look at all like Brad, who had been, when he bothered to shave and cut his hair, almost classically handsome. Yet for some unaccountable reason Diana was briefly reminded of her brother.

"I smelled roses," she admitted. "Every time I heard the music. And again last night, when I opened the kitchen door and saw a garden where nothing exists now except bare topsoil."

"Ah." It was a small sound, acknowledging her capitulation. "I saw it too. Violets in the bed by the steps—"

"Daffodils and tulips, lilacs in bloom. But it was roses I smelled."

"I saw them," Andy said. "Below the wall of the terrace. I had sneaked around the house and was about to climb the steps. The door opened. That was when it happened, in a split second, like a picture projected onto a screen. Violets, deep purple in the light from the open door. Flowers where there had been none. Silhouetted against the light . . . It was a woman's shape. Slender, young, eager, leaning forward as if in expectation. Her hair was loose around her shoulders and her long skirt belled out from her narrow waist down to her feet . . ."

"Then," he added, in quite a different voice, "you let out a yelp, and she was gone."

"I did not yelp. What a word!"

"Cry, squeal, gasp—some kind of sound. You couldn't have seen me; you were looking out, into the dark."

"I saw something—someone. It wasn't even a silhouette, only a moving darkness. You."

"But it was there earlier? In the garden?"

"I . . . I'm not sure. It all happened so fast."

"Okay. What else? I know you heard the music on other occasions; any other unusual phenomena?"

Diana was beginning to have doubts about what she was doing; the gleam in Andy's brown eyes wakened dire suspicions. However, she had made her decision and this didn't seem to be the time to waver. Having begun, she made a thorough job of it, dutifully reporting even those incidents whose applicability might be questionable.

Andy was a wonderful audience. His mobile features stretched into a variety of expressions, ranging from interest to concern to openmouthed wonder. When she had finished he could contain himself no longer.

"Hot damn! It's almost too perfect. Those flashes of what you call déjà vu fit the rest of the pattern."

"Don't do it, Andy!"

"What? I was only—"

"Mary Jo was right, you're a hopeless romantic! I know what you're thinking—I saw the look on your face when you described that woman's shape. All you saw was an outline; how did you know she was young, eager, and—and all the rest? You're trying to make a pretty little romance out of this. What we saw last night wasn't pretty, and there's nothing romantic about murder!"

There was more she might have said, but anger robbed her of breath. For once Andy didn't interrupt, or try to defend himself. Unmoving, perfectly relaxed, he waited until she had stopped talking before he spoke.

"I'm not proposing a solution, Diana, I'm still looking for one. Go along with me for a while, can't you? I do see a pattern in this. It may be the product of my deranged romantic brain or it may be something more. I thought lawyers were trained to examine evidence."

"You have a more tolerant attitude toward my profession than most people," Diana muttered. "Oh, all right. I suppose if I can defend a savings-and-loan officer I can put together a case in favor of your girlish ghost."

Andy bowed from the waist. "Thank you, Counselor. Start with the garden. That's the most concrete vision, and one that was viewed by two independent observers. What flowers did you see?"

"Violets, daffodils, lilac. They blossom in late April or early May, depending on the weather. But the roses—"

"They weren't in bloom," Andy said. "I didn't even see any buds. Not that I was paying close attention to horticultural details right then."

"That doesn't fit, then. If we saw . . ." She hesitated, and then forced herself to say it. "If we saw some past April, the roses wouldn't have been in bloom, or giving off perfume."

"They seem to be part of the theme, though—the scent, not the actual flower. Aren't most modern roses scentless?"

"Not all. But the old roses are noted for their powerful perfume."

Andy gave her a kindly smile. "You're cooperating admirably. Now. Put it all together. An eighteenth-century dance, the perfume of old roses, a woman in an old-fashioned costume."

"I'll only go so far, Andy," Diana warned him. "If you think you can make me believe in a sort of guardian angel—"

"Ha!" Andy's voice rose in a crow of triumph. "You said it, I didn't. She—it—something—saved you from a nasty accident—"

"And showed me Brad's rotting corpse."

"Uh." Andy grimaced. "That's a little hard to explain. Maybe there are two—"

"No! I might buy one ghost. Two is at least one too many."

"You felt her feelings," Andy argued. "Thought her thoughts. She was waiting for someone, a man who went away and never came back."

Diana was silent. His reminder brought it back—the poignant longing, the eager expectation. She had thought, at the time, that it was nothing more than a reflection of her own yearning for Brad's return. At last she said, "She. Who?"

"It's only an idea—"

"Why did you suggest we meet here, in the rose garden?"

Andy gave her a sheepish smile. "Because I had a feeling you'd refuse to confer in the presence of the tombstones."

"I'm not superstitious."

"Come on then." He rose in a single lithe motion and held out his hand.

The evening light bathed the standing stones in blue shadows. "George" lay where she had seen him last, face-down upon the carpet of brown needles. Andy went straight to the third, mutilated, stone.

"She was nineteen," he said. "A daughter of the house. Unmarried—"

"Damn it, Andy, there you go again! How do you know she wasn't married? You don't even know it was a woman. The name is gone."

"A married woman would have been buried in her husband's family plot. A grown son would have had a more impressive stone."

"That's plausible," Diana admitted. "But not evidential."

"So I'll find out."

"How?"

"There's got to be a record someplace. They kept registers of births and deaths, wills, deeds. The stone gives her age."

"Stop using the feminine pronoun. You're trying to prejudice the court."

Andy laughed and put his arm around her. It was a casual, undemanding embrace, that of a friend or brother. "Far from it. I want you to be the resident skeptic. Shoot me down when I go off the deep end."

"With a harpoon, I suppose." Andy chortled politely at her feeble joke, and she went on, "We already have two skeptics."

"I'd rather we kept this to ourselves. Walt would never let me hear the end of it, and Mary Jo—"

"Sssh." She turned, breaking his hold on her. "Someone's coming."

Mary Jo's voice was some distance away. "Diana? Where are you?"

"I'm coming," Diana called back. "Where are you?"

They met near the rose garden. Mary Jo must have run all the way from the house; she was gasping for breath. "Phone call," she panted. "For you."

"Why didn't you say I'd call back?" Diana asked. "You didn't have to rush out here."

"Just what I told her." Walt had followed, at a somewhat slower pace. He was frowning.

"It's your father," Mary Jo said.

Diana caught her breath. "Mother. Did he say anything about Mother? She hasn't been well . . ."

"No. He sounded normal—not worried or anything."

"He would," Diana muttered, starting for the house. The others followed.

"I'm sure there's nothing wrong," Mary Jo said. "He didn't say it was an emergency. I don't know why I ran."

"He has that effect on people," Diana said.

It was unlike him, though, to waste time and money waiting for someone to come to the phone. Sunday afternoon . . . But he was probably at the office. He usually was, weekends and holidays as well as workdays.

She forced herself to talk slowly and speak without panting. "Father. It's Diana."

"Where were you?"

She had to bite her tongue to keep from apologizing for the delay. "Outside. I would have called you back."

"I dislike waiting for people to return my calls." He went on without giving her a chance to reply. "I'll be in Washington tomorrow. You seem to be in a hurry for those letters; if you like, I'll bring them with me and you can drive up and meet me."

"You got the copies?"

"Certainly."

"All right," Diana said slowly. "I could do that, I suppose. Thank you. I appreciate your taking the trouble."

"It's no trouble for me. Shall we say Maison Blanche, at one?"

"Yes. That's fine. How is—"

He had hung up.

Diana replaced the phone. Mary Jo had left the room, dragging Walt with her, but she hadn't been able to persuade Andy to demonstrate similar courtesy. He stood at the refrigerator, his back to her—but his ears were pricked like a fox's. Taking out a can of beer, he popped the top and turned to smile ingratiatingly at her.

"What copies?"

"Close the refrigerator door," she said automatically.

Andy obliged, using his foot. "Copies of what?"

Diana sighed. "Brad's letters." She raised her voice. "You may as well come in, you two, I don't want to have to repeat this."

"Have a beer," Andy added hospitably, as they sidled into the room.

Mary Jo's face was flushed. "I wasn't eavesdropping."

"I was," said Walt, looming over her. "But your voice is too soft, Di. Copies of what?"

"The letters Brad wrote me after he left home. Mother won't part with them; she's convinced he is dead, and she . . . Severe depression is the clinical term, I suppose. I thought there might be a clue I'd missed on the first reading, so I asked Father to make copies for me."

"Good idea," Walt said, accepting the can of beer Andy handed him. "He's mailing them?"

"That's what I asked him to do. But he has to be in D.C. tomorrow and he offered to bring them with him. I'm to meet him for lunch."

"Very thoughtful," said Walt, in a tone that contradicted the words.

"Don't be so cynical, Walt," Mary Jo said. "Of course he'd do anything possible to help Diana find out . . ." She looked doubtfully at Diana. "Wouldn't he?"

"If you'd ask me that an hour ago, I'd have said no. I didn't tell him what I planned; he didn't know I was here until I called the other night. He's insisted all along that Brad was dead. Maybe I misjudged him. All the same, I can't help wondering what he's up to."

It was a two-hour drive to Washington. Diana was up early; she had had a restless night, tossing and turning and speculating. She dressed to the now-familiar rumble of machinery and men's voices. When she came downstairs she found Andy alone in the kitchen. He looked up from the newspaper he had been reading and pursed his lips in a whistle.

"Very sharp. The young lady professional. I liked your hair better in a ponytail."

"Ponytails aren't professional." Diana went to the counter to get a cup of coffee. "You look fairly sharp youself. Except for that awful tie."

"It's the latest power tie," Andy said, squinting complacently at the bright crimson streak down his front. "I thought I'd better dude myself up if I'm going to lunch at a classy joint like Maison Blanche."

Diana scowled at him. They had argued that and several other subjects the night before. One argument had developed into a full-fledged shouting match between Mary Jo and Walt when Mary Jo declared her intention of going to work as usual.

"Why don't you just paint a target on your back?" he demanded furiously. "You aren't going anywhere until they catch the bastard. He knows your schedule—"

"He's only violent when he's drunk."

"What makes you suppose he isn't drunk?"

Walt had lost that argument, though he insisted on driving Mary Jo to work and picking her up afterward. The other argument, between Andy and Diana, had been less strident. She had believed she had won it.

"You aren't having lunch at Maison Blanche," she repeated. "We settled that last night."

"I'd love to get an expensive free lunch out of the old iceberg," Andy said.

Diana had to smile. "It's a tempting thought. No, Andy."

"Okay, okay. I'll have lunch alone at some place classy like McDonald's. But at least you can let me ride in with you. I want to start that research we discussed last night."

She knew that wasn't his real reason. The genealogical information he wanted would be found, if it was to be found anywhere, in local courthouses and historical societies. Did he see himself as riding shotgun, watching out for ambush on the lonely stretches of back road? It was absurd, but it was like Andy. She didn't know whether to be flattered at his concern or aggravated by his assumption that she couldn't take care of herself.

"All right," she said ungraciously. "Let's go."

He didn't offer to drive. Slouched and seemingly relaxed in the seat beside her, he kept an unobtrusive but keen eye on passing traffic. It wasn't until they reached Route 29 that he broke a long— for him—silence, and from then on he chattered like a magpie about everything except the subjects that mattered. Her ears were ringing by the time she reached the city.

"The Maison Blanche is that way," Andy said, pointing to the right as she signaled for a left turn.

"I know."

"Where are you going?"

"To the nearest McDonald's."

Andy grinned. "I was only funnin', as we say in the boonies. Let me off at the Metro. I'll meet you—where and when?"

"Three o'clock. I'll pick you up. Where will you be? Library of Congress?"

He agreed so readily that she knew he was not going to the Library of Congress.

She parked in a garage a block from the restaurant and checked her makeup before leaving the car. As she walked along she could feel her stomach knotting up, and wondered why she was so nervous. She hadn't felt this way about confronting her father since she was a child. Was it because she was trying to change the terms of that relationship? It had not been warm or affectionate, but it had been stable. She had learned long ago how to avoid arousing his anger or disapproval. All she had to do was behave exactly the way he wanted her to.

She was ten minutes early, but he was there before her. As she followed the waiter toward his table he rose punctiliously to greet her. She hadn't realized how drastically her feelings had changed until she actually saw him; it was as if she beheld a stranger, a man about whom she had heard a great deal but had never met.

A fine-looking man. A number of people had referred to him that way; handsome wasn't the right word, his features were too rugged, his eyes deep-set under heavy brows, his mouth disfigured by habitual tightness. Fine-looking, though. He was tall and straight and still trim of figure; his dark hair was untouched by gray except for two dramatic streaks that swept back from his temples. Distinguished. That was another word people often used.

He gave her his usual kiss on the cheek and waited until the waiter had seated her before resuming his chair. Diana began to relax. If he had been angry with her he'd have let her know. Omitting the kiss, for one thing.

"You're looking well," he said, as he might have said to an acquaintance whom he had not seen for some time. "The bucolic life seems to agree with you."

"I'm glad you think so." Diana turned her attention to the menu. He would go on making his version of small talk until after the

VANISH WITH THE ROSE

waiter had taken their orders. She knew his habits very well.

Not until that business had been disposed of did he take a folder from his briefcase. "Here you are."

"Thank you." She slipped the folder into her own case. Two lawyers, doing business over lunch . . .

His next statement was not so impersonal. "I don't know what you hope to accomplish by this, Diana. Some form of catharsis, perhaps. You will achieve nothing else."

"How do you know?" The challenge took as much courage as she possessed; she didn't dare add what she was thinking: "You aren't God Almighty."

"I don't know, of course. But it is a reasonable certainty that your brother is dead—killed in an accident or brawl in New York. People die like flies in large cities, anonymous and unremarked. That sort of violence doesn't happen in a small town."

"It happened Saturday night," Diana said. "To me. Six bullets from a forty-five."

"You'd better explain," he said after a moment.

"The same man may have killed Brad. He's pathologically jealous of his ex-wife, who was . . . friendly with Brad. She's been staying with me. It was she he was after, actually, but he was blind drunk and quite capable of blowing away anyone who got between him and Mary Jo."

"I see." He took a bite of his salad and chewed it thoroughly. "No body was found . . ."

"There are hundreds of acres of woodland and pasture around the town. Larry is a big hulk of a man. He could dig a very deep grave."

Her father gave her a steady stare. "You surprise me, Diana. Perhaps you aren't as unreasonable as I had believed. How do you plan to proceed?"

His tacit admission of approval—she knew she would get no other—gave her confidence, and his concern, when she told him Larry was still on the loose, was unexpectedly warm. "I don't like to think of you there alone. Come back to Philadelphia until they capture him."

"I'm not alone."

Her father snorted. "The ex-wife? You'd be safer alone than with her there, drawing him like a magnet."

Diana explained. Her father's reaction was not the one she had expected. One corner of his mouth turned up in his version of a smile. "A ménage à quatre?"

"Hardly that."

"I was joking. I know you have better sense than to become involved with some gallant, semiliterate country boy. Well. It appears that for once you may have been right and I may have been wrong. I commend you. And I'll help in any way I can. A private detective, perhaps? These country cops—"

"At least they know the area. A city PI wouldn't be of any use."

"Possibly." He ate in silence for a time, pondering. "Let me know at once when they find the fellow. I'd like to talk to him."

He meant interrogate, not talk, but she was glad of the offer. No one could browbeat a witness as effectively as he. They discussed other possibilities, with a camaraderie and friendliness they had not shared for months. Diana was glad she had been wrong about his motives for asking her to lunch. He did care about Brad. It was a pity he couldn't demonstrate affection more easily, but one had to make allowances . . .

Not until the meal was over and they had ordered coffee did he drop the bombshell.

"There's something I must tell you, Diana. I wanted to do it face-to-face instead of over the telephone. I have filed for divorce."

He waited a moment for her to reply, and then said, "No recriminations? No outcries of outraged surprise?"

"I suppose I must have expected it," Diana said. She was surprised—at her own calm.

"You ought to have. You're a sensible woman. Naturally I'll take care of your mother as long as she lives. It will be in a nursing home, I'm afraid."

"No! She hated that place. You can't—"

"I came home the other night to find her in a coma," her father said coolly. "Another half hour and she'd have been gone. She's taken to drinking heavily. Added to the tranquilizers . . ."

"Oh, God." Diana fumbled for a tissue.

"She's trying to kill herself, Diana. If I were the monster you think me, I'd let her do it. Then I'd be free. I can't do that, of course. But neither can I face the prospect of another thirty years of this living hell." His voice held emotion for the first time. He conquered it, and went on steadily, "I'm only fifty-six. That may seem elderly to you—"

"No," Diana said. She was thinking of Charles and Emily. It wasn't a first marriage for either of them. Could she condemn her father for wanting a relationship like theirs?

"I don't blame your mother for what has happened to our marriage. The blame is never completely one-sided. But it's too late for us. Even if she recovers she'll never forgive me for Brad. And blameworthy though I may be, I don't think I deserve to lose all hope of happiness."

Diana wiped her eyes and stuffed the tissue back into her purse. "Is there someone else?"

"I don't think that need concern you."

"I suppose not. If there isn't, there will be. What do you want me to say—you have my blessing, go forth and be happy?"

"I'm sorry you're bitter about this," he said quietly. "I don't blame you. But I hope that in time—"

"I'll let you know." Diana pushed her chair away from the table.

"Your eye makeup is smeared. You'd better repair it before you go out into the street."

When she came out of the powder room he was waiting, briefcase in one hand, gold-handled stick in the other. He inspected her and then nodded approvingly. "That's much better. I meant what I said about helping with your investigation. I hope you won't let your present anger against me interfere with that."

"I'll let you know," Diana repeated.

They emerged from the restaurant into the bright spring sunlight. Diana's eyes were caught by a particularly vivid patch of scarlet.

"Hi, there," Andy said cheerfully. "I finished early, so I thought I'd save you the trouble of picking me up."

She had to introduce them. Standing slightly behind her father, she watched Andy's performance with exasperated amusement. His handclasp was firm but not too firm; his shoulders were slightly bowed and his head was slightly tilted, as if he were hanging on every word that fell from the other man's lips. He used the word "sir" twice in a single sentence.

If her father was conscious of caricature he showed no sign of it. He was, for him, absolutely cordial. He was also, as usual, in a hurry. Glancing at his watch, he hailed a taxi, took polite leave of Andy, kissed Diana's averted cheek, and was gone.

"You low-down bastard," Diana said. "How long have you been propping up that 'No Parking' sign?"

"Only a few minutes. You were earlier than I expected." Andy burst out laughing. "Did you see the look on his face when he spotted my tie? He could hardly take his eyes off it."

"You really are the most—"

"Well, I wanted to meet him. Now I can understand why Brad ran away from home, and why you genuflect every time you refer to him."

"Not any more."

"What happened?"

"I don't want to talk about it."

"Okay." He ambled along beside her in silence until they reached the car. "Want me to drive?"

"Not unless I had two broken legs and a dislocated shoulder," Diana retorted. "Get in and don't argue with me."

He remained tactfully silent while she negotiated the maze of traffic-infested streets. When she reached the ramp to the freeway he ventured to speak. "You got the letters?"

"Uh-huh."

"Can I see them?"

"I don't see how I can stop you without wrecking the car," Diana snapped. "Get your paws out of my purse. The letters are in the briefcase. And fasten your seat belt."

Reading the letters, he left her alone with her own thoughts for some time. They were not pleasant company; she was actually relieved when he spoke, in a voice that refused to acknowledge her evil mood.

"I can't see anything pertinent off-hand. He wasn't a very chatty guy, was he?"

Diana's hands tightened on the wheel. "Sometimes he was."

"He was quite forthcoming the times I talked to him. Maybe," Andy speculated, "He was one of those people who can't express themselves in writing. Some of my friends are like that. Talk your ear off, but never—"

"What did you do today? Don't tell me you were at the LC, I never believed that one."

"I was, actually." Andy folded the letters and returned them to her briefcase. "Just long enough to find out they don't have what I'm after. The Fairweathers weren't historical personages. I'll have to try the county courthouse."

"I could have told you that."

"So what did your old man have to say?"

Diana was ready to talk by then. In his own, quite different way, Andy was as effective as her father in inducing confessions.

"He was more cooperative than I expected. He even told me I had been right and he . . . might have been wrong."

"That, I gather, is a rare admission."

"He usually is right."

"Oh, yeah? In my opinion he has royally screwed up as a father."

"I didn't ask your opinion."

"I never wait to be asked," said Andy calmly. "So what changed his mind?"

"Larry."

"Mmm. You told him what happened?"

"Yes. He wanted me to leave the house. So you see he's not entirely indifferent . . ." She broke off. Why should she defend her father to Andy? But it wasn't he she wanted to convince.

"He offered to hire a private detective," she went on. "And come to question Larry when they catch him."

"Both good ideas."

She glanced quickly at him. "You think so?"

"A city gumshoe wouldn't be much use tracking Larry down unless he's left the area. I don't think he has; his truck's being held by the cops and there were no reports of stolen vehicles last night."

"How did you find that out?"

"A wonderful invention called the telephone. That was the situation as of noon today. Larry's probably holed up in the woods somewhere. He's got buddies in town who would slip him food and booze; some of the boys don't see anything wrong with a man using force to get his woman back."

"Charming."

"No, it's not; but I'm afraid it's a fact of life. That's where a private detective might be useful—locating his buddies, questioning them, following them. If Larry doesn't turn up in the next day or two, you ought to take Daddy dearest up on his offer."

"Do you have to speak of him so disrespectfully?"

"Making fun of people is a good way of cutting them down to

size," Andy said. "Now do you feel like telling me what else he said? It wasn't his offer of assistance that got you so worked up."

"None of your business." That was what she meant to say. Instead she heard herself blurt out, "He's going to get a divorce."

CHAPTER TWELVE

The General Rose—decay—
But this—in Lady's Drawer—
Make summer—When the Lady lie—
In ceaseless Rosemary—

—EMILY DICKINSON

"*P*ull off the road," Andy said.

"I'm all right."

"The driver of that van you just passed is shaking an appendage at us. Let me drive."

"I missed him by a mile." Diana drew a long breath. "I'm perfectly capable of driving safely."

"The news was obviously a shock," Andy mused. "Why? People get divorced all the time. You're a big girl now, you should be able to accept—"

"You're a fine one to talk! Have you accepted Charles? Hanging around the house all the time, leaving cars and dogs and other bits of your property, as if you were staking a claim—"

Andy didn't speak, but his harsh, indrawn catch of breath stopped her as effectively as a shout would have done. She had been incredulous when Mary Jo described him as quick-tempered, but when she saw his hands, clenched so tightly that the knuckles were as white as bare bone, she realized that only her gender and the fact that she was driving sixty miles an hour prevented him from striking out at her.

After a moment she said, "I apologize. I had no right to say that."

Andy's hands uncurled. "I guess I had it coming. I wouldn't resent it so much if it weren't true."

"Is it?"

"Sure."

"They're so happy."

"That makes it worse. If," Andy added, in a voice rough with self-contempt, "you're a selfish, emotionally retarded jerk like me. I can't seem to cut the damned apron strings."

"She's a pretty terrific lady. I can see why you love her."

"Love is supposed to mean desiring the happiness of the beloved."

"It's a lot more complicated than that," Diana said wryly.

"You're telling me? She adores Charlie and he's goofy about her. She's never been happier. My old man made her life miserable. Since I am a normal contemptible human being, I resent Charlie all the more on that account."

"What happened to your father?"

"Oh, he's around." Andy slumped down in his seat and stared straight ahead. "I see him now and then. He's not so bad—just lazy and shiftless and charming. Like me."

"You can be charming," Diana said cautiously.

Andy started to laugh. "Mercurial" was an even more appropriate word for him; he had apparently dismissed his anger against her and his disgust with himself.

"Go ahead, flatter me some more. I'll grow up one of these days, I guess. Now it's your turn. I've bared *my* soul and admitted *my* failings. How about you?"

"Why am I so upset about the divorce?" Diana tried to think. "I shouldn't be. I know the stats, and Father's at that age—mid-life crisis, status wife, all the rest of it. But Mother . . . She's such a damned mess! No sane man would want to live with her—but he helped to make her what she is, and now he's just discarding her, like a sack of garbage."

"She let him do it, didn't she?"

"Oh, shut up! What do you know about it?" Diana rummaged through her vocabulary for a sufficiently scathing epithet. None of the common expletives seemed strong enough. "Men!" she finished bitterly.

Andy would not be provoked. "Would she improve, do you think, if she knew what had really become of her son? The truth could be worse than uncertainty."

"Nothing could be worse," Diana said. "The wives of MIAs

and the parents of missing children are only too well aware of that. Yes; I think she might improve if she knew for certain. Why do you think I got into this crazy masquerade? She has to know." After a moment she added in a low voice, "I have to know."

"Still no trace of him," Andy reported, hanging up the phone. He had called immediately upon their return. "What are those incompetent idiots doing? You'd think by now—"

"Give them a break." Walt was taking one himself; he had come in to get a drink of water and learn the results of their expedition. "They haven't the manpower to mount a thorough search in this terrain. He has to come out eventually, he hasn't got supplies or even a change of clothes."

"He may come out shooting," Andy said pessimistically.

"He doesn't have a gun," Diana pointed out.

"He doesn't have *that* gun. It wouldn't surprise me to learn he was carrying a spare. He isn't going to be in a happy frame of mind after roughing it for several days. And it's supposed to rain tonight."

"It is? Damn." Walt got to his feet. "Got to get those tarps ready. Andy, will you collect Mary Jo? She should be getting out of work soon. Stubborn broad," he added.

The rain began shortly after Andy had left—not a storm, but a drizzle that gradually increased to a moderate downpour. Walt kept the men at work until the darkening skies forced a halt. When he came in he was drenched and grumbling. "I wanted to lay the foundations of the gazebo tomorrow. If this keeps up all night—"

"Quit worrying about the goddamn landscaping," Andy said irritably. "Ma will understand that we've had a few other things on our mind."

Diana nodded. "Especially after she finds out her supposed expert was a fraud."

Mary Jo was at the sink, peeling potatoes. "She won't be mad, Di. She's the most tenderhearted woman alive."

Andy chuckled evilly. "Charlie isn't. I don't envy you, Diana. He'll have the hide off you. Metaphorically, of course."

"Shut up, Andy," Mary Jo ordered. "And Walt, you get out of those wet clothes. You're dripping all over the floor."

Walt started to object. Then, with a glance at the others, he obeyed. Stripped to his shorts, his lean body was as functional and sleek as that of a classic statue, undistorted by the exaggerated muscles of modern body-builders. Mary Jo was not impressed; she gave him a stony stare and Andy muttered something rude under his breath.

Diana laughed—at the reactions of the other two, not at Walt— but he misinterpreted her amusement. Reddening, he gathered up his wet clothes and left the room.

One explanation for Walt's annoyance at further delay was apparent when they went to the library after dinner. He had taken some of his men off the job to repair the broken window and install a row of floodlights. The glare was hard on the eyes, but it illumined a wide stretch of lawn. Basking in the compliments of the others, Walt explained, "I told Charles months ago he ought to let me install outdoor lights. Especially here—these doors are practically an invitation to burglars."

Assisted by Miss Matilda, Diana began to read Brad's letters. She passed each one on to Mary Jo and Walt as she finished it. Andy, who had already read them, wandered to the fireplace and began picking at the edges of the hole in the wall. If he hoped his activities would go unnoticed, he was disappointed.

"At least spread some newspapers on the floor," Mary Jo snapped.

After doing so, Andy went on tapping at the plaster. His activities didn't distract Diana. It was an odd sensation to reread those brief letters, with part of her mind writhing in guilt for having failed to notice their reticence, and another part coolly analyzing their meaning. When she had finished the last of them—there were several dozen in all—she handed it to Mary Jo and sat with her hands limp in her lap.

Mary Jo was a fast reader. She shook her head in disgust as she gave the final letter to Walt. "Maybe I missed it, but I couldn't find anything."

"He had some nice things to say about you." Walt put the letter atop the pile.

"He said nice things about almost everybody," Mary Jo retorted. "Even you."

" 'Honest, hard-working, loyal . . .' Makes me sound like a god-damn Boy Scout." Walt sorted through the letters. "He even had

a good word for Miss Musser. I think. Who's this 'Miss Havisham' he compares her to? 'A tighter-lipped, part-time Miss Havisham.' "

"She's a character in a Dickens novel, you ignorant redneck,"
Mary Jo replied. "Didn't you have to read *Great Expectations* in
high school?"

"It was a dumb, long-winded book. I read Cliff Notes. Was Miss
Havisham the crazy old lady? That's pretty good. Miss Musser
was only part-time crazy, up to pretty near the end. She'd mumble
away, making no sense, and then suddenly come out with some
sharp comment or criticism. Caught you off-guard. I wondered
sometimes whether she was playing senile on purpose."

Mary Jo searched through the pile. "There was one interesting
comment—about the old lady's lawyer. Yes, here it is. 'No writer
would have the nerve to invent a name like Frank Sweet for a
shyster lawyer. He makes me glad I decided to become a dropout
instead of following in your footsteps.' "

"That's about the only negative comment, though," Walt said.
"Even Andy got a pat on the head. What'd he say—something
about meeting a fellow lover of poetry and folktales . . . Andy?
Hey, Andy!"

Andy turned toward them. His eyes were alight. "It's a door,"
he said. "I found a door. Come look."

He had to find a flashlight and shine it directly into the hole
before the skeptical Walt would concede he was right. "Looks like
a keyhole," he said grudgingly. "And the remains of paneling."
He jabbed a casual, efficient fist into the hole, producing a dry
splintering crunch.

Andy let out a yelp of protest. "Hey! You just destroyed a piece
of history, you vandal."

"It was worm-eaten and rotten," Walt said. "No wonder they
plastered over it." He sniffed, his nose wrinkling. "Air's as stale
as some old tomb."

The whiff of dead air that reached Diana's nostrils smelled of
dust and musty age. She stepped back. Andy grabbed the flashlight
from Walt and tried to get it, and his face, into the ragged hole
simultaneously. "Stairs," he reported, his voice echoing weirdly.
"It's a flight of steps!"

"Anything else?" Diana thought her voice was under control,
but Mary Jo took her arm and Andy turned with a quick denial.

Walt was less tactful. "We'd have smelled it," he said. "Anyhow, that door's been blocked for many years—centuries, maybe."

"Get a chisel and a hammer and give me a hand," Andy ordered.

"Wait a minute," Mary Jo said. "Just listen to me, before you start tearing the place to pieces. I wonder if this leads to that door in the bedroom upstairs. It's almost directly above."

"Door? What door?" Andy stared at her.

"It's behind the big wardrobe."

"You mean—you mean you found a mysterious door leading God knows where and you never even bothered to open it?"

"My job is cleaning, not snooping. I couldn't have opened the door anyhow. The doorknob's missing and it's been painted shut."

"The unnatural, inhuman curiosity of some people leaves me breathless," Andy muttered. "How could anyone resist . . . Come on, then. Maybe we can get at the stairs more easily from above."

Walt glanced at the window, as he had done every few minutes all evening. "I haven't got time to waste on historical research. Haven't you made enough of a mess?"

"We might as well help him," Mary Jo said with a sniff. "The sooner his curiosity is satisfied, the sooner we can start repairing the damage."

Diana said nothing. She had a certain sympathy for Andy. Who could resist a door that seemingly led nowhere? Common sense, a commodity in which Andy seemed to be deficient, told her they wouldn't find any mummified bodies or cache of stolen jewels. On the other hand, common sense would have denied her vision of the April garden.

The room in question was the one farthest from the stairs in the older, central section. It was still awaiting final renovation; patches of plaster marked the walls. The wardrobe, a massive, rather ugly Victorian piece, must have been left in the house because it was too big to go through the doorway. No doubt some ancestor of Miss Musser's had had it assembled in situ.

It took both men to shove the monstrosity away from the wall. "You moved this by yourself?" Andy asked Mary Jo respectfully.

"I clean behind things, not just around them," Mary Jo said, flexing her thin arms. "I waxed the floor in front of it with a candle stub."

"There sure as hell isn't any wax on the floor now." Andy wiped his perspiring brow.

"I cleaned it off afterward, of course. Wouldn't want Mrs. Nicholson to slip and fall."

Walt had already gone to work on the layer of paint that sealed the door to the frame. He was using a thin chisel and a lot of patience; after watching him for a time, Andy snatched up another chisel and squatted down to attack the lower portion. Walt nudged him aside. "Get away from that, Andy. I know how you work; you'll tear the door and the frame to shreds."

"Well, hell, what's the difference? They'll have to be replaced anyhow."

"They would after you got through with them. This is a perfectly good, solid old door. I thought you were in favor of historic preservation."

However, it proved necessary to destroy part of the frame after all. The door had been locked. Walt's proposal, that they clear the keyhole of paint and try to find a key that would fit, was so impractical that even he was forced to give way when Andy started hacking away at the doorframe.

"I don't know what the point is," he grunted, watching Andy with raised eyebrows. "That door hasn't been opened for fifty, sixty years."

"Longer, maybe," Andy murmured. Having widened the crack next to the lock, he inserted the heaviest of the chisels and heaved with all his might. With a loud crack the rusted bolt gave way and the door flew open, sending Andy staggering back into the unwilling arms of Walt, who set him on his feet with an exasperated grunt.

The motion of the door had drawn a current of air through the hole at the bottom and up the length of the staircase. It was so mephitic with old decay that Diana pinched her nose shut with her fingers. But it was not the stench that made them stare in mesmerized silence at the open rectangle. A filmy surface like a curtain of gray gauze blurred the darkness beyond, wavering and fluttering as if something behind it were trying to brush it aside in order to emerge.

Mary Jo was the first to recover. "I never saw a cobweb like that in my life! How could spiders get into a sealed space?"

"Bugs can get in anyplace." Andy picked up the biggest chisel and swept it across the opening. The giant cobweb dissolved into tatters of ugly gray. He tossed the chisel aside, picked up the flashlight, and started forward. "Steps," he crowed. "A hidden staircase. Shades of the Hardy Boys! Or was it Nancy Drew?"

Mary Jo grabbed him by the collar. "Watch it, Andy."

Andy squirmed. "Let go, Mary Jo. You don't think I'd be dumb enough to—"

The topmost stair promptly collapsed as he put his weight on it. Mary Jo yanked him back from the edge of what had become a sheer drop. The strength of her wiry arm was remarkable; Andy had to execute a few fancy dance steps to keep from falling over backward.

"Now you've done it," Walt said, peering down into the darkness. "The whole thing's collapsed."

"Just as well," Andy said calmly. "It must have been too rotted to support any weight. I'll get a rope and you can lower me—"

"Not me," said Walt, folding his arms.

Mary Jo was more emphatic. "You've wasted enough time on this nonsense. A hell of a lot of help you'll be if you break an arm or a leg or your stupid neck."

The argument was convincing. With a last forlorn look at the cobweb-fringed opening, Andy closed the door.

"And's what's more," Mary Jo continued. "You mix up some plaster and start filling that hole in the library wall. They're coming to install the mantel tomorrow, and I won't have . . ."

She continued to scold him all the way downstairs. Diana began to wonder whether her matchmaking instinct had been accurate. Andy certainly deserved the lecture, but constant hectoring wasn't conducive to romance.

Mary Jo returned to the computer and Walt sat down at the library table to go over lists of plant materials he had ordered. Andy sidled toward the hole in the wall.

"I told you to cut that out," Mary Jo snapped, without looking up from her work.

"I can't patch it till I clear away the loose pieces," Andy said in injured tones.

"Do it quietly, then. I have to finish this paper."

"I thought it was due today," Diana said.

"I got an extension. Professor Andrews allowed as how being shot at by your ex-husband was a valid excuse for being a day late."

Andy left her in peace for almost a quarter of an hour. Then he said, "Come and look. There's all kinds of interesting debris at the bottom."

Mary Jo whirled around. "For God's sake, Andy, will you stop that? I told you to fill that hole up, not enlarge it; it's twice the size it was before."

Unexpectedly, Walt came to Andy's defense. "He has to plug up the piece I knocked out of the wooden paneling before he plasters. There are some scraps of plywood in the barn you could use, Andy."

Stretching and yawning, he rose from his chair and joined Andy, taking the flashlight the latter handed him. "Yeah," he said, after a brief inspection. "That should work. I'll give you a hand."

"You're not going into the barn tonight, I hope," Diana exclaimed. "You were the one who warned me—"

"It's perfectly safe if you know what you're doing. That reminds me—I want to get the barn cleared out so we can start the repairs before Mrs. Nicholson gets home. Where do you want me to put those old wrecks of yours, Andy?"

"Damned if I know," Andy muttered, retrieving the flashlight and squinting into the hole.

"You better make up your mind or I'll have them hauled out into the pasture and dumped. What the hell are you looking at? There's nothing down there except rusty nails and splintered wood."

"I thought I saw something shiny."

"A gold-and-diamond tiara, probably." Walt's voice dripped sarcasm. "I'm serious, Andy. The barn goes down tomorrow, rain or shine, hell or high water, with your cooperation or without it."

"You aren't going to tear the whole thing down, are you?" Walt's tone had convinced Andy that the threat to his beloved wrecks was genuine. "Or dump Ma's boxes and bundles out in the pasture? Why can't you just shove everything back out of your way?"

"Let me explain it in words of one syllable," Walt snapped. "We've got to clear the whole interior before we start ripping out the damaged sections—roof and walls and flooring. I had hoped to save part of the floor, but when the gate fell it demolished a big section; there's not enough left intact to be worth the effort."

"But Ma's boxes, and the tools—"

"I'm putting up a temporary storage shed. It won't hold your goddamn wrecks, though."

"Well, how about—"

"I'll make some coffee," Diana said, getting to her feet.

Andy was obviously prepared to argue all night and Walt's temper was on the verge of cracking, but that wasn't why she sought an excuse to leave the room. Suddenly she was too restless to sit still. She had the sense that there was something she had neglected to do—something vitally important.

It was better in the kitchen—peaceful and still, without the sound of angry voices that had affected her so unpleasantly. Men's voices, raised in anger . . . But there was still that nagging sense of a task forgotten and unaccomplished. Moving without conscious volition, she went to the back door and opened it.

He was there, waiting, in the usual place. Their place. She could see him, a dark slender form in the darker shadows under the trees, but she couldn't move to go to him. It was as if her feet were glued to the floor, as if a hard invisible hand covered her lips. Paralyzed and mute, she stood watching as the other shape crept toward him, silent as a shadow. She heard a twig snap—she couldn't have heard it, they were too far away, but she heard— saw him turn in eager welcome, stiffen in fearful recognition, step back . . . There were no shouts of anger, only whispers, but she heard them too. The shadowy figures merged into a single monstrous shape, writhing and twisting in unequal struggle. The muscles in her throat felt as if they would snap, so painful was her effort to speak, to cry out . . .

She must have cried out, though she didn't remember doing so. When she opened her eyes they were all there; Andy's arms were around her, and Mary Jo was yelling at him. "Put her down, you jackass. You should elevate her feet, not her head. What kind of idiot—"

"Shut up," Walt said. He bent over Diana. "What happened?"

"Someone . . . out there." Too late, she realized she shouldn't have said it. "No—Walt, don't go out—"

He was already gone, leaving the door wide open. Mary Jo

hesitated for only a moment. Snatching a flashlight from a drawer, she went after Walt.

Diana shoved ineffectually at Andy. "Let go of me. Call them back."

Andy hauled her to her feet and dumped her unceremoniously into a chair. "You okay?"

"Yes. Go after them!"

"No sense in all of us rushing out into the night," Andy said coolly. "It wasn't Larry, was it?"

"No." The reaction hit her hard; she slumped forward, and only Andy's quick hands against her shoulders held her upright. "Oh, God! He killed him! I saw it—I heard the sound when his head hit . . ."

"Who? Who was it?"

"I don't know." Andy's fingers were biting into her shoulders. "Stop it, Andy, that hurts. I'm not going to pass out."

"Again, you mean? I'd say you were entitled. Put your head down."

He pushed her head onto her knees with a vigor that made her neck crack. When Diana ventured to sit up he was offering her a glass.

"I hate brandy," she said sullenly.

"Drink it anyhow." He sat watching her as she sipped and sputtered. Then he said, gently but inexorably, "You've got to think, Diana. Try to remember. There were two people? Must have been; you said, 'He killed him.' Was one of them the same man you saw—sensed—before?"

"I tell you, I don't . . . It could have been."

"Victim or killer?"

"Victim. I think . . . Andy, quit badgering me. I've never had any clear knowledge, only impressions. Not even a name."

Andy looked skeptical. "She must have been aware of his name. 'Come to me, Frederick, my love; Romeo, Romeo! wherefore art thou Romeo?' "

"Please don't, Andy."

Andy's head turned toward the door. "They're coming back. Mary Jo is really giving him hell. Maybe if you told them what you saw it would take her mind off—"

"No!" The words she had been reluctant to speak, or even think, tumbled out in a harsh, urgent whisper. "If I saw anything except the product of my own deranged imagination, it wasn't an imaginary eighteenth-century lover. Who else could it have been but Brad?"

When Diana woke next morning the sun was barely over the horizon. Mist drifted over the meadow in a pearly haze. Quickly she dressed and ran downstairs, hoping to get breakfast before Mary Jo came down, but the smell of coffee warned her she was too late. The others were at the table. Andy turned from the stove with a flourish of his spatula. "Bacon and eggs coming up."

"I don't want bacon and eggs. Just a piece of toast."

"Fat-free bacon and eggs."

"There is no such thing as—" Andy put a plate in front of her. With a resigned shrug Diana picked up her fork, and Andy resumed the argument he and Walt had been enjoying.

"Just give me another day. I'll get one of my buddies to come out and help me move them."

"I warned you weeks ago, and so did Emily." Walt shoved his chair back from the table and stood up. "Here come the boys. You better get out there if you want any say as to where we dump those wrecks."

Andy tried one last delaying tactic. "I thought you were going to work on the lily pond today."

"Too wet. The tarps helped some, but not enough." Slowly and deliberately Walt rolled his sleeves to the shoulders. "It's going to be a hot day, so we can probably get at it this afternoon."

He went out. "I wish he'd stop flexing his goddamn muscles," Andy muttered. Tossing his spatula in the direction of the sink, he followed.

"Sometimes I think men are more trouble than they're worth," Mary Jo remarked. She picked up the spatula and mopped the spattered grease from the floor with a paper towel.

"I feel better having them here," Diana admitted. "I guess I'm not as ardent a feminist as I used to believe."

"There's safety in numbers, male or female. Women have enough handicaps; we may as well take advantage of male chauvinism when we can. Larry would be more likely to barge in here if he thought he'd find two women alone. And," Mary Jo added coolly, "Walt's a better shot than I am."

Diana shivered. "Are you okay?" Mary Jo asked.

"Yes, fine. I'm sorry to have made such a fool of myself last night."

"You must have seen a deer or some other animal. But I don't blame you; I'll start screaming at shadows too if this goes on much longer."

"They'll get him. He can't hide forever."

"Yeah. They'll get him. And he'll be out on bail in a few hours. Oh, well." Mary Jo began collecting the dishes from the table. "You finished with your eggs?"

"I didn't want them in the first place. What's on the agenda for today?"

"School. I have two classes, and finals next week. Got to spend some time at the library."

"Is Andy going with you?"

"Uh-huh." Mary Jo's smile held little humor. "They're switching guard duty. Jesus, I hate this. Makes me feel like some helpless kid."

"As you just said—"

"So I'm inconsistent." Mary Jo's smile broadened and the dimple made a tentative appearance. "That's a woman's prerogative, isn't it?"

Diana laughed. "Not just a woman's. 'A foolish consistency is the hobgoblin of little minds.' "

"Emerson," Mary Jo said automatically. "The only thing is . . . I'd hate to think you were sticking your neck out on my account. You could get the hell out of here."

"If I had no other reason for staying, that would be enough," Diana said. "You'd do the same for me."

"Yes, but—"

"But you're a finer, nobler person than I am?" Mary Jo's mouth opened in indignant protest. Diana cut her short. "We're friends—aren't we? Anyhow, I have plenty of other reasons, including the one for which I came. I'll be damned if I'll let a piece of shit like Larry scare me off until I find out what happened to Brad. I hope you don't mind my referring to your ex so rudely."

Mary Jo grinned. "You couldn't call him anything worse than I've called him. I had an idea last night, about Brad. Now that you're out of the closet, maybe I could tell the people at school who you are and why you're here. He knew some of my friends;

I don't have many, I don't have time to socialize, but I introduced him to a few of them. I could say he's turned up missing and that you've come to see if you can trace him. The only objection is that the word will get around and it could turn you into a sitting duck if—well, if we're wrong about Larry and Brad."

"Tell anyone you like. It's an excellent idea."

"You sure?"

"I had already decided to spread the word. It was stupid of me to think I could learn anything without announcing my identity." Diana glanced at the door. "I'd better go out and see what those two are doing. Andy will stand around arguing all morning if Walt lets him."

"Walt won't. His temper is already on the ragged edge."

"He seems to be controlling it well."

"Yeah, well, that's when he's most likely to explode. Andy gets on his nerves something terrible."

However, when Diana reached the scene she was relieved to learn that an amicable agreement had been reached. Several of the men were putting together a prefabricated storage shed. It would be large enough to hold the tools and the boxes and crates containing Emily's collection of garden implements. Andy's "vintage cars," as he insisted on calling them, were to be moved into the field, but Walt had promised to cover them with tarps.

Diana addressed the unhappy collector, who stood watching gloomily as the boxes were carried out. "You'd better get ready to go, or Mary Jo will leave without you."

"Yeah, I guess." Hands in his pockets, Andy turned away. "Make sure Walt covers those cars, will you? I don't trust him."

"Aren't you coming back?"

"Not till tonight. I'm going to spent the day at the Historical Society, then pick Mary Jo up and bring her home."

"Okay." Diana tried to escape, but she was too slow. Andy's hand shot out and caught her arm. "I wish you'd stop that," she complained. "I'm getting bruises on top of bruises."

" 'My strength is as the strength of ten, because my heart is pure.' " Andy gave her a sunny smile, his ill humor forgotten. "If anything interesting occurs today, please make copious notes."

She knew what he meant. "Nothing is going to occur."

"The phenomena seem to occur most frequently after dark," Andy said. "I rather hoped we'd have another concert last night."

"I didn't."

"You said it happened once when Mary Jo was here. Maybe Walt's the inhibitor. The presence of a skeptic—"

"For God's sake, Andy, you sound like Madame What's-it the spiritualist medium." She regretted the words as soon as she had uttered them. A thoughtful expression spread across Andy's face.

"No," Diana said.

"No what?"

"No séance. No way. Not under any circumstances whatever."

"Hmm," said Andy.

"I mean it, Andy!"

"I better go. You stick close to the house today."

"I have to. The men are coming to install the new fireplace. You did plug up that hole, I hope."

"Oh, sure." He wandered off, hands in his pockets, head cocked at a thoughtful angle.

"Damn," Diana said.

"Damn what?" Walt came tramping toward her. "If you're referring to Andy, I'll second it. You stick close to the house today—"

"Damn you too," Diana said.

A bulldozer came rumbling toward her. She retreated, swearing randomly.

Andy had not, of course, finished plugging the hole. She found him in the library prying the lid off a can of pre-mixed Spackle while Mary Jo yelled at him.

"I couldn't finish it last night," he yelled back. "You know you have to do this a layer at a time and let one dry before you put the next—"

"I'll go without you." Mary Jo spun on her heel and started for the door.

The idea of having Andy around all day was too horrible to contemplate. "I'll do it," Diana said. "Give me that trowel."

"There's plenty of time," Andy argued. "It's only eight o'clock, for God's sake."

"The library opens at eight-thirty."

"She means it," Diana said, wrestling the trowel from Andy. "Hurry up."

"You don't know how—"

"Get out of here!"

He went. The sound of Mary Jo's voice, raised in strident criticism, was drowned out by a crash of collapsing timbers from the back.

The racket continued all morning. Diana could understand why Walt wanted to finish this part of the job before Emily returned; it was the sort of noise she particularly hated. Diana didn't like it either. She couldn't bring herself to watch the demolition or sit in the kitchen, where the sound was loudest. The arrival of the men to install the fireplace mantel in the library drove her from that room as well, and the pounding inside the house echoed the crashes from without. Diana sought refuge in her bedroom, along with a number of indignant cats, and read about old roses with her fingers plugging her ears.

An eternity later, a voice bellowing her name brought her to the head of the stairs. The noise had stopped, indoors as well as out; blessed peace reigned. It was twelve-twenty. Walt's crew must have stopped for lunch, and the men working on the fireplace must . . . Was it possible?

It was. Summoned to the library, she exclaimed with genuine admiration while the foreman preened himself and beamed. "It looks wonderful. I'm sure Mrs. Nicholson will be delighted."

She had to listen to a detailed description of the difficulties that had been encountered and overcome before the foreman took his departure, but she didn't mind giving him his due; the result had been worth the wait. The marble facing matched the mantel almost perfectly. One of the graceful maidens covered Andy's hole. Diana ran an appreciative finger down the carved folds of the marble robe. Or was the garment called a chiton? She was a Greek maiden, reminiscent of the draped women whose shoulders supported the porch of the Erechtheion in Athens.

Trailed by Baby, Diana went to the kitchen. The big dog had stuck close to her all morning; perhaps the presence of strange men in the house aroused its protective instincts. Diana half-expected to find Walt there, but apparently he had elected to eat his lunch with the men. She managed to eat half her sandwich in peace—except for the efforts of various cats to take bites out of it—before the noise began again. Abandoning her sandwich to the cats, Diana gathered cleaning materials and a stepladder, and returned to the library.

Two hours' intensive labor produced a satisfying change. The room was habitable again: dust and cobwebs vacuumed away, rugs back in place, furniture gleaming with polish. The mantel had been cleaned, it required only dusting, and now it glowed with a soft ivory patina. Mopping her streaming brow with her sleeve, Diana carried the ladder back to the kitchen. She was covered with a sticky mixture of dust and perspiration, but she decided to postpone taking a shower. The big dog had been inside all day, it deserved to be taken for a walk, and as she knew by experience, walking with a dog through field and forest would necessitate bathing again. It was hot even inside the house. The temperature outside, in the sun, must be unseasonably high.

One of the men warned her back with a shout and a wave of his arm as she approached the barn. It had been reduced to almost half its former size. The scorched timbers and beams had been ripped off, and the fabric remaining appeared to be sound.

Without regret Diana turned away. She hadn't seen Walt; he must be with the crew working on the lily pond. Instead of heading in that direction, she struck out across the pasture, toward the stream.

She had not gone far when a peremptory shout brought her to a stop and produced a menacing growl from Baby. She turned to see Walt running toward her. He had taken off his shirt; his chest and shoulders shone with sweat and vibrated with the quickness of his breathing. "Where the hell do you think you're going?" he demanded.

Baby growled louder and pressed close to Diana. The dog's weight threw her off-balance; she had to clutch at its thick coat to stay on her feet.

"That dog doesn't like me," Walt gasped.

"She doesn't like your tone of voice. Neither do I."

"I told you to stay close to the house." His fingers contracted as if he were itching to grab her and drag her back. He probably would have, Diana thought, if it hadn't been for the dog. Walt was no coward, but he was no fool either.

"I've been inside all day," she protested. "I just wanted to walk down to the creek."

"Larry's already left one souvenir there."

"Do you think he was the one who killed the deer?"

"Seems likely. He's a good marksman."

"But he doesn't have a gun."

"He wouldn't need a gun if he caught you alone," Walt said grimly. "Besides . . ." He hesitated, and then went on, "He does have a weapon. Emily's dog was killed by a shotgun, not the forty-five he used later. They haven't located the shotgun. He must have taken it with him."

"Why didn't you tell me before?" Walt did not reply. Diana said angrily, "Damn it, Walt, I resent being patronized and protected for my own good. If I'd known that—"

"You're bullheaded enough to go ahead anyway."

"I may be bullheaded but I'm not suicidally stupid!" The dog gave Diana an urgent push, and she staggered again. "If you don't stop yelling at me, this dog is going to knock me down."

A smile tugged at the corners of Walt's mouth. "Whoever taught her that trick must have been crazy. Anyhow, you were the one who was yelling. Diana—please come back to the house with me."

"All right."

"Huh? That easy?"

"You said the magic word."

"Oh." Walt pushed the damp hair away from his forehead. "I'll try to remember. Wait a minute. Do you hear anything?"

"No."

"Neither do I. They've stopped working. Lazy bastards, you can't leave them alone for five minutes. Come on. Uh—please come on."

The bulldozer stood silent and unoccupied. All the men were gathered together at the far end of the barn. As Walt came storming toward them, Jack hurried to meet him.

"We found something funny, Walt. Figured you'd better have a look."

The men fell back as they approached. Most of the flooring was gone now, along with the beams that had supported it. The bulldozer had scraped off the top six inches of weedy ground down to a relatively flat dirt surface. Low mounds and depressions marked it; but one depression, where the men had gathered, seemed larger and more regular in outline than the rest.

"Funny," Jack said again. "Funny shape. Almost like—"

"Is that all?" Walt demanded. "You stopped work because of a funny shape in the ground?"

"That's not all. Give it to him, Jimmy."

One of the men had been turning it over in his hands. It looked like a smooth stick. Silently he handed it to Walt.

"It's a bone," Jack said. "Long bone. Leg, I think."

The object was stained reddish-brown. It was very brittle; one end had been broken off, perhaps by the bulldozer; the sharp splintered break was paler in color than the rest of it. The other end was rounded and thicker, like the knob of a cane.

"Deer," Walt said in a stifled voice.

Jack shook his head. "I know deer. Horse, too. Looks like a human leg bone to me."

CHAPTER THIRTEEN

Why is it no one ever sent me yet
One perfect limousine, do you suppose?
Ah no, it's always just my luck to get
One perfect rose.

—DOROTHY PARKER

*D*iana could feel the blood draining from her face, leaving it as stiff and cold as that of the marble maiden in the library. Walt dropped the bone and swung her up into his arms. Baby lunged at him, barking furiously. One of the men caught the dog's collar, but it took two of them to pull her away from Walt.

"Put me down," Diana gasped. "I'm perfectly all right. I wasn't going to . . . Dammit, put me down!"

Jack stooped to pick up the bone. He was older than most of the other men; his hair was thinning and his belly sagged over his belt, but his face was wrinkled with remorse as he looked at Diana.

"Sorry," he said. "I shouldn't of said that. It prob'ly is a deer bone. What do I know?"

"Stop waving it in her face," Walt said. "Hold everything, boys. Including the damned dog. I'll be back after I take her—"

"You aren't taking me anywhere." Diana squirmed and pushed at him. Her struggles had about as much effect as they would have had on a robot. "Walt, if you don't . . . Please?"

His long strides had already taken them out of the barn. Now he stopped and peered closely into her face. What he saw apparently satisfied him, for he produced a strained smile. "The magic word. At least sit down, superwoman. Catch your breath."

He deposited her on the lowered tailgate of a truck and put a steadying hand on her shoulder. Jack had followed them, mumbling apologies. "I forgot some ladies feel funny about seeing—"

"That's not it," Diana said. She took a long breath. "You don't understand, Jack. It could be Brad. My brother."

Jack's mouth dropped open. Walt's grip tightened. "Diana, do you think this is the time—"

"Now's as good a time as any." She felt peculiarly calm and detached. "I'm not a landscape architect, Jack. I tricked Walt into recommending me to the Nicholsons. I came here searching for my brother. You may remember him, he worked for Walt last summer and then moved into the cottage—the one that was demolished—to look after Miss Musser."

Jack shook his head dazedly. "Sure, I remember him. He walked out on the old lady, left her without a word. Walt was mad as hell about it."

"I don't think he walked out," Diana said. "He hasn't been seen or heard from since last August."

"Jesus." Jack's eyes popped. "You mean . . . Hey, no. That's crazy. Why would he be there? They'd have to take up the floor boards and dig . . . They'd have to . . ."

His voice died away, but his lips continued to move as he mulled it over. Walt raised one eyebrow. "Jack's a little slow. You shouldn't have dumped it on him all at once."

Jack gave his boss an indignant look. "I may be slow, but I'm not dumb. Look, honey, that couldn't be him. I know bones, I've dug up plenty of 'em. Animal bones, that is. They turn brittle and brownish-red, from the clay in the soil. That one's been in the ground for years, not months."

"By God, you're right," Walt exclaimed. "It's true, Diana. I should have seen it myself."

"Damn right you should've," Jack said self-righteously. "If you wasn't so busy calling people names . . . You believe me, don't you, hon— I mean, miss?"

"Honey is fine with me." Diana smiled at him. "Thanks, Jack. But if it isn't Brad, it's someone—a human bone, you said. What are you going to do about it? Shouldn't you call the police?"

Walt swore, lengthily and luridly. "The goddamn county archaeologists could get in on the act too. I've run into them before. God damn it! This could hold us up for weeks."

"Got to do it, though," Jack muttered unhappily. "Remember that time Alec Williams dug through an old Indian cemetery when he was building the subdivision? He got death threats!"

Walt nodded in reluctant agreement. "Diana, go back to the

house and call the cops, tell 'em we found what looks like a human leg bone. They can take it from there."

He swung her down from the tailgate and set her on her feet.

"I'll go with her," Jack offered.

"Maybe you better," Walt said. Diana started to protest; he cut her off with a curt reminder. "Unless they've located Larry in the last few hours he's still on the loose. Go with her, Jack. If it isn't one damned thing it's another!"

Baby's holders had relaxed; she broke free and came rushing to Diana, tail flailing, tongue flapping. It took several minutes of reassurance to convince her the situation required no action on her part, but she stuck close to Diana as they returned to the house.

"I'll just have a look around," Jack said. "If that's okay with you."

It was more than okay with Diana. She doubted Larry would have the nerve to sneak into the house, but she was perfectly content to err on the side of overcaution. She had completed her telephone call and was pouring iced tea into glasses when Jack returned.

"No sign of anything," he reported, accepting the glass she handed him with a nod of thanks. "You oughta keep that front door locked, though."

"You're right, I should. I won't forget after this."

"What did the cops say?"

"They'll send someone. They didn't say when, but they were definitely interested—after I reminded them about Larry."

"They can't pin this one on him," Jack said. He polished off the rest of the tea. "Thanks, that hit the spot. I better get back now. You sure you're okay?"

"I'm fine, and I'm coming with you."

It took both of them to shut Baby in the kitchen. Her howls of protest followed them.

Diana had suspected what Walt meant to do; she was not surprised to behold a scene of furious activity at the far end of the barn. At least they were digging by hand instead of using the bulldozer.

Walt straightened, leaning on his shovel, and wiped his streaming brow with his arm. "They coming?"

"Yes. They didn't say when."

"Won't be long, I expect." He turned and called out to the men working at the north end of the section. "Anything yet?"

The reply was negative. Walt jammed the spade into the dirt. He had reserved the area where the bone had been found for himself.

"The police probably won't approve of this," Diana said.

"So we're a bunch of ignorant rednecks," Walt grunted, lifting a load of dirt. "We don't know any better."

"What have you found?"

"Over there." He deposited the dirt on a growing mound and bent to sift it with his fingers.

The pitiful, ugly collection had been deposited on the short stretch of remaining floorboards. Diana knew enough anatomy to identify some of the specimens: yellowed teeth, delicate fragments of fingers or toes, a curved section of pelvis. And a skull. That at least was unmistakable. The jaw was missing; the rounded cranium seemed to have more cracks than it ought to have. Next to the skull, in a separate pile, were a few rotted scraps of fabric.

"There's only one skeleton," Walt said. "We've dug down the same depth all around without finding anything."

"So it wasn't a cemetery."

"I don't think so. That's what I wanted to find out. If there's only one body, we may be able to keep the goddamn archaeologists out of this. The cops will be . . . Oh, shit, that's them now. Keep digging, boys."

Diana hurried back to the house. Why the police had chosen to arrive with sirens screaming she could not imagine, nor did she bother to ask. The troopers seemed confused enough by the tale she told them.

"Thought you'd sighted the perp," explained one, a downy-faced youth who looked like a teenager dressed in his father's clothes. "You found one of his victims? In the barn?"

Diana explained, slowly and carefully. Once on the scene, the young officer forgot official dignity in indignation.

"Damn it, Walt, what the hell are you doing? You know better than to disturb the scene of a crime."

"How do you know a crime was committed?" Walt asked innocently.

Under other circumstances Diana might have enjoyed the debate, which Walt seemed certain to win. The pathetic mementos of humanity lined up on the floor weighed heavily on her mind, however; she believed, because she wanted to believe, that they had no importance to her, but they had been important to some-one, sometime. She retreated to the house.

The answering machine was blinking but she was not in the mood to listen to messages. She sat at the table soothing the ag-itated dog until she heard a car approaching. It stopped with a shriek of abused brakes and a hailstorm rattle of gravel, and she got quickly to her feet. She couldn't complain of Andy's careless driving this time; seeing a police car in front of the house, he must have feared the worst.

The front door reverberated to his kicks and blows; she called out, but doubted he heard her. She opened the door and stepped quickly back. Baby did not; rushing in, Andy fell over her and measured his full length on the floor. Behind him, Mary Jo let out a cry of relief.

"You're all right. What happened? Did Larry—"

"No. No, it's something else altogether. I'll tell you. Andy, for heaven's sake, stop whimpering."

"I'm not whimpering, I'm trying to repress a scream of pain. Get the dog off me, can you? I thought she only did this with women."

They extracted Andy from under the dog and led him to the kitchen, where he demanded beer and explanations. The first hav-ing been supplied, Diana started on the second. Andy interrupted her before she had gotten far.

"Holy Christ! It isn't . . . Is it? Are you all right?"

"The next person who asks me that is going to get a punch in the mouth," Diana said ungratefully. "I'm tired of being treated like one of those tight-laced Victorian women who fainted all the time."

"All I said was—"

"Shut up and let her talk," Mary Jo said.

Andy allowed her to get a few more sentences out before he interrupted again. "Old. Old bones. How old? Never mind, I get it; they'll have to study . . . I've got to see this!"

He bolted out the door.

Mary Jo dropped into a chair and gave Diana a twisted smile. "Other than that, Mrs. Lincoln, how was your day?"

"No worse than yours." Diana ventured to put her hand on

Mary Jo's. "It must have been a horrible shock, seeing that police car. I should have been waiting, to warn you. I didn't expect you so early."

"Andy dragged me out of the library and insisted we come back. He's exploding with excitement over something he found, but he wouldn't tell me what it was." Mary Jo gave Diana's hand a brief squeeze before withdrawing hers; Diana felt as if she had won a prize. "It's been a shitty day all around, I guess. You're sure that isn't . . ."

"We won't be certain until the pathologists have a look at the bones. But I don't think—I don't *feel* it's Brad. That doesn't make sense, I guess."

"Makes sense to me. Sometimes feelings are as important as logic." Mary Jo got to her feet. "It's not as early as all that. We might as well start dinner. Nothing like a little menial labor to take your mind off attempted murder and a pile of bones."

The police car finally left, sans sirens this time, but Andy did not return. The sun had dropped below the trees, leaving the western sky glowing with old-rose colors of lavender and mauve, before he and Walt came in together. Walt had stuck his head and arms under the outside tap; they were clean only by comparison to the rest of his mud-streaked body.

"Get upstairs and wash," Mary Jo ordered.

"Give me a break." Walt dropped heavily into a chair. "How about something to drink first?"

"Have a beer." Andy was already at the refrigerator. He was almost as filthy, but unlike most of the other men he had not taken off his shirt. Diana wondered whether he was reluctant to risk comparisons. It would have been hard to compete with Walt.

"Later. Right now I need plain water."

Diana filled a glass, added ice cubes and handed it to Walt. "Did the police give you a hard time?"

"What could they do? I've known Billy Jack since he was a snotty-nosed kid following me and his brother around all the time. That scene-of-the-crime stuff was a bunch of crap. They won't know whether the guy died a natural death till the coroner has a look at him."

"Somebody buried him," Diana argued. "That suggests—"

"Look, I just went through this with the fuzz and Mr. Imagination there." Walt gestured at Andy, who was leaning against the fridge. "He could have been a tramp or vagrant who laid down and died, long before the barn was ever built. We don't know how long he's been there."

"Oh, come on, Walt, that's ridiculous." It was Mary Jo, not Andy, who objected. Puzzles intrigued her, and her quick intelligence saw the flaw in Walt's argument. "The barn area isn't that far from the house. Don't tell me somebody wouldn't have noticed him—or smelled him. Animals would have carried off the pieces—"

She stopped, with an apologetic look at Diana.

"That's right," Diana said coolly. "The bones weren't scattered, were they? You found them all together. He must have been buried, but that doesn't mean he didn't die a natural death, at some time before private cemeteries were declared illegal. A member of the family would have been interred in the family plot, but he could have been a servant or an itinerant workman."

"I don't see any sense in playing guessing games." Walt drained his glass. "What pisses me off is that we can't go ahead in the barn until the cops give us their okay. Billy Jack had a great time stringing tape around his crime scene."

"What's going to happen?" Diana asked.

"Well, first the county coroner has to examine the remains. They'll probably have to call in some anthropologist from the university to assist him. If the bones are Indian, we're in big trouble. Could hold us up for weeks if the archaeologists start poking around looking for a burial site. That's become a sensitive subject. Best we can hope for . . ." Walt ticked the points off on his fingers. "The person was white; there are no indications of foul play; he's been there no less than forty, fifty years and no more than a hundred. The cops aren't interested in missing persons if they've been missing for half a century and the archaeologists aren't interested in anything less than a hundred years old."

"Billy Jack can't be as stupid as you imply if he told you that," Diana said, impressed.

"Billy Jack doesn't know his ass from his elbow. It's just common sense." Walt got up and stretched painfully. "I haven't done that much digging by hand since last fall. Come on, Andy, let's remove our disgusting bodies from Mary Jo's nice clean kitchen."

Andy followed without a word. Diana watched his retreating form curiously. There must be something wrong with him. He hadn't argued or even commented.

He remained demurely reticent during dinner; the very quality of his silence reeked of self-satisfaction, and there was a curve to his lips Diana had learned to know well. However, the body in the barn continued to be the main topic of conversation; it wasn't until they had finished eating and Andy was making coffee that she was able to question him.

"What did you do today, Andy? Mary Jo said you'd discovered something interesting."

Andy glanced at her over his shoulder, eyebrows soaring, but he answered readily enough. "I was at the Historical Society. I think I've found out who that third tombstone belonged to."

Walt grunted disgustedly. "We've got a lunatic with a shotgun in the woods and a skeleton in the barn, and you're looking up genealogies? Jesus Christ, Andy, even you—"

"We can't do anything about either of those things tonight," Diana interrupted. "I'm interested, Andy, and so will Emily. Let's go to the library, and you can tell us all about it."

Andy scowled at her; she had spoken to him as she would have spoken to an enthusiastic ten-year-old who wanted to lecture them about dinosaurs.

"We better listen to the phone messages first," Mary Jo said, rising. "The answering machine's blinking like crazy. Haven't you taken any messages today, Diana?"

"I just didn't get around to it."

They listened to the whir of the tape rewinding while Andy got the coffee tray set up. The first voice was that of the decorator from whom Emily had ordered new draperies for the library, confirming the appointment for the following day and announcing he would be there at ten. The second message was from Emily herself, explaining that she couldn't talk long because Charlie was mad at her for calling during prime time, and then going on at length to tell them what a wonderful time she was having and hoping they were the same. She was reeling off a list of new plants she had seen and desired when a shout from Charlie stopped her. A giggle and a click ended the message.

"She obviously hasn't heard anything about our little adventure," Diana said, relieved.

"A small-town shooting isn't important enough to make the national news." Andy's brow furrowed. "I only hope to God this latest discovery . . . Who's that?"

The voice was male, slow and uncertain. "I'm trying to reach—er—Ms. Diana Reed. I—er—hope I have the right number."

The ers and hems increased as he proceeded. It wasn't until the end of the message that he remembered to give his name, by which time Diana had already identified the speaker.

Andy reached for the cut-off switch. Mary Jo pushed his hand away. "We'll have to listen to the whole string of them over again if you stop it now," she scolded. "Be quiet, Andy."

The next message was for Andy himself. The speaker was obviously one of his "buddies," this time a buddy from the office. "Henderson says he's going to skin you alive if you don't report in. He hasn't heard from you for almost a week, and he wants to know what, if anything, you're doing. You better show up, Andy, you could lose this job."

It was the last of the new messages. Andy pushed the switch and the tape began to rewind. "Screw Henderson," he remarked.

"Andy, I won't let you lose your job on my account," Mary Jo exclaimed.

"I was going to quit anyway. Who was that guy?" He fixed Diana with an inquisitorial stare.

"What . . . Oh. He's the librarian I mentioned, the one in charge of the Historical Documents Collection."

"You never mentioned him," Andy said.

"Maybe not to you. I didn't know I was supposed to report all my activities in detail."

"Huh," said Andy, unimpressed by her sarcastic tone. "You going to accept his invitation to lunch tomorrow?"

"Probably." Diana resisted the childish impulse to inform him it was none of his business. "You heard him say he'd found something in Miss Musser's papers. It was kind of him to take the trouble to look, and the least I can do—"

"Look for what?" Walt's voice was as critical as Andy's. "I assume you didn't announce your identity, so he wouldn't be searching for information pertaining to Brad."

Ignorant redneck? He was nothing of the sort. Diana was beginning to wish her companions weren't so inconveniently intelligent.

Mary Jo came to her rescue. "Quit hassling her, both of you.

We're going to the library. You can join us after you've cleaned up. Don't forget to wipe the table."

Hoisting the tray with a waitress's trained skill, she marched out, herding Diana ahead of her. As they left the room Diana heard a chuckle from Andy and a low-voiced but obviously profane comment from Walt.

She had neglected to mention the arrival of the mantel. Mary Jo stopped short in the doorway and exclaimed with pleasure.

"You must have busted your butt cleaning in here. It looks great."

"As you said, there's nothing like menial labor to take one's mind off other things. The room will look lovely once the new drapes are up."

"Coffee is served, madam." Mary Jo deposited the tray on a low table and sank luxuriously into the soft embrace of the sofa. "Boy, is this class. I could get used to this kind of life. It's so elegant and peaceful here. Except for those two loud-mouthed male chauvinists."

"Apparently they can be trained," Diana said with a grin. "Walt didn't object when you told him to clean up the kitchen."

"He's probably bitching at the top of his lungs right now. They'll do a lousy job; we'll have to do it all over again."

"It's the principle of the thing," Diana said, amused at Mary Jo's tone of pessimistic conviction and pleased at her use of the plural "we."

Her pessimism was substantiated by the short interval of time that ensued before the appearance of the kitchen help. Andy looked virtuous, Walt was obviously sulking. However, he made no comment and Mary Jo wisely refrained from voicing her doubts. The surroundings might have had something to do with their more mellowed attitudes. It was a lovely room, even though it had not yet attained the elegance Emily had planned. I hope she doesn't get too carried away, Diana thought. The rows of books lining the walls, the shabby comfortable furniture gave an air of welcome no decorator's design could improve upon.

After the new mantel had been admired—it did not occur to either man, of course, to notice the results of Diana's hours with vacuum and dust cloth—she returned to the subject of Andy's research. Her question distracted him from his complaint that his precious hole had been covered up.

"Her name was Martha," he announced proudly. "Martha Fairweather. She was George's eldest daughter. Unmarried." He gave Diana a triumphant glance.

"Quick work," she said composedly. "You're certain?"

"Dates fit." Andy squirmed around so he could reach his back pocket, from which he withdrew a wad of crumpled papers. "She was born . . . I have it here somewhere. Oh, hell. Well, anyhow, you can take my word for it. She was exactly nineteen years, three months, and seventeen days old when she died."

"It's a pretty name," Mary Jo said. Her voice was gentle; only a person completely devoid of imagination could fail to be moved by the poignancy of a young life ended before its time. "How did she die?"

"I don't know. The truth is," Andy admitted, "I was lucky. Searching birth and death records could take weeks. But somebody had done a genealogy."

Even Walt had become interested. "I thought the family died out in the middle of the last century. Usually it's a relative who does that genealogy stuff—trying to get into the DAR or some such organization."

"That's who it was. The direct line died out, but there were cousins—women, they didn't carry on the Fairweather name. The collateral descendants were scattered all over the country by then; I guess that's why the house was sold, nobody wanted to move back to the ancestral acres. Some woman name of Moody had the genealogy traced back in the thirties. I figured she was aiming at the DAR or the Colonial Dames or some such thing because she went all the way back to—"

Walt's interest had faded again. Too restless to sit still, he jumped up and began pacing. "Who cares? I don't know how you can waste your time on junk like that when you could be—"

"Doing what?" Andy demanded.

"Holding a job, for one thing."

As soon as he spoke he looked as if he wished he hadn't, but the words could not be retracted. Andy's cheeks flushed. "My employment situation is none of your goddamned business, Walt."

"Stop it," Mary Jo said sharply, as Walt whirled, his hands flexed and quivering with tension. "That's all we need, for you two to start beating on each other."

"We're all on edge," Diana added. "Let's try to keep our tempers."

Walt relaxed. "Right." He added stiffly, "Sorry, Andy."

" 's okay." Andy's voice was equally cool.

Walt went to the window. Instead of turning on the outside lights he stood staring out. Then he slammed his fist into the window frame with a crash that made the others jump. "Where is the son of a bitch? The suspense is killing me."

"If you stand there silhouetted, it won't be suspense that kills you," Mary Jo said. "Please don't . . . Walt? What is it?"

He had gone rigid, leaning forward as if to see more clearly. "A light. Some way off, flickering . . ."

Andy was on his feet and at the window in a second. "Where? I don't see anything."

"Gone now. Could have been a flashlight." Walt was heading for the door as he spoke.

"For God's sake, Walt!" Mary Jo's voice rose hysterically. "Don't go out there! I couldn't stand it if he . . ."

She had found the best, perhaps the only, way of stopping him. He stood still, his back to the others, fairly shaking with frustration; and Andy went to the telephone.

"Dial nine-one-one," he said cheerfully. "What's the name of your buddy on the force, Walt?"

Billy Jack was not on duty, but his associates shared his fondness for sirens. In this case they probably served a useful purpose.

"He'll have headed for cover when he heard us coming," the officer said. "Assuming it was him you saw. Could've been a firefly."

"It wasn't a fucking firefly," Walt said, his face crimson. "You think I don't know the difference between—"

"A poacher, then, or kids camping out. We'll have a look around tomorrow. It's too dark to see anything tonight—and," the officer added in a burst of candor, "I'm not stupid enough to go crashing around in the woods yelling and waving lights if he's behind a tree with a shotgun."

He took his departure. Walt turned on the others.

"It was not a—"

"Couldn't have been, it's too early for fireflies," Andy said.

The casual, conciliatory comment struck a chord in Diana's memory. Someone had said that earlier, or thought it . . . Before she could pin the thought down, Mary Jo said, "He was right about the stupidity of crashing around in the woods in the dark. Were you listening, Walt?"

She was herself again, acerbic and critical, but there was an underlying note of anxiety that was clearly audible to Diana. Not, it seemed, to Walt. "I was listening," he growled. "Does anybody mind if I stupefy my dumb brain a little more by watching TV?"

"Is there anything good on?" Diana asked, trying to placate him.

"I don't give a damn what's on so long as it's mindless and violent. With lots of shooting and car chases." Walt flung himself into a chair and reached for the remote control.

Lips tight, Mary Jo gathered an armful of books. "I'm going upstairs to study."

She marched out, leaving a strained silence in her wake. It was Walt who finally broke it. "She can't take much more of this," he muttered, eyes fixed on the screen, where two men mouthed silent and—to judge by their expressions—pejorative comments at one another. "I'm surprised she hasn't walked out of here already."

"We can't let her do that," Diana said.

"Stopping Mary Jo when she's determined to do something is like beating your head against a brick wall. One thing for sure— if they haven't found Larry by the time the Nicholsons get back, she'll take off. She won't risk Emily getting hurt."

"Neither will I." Andy looked perturbed; the idea had obviously not occurred to him before. "But we can't throw Mary Jo to the wolves. Maybe we can talk Ma and Charlie into prolonging their trip."

"You can try." Walt was pessimistic. "But if Emily finds out what's been going on—and the discovery of the skeleton may be weird enough to appeal to one of the wire services—she'll be back like a shot. No. We've got to find Larry." He was flexing his hands as he spoke; the tendons knotted and moved like stretched cords under the skin. "I can't understand how the bastard has managed to stay undercover so long. He lit out with only the clothes on his back and his shotgun—no food, no booze, no nothing. He hasn't been back to his apartment; the cops have that staked out. There haven't been any break-ins or car thefts."

"Unless he's trapping animals for food," Andy began. Walt's irritable gesture denied this suggestion. He went on, "Then he's hiding out with a friend, or somebody is getting supplies to him."

"His so-called friends have been questioned. Trouble is, the cops don't have the manpower to watch all of them all the time." Walt glowered at his clenched hands, ignoring the car chase on the screen. After a few moments he looked at Diana and his face smoothed out into an artificial smile. "They'll get him. Bound to. Not much we can do but wait. Diana, if you are going to the library tomorrow, you could drive Mary Jo to school."

"Isn't tomorrow one of her work days?" Diana asked. The apparent change of subject was nothing of the sort, she knew.

"You should be able to talk her into taking a day off. Exams are coming up, aren't they? I don't know where she's supposed to be tomorrow, but all her jobs are in and around Faberville. I want her as far away as you can get her. Larry won't take a chance on going to the college."

"I can drive her," Andy began.

"You could give me a hand here," Walt said.

He didn't look at Andy, but some sort of silent message must have passed between the two men. Andy looked surprised, then thoughtful. "Right," he said.

"Right," Diana repeated.

She knew perfectly well what Walt intended to do next day: send the helpless females to safety and then go looking for Larry. He must intend to use his whole crew in the search, which would leave the house unguarded. There was no point in arguing with him when he was in this mood, but if he was going to play the protective male with her, she felt no obligation to tell him of her plans. After a while she excused herself and went to the kitchen.

She had almost finished the second telephone call when Andy's insatiable curiosity brought him in pursuit. He leaned against the wall, arms folded, and listened.

"I won't be here tomorrow during the day," Diana said, scowling at the eavesdropper. "You can leave a message—or I'll call you. Around eleven-thirty? Good. Yes, I've already done that. Thanks. I do appreciate . . . What? Yes, certainly, I'll keep you informed."

She hung up. Andy shifted position. "The old man?" he inquired.

"Yes."

"The private 'tec?"

"Yes."

"What have you already done?"

"Offered a reward."

Andy nodded. "Good idea. I doubt if Larry has any buddies who love him more than money. How much?"

"A thousand."

"Are you going to say more than three words at a time?"

"No."

"I don't know why you're mad at me. It wasn't my idea to—"

"Blunder around the woods looking for an armed and dangerous crack shot?" Diana dropped heavily into a chair. "I don't know which of you is the worst. Walt's so obsessed with finding Larry he's willing to endanger himself and his friends, and you are so obsessed with your ghost story—"

"That'll have to go on hold for a while. Believe it or not, my mother's safety is more important to me."

He sat down in the rocking chair and set it swaying back and forth with a vigor that emphasized his words. "She's such a screwball," he went on angrily. "The woman hasn't got any sense. I know her; she'd invent all kinds of wild schemes to protect Mary Jo—locking her in a room for her own good, or dragging her off to some exotic resort in disguise and under an assumed name—and then she'd try to lure Larry out of hiding with sandwiches and brownies. And when she finds out about the bones . . . Jesus! It makes my blood run cold to think about what she might do."

His horror was so genuine it provoked Diana to laughter. "Maybe we can persuade Charles to lock *her* in her room, for her own good."

Andy was not amused. "If worst comes to worst, I'll tell Charlie what's going on. He'll think of some way of keeping her unwitting and distracted. I hate to resort to that, though. He'll blame me for the whole mess."

"Don't be silly. Why should he? None of it is your fault." She couldn't help adding, "Except for the psychic-research stuff. He won't like that."

"Ma will, though." Andy looked more cheerful. "Once this other business is cleared up we can have a great time . . . Oh, hell, I'm sorry. I forgot. I mean, I didn't forget, I—"

"It's a game to you," Diana said. "Not to me."

"Nor me. I swear. But it's all connected, Diana, it has to be.

Larry may have the answer to what happened to your brother. You said yourself that knowing the truth would be less painful than a lifetime of uncertainty."

"I said it, but I'm not sure I believe it." In her mind, vivid as an image projected onto a screen, was the memory of that random collection of brown and brittle bones.

CHAPTER FOURTEEN

*Rose, O pure contradiction of desire; to be
nobody's sleep amongst so many eyelids.*

—Rilke

Diana had braced herself for an argument with Mary Jo. Since
she usually lost those arguments she was relieved to learn that
Mary Jo had not intended to work that day. She had a final exam
that afternoon, and she was up and dressed by seven, meaning to
get to the library as soon as it opened. Walt had already eaten
breakfast and gone out to join his crew when Diana came down
but Andy managed to draw her aside for a few words in private
while Mary Jo collected her books and papers.

"Nothing happened last night?"

Diana chose to ignore the rising inflection at the end of the
sentence. She searched busily through her purse for her car keys.

"I think I know why," Andy said.

"Andy, I don't have time for—"

"Walt. He's been sleeping in the library."

"Oh, really. Well, it makes sense; those windows are the most
vulnerable point."

"But his presence may be deterring our musician."

"That's fine with me. Andy, for heaven's sake, keep your mind
on essentials. And if you possibly can, try to talk Walt out of—"

She broke off as Mary Jo came trotting down the stairs.

"Yeah, sure," Andy said. His voice lacked conviction. "Break a
leg, Mary Jo. And do have a nice day."

As soon as she buckled her seat belt Mary Jo opened a book.
"You don't mind, do you?" she asked.

Diana did mind. She had looked forward to talking with Mary

242

Jo alone, without Andy's constant chatter and Walt's scowling presence, but the other woman's preoccupied frown told her Mary Jo was worried about the exam and in no mood for idle conversation.

She dropped Mary Jo off at the library and found a newsstand and a coffee shop. She had four hours to kill before her lunch date, and two hours before she could even confirm it. Louis had informed her, among a flurry of ers and uhs, that she didn't have to let him know, he would be at work after ten, ready and waiting if she wanted to come, but she didn't have to bother, if she couldn't make it that was fine, but in case she did . . . Diana felt rather sorry for him, and almost as sorry for herself. She was in no mood to waste time in social engagements and she didn't suppose Louis had found anything of interest. How could he, when he had no idea what she was looking for? She didn't know herself. If he considered taking her to lunch sufficient reward for days of boring labor, that was the least she could do for him.

She spent an hour reading the newspapers, not only the local papers but the Washington *Post*. She had been out of touch with the "real world" for so long she felt like an exile; but as she read about violence in the city streets and political maneuvering on the campaign trail and futile debate about the budget crisis—everybody complained about it but nobody wanted to do anything—she felt a mounting impatience. That wasn't the real world. Reality was the day-by-day struggle of ordinary people with the problems of their own lives. Her own private agony had seemed to her peculiarly tragic, but she had come to realize that pain is immeasurable. How could she claim she had suffered more than Mary Jo, who had seen the man she once loved turn into an enemy intent on destroying her? For years he had tried to kill her spirit and her ambition by methods less direct but perhaps even more painful. Mary Jo wasn't unique; there were thousands, millions, of women like her.

Diana forced herself to concentrate on the local news. The only reference to their recent activities was a short item on a back page of the county paper: SEARCH CONTINUES FOR GUNMAN. It told her nothing she did not already know. There was nothing in the *Post* or the Richmond and Charlottesville papers. No news was certainly good news, in this case; Emily and Charles wouldn't be likely to find the local paper on newsstands in North Carolina. It was too early for the story about the skeleton to have reached the press. She could only hope Walt was wrong when he claimed it was bizarre enough to attract widespread media interest.

Having occupied the booth for an hour and consumed two cups of coffee, she decided she couldn't decently linger any longer. A brisk walk along streets lined with pleasant old houses and nicely kept yards occupied her for another hour. Some of the gardens were pretty enough in their spring bloom to distract her from her gloomy thoughts. Would Emily want a magnolia? Knowing Emily, she supposed Emily would—a magnolia already thirty feet tall. The classic Southern magnolia, with its huge waxy-pale flowers, was not yet in bloom, but there was another variety—tulip magnolia?—with vivid shocking-pink blossoms that made a spectacular show. Almost every yard boasted one. No, that was wrong; it wasn't a true magnolia, it was . . . She had forgotten. Diana's spirits sank. In addition to her other problems, she had confession and penance yet to face.

Maybe the stores would be open by now. Shopping was supposed to be a suitable distraction for feeble female brains. Hers was feeling particularly frail at the moment. Retracing her steps, she found herself passing a handsome old mansion, with white pillars and a flight of stone stairs framed by curved wrought-iron railings. She stopped to admire the tracery of the fanlight over the door, and saw the sign.

This was where Andy had been the day before. And it was open—ten to four, the sign said.

First she made her telephone call, from a box on the corner. Louis was reduced to virtual incoherence by her acceptance of his luncheon invitation, but he managed to stutter out agreement when she proposed to meet him at the library. Diana looked at her watch. Still almost two hours to go. She might as well spend it at the Historical Society rather than wandering the street or buying a lot of junk she didn't need.

The first floor was devoted to exhibits. She paid the modest requested "donation" and wandered into the first room. Cases filled with arrowheads and stone tools, scraps of pottery and basketry stood under placards describing the prehistory of the county. Apparently history proper didn't begin until the arrival of European settlers.

No doubt it was all very interesting to an expert, which she was not. A bustle of activity in an adjoining room drew her onward. The open arch was barred by a rope, but there was nothing to prevent her from standing and watching, which she proceeded to do. This exhibit was more to her taste.

The room had been furnished with antiques of the late-eighteenth century, from which period the house itself dated, and with several mannequins wearing period costume. The room was a drawing room, and a tea party was in progress. One figure, seated on a brocaded Chippendale sofa, stretched out her hand toward the silver tea service on the table before her. She wore a powdered wig and a panniered gown of pale-green watered taffeta, pulled back to display an embroidered petticoat. Lace, delicate and fragile as cobwebs, framed her shoulders and hung in graceful gathers from the elbow-length sleeves of her gown. Two other female figures stood nearby.

After a fascinated inspection Diana realized that the costumes were the genuine article—antiques like the furniture around them, and probably as old. The young woman who was busily arranging the exhibit looked out of place in her faded jeans and tie-dyed shirt. She adjusted the wig of the last figure, a gentleman wearing knee breeches and buckled shoes. His matching coat and waistcoat were lavishly embroidered with bright silks and gilt thread.

Looking up, she met Diana's eyes and gave her a friendly grin. "Hi. Come on in."

"You're not open, are you?"

"Just about to be. This exhibit should have been finished last night, but I didn't quite make it." She lifted the rope that had barred the doorway and hooked it up out of the way. "You interested in costume?"

"I wasn't. But these are gorgeous."

"The prizes of the collection." The young woman ran her hand through her fashionably tousled hair and contemplated her work with rueful pride. "They really shouldn't be here. Small local museums like ours don't have the funds or the expertise to handle objects like these. I'm only a part-time volunteer, and I should be at work right now; had to take annual leave to finish up."

"So you're a point of light," Diana said, smiling.

The young woman's answering smile was decidedly sour. "If you've got a few hours free, I'll tell you what I think of that points-of-light baloney. Volunteers can't supply what's really needed—

cold, hard cash. Fabric is fragile; it ought to be kept in temperature and light-controlled storage areas to prevent further deterioration, and that kind of equipment costs a bundle. I suppose historic preservation is less important than a lot of other things that are underfunded these days—in fact, I know it is. But I get so frustrated sometimes, trying to save objects that can never be replaced, when a few lousy bucks would make such a difference . . . Oh, well. You don't want to hear me lecture."

"It's very interesting. I expect you have to get to work, though."

"I took the morning off. If you've got questions I'll be glad to answer them. My name's Marily Garner, by the way."

Diana gave her own name, somewhat abstractedly. One of the gowns had already caught her eye. Roses again; they kept popping up in the most unlikely places. Sprays of embroidered blossoms and trailing stems covered the fabric of the skirt, which was looped up at the back to display a quilted underpetticoat. The tight-fitting bodice was of the same fabric as the skirt. A gauzy shawl covered the figure's shoulders.

"That style is called a polonaise," said her friendly informant. "It was popular in England in the 1770s. Lasted a little longer here in America; fashions were always a few years late in the Colonies."

"That old? I can't imagine how it lasted so long. It's in remarkable condition."

"Well, we had a bit of luck with this one. The girl for whom it was made died young, just before her wedding. This was part of her trousseau. Her grieving parents packed the clothes carefully away, and there they stayed, in sealed boxes, for almost a hundred years. Since the dresses had never been worn, there were no perspiration stains to weaken the fabric, and light never touched it."

The feeling that came over Diana was stronger than a premonition or even a suspicion. She was sure she knew what the answer would be when she asked, "Do you know her name?"

"Oh, sure. Martha's sort of a romantic legend with the staff here. The Fairweathers were a local family. The house is still standing, it's one of our stately mansions, but the heirs sold it and moved away a long time ago. That's how the Historical Society got the clothes. They'd bring high prices at auction today, but in the 1860s they had only historic and sentimental value. We get a lot of contributions that way—including a lot of junk! Families hate to throw out Grannie's nightcap or horrible hand-painted chamber pot, but they don't want to give them house room."

She would have gone on chatting—loquacity was apparently a local habit not restricted to the Nicholsons—if Diana had not interrupted. "You have more of her clothes, then?"

"Uh-huh. Including her wedding dress. They're stored away, but if you want to come by this weekend I'd be glad to take them out for you. Saturday's my regular day."

"That's awfully kind of you. I can't imagine a museum curator in Philadelphia or New York taking so much trouble for a perfect stranger."

"It's no trouble. I don't get that many sympathetic, intelligent visitors, believe me. Is there any particular reason why you're interested in Martha?"

Diana gave her an expurgated explanation. Marily's eyes lit up.

"What fun! I read about that couple winning the lottery and buying the house. Everybody's been dying to see what they did to it."

"I'm only a guest of theirs," Diana began.

"Sure, I understand. But put in a good word for us poor underfunded institutions, will you? We sponsor a house-and-garden tour every year to raise money; that place would really draw the paying customers." She glanced at her watch. "Got to run, I want to grab a sandwich before I get to work. I'll be here all day Saturday; just come by and ask for me."

Gathering up her purse, she dashed out.

Left alone, Diana dared to brush the edge of the lace-trimmed sleeve with a feather-light finger. No psychic shock or shiver of ancient memory touched her; no recaptured emotion shadowed her mind, only remote pity for a long-dead girl who—like millions of other long-dead girls—had died young. Andy would probably claim the ambience was wrong. Andy would go out of his mind when he learned that Martha's very clothing had been preserved, and that his romantic scenario was even more sickeningly sentimental than he had supposed. He would probably want her to steal, beg, or borrow Martha's trousseau—fondle the fabric, try on the gowns . . .

Diana's lip curled in instinctive distaste. She had no intention of feeding Andy's fantasies.

She might come back on Saturday, though. The clothing was

beautiful. Emily would certainly be interested. Any intelligent, imaginative person would.

Lunch with poor Louis (as she was coming to think of him) was not as tedious as she had expected. Poor Louis's efforts to spruce himself up for the encounter were a disaster; he had been a good deal more attractive in his casual work clothes than in a sport jacket whose excessive shoulder pads only emphasized the meager frame beneath it. However, once he got over his nervousness, and Diana's tactful direction of the discussion turned it to his own subject, he proved to be an interesting conversationalist. The underlying theme was sadly similar to the one she had heard from Marily: not enough money, not enough support, resulting in the irretrievable loss of knowledge and beauty. Diana felt ashamed of herself as she listened to his indignant comments. He and Marily and others like them were a small, valiant army fighting impossible odds. They didn't even get respect. She wondered how often Louis had been told he ought to have majored in something that paid good money. Computers, for example.

Shame made her exert herself to be gracious, with the unfortunate result (as she later realized) of arousing expectations in poor Louis that not even respect could induce her to fulfill. She managed to escape without committing herself to an official "date," but she could see trouble ahead.

The interesting information that poor Louis had found consisted of a bundle of letters, from a friend and former teacher of Miss Musser's. Louis believed they had been preserved because the friend had been a writer, and Miss Musser cherished the illusion that her correspondence would be of interest to literary historians. Diana had never heard of "my friend Amelie DuPrez, the authoress," nor, Louis admitted, had he until he looked her up. She had written a number of sentimental novels with titles like *The Rosebud Girl* and *The Lament of the Lonely Heart.*

"Oh, dear," Diana said.

"I gather they were as bad as the titles suggest," Louis agreed. "She enjoyed moderate popularity in the late teens and early twenties, but she was never a best-seller, and the taste for such sentimental tripe started to die out after World War One. I guess Mrs. Nicholson wouldn't be interested in them."

Diana assured him Emily would—which was probably true, Emily was interested in everything—and took the copies he had made with appropriate thanks. She told herself she had no reason to be disappointed. She had not expected anything, had she?

At least the letters kept her amused while she waited for Mary Jo. Emily would enjoy them. The "authoress" was certainly impressed with herself; there were florid descriptions of lavish gifts from gentlemen admirers, extravagant lunches with New York publishers, and travels to Europe on great ocean liners where, of course, the famous authoress had been seated at the captain's table. No wonder poor Miss Musser had kept the letters; to a country girl they must have represented a world of glamour and glitter which she would never experience. She hadn't bothered to keep copies of her own letters.

Mary Jo finally emerged from the building, rumpled and tired but with a visible look of triumph. "I think I did okay," she announced, dropping into the seat next to Diana.

"I'm glad but not surprised," the latter answered. "When are you going to find out about the scholarship?"

"I've got it." Mary Jo tried to sound casual. She didn't quite succeed.

"But that's wonderful! Congratulations. I'm so pleased!"

"I'm still sort of numb," Mary Jo admitted. "I guess I never really believed it would happen. When it dawns on me I'll probably go nuts. Can't afford to do that now. If I don't graduate, the whole deal falls through."

"There's no reason on earth to think you won't graduate. But I know how you feel. When you're that close to something you want that badly, you start looking over your shoulder for unexpected and illogical disasters. But that's pure superstition, Mary Jo."

"No, it's what they call the natural perversity of things." Mary Jo leaned back with a sigh.

"I bet you didn't eat lunch."

"You kidding? I needed every minute of that time in the library. My normal study hours have been somewhat— Where are you going?"

Cutting neatly across two lanes of traffic, Diana pulled into the parking lot of a shopping center. "When I was in high school, my best friend and I used to go out and gorge on ice cream whenever we passed an exam or did anything else we considered worthy of celebration. Seems to me that a scholarship deserves at least a banana split."

"I haven't had a banana split in years." Mary Jo looked horrified. "Maybe a cone—"

"No, no. The biggest, unhealthiest, most fattening concoction on the menu. With everything on it—whipped cream out of a can and ersatz cherries and stale nuts. And you have to eat it all."

For a moment she didn't know whether Mary Jo was going to laugh or swear. She did neither. Diana caught a glimpse of trembling lips and overflowing eyes before Mary Jo folded her arms on the dashboard and hid her face against them.

"Hey, if the idea repels you that much, you only have to eat half of it," Diana said cheerfully.

A stifled snort was the only reply. Finally Mary Jo sat up, wiping her wet cheeks with her fingers. "You're really something, you know that?"

Diana presented a handful of tissues. "I was tempted to say, 'Everything is going to be all right.' But it probably isn't."

"I don't see how it can be."

"In the short term, probably not. But in the long run, there's escape for you and peace of mind for me. And in the meantime there are things like banana splits."

"Only if you eat one of the revolting things too." Mary Jo gave her a watery smile.

"Damn straight," Diana said.

The brief euphoria produced by their descent into schoolgirl silliness was beneficial. Not until they crossed the bridge and were approaching the house did Mary Jo stop chattering about her college plans and fall silent. Diana felt her stomach begin to knot up, and knew the ice cream—which had been just as rich and revolting as Mary Jo predicted—was not responsible. When she saw the car parked in front of the steps she exclaimed in annoyance. "Who the hell is that?"

"At least it's not a cop car," Mary Jo said.

"Right. Thank God for small blessings. Do you recognize this one?"

"Never saw it before. And I don't know anybody who'd be likely to drive an aesthetic catastrophe like that."

The car missed being a limo by only a few feet, but it was the color even more than the size that had prompted Mary Jo's critical comment. It was white—not plain ordinary white, but the glimmering iridescent shade of . . . "I think I can guess," Diana said.

They found Pearl in the drawing room being entertained—or vice versa—by Andy. She was doing all the talking. Andy, who was in an indescribable state of tatters, scratches, and general dishevelment, gave them a hunted look and leapt to his feet.

"Ah, here they are. I'll be ready in a minute, ladies, soon as I shower and change."

This feeble subterfuge had no effect on its object. Pearl settled herself more comfortably on the sofa. She was wearing a four-strand choker of her favorite gems and a bright-coral jersey dress that fondled every curve. She nodded at Mary Jo and gave Diana a smile full of teeth. "I just happened to be passing by."

Diana was not in any mood to tolerate Pearl. "It happens often. People just passing by. This is such a well-traveled road."

Pearl's jaw dropped, but she recovered quickly. "I mean, I happened to be out this way. So I thought I'd stop by and see what Miz Nicholson wants to do about that birdbath. Seeing as how I've got another customer that's interested—"

"Let him or her have it," Diana cut in. "I haven't had a chance to talk to Mrs. Nicholson about the birdbath. She certainly wouldn't expect you to hold it indefinitely."

"Oh, hell, I don't mind doing a favor for a good customer like Miz Nicholson. But I have to know pretty quick."

"I'll let you know as soon as I can, but feel free to make other arrangements if you choose." Diana glanced at the clock and went on, without pausing. "You'll have to excuse us now. We have an appointment and we're going to be late."

Even Pearl couldn't ignore that. She heaved herself to her feet, coral convolutions wobbling. "I was expecting you'd stop by my store. Got some new stuff, from a stately home up by Winchester, bought the entire contents—"

"One of these days. Let me see you to the door."

After she had herded Pearl out she gave herself the satisfaction of slamming the door. The others had followed her into the hall. Mary Jo was trying to contain her laughter; Andy's face was rapt with admiration.

"How did you do that?" he demanded. "It was the coolest piece of rudeness I ever saw."

"I learned from an expert," Diana said briefly. "You look like hell, Andy. What have you been—"

She realized then what he had been doing and broke off, with a glance at Mary Jo.

"I know what he's been doing," the latter said. "Walt too. I can read that ignorant redneck like a book. I didn't see any sense arguing with him, it's like beating your head against a stone wall. Of all the stupid-ass things to do! Look at you, Andy! That shirt's in rags and your face looks like you stuck it in a barrel full of cats. I hope you're covered with poison ivy and ticks and chiggers!"

A fatuous smile spread across Andy's face. "She loves me," he exclaimed, advancing on Mary Jo with outspread arms.

"I hope Walt's covered with 'em too," Mary Jo snarled.

"Crushed again." Andy let his arms drop heavily to his side. "How did the exam go?"

"Okay."

"She got the scholarship," Diana said.

"Yeah? Fantastic! This calls for a celebration. I'll make my most famous dish, spaghetti con funghi, and we'll . . . Oh. Hell, I forgot. Can't do it tonight, I have a date."

"Just as well, I won't be able to eat anything for hours," Mary Jo said, smiling at Diana.

"Rain check," Andy said. "Tomorrow nght. Who knows, we may have something else to celebrate by then."

He refused to elaborate on this enigmatic statement, even after Mary Jo had gone in search of "the ignorant redneck," so she could tell him what she thought of his ideas.

"Did you find something in the woods?" Diana demanded. "I know you didn't locate Larry; you'd have had the decency to say so at once if that had been the case. Wouldn't you?"

"I'd have been waiting for Mary Jo when she came out of that classroom," Andy said soberly. "Walt had some idea Larry might have holed up in a cave up the creek a piece, as they say in these parts. It's not really a cave; more of a rock overhang. It didn't seem likely to me, since according to Walt most of the local kids know about it, but we did find indications that Larry'd been there—charred wood from a fire, cigarette butts."

"My God, Andy! Mary Jo is dead right, that was stupid. Why

didn't you tell the police instead of barging in there yourselves?"

"I let Walt go first," Andy explained, grinning. "No, but seriously—I think he was there only temporarily, the first night. As soon as he sobered up he'd have sense enough to move on. We didn't find food wrappers or cans."

"Maybe he had sense enough to bury them."

"We dug," Andy said, with a sour look at his scraped, bruised hands. "God, did we dig!"

"Then what did you mean when you said we might have something else to celebrate?"

"Sorry, I've got to get cleaned up. This is one lady I particularly want to dazzle."

He was halfway up the stairs before she could reply, the tatters of his jeans flapping around his ankles.

The kitchen was full of furry forms and wagging tails. Mary Jo was feeding the animals. Diana patted Baby, who had greeted her with a "wuff" and a lunge, and went to help.

"It's done," Mary Jo said brusquely. "Sit down before that damned dog knocks you down."

Diana knew Mary Jo's anger wasn't directed at her. She felt she had made enough headway in winning the other woman's friendship to risk a critical comment. "Why are you so hard on Walt? He's doing this for you."

"You think he's doing me a favor by risking his neck?" Mary Jo swung on her, brandishing the spoon she had used to stir the dogs' dinners. "If Larry killed him or hurt him badly I'd have to live with it the rest of my life. I can do without that kind of favor."

"I know. I agree with you. But—"

"Anyhow, what makes you so sure he's doing it for me? Your neck's in the noose too, and he . . . he likes you. I can tell."

"He has a funny way of showing it. Okay, you've made your point. I don't want him getting killed on my account either. I don't suppose the police have called with good news? That would be too much to expect."

"I haven't checked the messages." Mary Jo cleared the kitchen of dogs, setting their bowls on the porch and stepping smartly away from the mad rush that ensued. Diana switched on the answering machine.

The only message of interest was from her father. "I believe I've found someone for you. The firm is highly recommended, and one of their operatives knows the area well. He will arrive tomorrow around eleven. Please be there. I've given him as much of the background as I could, but naturally he wants to talk to you. Call me after you've spoken with him."

"He doesn't waste words, does he?" Mary Jo commented. "Is it a private detective he's talking about?"

"No and yes, in that order. I hope you don't mind."

"I'd welcome Attila the Hun if I thought he could find Larry. Anyhow, it's not up to me to mind or not mind. Brad's the one your dad is thinking of. As he should be."

"Nothing from the police," Diana muttered. "Damn it! I'm going to call."

There was no information on Larry or on the bones. Billy Jack, with whom she had asked to speak in the hope that he would be more forthcoming than his colleagues, informed her that they had been turned over to the forensic anthropologist at the university in Charlottesville, but that no report was expected for several days.

Miss Matilda jumped onto Diana's lap and began washing herself. Stroking her, Diana repeated the information to Mary Jo. "I don't approve of what Walt did today, but I can sympathize with his feelings. It's so maddening to sit around waiting for other people to do things. I'd like to rush over to the university and force Professor What's-his-name to drop everything and start working on those bones."

"They don't have anything to do with us." Mary Jo said firmly.

"I'm ninety-nine percent sure of that . . ."

"But you wish you were one hundred percent sure." Mary Jo thought a moment. "Did you tell your dad about them?"

Diana stared at her in chagrin and admiration. "My God, you're sharp. Why didn't I think of that? I'll call him right away. If anybody can pull strings and exert undue pressure, it's my father."

She was unable to locate her father, at the office or at home. A strange woman's voice answered the latter call and identified herself, after Diana had done so, as a nurse. "I'm sorry your mother isn't able to speak with you, Miss Randall. No, there's nothing to worry about. She's sleeping. No, I don't know when Mr. Randall will be here. He's working late."

Diana hung up and dialed again. Watching her stony face, Mary Jo refrained from question or comment until after Diana had recited her message into the machine at the other end.

"You don't waste words either," she remarked. "That was pretty blunt, wasn't it? You could have told him you don't think it was his son."

"Blunt is how he likes it. He's working late. Not at the office."

"Entertaining a client—"

"Entertaining somebody. He's divorcing my mother. He told me that the other day."

"I'm sorry."

"No. I'm sorry to behave like such an adolescent fool. I shouldn't let it bother me. Happens all the time."

"It could be the best thing for her," Mary Jo said. "Your mother."

"How could it be—" Diana stopped. "I never thought of it that way," she said after a moment. "I'm afraid it's too late for her, though. She's been in that cage too long."

"I don't see how she could be worse off than living with a man she blames for the death of the person she loved best in the whole world . . . Oh, shit, I didn't mean that. I meant one of the people—"

"You were right the first time." Diana slumped lower in the chair. "Why does everything have to be so complicated? I think I could deal with Larry on the loose and mysterious bones in the barn, and even Brad's disappearance—all the standard plot clichés of contemporary thrillers—if they weren't so weighted down by emotional baggage. I've faced more uncomfortable truths about myself in the last week than I have for twenty years."

"And it didn't cost you a cent," Mary Jo said sardonically. "Imagine how much a shrink would have charged."

"There is that. I wonder if it's been the same for Andy and Walt."

"Walt doesn't face uncomfortable truths about himself." Mary Jo got up. "I'm going to study. I'll grab a sandwich later, if my stomach ever settles down, so don't bother cooking anything for me."

Diana detached Miss Matilda from her skirt and went to the back door. In the distance she could hear the growl of machinery and a rhythmic beat of hammering. She wondered what Walt was doing—the gazebo?—but didn't have the energy to go out and see. The new sod on the upper terrace was a brilliant healthy green in the rays of the setting sun. When Walt had found time to do it she could not imagine, but since she last looked he had laid out formal beds on either side of the path leading from the back door to the terrace steps, and had planted some of them with pansies, those toughest of early-blooming annuals. It was too early to plant anything else; hard frosts could occur as late as the first week in May. Somehow Diana found the pansies oddly touching. Walt was determined that Emily should find flowers, some kind of flowers, in bloom when she returned.

The austere unfinished terrace was quite a contrast to the garden she had seen in that uncanny fleeting vision—a garden bursting with bloom, with flowering trees and spring bulbs. Had it been Martha Fairweather's garden she had seen, Martha's favorite roses whose scent she had inhaled, in a distortion of time no less impossible than the one that had inspired the vision itself?

Diana shivered. The evening had turned sharply cooler; the warmth of Miss Matilda, clinging like a limpet to her shoulder, felt good. The pansies nodded in the breeze.

Darkness was almost complete before she heard Walt's heavy footsteps. He flung the door open, swore at a dog lying on the threshold, and turned a scowling face to Diana. "I told you to keep the doors locked."

Pansies, Diana thought. Remember the pansies. "I felt perfectly safe with you and the other gentlemen on guard. Dinner will be ready in a few minutes. Do you want something to drink before you change?"

Walt studied her suspiciously. He was not as battered as Andy, having had the sense to wear heavy work clothing and boots instead of sneakers, but his face was crisscrossed with scratches. "I could use a cup of coffee," he admitted grudgingly. "It's getting cold out there."

"I hope the pansies won't be nipped." She filled a cup and brought it to him. "Sit down and relax for a minute. You look exhausted."

Even to her the speech sounded forced, like a caricature of womanly concern. Walt's scowl intensified until his eyebrows met in the middle of his forehead, but he sat down at the table and picked up the cup.

"I'm not exhausted. I feel fine." After a moment he added, "The pansies will be okay. It isn't going to freeze."

"They were a nice thought, Walt."

"You're easy to please, aren't you?" But his voice was softer and his face had relaxed.

Diana didn't answer. She filled a cup for herself, not because she wanted coffee, but as a companionable gesture, and sat down at the table. "Mary Jo got her scholarship."

"Great. Now all we have to do is make sure she lives long enough to accept it."

"Nobody could do more than you're doing."

"Apparently not." Walt was determined not to be flattered or optimistic. "Any calls?"

Diana filled him in on the news of the day. She had wondered if Walt would resent the idea of an outsider intruding on what showed signs of becoming a private vendetta, but he reacted with the first show of enthusiasm he had demonstrated.

"Good idea. You mind if I talk to the guy?"

"I wish you would. You can fill him in better than I could."

"I'm running out of ideas," Walt admitted. "Somebody's got to be sneaking supplies to him, but the cops can't keep tails on all his buddies twenty-four hours a day."

Worry and fatigue had drawn new lines on his face. Impulsively Diana put her hand on his. "Maybe we're overreacting, Walt. He may have given up the idea of getting at Mary Jo. He only turns violent when he's drunk, she said; it could be that he's concentrating on how to save his own skin."

"Maybe. But we'd be insane to count on it. And there's the minor matter of whether he killed your brother."

Somehow the positions of their hands had become reversed; Walt's calloused palm held hers and his eyes were fixed on their twined fingers. "Don't get any sloppy sentimental ideas about me and Mary Jo, Diana. I've known her since she was a kid. I admire her guts, and I hate Larry's. That's all there is to it."

CHAPTER FIFTEEN

The rose-lipt girls are sleeping
In fields where roses fade.

—A. E. HOUSMAN

Walt left rather abruptly, without giving Diana time to reply. As she moved around the kitchen rattling pans and slamming dishes on the table, she gave vent to her feelings in a series of mumbled comments. "Who does he think he is? Conceited bastard! That was supposed to make my day, I guess." And, more betrayingly: "I don't need this!"

She had never been inclined to seek comfort or forgetfulness by jumping into bed with the first medically certified and sexually attractive man available. There had to be an emotional element in such a relationship, and now of all times she couldn't handle that kind of stress. It was hard enough dealing with the turmoil of emotions that battered her from all sides—fear and uncertainty, guilt and grief, love and . . . hate? She didn't hate Larry; she despised and feared him, but hate was too strong a word for such a contemptible object. If she hated anyone . . .

The ringing of the telephone saved her from that unpleasant admission. She leapt at it as at a lifeline.

Emily's voice gave her spirits a brief lift until Emily explained the reason for her call. "I've been worrying about you all day. Is everything all right? I can't reach Andy, and I had a horrible nightmare last night. The house was under attack and you were inside, and I tried to run to help you and fell out of bed, and now I have a big bruise on my bum and Charlie's mad at me because I woke him up and because he doesn't believe in premonitions. But I do, and I'm sure something must be wrong because you and

I are en rapport and I want you to tell me the truth and not try to spare my feelings."

She might have gone on if she had not had to stop to breathe. Diana tried to gather her wits, which were in a state of pitiful confusion. Emily's conversational gambits were difficult enough to follow under normal circumstances, and the uncanny accuracy of her premonition—guess, maternal sympathy, whatever it was—had an unnerving effect.

Andy's appearance in the doorway gave Diana the hint she needed. "Andy's right here," she said. "He's just fine. In fact, he's all dressed up for a date and looks pretty as a picture." Andy shook his head wildly and mouthed, "I just left!"

"Do you want to talk to him?" Diana asked.

Emily did. Andy bared his teeth at Diana and took the phone. "Hi, Ma. How are . . . Sure, I'm fine. I've been busy. You know, in and out. Well . . . yeah, since you ask, I've been here most of the time. Giving Walt a hand. My job? Look, Ma, I'll explain when you . . . What?" He listened in silence for a time, and Diana was entertained to see his face reflect, in exaggerated mime, her own reactions to Emily's story—consternation, guilt, surprise, and, finally, amusement. "Did you say aliens?" he inquired, grinning at Diana. "Green aliens with tentacles? Oh, I see. They were shooting their ray guns at the house. Yeah, Ma. Sure. Yes, they were here last night, but we fought 'em off with . . . No, Ma, I'm not making fun of you. I'm sorry about the bump on your bum."

He handed the phone to Diana. "Over to you, kid. Lots of luck."

However, his levity had had the desired effect; Emily required very little more reassurance. "Well, just be careful," she said seriously. "I'm sure that dream meant something. It may have been precognition instead of clairvoyance, so make sure you keep a close watch tonight and tomorrow . . . Oops, Charlie's at the door. I have to hang up. I don't want him to know I called, he was very rude about my dream."

Andy had gone to the stove and was ladling food onto a plate. "I thought you didn't have time to eat," Diana said.

"I didn't say I didn't have time to eat, I said I didn't have time to cook."

He did look nice, if not exactly pretty as a picture. The scratches on his face marred the image somewhat, but his hair lay in shining waves and he had brushed most of the cat hairs off his jacket.

After swathing his neatly knotted tie in a napkin, he put his plate and his elbows on the table and began to eat.

"It was odd, wasn't it," Diana said. "That she should dream about danger."

"Nah," Andy said calmly. "She's always having premonitions."

"But this one was accurate."

Andy put a chicken bone on the plate and wiped his fingers daintily. "It wasn't all that accurate. Larry's mind-set is certainly alien to me, but I don't think of him as having green skin and tentacles. She said you were pelting him—them—the aliens—with roses."

"The symbolism of that eludes me," Diana admitted.

"It's a symbol of how Ma thinks of you. Rather touching, really."

"She won't think of me that way when she learns the truth."

"She'll forgive you. Ma's hopelessly romantic and a sucker for a good sob story. Oh, hell, there I go again, putting my foot in my mouth."

"You have an unfortunate way of expressing yourself," Diana said.

"I've gotten into the habit of making fun of everything, including myself. Sometimes the only way of keeping your problems in perspective is to laugh at them."

"You should collect your clever sayings into a book. 'The Wit and Wisdom of Andrew Davis.' "

Andy winced. "Ouch. Look, Diana, I'm trying. You may have noticed I've abandoned my—let's call it genealogical research."

"I did notice."

"I still believe that it, and the experiences you've had, are somehow connected with our current difficulties. But finding Larry has become my top priority. He could have the answer to your brother's disappearance."

She hadn't expected him to give that reason. Before she could reply he went on, "That skeleton isn't Brad. No way. I'm convinced of that, but you'll never be completely convinced until you find out what did happen to him."

"Why are you so sure?"

"Among other reasons, because Larry wouldn't have buried him there. He—or whoever it was, got to give the bastard the benefit of a doubt—he'd have had to take up the floorboards before he dug the grave. Why go to all that trouble, with the old lady only a hundred yards away, when he could have carried the body into the woods?"

Diana had gone through that reasoning herself, but it was comforting to hear someone else voice the same conclusion. "Then who—"

"You know who. You saw the murder."

"I don't want to talk about it."

"Just as well," Andy said calmly, as footsteps were heard in the hall. "Here's Walt. Neat as a pin and clean as a whistle and ready for—"

"Ready for what?" Walt ran a self-conscious hand through his damp hair and scowled at Andy.

"I wouldn't risk it," Diana advised.

"I think you're right," Andy murmured. He glanced at the clock and gave a theatrical start. "Good gracious me, look at the time! I must fly. Can't keep a lady waiting."

Walt picked up a plate and went to the stove. "That mouth of Andy's is beginning to get to me," he said, without bothering to lower his voice.

"He doesn't mean to be annoying."

"Oh, yeah?" Walt came to the table and sat down. "Aren't you going to eat?"

"I'll wait for Mary Jo. She and I stuffed ourselves with banana splits a few hours ago. To celebrate her winning the scholarship."

Walt's stiff face relaxed. Diana realized it had been a long time since she had seen a genuine smile on his lips. "That was your idea, I guess. Mary Jo wouldn't have thought of it."

The smile was really devastating at close range. Diana's eyes fell. "Emily called a few minutes ago," she said.

That took care of the smile. "She hasn't found out—"

"No. It seems she had a bad dream."

She told him what Emily had said. The look of affectionate amusement that softened his features was almost as demoralizing as the smile, but at least it wasn't directed at her. "She's really something," he said fondly. "Aliens, yet. I'm surprised she didn't haul Charlie out of bed and make him drive her straight home."

"Charlie doesn't believe in premonitions."

"She doesn't either, it's just one of her little games. She's too sane to believe in that kind of crap."

Diana was glad she hadn't confided in Walt or allowed Andy to do so. Walt would order straitjackets for two if he found out. Yet his dogmatic rationalism annoyed her as much as Andy's only too willing suspension of disbelief.

The sky was a boiling caldron of black clouds, laced with light-ning. Thunder surrounded and assaulted her, but she was helpless to resist the unseen force that drew her forward, through weeds and brambles and over bare beaten earth, toward the structure that loomed ahead. The sallow light smeared the stones like lichen; the walls were intact, unmarked by fire or decay. The heavy wooden doors had been pushed back. The opening was a rectangle of blackness, yet she could see inside, for a cold green light from some unknown source filled the interior like water or gas. The stalls were empty, but traces of the former occupants haunted the air; it smelled of hay and manure and stale grain.

A long aisle, dusty and unmarked by prints of feet or hooves, stretched from the door to the far end, between the stalls. In the breathless hush between rolls of thunder she heard it—a series of sharp snapping cracks, the sound of wood splintering under pres-sure. Slowly at first, then in a rush, one of the heavy planks of the floor lifted.

It was a shadow at first, formless and dark as a fallen storm cloud. Drifting up from the opening in the floor, it hovered and spread and took shape. She saw the gleam of bare bone, ivory-pale before flesh and fabric clothed it in layers of gradual accretion. Pale flesh, soft with decay; tattered fabric that had once been a man's coarse work garments.

The face was the last to form. At first the features were unfa-miliar, the nose bold and prominent, the mouth half-veiled by something that looked like a mass of filthy cobwebs, the eyes . . .

She tried to cry out when she saw them, tried to turn and run away. The terrible face writhed, shifting like melted wax, and solidified again. It was familiar now. The eyes were the same, empty sockets under ridges of fleshless bone, but the other features were Brad's.

Choking and gasping, she fought her way out of sleep to wake-fulness. The cold sad light of predawn grayed the room. Her hair was sticky with sweat and she was clutching her pillow in a fierce grip.

It had been so bad that even the relief of waking wasn't enough. Throwing the pillow aside, she got out of bed and stumbled toward the door. She had no intention of waking anyone to plead for comfort like a child afraid of night monsters; she just wanted to see them, know they were there.

As she approached the head of the stairs, noiseless on bare feet, she heard voices in the hall below. They were muted, but in the silence of the house the words were clearly audible.

"I didn't ask you to wait up. Think you were my mother or something."

The blurred, belligerent voice was Andy's. Walt's reply was no less savage. "Being related to you is a punishment nobody deserves. I expected you back hours ago."

"You know what I was—"

"I finally figured it out. Hoped I had, anyhow. You've got shit for brains, Andy. What the hell did you—"

"Ssssh!" Andy's hiss was louder than any sound either had yet made. "You'll wake 'em up. I almost had her tonight, Walt. She's weakening— What was that?"

"That" was a gasp of outrage from Diana. She hadn't found the comfort she wanted, but Andy's performance had been almost as effective in weakening the impact of her dream. Staying out all night, coming home drunk, bragging about his conquests . . .

He hadn't drunk enough to affect his running ability. He must have caught a glimpse of her pale face looking down, for he took the steps three at a time and caught up with her in the doorway of her room. "What are you doing up at this hour?" he demanded.

The accusing tone was the last straw. Diana pulled her arm back and struck out blindly, not with her open palm but with her clenched fist. Andy clapped his hands to his face. His eyes filled with tears.

Tearing eyes are an involuntary reflex reaction to a sharp blow on the nose. Laughter is not. The muffled sounds from behind Andy's fingers were unmistakably those of amusement.

"Sorry," she said. It was an apology, not only for the punch in the nose but for her suspicions.

Andy took hold of the tip of his nose and wriggled it gingerly. "I don't think anything's broken. Can I come in? If you're planning to hit me again, I don't want to scream and wake Mary Jo."

She followed him to a chair and stood over him, hands on her hips. "Walt is right, you do have—"

"Ladies don't use that kind of language," Andy said. "Nor, as a matter of fact, do they punch people in the face. I'm willing to overlook that, however, since jealousy is an understandable, indeed flattering motive for—"

"Who is she? That girl who was with Larry at the Fox's Den?"

"I wasn't at the Fox's Den on the occasion to which you refer," Andy began. Seeing her expression, he added hastily, "It probably was the same. She's his current . . . the word she uses, poor stupid wench, is fiancée. Pronounced 'fi-ant-see.' "

Diana collapsed onto the edge of the bed, narrowly missing Miss Matilda, who let out a squeak of alarm. "He can't be coming to her. He's not stupid enough to risk being seen. And you," she added nastily, "wouldn't risk Larry catching you in bed with his current fi-ant-see."

"I'd be risking several equally unpleasant things if I did," Andy said. "There are limits even to my dedication to duty."

"I'm pleased to hear it. So you sat, or stood, outside her apartment all night."

"Sat. In my car."

"And she didn't stir."

"I don't know how much stirring she did, but she didn't leave the building. It's on a corner, and her back porch is at the side. I could see the back stairs and the front door from where I was parked."

"Which proves—"

"Nothing." Andy's face no longer showed signs of amusement. "She may not go to him every night. But she's been in touch with him, Diana, I'm sure of it. She practically licked her lips when I mentioned the reward, but she's terrified of him, and I couldn't convince her we'd keep her name out of it."

"He'd probably hold her accountable in any case, if she's the only one who knows where he is."

"I made that point too. She was definitely weakening. She agreed to see me again tomorrow night—"

"Tonight, you mean. The detective Father hired will be here in a few hours, Andy. Let him handle it. Please."

Andy considered the idea. "It's a thought. He might be a more persuasive advocate. Okay, I'll talk to him."

It was not the total capitulation she had hoped for, but it was more than she had expected. "Grab a few hours' sleep, why don't you? He won't be here till eleven."

"Okay." But he didn't move. "Do you want to tell me what woke you? It couldn't have been me, I hadn't been in the house ten seconds when I saw you at the top of the stairs."

The sun had risen; the room was no longer sickly with shadows. She was able to remember and to relate the dream with some degree of detachment, but Andy's expressive face reflected the effect of even the bald details.

"Nasty," he said, after she had finished. "They're getting progressively worse."

"They? How can there be any connection? At first it was so gentle, so innocent. Roses and music and laughter; I could have accepted that, a lingering impression of happy years in this house, of gentlemen and ladies, quiet dust . . . This was a nightmare, pure and simple. And only too easy to interpret."

Andy started to speak. He stopped; when he went on she knew it was not what he had started to say. "Can you sleep now?"

"I had plenty of sleep. I feel better, if that's what you mean." She smiled at him. "In your own weird way, Andy, you do have a certain cathartic effect."

Andy did not appear pleased by the compliment.

It was some consolation to find that Mary Jo, at least, had no idea what Andy had been up to. She'd hit the ceiling if she found out he had taken such a risk—and a certain element of risk had been present, despite Andy's airy disclaimers. Larry *was* stupid enough and perhaps desperate enough to venture into town.

Mary Jo's caustic comments to Andy when he finally made his appearance, yawning and rubbing his eyes, were more amused than censorious; she even whipped up a revolting hangover remedy and forced him to drink it. Knowing that lack of sleep, not alcohol, was responsible for his pallor and heavy eyes, Diana felt a certain sympathy for him—until, behind Mary Jo's back, he clapped one hand to his brow and the other to his chest in a pose meant to suggest a hero suffering in silence to preserve his lady's honor.

Diana was a little out of temper with Mary Jo, however. She had had to argue, yell and threaten in order to persuade the other woman to stay at home and not go to her job. None of those devices had worked, so she was forced to resort to the one she should have employed in the first place—an appeal for help.

"The decorator is supposed to come to hang the library drapes.

Somebody ought to supervise him, but the detective is coming at eleven, and Lord knows how long he'll stay."

Mary Jo looked mutinous. "Why can't he supervise?"

She gestured at Andy, who promptly let out a heartrending groan and collapsed face-down across the table. "Oh, all right," Mary Jo said with an unwilling grin. "I'm off-schedule with the cleaning anyhow. I'll start upstairs and do the library after the drapes are up."

Suiting the action to the words, she collected dust cloths and polish and marched out.

Andy sat up, brushing the hair out of his eyes. "So far so good. Do you think you can persuade your tame PI to refrain from mentioning my brilliant scheme in Mary Jo's presence? She'll have the hide off me if she . . . That sounds like a car. He's early."

Windows and doors were open; the early-morning chill had given way to a bright balmy spring day. Diana got up. "Almost forty-five minutes early. I'll go see if it's him."

Followed by Andy, Baby, and an assortment of cats, she went to the door. The dusty, battered Honda was unfamiliar, but it suited the image she had formed from films and detective stories. However, when the occupant got out and approached the house she felt a horrid qualm. He was too young to be an established professional. She was pretty sure she knew what he was; she had encountered the breed before.

So had Andy, to judge from the vehemence of his brief, profane comment. He reached for the screen door. Diana slapped his hand away.

"I'll handle this. Get out of sight."

"But—"

"You've got a big mouth and a quick temper and you're the son of the owners. Go away."

Muttering, Andy retreated. The young man had reached the door; he shifted, trying to catch a clearer view of Andy. Diana shifted position too.

"Can I help you?" she asked.

"Sure hope so, ma'am. Miss, I should say; you can't be Mrs. Nicholson."

He had a broad, brash smile and wavy blond hair and a soft accent that lengthened vowels and slurred final consonants. Diana did not return the smile.

"Mrs. Nicholson isn't here. Now if you'll excuse me—"

She started to close the door. Seeing he had lost the first round, the young man was forced to announce his identity. "Joe Blackstone, from the *News Post*. And you are—"

"A guest of the Nicholsons. I have nothing to say, Mr. Blackstone, so you may as well go away."

She hadn't expected it would be that easy, and it wasn't. He had heard about the bones from an informant in the police department; sensing a story, he had decided to pursue it. It might have been worse, Diana thought; he was from the local paper, not one of the wire services, and what he had learned from the police wasn't enough to rate extended coverage. She decided to change her strategy, and gave him a wide, sweet smile.

"Honestly, Mr. Blackstone, I don't know anything more about this than you do—if as much. The workmen found the remains in the course of some renovations that are being made, and of course they immediately notified the police. We haven't heard from them."

"The workmen," Blackstone repeated. "The guys working out in back? Do you mind if I talk to them?"

"I can't give you permission to do anything, Mr. Blackstone, I am not the owner of the property. And," she added pointedly, "I wouldn't advise you to approach the foreman of the crew right now. He's furious because he had to stop in the middle of the job, and he's a quick-tempered man."

It wouldn't have worked with a big-city reporter, but he was young and inexperienced. Diana half promised him an interview at some indeterminate future time, assuming the police investigation produced any real information, and finally he took his departure.

The annoyance was minor and one she had half expected, but she was getting to the point where even a minor annoyance was one too many. Leaning against the doorjamb, she watched the Honda disappear into the trees and tried to find a silver lining to this latest cloud. If Blackstone did decide to write the story, it wouldn't appear until the following day, and only in the local paper. It was too vague and incomplete to attract the interest of the wire services—yet. Assuming such a catastrophe did ensue . . . Well, they only had a few more days in any case. Emily and Charles would return on Monday. Some resolution of at least some part of the matter had to occur by then. It had to!

She was about to turn away when she saw another vehicle approaching. If it was the decorator, he was late; if it was the detective, he was fifteen minutes early. She didn't recognize the Mercedes—couldn't accept that recognition—until it turned to follow the curve of the driveway.

Andy's reflective voice, behind her, made her start. "You aren't surprised, are you? I thought he'd come himself."

"Why?"

"He wouldn't trust anyone else to do the job right."

"Do you always assume the worst about people?"

"It's safer. Take them to the kitchen. I'll go get Walt."

The other man was the first to get out of the car, his movements as quick and decisive as her father's were deliberate. As protective color went, his was excellent; he had the same weather-beaten face and thinning graying fair hair as many of the local men. Slouching, hands in his pockets, he stood looking interestedly at the house until her father joined him. They started up the steps side by side.

His name was Samuel Bellows. Diana shook his hand and turned her cheek for the expected kiss from her father, then led the way to the kitchen. Bellows accepted the coffee she offered him; her father refused. As she filled the cup she said, "I wasn't expecting to see you, Father. You must have left at the crack of dawn."

"I drove to Richmond last night."

Diana felt the color rise in her cheeks. Her father observed her flush—he missed very little. He made no comment, but the corners of his mouth quirked in a way that assured her he knew what she had suspected. "I got your message," he went on. "I have an appointment with Professor Handson in Charlottesville later this afternoon. I spoke with him only briefly, but he considers it unlikely the remains could be those of your brother. He hopes to have a definite answer by the time I arrive. I will call you as soon as I have spoken with him."

With almost surgical precision he was demolishing the wall of angry resentment she had raised against him. She didn't have to ask how he had bullied a busy professor into laying aside his other work. She knew the technique, if not the actual intermediary. It could be anyone from the governor of the state to a Supreme Court justice.

The back door opened and Andy entered, followed, not too closely, by Walt. Andy greeted her father like an old friend. "Good to see you again, Mr. Randall, sir. And this is Mr. Bellows? Nice meeting you. I'm Andrew Davis, Mrs. Nicholson's son. My mother and her husband are out of town right now. They don't know anything about this. I hope we can clear the matter up before they find out. My mother is not a young woman and she's led a very sheltered life. I'm sure you can understand why I want to spare her unnecessary anxiety."

Oh, well done, Diana thought, hugging herself in secret delight. Andy's suggestion of the kitchen had been a stroke of genius; her father's pursed lips and raised eyebrows had told her what he thought of that ambience. Now Andy had established his position as host and heir, and established a sentimental image of frail motherhood to support his bland assumption of authority. He had made it clear that the other men were guests and that they had damned well better behave like guests.

It was clear to a pro like her father. A glint of what might have been admiration shone in his eyes as he studied Andy's frank, smiling face. Seeking a more vulnerable assailant, he turned to Walt, eyebrows raised. "And this gentleman is—?"

Watch it, Andy, Diana thought. She felt like a spectator at a tennis match. Advantage Mr. Randall. Walt was clearly uncomfortable and sensitive to her father's patronizing manner.

Andy was quick to recover. He introduced Walt, waved him to a chair, and—a nice touch, Diana thought—served him coffee, talking all the while. "He's been like a son to dear old Ma. I don't know what she would have done without him. I don't know what *we* would have done without him. Especially Diana. Right, Di?"

"Absolutely," Diana said, hoping Walt wouldn't explode before she could change the subject. Her father was inspecting Walt as he would have inspected a horse he was thinking of buying. She went on, "More important, Mr. Slade is the man you need to consult, Mr. Bellows. He knows Larry's friends and habits and he's familiar with every foot of the terrain. I'm deeply grateful to him for consenting to share his expertise."

Bellows didn't conceal his relief at finally getting down to business. "Me too, Miss Randall. Your father's filled me in on what he knows of the case, so if it's okay with you, Mr. Slade, I'll ask questions about the things he didn't know. That way we can avoid unnecessary repetition."

Walt had relaxed. "Suits me."

Bellows was good at his job. His questions were brief and to the point. He took copious notes, especially of names. He was particularly interested in Larry's women friends. When Andy interrupted with an account of his "date," the detective's brows lowered and he shook his head. "You shouldn't've done that, Mr. Davis. Could have been dangerous, not to mention counterproductive."

Andy was unrepentant. "I softened her up for you, Mr. Bellows. She's ready to talk."

"I appreciate that," Bellows said, with the suspicion of a smile. "Leave it to me now, all right?"

It was almost an hour before Bellows declared himself satisfied. "I'll want to talk to you—all of you—again. And to the suspect's wife."

"Ex-wife," Andy said sharply.

"Right. How can I get in touch with her?"

"She's here," Diana said. "Shall I—"

"If you don't mind."

She had heard the decorator's van arrive, so she knew where to look for Mary Jo. The sound of hammering greeted her as she approached the library. The men were standing on ladders putting up the hardware and valances; opulent swaths of fabric draped the sofas. In the midst of it sat Mary Jo, hands folded in her lap, silent as a sphinx.

"He wants to talk to you," Diana said.

"I figured he would. Carry on, boys," she added, with a rather pathetic attempt at insouciance.

Diana felt she ought to be warned. "My father's here too," she said, as they walked toward the kitchen.

"I thought so. That Mercedes didn't look like a PI's car."

"Don't let him intimidate you."

"Me? Never."

But she looked smaller and shabbier than usual, her narrow shoulders squared under the faded plaid blouse, the hole in her sneaker exposing a pink toenail. Diana felt a wave of fierce protectiveness fill her. She wanted to put her arm around Mary Jo, introduce her as "my friend," force her father to show the same deference he would have demonstrated to a wealthy, well-dressed client. She knew better; all she could do was lead the way and sound as proud as she felt when she introduced Mary Jo.

The men all got to their feet, even Walt. In fact, he was the first to rise. When he pulled out a chair for her, Mary Jo stared at him as if he had sprouted a second head.

In fact, Mary Jo had little to add; as she pointed out, she had done her best to distance herself from her ex-husband and his friends. There was an aunt . . . Walt had already told him, Bellows said.

Finally he closed his battered notebook and replaced the rubber band that held it together. "Thanks very much, Ms.—Heiser? You took your maiden name back? Right. That should do it for now. I can reach you here, can I?"

"Yes," Diana said, before Mary Jo could answer. "We'll all be here. And you'll let us know as soon as you . . . If you . . ."

"As soon as, not if," the detective said coolly. "I don't make a habit of holding out false hopes, but this isn't one of your Sherlock Holmes—type mysteries. I don't think it will take long."

"Good, good," Andy said. "Glad to hear it. My dear old mother . . ." He caught Diana's eye. "Uh—that is—can I offer you gentlemen a spot of lunch?"

"Thanks all the same." Bellows rose. "I've taken enough of your time. That is, unless Mr. Randall . . ."

With a twist of his lip and a tilt of one eyebrow, Diana's father made it clear that sandwiches and coffee in the kitchen weren't his idea of a spot of lunch. "I must drive Mr. Bellows back to town. He left his car at the motel. I have to be in Charlottesville by four, but if you'd care to follow us, Diana, you and I could have lunch somewhere. There is a restaurant of sorts, I presume."

Andy's lips twitched. "Bettie's Café serves great fried catfish. The blue-plate special is only—"

"I'll show you to the door," Diana said quickly.

When they reached it, Bellows stopped. "You know how to reach me, Miss Randall. You will inform me immediately if you learn anything?"

"Of course. Let me give you the number here."

"Mr. Davis gave it to me. I'll be in touch, then." He added, "I'll wait in the car, Mr. Randall."

Her father still hadn't caught on, though Bellows obviously had. "If you want to freshen up before we go," he began, with a critical look at her jeans and mud-soiled sneakers.

"I'm not coming. There's no point, Father. You wouldn't care for Bettie's catfish, and . . . What is there to talk about? You seem to have the matter well in hand."

He didn't argue with her. If people chose to ignore his suggestions, that was their problem. "The worst is yet to come, you know. Once this man confesses—"

"Whatever happened to presumed innocent?" Diana interrupted. "He may not have done it."

"Well, we'll find out, won't we? If there is a confession and a trial, I won't be able to keep the matter quiet. I hope you're prepared for the inevitable publicity."

"I had a reporter here this morning."

"From the local paper?" He was terrifyingly quick-witted; all the implications were instantly clear to him. "They can't have made the connection between this missing lout and your brother; what was it, the skeletal remains?"

Diana nodded. "That has nothing to do with us," he went on. "I'll see to it that Professor Handson issues a statement first thing in the morning. That should take the spotlight off you. I want to see you away from here, back where you belong, before the real story breaks."

"I'm sure you do," Diana murmured.

"I beg your pardon?"

"Never mind. Good-bye, Father. Thank you for your help."

She was still standing at the door, staring at the empty driveway, when Mary Jo joined her. "I thought you were going with them."

"No. But I'm starved. How about you?"

"Andy's making sandwiches. First I thought I'd better see how that crew in the library is doing. Never thought it would take so long to hang a couple of curtains."

They inspected the work together, listened skeptically to the designer's assurance that another hour or so would finish the job, and started back to the kitchen. The silence was so awkward Diana knew she had to be the one to break it.

"Well, now you've met him in person. Was it better or worse than you expected?"

Mary Jo hesitated. "He's a very fine-looking—"

"Stop being polite or I'll shake you. In fact, he behaved better than I expected. That was Andy's doing; Father was briskly cutting me down to size when Andy turned the tables on him."

"I missed that. What did he do?"

"Ask Andy. He's probably still gloating."

Andy heard the last remark. "Damned right," he said, bringing a carving knife down on a sandwich with a solid thwack. "Ham or chicken, Diana?"

Gathered around the table, the three of them joined in a satisfying critique of the interview. Walt had already joined the crew, taking his sandwich with him. "It was the way he looked at Walt that made me mad," Mary Jo admitted. "Like he was a laboratory specimen with a particularly low IQ."

"Probably sizing him up as a prospective son-in-law," Andy said wickedly. "If you're looking for a way of getting back at the old goat, Di, you couldn't do better than marry into the lower classes."

"You're an evil-minded snob, Andy," Diana said.

"I wasn't insulting Walt, I was insulting your father. He's an efficient bastard, though, isn't he? Bellows impressed me. And did I hear something about getting a report on those bones?"

"You couldn't have heard that unless you were eavesdropping," Diana said accusingly.

"I was. I have to, nobody ever tells me anything."

"Then you heard him say the preliminary report indicates they have nothing to do with us."

"No, I didn't hear that part," Andy said calmly.

"So sorry. I'll be sure and report immediately from now on."

Sarcasm was wasted on Andy. "Thanks, I'd appreciate that."

The call came through later that afternoon. Diana was in the library waiting for it.

Professor Handson was certain. The remains found in the barn could not have been Brad's. His report would go to the police the following day.

CHAPTER SIXTEEN

*Here grow fine flowers many and amongst those
The fair white lily and sweet fragrant rose.*

—Governor William Bradford, *History of
Plymouth Plantation*

Reactions to the news varied. Mary Jo was pleased for Diana but
otherwise uninterested; Walt said that was what he had expected,
and now maybe he could get clearance to resume work.

Andy was outraged. "Is that all he said, that it wasn't Brad?
How does he know? Why didn't you let me talk to him? Why
didn't you ask him—"

Walt interrupted the tirade. "Christ Almighty, Andy, you're as
curious as a cat. What difference does it make who it is, so long
as it isn't her brother?"

Andy had concocted the promised gourmet spaghetti dinner.
Quantity as well as quality marked his talents as a chef; they
continued to sit at the kitchen table, too stuffed to move. It was
not only too much food and too little sleep that had produced a
shared mood of relaxation. Diana knew they all felt as she did—
that the news was a good omen and a portent of even better news
to come.

Walt's increased optimism expressed itself in plans for future
activity. "That's one thing off our minds, anyhow. The fuzz probably won't let me go ahead with the barn for a few more days,
but that perennial order Emily and I placed is ready; if I pick it
up tomorrow or the next day, I can get most of the plants in the
ground before she gets back. Have to be day after tomorrow, I
guess; Tom Wilson will be here tomorrow to install the plumbing
for the lily pond."

Mary Jo was only pretending to listen and Andy had relapsed into frowning introspection. Diana felt that Walt's dedication to duty deserved more commendation. "I don't know how you got so much done with all these distractions," she said. "Maybe I could pick up the order for you."

"Can you drive a truck?"

"Certainly," said Diana, with more confidence than she felt.

Walt grinned. "I shouldn't have asked. It's a big order, lots of trees and shrubs. I guess the guys at the nursery would load it for you . . . Yeah, that would be a big help. The nursery is near Gordonsville. It's almost eighty miles from here, so by the time you get there and load up and then drive back, it'll be an all-day job."

"No problem. I've nothing else to do. You want to come along, Mary Jo?"

"I'm going to work tomorrow." Her voice held a rocklike finality that forbade argument, but she added, with a reassuring glance at Diana, "It's the bakery. He won't dare come there."

Andy, who had been feeding strands of spaghetti to a cat with unusual food preferences, looked up. "I'll go with you, Diana."

"Only if she drives," Walt said firmly.

"But she doesn't know how—"

"She knows how to drive without scattering a load along the highway. They'll tie the plants down and cover them, but the damned things are fragile. I don't want them banging around the truck bed or getting branches snapped off."

His tone was as final as Mary Jo's. Andy shrugged. "Whatever you say, boss."

He came to her room late that night, after the others were asleep, heralding his presence by a soft knock but not waiting for a response.

Diana looked up from her book. "Now what, Andy?"

"Can't you sleep?" He started to sit down on the edge of the bed. It was lined with a multicolored row of cats, from calico to white, all of whom stared stonily at him. Andy pulled up a chair. "Or are you afraid to?"

"I was thinking of taking a sleeping pill," Diana admitted.

"Better not. Want me to stay?"

The suggestion had an unexpected appeal, like the sight of food to a man who had not realized he was hungry. She tried to speak coolly. "What did you have in mind?"

"I'd be helpless to resist if you forced yourself upon me," Andy said. "But that wasn't what I had in mind. It's a big bed. Or I can sit here, like Sir Galahad guarding the Holy Grail."

"Don't be a fool. You need your sleep."

"Be still, my heart!" Andy bounded to his feet. "You mean you want me—"

"I mean I want you to go to bed. Your bed. I'll be all right."

"It was worth a try," Andy said. "If you change your mind, let me know. I'll be around."

Several cats followed him out, including the spaghetti eater. He left the door slightly ajar.

Diana turned out the light. She was exhausted; as sleep weighed her eyelids she remembered Andy's promise. Around where? she wondered. Guarding her door like a faithful dog? A sleepy smile curved her lips as she pictured Andy and Baby side by side across the threshold, but her last conscious thought was a faint regret that she hadn't taken him up on his offer. Any of his offers.

Andy was the last one to come down next morning. Mary Jo looked him over, from faded T-shirt to mud-stained jeans, and remarked, "The washing machine works fine, Andy. I hope you aren't waiting for me or Diana to do a wash for you."

"He's going to be loading plants, not having tea at Buckingham Palace," Walt said. "Here's the list, Diana. Make sure you check it as they load. The viburnum hasn't arrived yet, but all the rest—"

"You've been over that already," Mary Jo interrupted. "Hurry up, Andy. I don't want to be late."

She had agreed to let them drop her off at the bakery on their way, but she disliked having to make that concession and she continued to nag Andy until he fled from the room, leaving half his breakfast uneaten. Walt insisted on giving Diana a lecture on the handling of the truck and sat beside her, poised like a driving instructor on the first outing with a nervous client, while she backed and turned the heavy vehicle and drove to the front of the house. It had been some time since she had dealt with a stick shift, but the truck was one of the newer models, with power steering, and the expectant grins of the other men, who stood watching, inspired her to perform well.

"I hope you're satisfied," she said, bringing the truck to a smooth stop. "I told you I could—"

"What's that?" Walt was staring out the window at some object on the topmost step.

It certainly had not been there the night before when she locked up. She couldn't have missed seeing the mass of crumpled brown paper, weighted down by a heavy rock. Walt reached it before she did, since she had to lower herself from the high seat.

Kicking the rock aside, he inspected the paper closely before picking it up. Diana saw it was a standard-sized grocery bag. The top had been tightly twisted and tied with string.

"Feels empty," Walt said. He shook the bag. A rattle from within proved him wrong. He took out a pocketknife and cut the string.

"I wouldn't reach inside if I were you," Diana said uneasily.

"I'm not going to." Walt upended the bag.

The object hit the stone step with a depressing crunch just as the door opened.

"What on earth," Mary Jo began. Behind her, Andy wrestled with Baby, who was trying to get out the door.

"Shit," Walt muttered. "I thought it might be . . . Anybody lost a watch lately?"

Andy shoved the dog and Mary Jo out of his way. "If I owned a watch that expensive I'd never take it off. That's a Rolex. Or was, before Walt demolished it."

He stooped to pick the watch up. Diana's hand intercepted his.

"It's Brad's," she said. "See, it has his name engraved on the back. Father gave it to him the time he won first prize in an essay contest. He was fourteen."

Bellows was waiting for them in the coffee shop at the motel. Diana's telephone call had wakened him, but he brushed her apologies aside. "I intended to call you this morning anyway. Shall I come there, or will you come here?"

Mary Jo had insisted on being dropped off at work. There was no point in her talking to Bellows—she knew no more than they did—and with this latest evidence of Larry's proximity she was obviously safer away from the house.

After inspecting the watch and the paper bag carefully, Bellows said, "Interesting development. This is the first solid evidence of a connection between the fugitive and your brother."

"That's what bothers me," Andy said. "If this was meant as a reminder to Mary Jo that he's out there watching for her, why didn't he leave something uglier and more threatening? The watch is practically tantamount to a confession."

"He's not too bright," Bellows said thoughtfully. He turned the empty bag over in his hands. "No message, no writing. No way of tracing the bag, it's a common type."

"How about fingerprints on the rock that weighed the bag?"

Bellows glanced at the plastic bag in which Andy had carefully encased the rock. "Too rough." He added with a kindly smile, "It was a good thought, though."

Andy resented the kindly smile. "What luck have you had?"

"That's what I was going to call you about," Bellows said calmly. He beckoned the waitress and indicated his empty cup. "Sure I can't offer you some breakfast? Toast, coffee—"

"We've got to be on our way," Diana said, before Andy could accept. "What did you want to tell me?"

"I had a talk with the girlfriend last night. You were right, Mr. Davis; she has been in touch with him."

"Ha!" Andy crowed.

"She was supposed to rendezvous with him a few days ago, but she didn't go. It was raining, she said. That wasn't the real reason, of course. The weather since has been fine. She's afraid to go and afraid not to go."

"She wouldn't tell you where?" Andy asked.

"Oh, she told me. That's where I was most of the night—near the ruins of a burned-down barn about three miles west of here. You people seem to have bad luck with barns."

"That was the local firebug," Diana explained. "He was the son of—"

"Who gives a damn about the local firebug?" Andy demanded. "Well? What happened?"

"Nothing. He didn't show up. Now we know why. He was at your place. Didn't you hear anything suspicious last night? Not even the dogs barking?"

"They bark at beetles, bats, and the full moon," Andy said morosely. "They bark so much I don't even hear it anymore. Damn! If that stupid wench had told me that when I talked to her, we might have got him. He's probably given up on her now."

"Exactly." Bellows's smile faded. He leaned forward and prodded Andy on the chest with a rigid finger. "Listen good, Mr. Davis. He'll be running out of supplies pretty soon, if he hasn't already. He'll have to come out of hiding. Up till this morning I figured he'd do one of two things—try to steal a car and some cash, or come calling on his ladyfriend. That seemed the most likely. He could get what he needed from her, plus the fun of knocking her around because she had failed him. Now—"

"But that's still a strong possibility," Diana exclaimed. "You've got to do something to protect her."

"She and her place will be under surveillance starting tonight, Ms. Randall. I requested additional men this morning. As I was about to say, the new evidence you brought me strongly suggests that he's shifted his territory. I want you—all of you—to get the hell out of that house."

Andy's lips tightened. "I'm not going to leave the house to him. Jesus Christ, Bellows, he could set fire to the place, kill the animals, God knows what."

"That's your choice," Bellows said. "But her father has made me responsible for Ms. Randall's safety. You can't patrol the whole perimeter, Mr. Davis. You say this creep is a crack shot. One bullet is all—"

"Okay, okay! You've made your point. I'm still not leaving, but Diana and Mary Jo—"

"No," Diana said. "Let's go, Andy. We're late already."

"But you—"

"No."

"Fight it out between yourselves," Bellows said. He was smiling again; Andy seemed to provide him with an endless source of quiet amusement. "I can't force you, Ms. Randall, I can only warn you."

"Which you have done." Diana reached for her purse. "Thank you, Mr. Bellows. I'll tell Father you did your best."

Andy lingered for a few words with Bellows. He caught up with her as she was starting to hoist herself onto the seat. Feeling at a disadvantage in that undignified position, she lowered her foot to the ground and turned to face him.

"I'm not going to argue with you, Andy. If you plan to hassle me for the next two hours, I'll leave you here."

"I wasn't going to argue. How about letting me drive?"

"Oh, all right. Just keep your eyes on the road and your mouth shut."

It was impossible for Andy to keep quiet, but he made no further attempt to persuade her to leave the house or induce Mary Jo to do so. His only reference to the subject was a remark to the effect that he considered Bellows's fears exaggerated. "Larry won't venture near the house in daylight, there are too many people around. If we stay inside after dark and avoid lighted windows, there's no real danger."

"I don't want to discuss it."

"Okay. We'll talk about flowers. That's a nice harmless subject. What's on that list Walt gave you?"

Some of the names were unfamiliar to her, but not to Andy. He seemed to know a little bit about practically everything. "*Nepeta mussini?* That's catmint. Trust Ma not to forget the pussycats . . . *Rudbeckia* is plain old black-eyed Susan, didn't you know that? I wonder where she's going to put that; it's a vulgar sort of flower, not suited to a formal garden. And what the hell is she doing buying *Cornus florida?* That's dogwood. The woods are full of them."

Diana refrained from commenting on his driving, though he was clearly intent on making up the time they had lost. But when they whizzed past a particular sign, she protested. "We should have turned off there, Andy. It said—"

"Didn't I tell you? I must have forgotten to mention it."

"No, you didn't forget. Where are we going?"

"Guess," Andy said coyly.

"I don't have to guess. We're heading for Charlottesville. Do we have an appointment, or do we just barge in?"

"I called him this morning. He said he'd expect us at . . . hmm. We're running late." His foot pressed heavily on the gas. The truck picked up speed, creaking and squeaking in protest.

Thomas Jefferson would not have recognized his home town; it was a small city now, with all the unattracative appurtenances of modern life—shopping malls, sprawling suburbs, and highways lined with fast-food restaurants. He would probably have found it fascinating, though, Diana thought. He had that kind of mind. However, she doubted he would have approved of the additions to the university, whose graceful classic center he had himself designed. The new buildings were functional but hardly decorative.

Andy parked illegally, ignoring Diana's objections. "You can't ever find a legal parking place around here," he explained airily. "So we get a ticket. Your old man can fix it."

Handson, a big, balding man with the build of a wrestler and a pair of keen dark eyes, was in his office. He waved Diana's breathless apologies graciously away. "Mr. Davis here explained the situation, Ms. Randall. I understand how you must feel, but I assure you you need have no doubts whatever. The remains can't possibly be those of your brother."

Andy had inspected the office as if hoping to see the remains laid out and waiting. Visibly disappointed, he turned back to Handson.

"How do you know? They're male, aren't they?"

"How do you know?" Handson countered, his eyes narrowing.

"I measured the long bones. They were the same length as mine, allowing for shrinkage. So the body was too tall to be that of a woman, if the proportions—"

"A big 'if,' " Handson said, smiling. "You've been reading too many of a particular kind of mystery story, Mr. Davis. It isn't that simple."

"I took a couple of anthro courses. I know it's not that simple."

"Well, your guess—excuse me—was correct. There are a number of indicators in addition to relative height, and all confirm the assumption. The subject was almost certainly a male Caucasoid, more than eighteen and less than twenty-six years old. However— and this is what concerns Ms. Randall—he did not die as recently as last year." He gave Diana a reassuring smile. "We're always hedging our statements with words like 'probably' and 'almost,' but I can safely omit the qualifiers when I tell you that. The poor chap has been dead not for months but for decades—perhaps centuries."

"Which?" Andy demanded.

Handson leaned back in his chair. "Where did you take those anthro courses?"

"Uh—sorry. I know you can't be precise, but I thought—"

"I've got a committee meeting in ten minutes," Handson said, glancing at his watch. "So this will be a brief lecture. The deterioration of skeletal material is affected by a number of conditions, some of which are unknown to me—the type of soil, the depth of the burial, the kind of wrapping or coffin employed, to mention only a few. However, I can say without equivocation that it would require at least seven to eight years to produce the condition I found. The staining of the bones suggests a much longer period. A century, give or take fifty years—that's my best estimate at the present time, and unless the police request additional tests, I don't intend to go any farther. I've relieved—I hope—Mr. and Ms. Randall's doubts, and that was my chief concern."

His tone was one of dismissal. Diana was perfectly willing to accept that; Andy was not, but she managed to get him out of the office and down the first flight of stairs before he broke free with a murmured "Forgot something. Go on, I'll catch up."

He did not do so until she had reached the truck. A ticket flapped breezily against the windshield. Andy plucked it from under the wiper and stuffed it in his pocket. "Cagey son of a bitch," he said irritably. "Fifty to a hundred and fifty years, and he won't even commit himself to that."

Diana allowed him to boost her into the passenger seat. "Where did you take those anthro courses?" she asked pointedly.

Andy's flexible features reshaped themselves into a modest smile. "Duke. I did good, too, if you can believe that."

She did believe it. Andy wasn't stupid. He seemed to have a problem, though; at his age he ought to have settled down to a career or a profession instead of flitting gaily from job to job.

In some disgust she realized she was thinking in the stereotypical terms her father might have used. But Andy's problem wasn't like Brad's. Brad had not been encouraged or even allowed to pursue the career he had chosen. He might have failed, but surely it was better to have tried and failed than never to have tried at all.

It took several hours to inspect and load the plants. After seeing the forest of waving boughs that filled the bed of the truck, even Andy realized the necessity of careful driving. One of the trees was a *Franklinia altamaha* almost twenty feet in height; though it lay propped and braced at an oblique angle, its branches obscured the back window. Andy's conversation during the return trip consisted primarily of profane replies to other drivers who expressed their resentment of his deliberate pace.

Walt came running to meet them when they pulled up in the driveway. "You should have been back two hours ago. What took you so long?"

He hurried to the back of the truck and began untying the ropes that held nets and tarps in place.

Andy jumped down and joined Walt. "Every time I pushed that

heap over forty-five it shook like a belly dancer. If it was as hard on the plants as it was on my butt—"

"I figured you'd con Diana into letting you drive," Walt said in a resigned voice. "Well, it could be worse. No major damage that I can see. Go pick up Mary Jo, will you? It's about that time."

"But—"

"Jesus H. Christ, can't you do anything without arguing about it?" Walt tossed him a set of keys. "Take my car. I was about to go myself. You know her, she won't wait."

Muttering under his breath, Andy obeyed. Walt turned to Diana. "How'd it go?"

"No problem." They watched Walt's car glide slowly away. Andy was doing approximately fifteen miles per hour. "She'll have to wait, won't she?" Diana asked. "How else could she get here?"

"Hitch a ride, borrow a bike—walk, even. She's stubborn as a mule. He's got plenty of time, though." A smile fought the rigid lines of Walt's mouth. "Once he's out of sight he'll floor it."

"Any news?"

"I've been outside all day. But I assume they'd send somebody to tell us the good news if they couldn't reach us by phone."

"I expect you're right. But I'll check the messages."

Walt followed her into the house, but not into the kitchen. She heard him moving around upstairs. He was taking no chances, not even minuscule ones. Remembering what Bellows had said that morning, Diana had no objections.

For once the answering machine was almost quiescent. A friend of Andy's had called, reiterating more emphatically the need for him to report to his boss; there was nothing from the police, or from Bellows.

Walt refused the cold drink she offered. "I want to unload, maybe get some of the plants into the ground. There are a couple of hours of daylight left."

"Can I help?"

He inspected her from head to foot and back again. It was an annoyingly impersonal survey; Diana felt as if she ought to flex her muscles and show him her teeth. "Sure, if you want," he said. "I'll bring the truck out back."

Gaping holes of varying sizes now marked the surface of the upper terrace. One, almost as deep as she was tall, was intended for the *Franklinia*. Diana knew better than to offer to help with that. Perched on the wall, feet dangling, she watched the crew wrestle the tree off the truck. It had been carefully propped so that it would not rest directly on the other plants around it, so it had to be lifted, not dragged across the rest of the load. Thrusting an impatient hand under one of the branches, Walt withdrew the hand even more quickly and inspected a bloody scratch. "What the hell—"

"Looks like some kind of a cactus," said Jack, peering under the branch.

"That's Andy's," Diana explained. "You know how he is about—"

Walt's response was brief and profane. However, when Andy appeared, offering his services, Walt accepted them without mentioning the cactus. "Mary Jo's coming to help too," Andy said. "Soon as she changes."

Walt nodded. Diana knew her help and Mary Jo's would be negligible and unnecessary. But it was better for them to keep busy instead of sitting around waiting for the phone to ring. Gardening offered a unique kind of therapy—plunging your hands into the cool gritty substance of the earth itself, knowing you were helping to create a living thing that might survive you and your children's children.

Gardening was also hard work. Walt made no condescending concessions, demanding of them the same perfection he expected of his men. "The hole's too shallow. You need another six, eight inches of topsoil under the root ball."

The sun had dropped below the trees before he called a halt. The men scattered thankfully to their trucks and cars, and Walt surveyed the remaining plant material, prodding at the burlap-wrapped roots to make sure Mary Jo had soaked them thoroughly. "That's everything except the perennials around the pond—if Tom finishes laying the pipes we can get them in tomorrow—and the shrubs. Azaleas, kolwitzia . . . What's this?"

"Roses." Leaning on her shovel, Diana rubbed her aching back.

"I know they're roses," Walt grumbled. "They weren't on the list."

"They're a present," Diana said. "To Emily, from me and Andy. It was his idea," she added defensively, as Walt turned to stare at her.

"What am I going to do with them?" he demanded. "The rose

garden won't be ready until fall. That's when you're supposed to plant the damned things, isn't it?"

"A lot of people prefer to plant in the spring. These aren't bare-rooted, they're in pots. And they aren't damned things. They're those new English roses, the ones developed by David Austin, that combine old-rose forms and scent with the everblooming qualities of modern roses."

"Oh, yeah, I read about them." Walt regarded the stumpy branches with more interest. "I didn't know Wolverhampton carried them."

"He just started this year. Emily will be thrilled to find that there's a source so close; she and I were talking about them the other night. I'm afraid we got a little carried away," Diana admitted. "They have such beautiful names—Admired Miranda, Fair Bianca, Cressida, Mary Rose, Proud Titania . . ."

"So you got one of each." Walt's face had softened into the look he usually reserved for Emily. "It was a nice thought. But I still don't know where I'm supposed to put them."

Andy cleared his throat. "At the bottom of the steps. Below the terrace wall."

Over supper they discussed the latest developments, such as they were. Mary Jo had heard from Andy about their talk with Bellows, but Walt had not; he insisted on having the conversation repeated word for word. "It doesn't make sense," he declared. "Is that the only explanation he could come up with—that Larry's not too bright? I don't buy it. Why would Larry take the risk of coming here to leave something that connects him to a crime nobody's even accused him of committing? And how did he get by the dogs?"

"Forget the dogs; they aren't even here most of the time," Andy answered. "He may have waited till they took off, or offered them food to distract them. As for the other question, I have a couple of theories."

Walt leaned back and folded his arms. "Some farfetched piece of psychological crap, I suppose. Guilt is preying on the poor guy's mind? Unconsciously he yearns to confess and be at peace with himself?"

Andy flushed angrily. "He may be a lout, but he's a human being, with the rudiments at least of human feelings. I'm not trying to defend the bastard, I'm trying to understand him, and I'm convinced that if he did kill Brad, it was in the heat of anger, when he was drunk. It could even have been an accident, during a fight. Sure, he feels guilt. Some part of him, part of the time."

"He's good at guilt." Mary Jo's voice was cold as ice and flat as a tabletop. "After he beat me up he'd cry and tell me how sorry he was."

Walt's fingers dug white-rimmed pits in the flesh of his arms. "If you'd told me—"

"You'd have beat *him* up? Helluva lot of help that would have been." Her voice was gentler, however. "Nobody can help a woman who's being battered until she decides she deserves help. That's the trap people lock you into—that feeling that you deserve what he's doing to you, that in some crazy way it's your fault. Don't tell me about guilt, I'm an expert."

No one spoke, but Mary Jo must have felt their silent sympathy and outrage; it was as palpable as a hot wind. She drew a long breath. "Don't know what came over me. What I started to say was that Andy could be right. Seems to me, though, that Larry's more likely scared than sorry. It could be that leaving the watch is his way of proposing a deal."

"That was my other theory," Andy said. "By this time he could have learned who Diana is. He has Brad's death on his conscience—oh, all right, damn it, so he doesn't have a conscience—on his mind—and here's Brad's sister, hot on the trail. He's not so dumb that he hasn't heard of copping a plea."

"Now that's starting to make sense," Walt said intently. "There's another thing. Is it only a coincidence that he delivered the watch last night, after we'd had a visit from Brad's father?"

"Jeez, I hope so," Andy said fervently. "He couldn't know about that unless he was watching us—from someplace too close for comfort. No, I don't buy that, Walt. How would he recognize Mr. Randall?"

Walt was too enamored of his theory to abandon it. He proposed several explanations, all plausible and all unprovable. They continued to discuss the matter without arriving at any conclusions, except the one Andy grimly reiterated—that it might be a good idea to stay away from lighted windows.

No one proposed a certain third theory. Diana felt sure it must have occurred to at least one of them; Andy's imagination was too fertile to have overlooked it. She knew why he had not said anything. She tried not even to think it. Uncertainty was not the worst thing after all. Hopes that were raised and then shattered were the worst—even a hope as forlorn and unlikely as the one that had crept into her mind. Brad couldn't be alive, held prisoner under some imaginable set of circumstances, for so many months. But there was the watch, unmarred by earth; there was the tacit suggestion of an exchange . . .

Of information. It couldn't be anything else.

They were all restless that evening, for readily comprehensive reasons. Walt brooded over his plans and lists, Mary Jo stared at a book without turning the pages, and Diana couldn't keep her eyes from the telephone. Andy . . . Where was Andy? He had offered to clean up the kitchen, but he was taking an awfully long time about it. She was about to go in search of him when she heard a clatter and a yelp from the hall.

They found Andy sprawled on the stairs, trying to untangle himself from the ladder that had trapped one of his legs between its rungs. "Damn," he said calmly. "I thought I could get upstairs without you hearing me."

Mary Jo knelt and yanked his ankle free with a vigor that brought another yelp from the victim. "You've been outside."

"Only to the shed. There wasn't—"

"You made us promise we wouldn't leave the house." Her face was crimson with fury. "If you do that again, I'll kill you. Where were you taking that thing?"

"Upstairs."

Diana sat down on the bottom step. "Don't waste your time asking questions, Mary Jo. I think I know what he has in mind. Andy, how on earth did you suppose you could climb down into that hidden stairwell and root around in the debris without us hearing you?"

Andy got to his feet and reached for the ladder. "By then," he said, "it would have been a fait accompli. Oops—sorry—watch out—"

Walt caught the end of the ladder before it hit his head. "It's not long enough."

"I think it is. Worth a try."

In the end they accompanied him. It was, as Walt glumly admitted, something to do. Anyhow, he added, the prospect of having to extract Andy's broken body from the bottom of the stairwell didn't really appeal to him.

The ladder wasn't long enough. However, the topmost rung was less than five feet below the threshold of the door. With Walt's profane assistance, Andy lowered himself until his feet touched the ladder.

Diana knelt by the opening and directed her torch downward. The beam cast hideous shadows across Andy's features. He blinked and ducked his head. "Don't shine it right in my eyes."

"Don't look at it," Diana retorted. "You're supposed to be looking at where you're going, not where you've been."

"Especially when you're standing on a ladder," Walt added. He knelt beside Diana, his shoulder hard against hers, his hands grasping the rope he had insisted Andy fasten around his waist. Diana suspected Walt was beginning to enjoy himself. Perhaps he was hoping he'd get the chance to drag Andy back to safety, inflicting painful but not incapacitating injuries in the process.

Mary Jo stood some feet away, her arms folded and her face a mask of disapproval. "If Walt does have to yank on that rope, he's apt to knock you over the edge, Diana," she remarked. "There's not room in that doorway for two people. If you're determined to see what's going on, lie flat so you won't be in his way."

It was sensible advice, and Diana followed it. Andy started to descend, sneezing and brushing away cobwebs with his flashlight. If there had been paneling on the walls, all traces of it were gone. The plaster might once have been painted; it was hard to tell, for it crumbled at the slightest touch. About halfway down Andy stopped.

"A little more slack on that rope, Walt. It's cutting me in two."

"Sorry," said Walt. He gave Diana a sideways grin.

"What are you doing?" she demanded. Andy's light was focused on the wall.

"Thought I'd found something. It's just a crack, though."

"You aren't going to find hidden cupboards in a stairwell wall."

"How do you know?" He continued his downward progress.

Before long they could see what lay at the bottom of the stairs—or rather, what had once been the stairs. Their splintered remains filled the lower part of the stairwell. Andy had forced the ladder through the scraps so that it presumably rested on solid flooring, but this could not be seen; the uneven surface bristled with jagged ends of wood.

Andy stopped, turned, and leaned forward at a precarious angle. "Watch it," Walt called, as the ladder swayed.

Andy grunted. His body and the shadow it cast obscured the view of the watchers; he seemed to be burrowing in the debris, throwing scraps to one side.

"He's going to pull the ladder away from the wall and fall face-down into a pile of splinters and rusty nails if he isn't careful," Diana said anxiously. "Andy, come up out of there."

"Throw down that paper bag," Andy called.

The bag fluttered down like a giant moth. Andy caught it and bent forward again. They heard the rustle of paper and a series of soft thuds and tinkles. Finally he straightened and started up. When he reached the top of the ladder he handed the bag to Diana, with a brief "Get out of the way."

Walt also moved back, keeping a firm grip on the rope. Andy caught the sill and pulled himself up. He took the bag from Diana. "No fair looking."

She had been holding it in her fingertips. Though it was wreathed with cobwebs and the mummified bodies of long-dead insects, it was not as disgusting a sight as Andy himself. She had seen mummies in museum cases that looked better.

The coating of dust-blackened plaster covering his face cracked into a smile of triumph. "Got it. Come over here to the table and I'll show you."

"I'm not coming any closer till you wash," Mary Jo said. "A person could catch half a dozen diseases being in the same room with you."

"She has a point, Andy," Diana said. "I hate to think of the garbage you've been breathing into your lungs."

Andy sneezed violently, started to wipe his face on his sleeve, looked closely at the fabric, and changed his mind. "Oh, all right. Promise you won't peek." He made certain they wouldn't by taking the bag with him. A cloud of dust accompanied him.

• • •

Mary Jo insisted on inspecting Andy before she let him come into the library, but refused his offer to let her look behind his ears. "What did you do with your clothes?" she asked suspiciously, as he brushed his damp hair back into place.

"Threw 'em in the wastebasket. Does that meet with your approval?"

"Only place for them. No, don't you dare dump that mess onto the couch. I spread newspapers on the table."

She had also brought dust cloths from the kitchen. Her foresight was justified when Andy spilled the contents of the bag onto the newspapers. They were so coated with filth that at first Diana couldn't make out what they were.

Andy's long lean fingers deftly fitted several of the scraps together. "It's a box, see? I caught a glimpse of it, a few steps down from the top, before the stairs collapsed. I couldn't find all the pieces, though."

"Here's another one." Mary Jo offered the section she had been rubbing. "Part of the lid, is it?"

"Yep. There's a hinge on one side." Andy tried unsuccessfully to match the scrap with another. "Damn. I can't tell how big it was, there's too much missing. Nice piece of work, though. Plain but well-made."

Mary Jo began dusting another scrap. "What's this? It's wood, but it doesn't look like part of the box."

"I don't know what it is," Andy admitted. "I just scooped up everything that looked different from the pieces of the stairs."

"Here's another one the same shape." When Mary Jo lifted it, something else came with it—a piece of cloth several inches long, attached to the wood. "There's a seam," Mary Jo said, inspecting the filthy cloth curiously. "I can see stitches. It's a hollow cylinder, almost like . . ."

"A sleeve," Diana exclaimed. "No, not a sleeve—the upper part of an arm. And this is the lower arm, this piece of wood—you can see where the fingers broke off. It's the arm of a doll! And here—this is the head."

The pieces were easily identified now that they had the clue. Traces of paint still remained on the round wooden ball—the faded red of a pouting mouth, a black circle of pupil. A wad of mildewed cloth proved to be a bonnet, trimmed with rotting age-browned lace. Another scrap might have been part of the body, but the rest, including possible legs and feet, was missing.

"I had one like this once," Walt said, examining a broken scrap of shell. "A big conch shell. My Uncle Tom gave it to me when I was five. Kept it for years."

"This looks like part of a fan," Mary Jo murmured. The carved, flat stick she held was ivory or bone; fringes of cloth, the remains of the silk body of the fan, still clung to it.

None of the other twisted lumps was identifiable. There were several pieces of metal, crushed and brown with rust, and bits of fabric that might have been the doll's dress. Studying the pathetic collection, Diana said gently, "It was a child's—a girl's—treasure box. How thrilled she must have been to find such a lovely secret hiding place for her toys."

Walt glanced at Andy's disappointed face and burst out laughing.

CHAPTER SEVENTEEN

Conserve of Red Roses:
The colour both of the Rose-leaves and the Syrup about
them will be exceedingly beautiful and red and the taste ex-
cellent, and the whole very tender and soothing and easie to
digest in the stomack without clogging it . . .

—SIR KENELM DIGBY'S *Closet* (1669)

*W*alt's gibes about diamond tiaras and skeletons in the closet were not well received, but Andy managed to hold on to his temper until Mary Jo finally came to his defense. Her tone implied that picking on Andy was her prerogative.

"Lay off him, Walt. I was against him going down there, but only because he was taking foolish chances. I swear, you haven't got any more imagination than a toad."

Her intervention didn't please either of the men. Walt's face reddened and Andy scowled at his champion. Diana decided to try her hand at peacemaking. "I wonder if that debris oughtn't to be cleaned out. It could be a source of infection—did they use asbestos back then?—as well as a breeding ground for snakes and insects."

The angry color faded from Walt's lean cheeks. "That would probably be a good move. There's years of dirt and plaster dust in there, if nothing worse."

The emotional temperature had dropped several degrees. When Walt addressed Andy his tone was curious instead of mocking. "What were you looking for? Something to do with your—what do you call it—genealogical research?"

"In a way." Andy hesitated. He was careful not to look at Diana; she waited with some curiosity to see if he could produce a sensible answer, for she doubted that he himself knew precisely what he had hoped to find.

"Diana and I talked some time back about designing a proper setting for those tombstones," Andy went on. "They don't mark the graves; the exact location of the old family cemetery has been lost. Now we've found a grave, or at least a skeleton, and according to Professor Handson, it's fairly antique. Maybe those bones have some connection with the tombstones."

He hadn't really answered Walt's question, but his response served the purpose he had intended—that of distraction. Walt looked aghast. "You mean the graveyard was where the barn is now? I'll never get that construction finished if we have to . . . No, it's impossible. They'd have found the graves when they built the barn. They had to dig foundations and postholes, and those suckers are deep."

"They missed one grave," Andy argued.

"Maybe, maybe not. If the guy was buried before the barn was constructed—well, yeah, they could have missed one. But not a whole cemetery. We did some digging ourselves before the cops arrived, all around the place where we found the bones. There wasn't anything."

"How long ago was the barn built?" Mary Jo asked.

"Good question." Walt considered it. "I don't know the answer. It's been there as long as I can remember. At a guess, I'd say somewhere around the end of the last century. But it could be older. Or more recent. They're a conservative lot around here, they stick to the old styles."

"You sound like Handson," Andy grumbled. "Approximately a century, give or take fifty years."

"It shouldn't be too difficult to find out when the barn was built," Mary Jo said thoughtfully.

"What's the point?" Andy demanded. "That won't tell us when the body was buried. The killer could have taken up the floorboards."

The word cast a chill, like a cold breeze. "Killer?" Walt repeated.

"The skull had been fractured," Andy said.

So that was why he had returned to Handson's office. Diana wondered why it hadn't occurred to her to ask the anthropologist whether he had been able to determine the cause of death. Was it because it seemed irrelevant, once she knew it wasn't Brad's death that was in question, or because she didn't want to know the answer?

"Fractured?" Walt let out a brief bark of a laugh. "It was in fragments."

"You ran over it with the goddamn bulldozer, that's why it was in pieces," Andy retorted. "Those were fresh breaks. Experts can tell the difference."

"That doesn't mean he was murdered," Walt argued. "Could have been an accident."

"Which is undoubtedly what the cops will claim," Andy said. "They've got enough crime on their hands; they won't waste time on a century-old corpse."

"That suits me just fine."

"Aren't you even curious?" Mary Jo demanded. "About who he was and how he came to be there? He was only—what did the professor say?—in his early twenties. Someone loved him, someone mourned him—" She broke off, with an apologetic glance at Diana. "Sorry. Maybe we shouldn't be talking about this."

"It's all right." Diana roused herself from disturbing private thoughts. "One can't help speculating, feeling curiosity and pity."

"Well, sure," Walt said. He sounded defensive; Mary Jo's comment about his lack of imagination had apparently hit home. "But what's the use? We'll probably never know who he was. It isn't as if we could do anything for him."

"There is one thing," Andy said. "We can give him a proper burial."

"Ghost stories," Diana snapped. She and Andy were in the kitchen taking care of the animals while Walt and Mary Jo checked locks and lights. "You've missed your true calling, Andy—writing screen plays for horror movies. You don't really believe that saying a few prayers over those poor old bones will give peace to a troubled . . . I can't say it, it's too absurd!"

"That's one of the classic motives for a haunting," Andy argued.

"But he's not the one who . . . Oh, for God's sake, now you've got me doing it. How about revenge as another classic motive? Missing wills, buried treasure?"

"You've read 'em too," Andy said, pleased.

"I've read every ghost story and fairy tale ever written. But they're stories, Andy! Pure fiction. Products of imaginations as uncontrolled as yours."

"It can't do any harm, can it?"

Diana gave up. Irony and reason alike were wasted on Andy. "Oh, I suppose not. Get out of there, you." She removed a pushy tabby from Miss Matilda's bowl. "Your mother will probably approve of the idea. Like her son, she's a hopeless romantic."

"It's only common decency," Andy insisted. "There aren't any next of kin to claim him. Would you like your bones to spend eternity wrapped in plastic on a laboratory shelf?"

"Once I'm finished with them I don't give a damn what becomes of them." Diana opened the door to admit the last of the cats. "But as you say, it can't do any harm. Anyway, the decision isn't up to me."

The night air touched her face with cool damp fingers. A bright star or planet—Venus, Jupiter?—shone out and then was hidden by a wandering cloud. "Come away from there," Andy said.

Diana closed the door, shutting out the night breeze and the faint, elusive scent it carried.

If Andy came to her room that night she was unaware of it. Ignoring his advice, she had taken a sleeping pill. It—or something—had the desired effect. She slept without dreaming.

The other three looked as if they should have followed her example. Andy kept yawning, Mary Jo's eyes were sunken and shadowed, and Walt was frowningly unresponsive to every conversational gambit. The most anyone got out of him was a grunt.

Finally he expressed one reason for his ill humor. "The weather isn't going to hold much longer. It feels like July, hot and muggy. If we get heavy rains the ground won't be fit to work for a week. I was only able to raise half a crew today; the boys say their wives are complaining about the long hours they've been working."

"Always blame it on the women," Mary Jo muttered.

"I'm not blaming them! I just said—"

"You've done wonders, Walt," Diana said quickly. "Emily will understand why you couldn't do more."

Walt's glum face darkened still more. That was the real cause of his discontent and that of the others. The resolution of the question of the bones and the arrival of Bellows, confident and seemingly efficient, had given them all a brief lift. But Larry was still on the loose and it was Saturday morning. The Nicholsons would return on Monday.

"I'll have to head her off somehow," Andy said, voicing their shared concern. "Better do it today; they could change their minds and start home tomorrow."

Diana roused herself. She felt sleepy and stupid from the effect of the medication. "She said they might stay over another day or two. Why don't you call and ask what their plans are?"

"That makes sense. If they weren't planning to get back till Tuesday—"

Walt's temper cracked wide open. He brought his fist down on the table with a crash that made the others jump. "Sunday, Monday, Tuesday—what's the difference? This could go on for weeks! That cocky bastard Bellows hasn't accomplished a damn thing that I can see."

"He's had less than two days," Diana said. "A few more days could make a difference. I admit it's horribly frustrating, there's so little we can do. But at least we can try to keep Emily out of this as long as possible, in the hope that it will be resolved soon."

Andy's forehead smoothed out and his lips curved in a smile. "She's going to be mad as hell, you know. Ma likes to be in the thick of things."

"I suppose we are being patronizing," Diana admitted.

"Oh, dear, I hadn't thought of that," said Andy in a shocked voice. "Let's give her a ring and tell her all about it."

"I'll give Bellows a ring instead," Diana said. "Damn it, he could at least report no progress."

"Right." Andy yawned. "Let's get organized. I call Ma, you call Bellows. What else is on the schedule for today? Walt will be digging holes and yelling at his crew—"

"I've got to stop by my apartment sometime today," Walt said. "I haven't picked up my mail for days."

"Check. Mary Jo?"

"I should go to the school library. My last exam is Monday."

"Check. I'll take you in. Want to come along, Di? You can visit your boyfriend at the library while I gad about the shops."

Diana knew better than to respond to the provocation. "You're going shopping? Easier to buy socks than wash them, I suppose."

"You do me less than credit, madam. I washed my socks last

night after you went to bed, slaving over a hot sink while you slumbered. A woman may work from sun to sun, but a man's work—"

"Is seldom done," said Mary Jo. She sounded more cheerful; Andy's conversation usually had that effect.

"I am going antiquing," said Andy loftily. "Poor pitiless Pearl called yesterday."

"I heard that message too, but I wasn't inspired to visit her shop," Diana said. "Pearl's taste is all in her mouth. As you can tell by her shape."

Andy produced a startlingly lifelike "meow." Several of the cats raised their heads and stared wildly around the room. "What Pearl didn't say, but what I know from other sources, is that she has some of Miss Musser's things. She claims she bought them at auction. Only God and Pearl know whether that's true, but I thought there might be photos or something Ma would like. She's keen on collecting before-and-after pictures of the house."

"She's already got a lot of them," Diana objected. "The lawyer brought them."

"With Ma, a lot is never enough. Come on, be a sport. You never know what treasures may lurk at the bottom of a cardboard carton of miscellany." He gave Walt a challenging look. "Like diamond tiaras."

Thanks to Andy's efforts, an air of holiday prevailed when he and Diana and Mary Jo set out for town. Emily had found another nursery worth visiting, and did not plan to return before Tuesday night, possibly Wednesday. Bellows had not answered his telephone, but Andy found a silver lining there too. "At least he's out doing something instead of sitting in his room watching cartoons and cleaning his toenails."

Mary Jo had even agreed to go with them to Pearl's before they dropped her at school. "You'll need all the help you can get," she said darkly. "That bitch will steal the teeth out of your mouth."

Andy immediately protested the implied slur on his bargaining talents, and they bickered more or less amicably for the rest of the drive.

Watching Mary Jo's animated face, Diana marveled at the change in the other woman. There had been no improvement in her physical appearance; if anything, she was thinner and more haggard, her clothes were as shabby, her hands as work-worn and calloused. The change was in her expression. The dimple was the genuine article now; it appeared with more frequency and didn't dart into concealment as often. Even her hair looked brighter and thicker.

More Pearls of Great Price was a rambling structure of cinder block strategically located near an exit from the interstate. Pearl's efforts to spruce the place up would have been pitiful if they hadn't been so god-awful. The tubs of geraniums and petunias flanking the door were plastic—tubs and flowers both—and dusty to boot. The cinder block had been painted shocking pink and white, in checkerboard style. The sign featured a portrait of Pearl herself, showing all her teeth and flaunting strands of pearls around her neck and woven through her hair.

Andy stared in horrified admiration. "Holy shit," he said simply.

"More inside," Mary Jo grunted.

At first glance the word did seem to apply to most of the merchandise. Depression glass, chipped china figures of pop-eyed cats, simpering shepherdesses and leering clowns, mementos of Elvis and forties' film stars covered table after table in grimy profusion. Pearl herself was not in evidence, but the clerk assured them she was due any minute. "The best stuff is in the annex," she said, sizing them up with a shrewdness an employee of Pearl's might not have been expected to possess. "This is just for the collectible trade."

"Who'd collect this?" Mary Jo demanded, inspecting a tangled heap of costume jewelry. "I wouldn't take it if you paid me."

"People collect all kinds of things," Diana said. "You'd be surprised."

"Not after seeing this I wouldn't," Mary Jo retorted.

They followed Andy into the annex, where they found him contemplating a rolltop desk. "I always wanted one of these," he said. "Look at all those little cubbyholes."

"It's filthy," Mary Jo said. "Ink stains all over the top. I don't see anything . . . Wait a minute. That quilt looks familiar. Miss Musser had one like it."

"It's a common pattern," Diana said. "Double wedding ring, I think it's called."

Mary Jo sorted through the pile of quilts and extracted one

appliquéd with red and yellow tulips. "That looks like one of hers too. My God, is this the price? It can't be!"

"Old handmade quilts are expensive." Diana glanced at the tag. "They've gone down in price lately, though; that's pretty steep, even by big-city standards."

There were a few pearls—cultured pearls, at least—among the trash. Andy's eye was unerring; he pointed out a Windsor chair, a woven coverlet, and a very dark oil painting in a massive gold frame. "That's a Maentel, or I miss my guess. Cleaned and restored, it would be worth twice what she's asking."

"Oh, yeah?" The idea of putting one over on Pearl restored Mary Jo's interest. "I never heard of Maentel."

"Itinerant portrait painter, circa 1830. It's in bad shape, though; probably cost a bundle to have it restored."

Mary Jo was kneeling, sorting through a basket of lace, and Andy was deep in an old issue of *Marvel Comics* when Pearl arrived, with a slam of the door and a shout of greeting. "Hey! Sorry I'm late, folks. What can I do you for?"

"You got a hell of a nerve asking these prices for some scraps of dirty old lace," Mary Jo said, rising up from behind the table.

"Oh, hi, Mary Jo," Pearl said unenthusiastically. "You looking for something in particular?"

"She's with us," Andy said. "You said something about snapshot albums, Pearl. I don't see them."

"I put 'em away for you. Don't be a rush, take your time, look around. Interested in china? Your ma'd like this Royal Prussian chocolate set, I bet. Don't see complete sets often, not Royal Prussian."

The pieces were in a locked cabinet, as they ought to have been, if Pearl's description was accurate. They looked authentic to Diana, with the profusion of gilt trim and lavishly scattered flowers characteristic of Royal Prussian, and of other far less costly examples of nineteenth-century European porcelain. She took a closer look. The flowers were—what else?—roses.

Pearl unlocked the cabinet for her and then went to work on Andy, who was studying the rocking chair. Diana examined the pieces. They were in good condition, with only a few small chips, and the bases bore the red marks that confirmed Pearl's description, but the price she had set was outlandishly high.

"That was Miss Musser's," said Mary Jo in Diana's ear. "I could be wrong about the quilts, but not that set of china. She stood over me breathing down my neck every time I washed it."

"There was an auction, wasn't there?"

"There was, and I went to it. This set wasn't listed."

"I know what you're thinking, but we could never prove it," Diana murmured. "I'd love to get this for Emily. I think she'd like it."

"She probably would, but I'd hate like hell to pay Pearl for something she—"

"Don't say it. She'd sue you and subpoena me and Andy as witnesses. I may be able to talk her down."

"Stop admiring it, then. You're practically drooling."

"You're right, I am. Poor strategy." She restored the sugar bowl to its place and closed the cabinet. Mary Jo went back to the basket of lace, emitting indignant cries at intervals, and Diana began to inspect the used books.

She loved old books, but there was nothing there to attract her, only the usual collections of paperback romances, long-forgotten best-sellers, and out-of-date textbooks. Pearl's attempt at classification was sometimes hilarious; she had put *The Case of the Giant Hogweed* in the gardening section and *From the Finland Station* under "Travel."

Diana was scanning the fiction hardbacks when a name caught her eye. She extracted the book from its place with some difficulty; the shelves were tightly packed and the layer of dust atop the volumes showed they hadn't been moved for months.

Yes, it was one of the books Louis had mentioned, written by Miss Musser's "authoress" correspondent. Opening the front cover she found what she had expected: Miss Musser's name written in faded copperplate, and a date—July 17, 1919. There were several others by the same author.

These forlorn examples of the fickleness of fame might well have come from the auction. Nobody would bother stealing them. Even Pearl had assessed their worth accurately. The price was two dollars apiece.

However, they had belonged to a former owner of the house; that might be enough to interest Emily. Nor would it surprise Diana to find that Emily liked to read books with titles like *The Maiden of the Mountain Mists*. Miss Musser had faithfully collected the entire oeuvre; Diana selected half a dozen, more or less at random. If Emily decided she wanted the rest, they would almost certainly still be there.

Andy had inspected the photo albums and was dickering with Pearl, ably assisted by Mary Jo. "I could make you a better price if you took the chair too," Pearl said. "It came from the house; I bought it at—I bought it from Cousin Matilda before she died."

"Well," Andy said weakly.

That was a mistake, as any salesman could have told him. When they left they had not only the photo albums and the chair, but two quilts, the books, and the chocolate set. Diana had paid a price for the last item that left Mary Jo sputtering, but it was considerably less than the one Pearl had first quoted.

"Lucky we brought my van instead of your car," Andy said complacently, as he loaded their purchases. "Plenty of room left; what do you say we check out a couple more antique shops?"

"Are all the dealers as crooked as Pearl?" Mary Jo asked. "You noticed how she started to say she bought that chair at the auction and then changed her story? She didn't buy it, she stole it."

"She probably stole it even if she did buy it," Andy said. "It's a hundred and fifty years old if it's a day, and well worth what she was asking. Miss Musser might not have known its value."

"That last year she didn't know her own name most of the time," Mary Jo said. "It makes my blood boil to think of leeches like Pearl taking advantage of the old lady. We could check the list of what was sold at the auction. I bet somebody's got a copy."

"Her lawyer, for one," Diana said. "But we couldn't prove anything, Mary Jo. Pearl could always say, as she just did, that she bought the items privately. Even if she paid peanuts for them, there's no law against getting a bargain."

"And to answer your question," Andy said, "no, most dealers aren't crooks. There's a certain amount of sharp dealing in the antique business, as there is in any business, but a reputation for honesty pays off in the long run in higher prices and faithful customers."

He stopped at the exit from the parking lot. "Which way? There's an Antiques Emporium ten miles south off the interstate, or we could have a bite of lunch first."

Mary Jo shook her head. "That was fun, but I've wasted enough time. Drop me off at school and then you two can carouse all you want."

They watched her march up the sidewalk toward the library, head high and thin shoulders squared. "You know, she wouldn't be bad if she'd use a little makeup and wear decent clothes," Andy remarked.

The comment infuriated Diana all the more because she had been thinking along the same lines. She got as far as "Smug, superficial, male-chauvinist—" before she realized Andy was trying to bait her. "Jerk," she finished.

Andy chuckled. "What shall we do now?"

"Four hours, did she say? That's a lot of time to kill. Maybe we should go back to the house."

"And sit around waiting for the phone to ring?"

"We could call Bellows again."

"There are pay phones. Out here in the backwoods they even work." Andy put the van in gear and pulled away from the curb.

"So what else can we do?"

"Eat," Andy said promptly. "I hope Mary Jo remembers to grab a sandwich at the cafeteria, as she said she would, but I prefer a more elegant ambience. How does pizza grab you?"

"I don't care."

"Then," Andy continued, "we could visit your admirer at the library."

Diana glanced at him. He had washed more than his socks, and there was some evidence that he had even gone so far as to plug in an iron. His pants were creased, his shirt shone snowily in the sunlight, and his glasses must be a new pair, for they held together without the aid of tape. His teeth gleamed white against the deep tan of his face, and his forearms displayed a respectable set of muscles. I can't do that to Louis, Diana thought. Not poor Louis.

"I don't even know whether he's working today," she said. "He'd have called if he had found anything of interest."

"There's not a chance in hell that he will," Andy declared. "The old lady was too goofy that last year to take notice of suspicious circumstances, assuming there were any. She didn't keep a diary, did she?"

"Nobody's mentioned one."

"Then what did you have in mind when you vamped that poor devil of a librarian? I have been accused of being a perennial optimist, but even I would not expect to find a diary with an entry like 'That uncouth ex-husband of Mary Jo's was here today threatening to shoot my gardener.' "

"I don't know what I had in mind," Diana said angrily. "That makes two of us, doesn't it?"

"Wrong. My brain is absolutely packed with useful ideas." Andy pulled neatly into a parking space. "The only thing I'm uncertain about is whether to have anchovies or olives."

He had both. The pizza was good, and the ambience was pleasant, though hardly elegant. Diana had finished her first piece and Andy was halfway through his third when she recognized a familiar face. The hand that went with it was waving at her.

"Who's that?" Andy asked.

"Uh . . ." Before she could think of a safe answer, Marily joined them.

"You did decide to come! I've got the clothes all ready for you." She looked hopefully at Andy. Diana had no choice but to introduce them, but she did not add any explanatory comments. It was useless; Andy's ears were pricked.

"How about a cup of coffee?" he suggested, pulling out a chair. "You work at one of the stores here in town, Marily?"

The inevitable explanations followed. "Fascinating," Andy said, ostentatiously not looking at Diana. "Mind if I come too?"

Marily didn't mind.

After she had gone, Andy turned his head very slowly and fixed Diana with a glare that would have done Medusa proud.

"I'm going to call Mr. Bellows," she said, and fled.

When she returned Andy had finished the pizza. "Serves you right," he said when she protested. "Eat the salad, it's good for you. Was he there?"

"No. I left a message asking him to call."

He said no more, only waited with ostentatious patience for her to finish her salad. They left the van where it was; the museum was only a block away.

The woman behind the desk directed them up two flights of stairs to the work areas, where they found Marily going through a plastic trash bag. "This is typical of our donations, unfortunately," she said, holding up a checked calico apron riddled with holes. "What am I supposed to do with it?"

"Dust rag," Andy suggested, with a meaningful glance around the room. It was a vast, echoing attic whose rafters were hung with cobwebs and whose windows hadn't been washed in years. The shelves lining the walls bulged with boxes, cardboard cartons, and objects wrapped in yellowing newspaper.

"It's a mess, isn't it?" Marily sighed. "But you should have seen it when I started. I managed to talk the board out of a few bucks for acid-free boxes and paper, so I could salvage the best of the costumes, but I'm only here one day a week."

"I wasn't criticizing you," Andy said quickly. "You're doing a great job under impossible circumstances."

Marily blushed. "I do the best I can. Anyhow, I won't have to waste time on this." She bundled the apron back into the bag and tossed it into a corner. "I'd throw it out, except that it came from one of our 'best' families. They get huffy if you reject their offerings. Here are Martha's things. They were the first to get acid-free boxes and garment bags."

She lifted the lid of a long gray box, freeing a strong stench of mothballs, and lifted out the topmost garment.

Petticoats of linen and quilted satin, cotton chemises trimmed with lace and ruffles, a corset of blue watered silk, knitted cotton gloves with lacy openwork patterns . . . The whites were white no longer; the fabric had aged to a creamy yellow.

"You sure these belonged to a woman nineteen years old?" Andy asked, holding up one of the chemises which, Marily had explained, were not nightgowns but undergarments. The head of the wearer would barely have reached his chin.

"People were smaller then," Marily explained. She picked up the corset. "Look at the size of her waist."

The prize of the lot was a wedding gown, which Marily carried in from an adjoining room. "There's an air conditioner in there," she explained. "I couldn't afford one big enough to cool this vault, so I commandeered the room next door."

"You couldn't afford?" Andy repeated. "You mean you not only work for free, you have to buy your own equipment?"

"I didn't have to. But the trustees wouldn't authorize it and I couldn't stand the idea of seeing these things rot away. Heat and humidity are hard on old fabrics, and they encourage all kinds of insects."

The dress had been carefully folded into a box, with rolls of tissue paper inserted to prevent creases; as Marily explained, hanging it would have put an undue strain on the material. Diana could understand why; there must have been fifteen yards of satin in the wide skirt, which was trimmed with ruched puffs and gathers of the same fabric.

"Never been worn. Never will be. Kind of sad, isn't it?" Marily said cheerfully.

Andy's expression was pensive. If the minuscule size of the dress hadn't convinced him it was futile to suggest that Diana try it on, Marily's lecture would have done so. It was clear that she would never permit such a thing.

They left Marily with thanks and compliments, stopping on their way out, as she had suggested, to look at the exhibit. Andy spotted the rose-woven fabric instantly. "Aha! Martha's favorite flower."

Diana sniffed. "Flower motifs were common. And those look more like peonies to me."

"Cabbage roses."

"What do you know about women's fashions?"

"I know a rose when I see one." He gave her a sidelong glance. "Any sensations of déjà vu? Cold shivers up your spine?"

"Not a tremor."

"Would you tell me if you did? Ah, well, it was an interesting experience. Come on, I'll buy you a cup of coffee. We've got another hour to kill."

Diana refused the offer, so they spent the time parked in front of the library. She also refused to respond to his attempts to discuss antique clothing, roses, and Martha Fairweather; becoming bored, Andy turned and reached a long arm into the back of the van. "Bought any good books lately?" he asked, dragging out the brown paper bag into which Pearl had placed Diana's literary purchases.

"I doubt they would interest you. I only bought them because they belonged to Miss Musser. The author was a friend of hers."

"Amelie DuPrez?" Andy repeated incredulously.

"It's a pen name. Her real name was Ida Maude something."

Andy opened one of the books at random and began to laugh. "Next time I make rude remarks about the literary quality of today's best-sellers, remind me that there once was a writer who penned the following sentence: 'Oh, God in Heaven, this cannot be! Let he whom she adored despise and loathe her for this vile act, but God, oh, God, save him at any cost!' I think the photo albums would be less painful."

They might have been less painful aesthetically, but they had their own pathos. All those faces, once known and loved—or hated—now anonymous, their identities lost in the passage of time.

The clothing, lovingly selected for its fashionable beauty, looked absurd to modern eyes.

"These must date to the late twenties," Diana said. "The flapper era. That's when they wore those short, shapeless dresses."

"Yep. That's a 1928 Packard they're sitting in." Andy squinted at the faded snapshot, his face alight with love. "What a great car! Who's the old sport at the wheel?"

"That's Miss Musser next to him, surely. Must be her father."

"Her boyfriend, maybe. Or would she have called him her beau?"

"He's too old. His hair is snow-white."

Mary Jo finally came, and Andy tossed the album into the back of the van. "It's too hot to cook tonight," he said, after a seemingly casual glance at Mary Jo's tired face. "Let's stop for takeout. Chinese?"

"Diana hates Chinese."

Diana laughed. "I thought I put on a good act."

"It was pretty good," Mary Jo conceded. "How about cold cuts and salad? I could make—"

"You aren't making anything." Andy zoomed out into traffic. "I happen to know a deli . . ."

He kept Mary Jo entertained on the way home by a description of his encounter with eighteenth-century underwear. "It was positively indecent. Not a pair of drawers in the lot. I never realized our ancestors were such a rowdy lot."

"I suppose it would be hard enough hoisting up all those skirts and petticoats," Mary Jo said, grinning. "No bras either?"

"No, but the corsets would kill you. I can see some frantic lover, clumsy with rising passion, trying to untangle the laces on one of those things."

"What a low, vulgar mind you have, Andy." Mary Jo sobered. "I wonder if Emily knows the Historical Society has those clothes. Bet you she'll want to buy them."

"She might at that," Andy said. "She's never been able to find anything that belongs to the Fairweathers. Except . . ."

"The tombstones." Mary Jo was unaware of his reason for failing to complete the sentence. "Have you thought about what you're going to do with them?"

The subject of landscape architecture occupied them for the rest of the drive.

The first thing that struck Diana when they reached the house was the silence. No growl of engines, no thud of rock and dirt loads, no voices. The crew had left, but Walt was still at work, spreading mulch around the newly planted perennials. He was stripped to the waist and shining with sweat. Even his hair dripped perspiration.

"For God's sake, quit making a martyr of yourself," Andy said rudely. "It must be over ninety degrees."

"I'm almost done." Walt pushed a damp brown lock out of his eyes. "Decided to let the boys leave early. I've been pushing them pretty hard."

"Yourself as well," Diana said. "Do stop, Walt. Maybe there's a good movie on tonight. You deserve an evening off."

"I just want to finish mulching. How does it look?"

"A tribute to your dedication, nobility, hard work, and bull-headedness," Andy said, before Diana could reply. "Who gives a damn about the goddamn garden?"

He stamped back into the house and slammed the door. Walt looked at Diana. Amusement instead of the anger she had expected warmed his eyes. "Poor old Andy. He's so obvious. Looks good, doesn't it?"

It all looked good, including Walt, who might have posed for a statue of a Greek athlete, with asphodel or some other appropriate flower around his feet. Diana expressed her admiration—of the gardening, not the gardener—and left him to it.

Andy was drinking beer and scowling at the answering machine. "I refrained from turning it on till you could listen with me. Thought you might be mildly interested in finding out whether your tame 'tec has discovered anything."

Diana didn't bother to ask why he was in such a foul mood. With a shrug she turned on the machine.

There were two messages from Bellows, one before he had received hers, the second afterward. The first was couched with cautious, professional indirection. The 'subject' under surveillance had not approached, or been approached by, the individual in question. That same individual had not returned to the location that had been discovered earlier. Further investigations along different lines were proceeding.

The second message was more encouraging. "I think I may have a lead," Bellows began. "I wasn't going to mention it because I don't want to get your hopes up and because we're still in the early stages; but you sounded kind of irritated when you called, so . . . I may know more late tonight or early tomorrow morning. I'll call as soon as I have more information."

"Late tonight or early tomorrow," Andy repeated, his ill humor forgotten. "I wonder what he's got—"

He broke off as another voice began to speak. The stammer was unmistakable. Louis wondered if Diana would like to go to a Bach concert at the college the following evening. It was short notice, he knew, and he was really sorry, but he hadn't been certain of being able to get tickets until that morning, and he figured she probably couldn't make it, so if he didn't hear from her he would just assume she couldn't make it, but if she could, he would be delighted to pick her up, just let him know . . .

Diana reached for the cut-off switch. "Wait a minute," Andy said, his voice choked with laughter. "There are a couple more messages. I counted the blinks."

The next message wiped the grin from his face. It went on for some time but could be summarized in two words. "You're fired." Walt, on his way through the kitchen to his room, heard the last part of it and grinned at Diana, but was wise enough not to pause or comment.

"I wonder how he got the number," Andy muttered. "Hell. I was going to quit before he could fire me. Who does that bastard think he is, talking that way when a lady, not to mention my dear old mum, might overhear?"

"Sssh."

The next voice was her father's. "I presume you will have received Bellows's message by now. He said he would call. I am coming to see him tomorrow to discuss the latest developments. It would be useful, I believe, for you to find time to talk with me. I should arrive around noon. Please call back and let me know what time is convenient. I would like to take you to lunch or dinner if you can endure my company that long."

Click.

Mary Jo had come quietly in while he was speaking. "He sounds sort of sad."

"Sad? Him?" Andy snorted. "He's trying to make her feel sorry for him. And succeeding."

"Oh, he never says or does anything uncalculated," Diana said wearily. "But I may have been unjust. Look at the effort he's making now—two trips down here in a few days. He's trying, and the least I can do is meet him halfway."

Mary Jo nodded. Andy looked skeptical, but he waited until after she had placed her call and left a message agreeing to the appointment before he spoke. "Actually, that's even more encouraging than Bellows's second message. Trying or not, he wouldn't make that drive again without a good reason. Bellows may have told him more than he told you."

They had to explain it to Mary Jo, who had not heard Bellows's messages, and again to Walt, when he came downstairs. Mary Jo didn't mind hearing it twice. "It's the best news yet," she said, trying not to look hopeful.

It turned out to be a pleasant evening, thanks to strenuous efforts on everyone's part to be agreeable. Andy rummaged through his mother's collection of video tapes, which ran heavily to slapstick comedy and golden oldies; they watched not one film but two, eating popcorn and trying to keep the cats out of the bowl. Diana had seen *The Producers* several times; the reactions of her companions intrigued her as much as the film. Andy's rubbery features reflected every emotion expressed by every actor; Mary Jo looked like a teenager as she chuckled and stuffed popcorn into her mouth; and Walt actually laughed out loud.

Diana's euphoric mood lasted until Andy drew her aside as she was preparing to follow Mary Jo upstairs. "Did you take a sleeping pill last night?" he asked.

Diana came down with a thud. "What business is it of yours?"

"Don't take one. Please."

She pulled her arm away from his grasp. "Damn it, Andy, I was feeling great until you reminded me. Go to hell or to bed, I don't care which."

The temperature had dropped but the night air was sticky and still. She was tired enough to sleep . . . but just to be on the safe side . . .

In the darkness she could not see them except as darker shapes. They were fighting, murderously and furiously, in a deadly silence broken only by gasps and grunts of pain and the sodden thud of blows. She knew she was dreaming. She tried to move; her feet felt as if they were glued to the ground. She tried to cry out, to tell them to stop. She could not utter a sound. Then one of the featureless forms staggered back, fell, and lay still.

The scream she had been unable to utter issued from her throat with the force of water bursting a dam. The grass was cool and damp under her bare feet. A white shroud of mist hovered over the lawn. The moon's gibbous outline was blurred by thin clouds. She was not dreaming. She was wide awake—and they were there, one man motionless on the ground, the other bending over him as if about to strike again.

He spun around when he heard her voice, and caught her, not in an embrace but in a hard, bruising grip. In the pallid moonlight she could see his features clearly, but she had already recognized him and the man he had struck down. Neither of them was Larry. It was Walt who held her, Andy who lay still on the silvered grass.

CHAPTER EIGHTEEN

I sometimes think that never blows so red
The Rose as where some buried Caesar bled . . .

—EDWARD FITZGERALD

*H*e had pinned her arms to her sides. Diana kicked out and stubbed her toe painfully on a shin that felt like bone covered with leather. Struggling furiously, she managed to free one arm. Her nails raked his face. That hurt him. He let out a breathless oath and pulled her close, so that her hand was pinned between his breast and hers. His strength was terrifying; he was only using one arm to hold her in a grip she couldn't break. She drew in her breath. He must have heard it and anticipated her intention; his free hand covered her mouth before she could cry out.

Pretend to faint, she thought. Go limp. Once he's off-guard . . .

Before she could act she heard his voice, low-pitched and harsh with strain. "Don't yell! You want to wake Mary Jo?"

It was such an inappropriate speech for a man bent on criminal assault of one variety or another, that she did go limp, not from calculation but from surprise. He bent his head, squinting as if he were trying to see her shadowed features more clearly. "Diana? Don't pass out on me. Are you okay now? Can you hear me?"

His hand was still over her mouth. As she tried to think of a way of reminding him of this fact, she heard another voice that added the final touch of unreality to the encounter.

"That's torn it," Andy said. "It's a wonder she isn't unconscious—or worse. Don't you know it's dangerous to wake a sleepwalker?"

He was lisping. When he loomed up behind Walt, Diana saw the dark stains around his mouth and understood why his voice had sounded so strange. Baring his teeth, he took an upper incisor gingerly between his thumb and forefinger. "Lucky you," he said indistinctly. "I'd have stuck you with a whopping dental bill if you'd knocked it loose. Take your hand off her mouth, why don't you? And let her go, you're squeezing the breath out of her."

Instead of following Andy's suggestion, Walt shifted his hold and lifted Diana in his arms. Dizzy and confused, she clung to him. The outlines of the trees beyond the meadow were dark against the moonlit sky; the air was muggy with pent moisture. What was she doing in the meadow in the middle of the night, barefoot and wearing only a flimsy nightgown? She had not the faintest recollection of how she had got there.

"Sleepwalking," Walt repeated. "That's the story, is it? And you were following her to keep her from hurting herself? How far were you going to let her go? She was heading for the barn—"

"No, she was not." Andy rubbed his mouth with the back of his hand. "She was going that way—toward the rose garden and the stream. I was just about to turn her back when you jumped me."

"I thought you were someone else."

"Like hell you did."

Walt turned without another word and started for the house. When she realized how far she had gone, unaware and unfeeling, Diana began to shiver uncontrollably. Clear across the upper terrace and down the stairs . . . Her feet hurt.

The back door was open. The kitchen was dark, but the outside lights spread a glow across the newly planted flower beds. "Put her on the sofa," Andy said, closing the door and pressing the light switch. "I'll get her a glass of brandy."

"I don't want any damned brandy," Diana mumbled. Walt had lowered her to the sofa; she felt suddenly cold without the warmth of his body against hers.

"Make some coffee," Walt ordered, tucking an afghan around her. "Good Lord, look at her feet. She must have stepped on some broken glass."

Diana yelped in protest as his fingers probed the cuts. A relieved smile lightened Walt's face. "Alive and kicking," he said with satisfaction. "Are you all right now?"

"No."

Walt sat down on the edge of the sofa. "I guess you *were* walking in your sleep." He took the bowl of water and cloth Andy handed him and began wiping Diana's feet. "You wouldn't go running around in the middle of the night barefoot—"

"She wouldn't go running around in the middle of the night, period," Andy said impatiently. "What does it take to convince you, you stubborn jackass? This is the second time. I found her in the kitchen last night, trying to open the door. Got her back to bed without waking her, the way you're supposed to. I must have dozed off tonight; didn't hear her until she opened the kitchen door. My room's right above it."

"Last night too?" Diana sat up, her eyes widening. "Why didn't you tell me?"

"Because . . . uh." Andy rubbed his chin. "Because I was playing the protective male. Sorry. I should have told you."

"And me." Walt got up and carried the bowl to the sink. "You could have spared yourself some pain, buddy. I was awake, looking out the library window, and saw your flashlight. Naturally I thought . . . well, you know what I thought."

He turned, bracing his hands on the counter. Andy hadn't gone down without a struggle; one of Walt's eyes was swelling and there were patches of reddening skin along his jaw. The bloody furrows on his cheek, Diana realized, were her contribution.

"I don't know how you're going to explain those bumps and scratches to Mary Jo," she said.

The combatants studied one another thoughtfully. "We'll tell her the truth," Andy said with a sigh. "All this crap about sparing people's feelings has to stop. It's insulting and it's dangerous. From now on we tell the truth, the whole truth and nothing but the truth."

"I have been," said Walt, his eyes narrowing. "What other little surprises have you been holding back, Andy?"

"Well . . ."

"Is the coffee ready?" Diana asked. She knew what Andy was about to say and she didn't think Walt was ready to hear it. She wasn't ready either; exhaustion, physical and emotional, weighed her limbs.

Walt saw it, if Andy did not. "You sure you want coffee, Di? What you need is rest."

"It won't keep me awake," Diana said wryly.

"Okay, one cup. Then it's beddy-bye for you." He sat down

beside her, holding the cup. "I've read about this sleepwalking thing, but I never saw it before. Do you remember anything? You didn't hear a noise, or see something outside?"

"Not a thing." She caught Andy's watchful eye. He had a point about being honest. Perhaps she could risk telling part of the truth. There was nothing abnormal or supernatural about bad dreams. "I was sound asleep the whole time. I dreamed about people fighting. I couldn't see who they were; it was dark."

"That was no dream," Walt said.

"Part of it was. It started in a different place. I can't remember . . ."

"Try." Andy leaned over her, his face intent. "What place? You were heading for—"

"That's it." Walt took the cup from Diana's hand and put it on the table. "Dream analysis yet! She's so tired she's about to fall asleep here and now."

He picked her up, afghan and all. Diana started to say she was perfectly capable of walking, but she didn't complete the sentence. Her feet were sore and her eyelids were heavy, and Walt was carrying her as if she weighed no more than a child. He felt so nice and warm . . . She was half asleep when he laid her on her bed and tucked the blankets around her with big gentle hands.

The kitchen door was open; she could hear them talking as she approached. The others must have overslept too, because Mary Jo was still in the initial stages of her lecture.

". . . like a pair of nasty little boys! Letting her stand there in her nightgown while you battered each other senseless! She could have caught her death of cold, not to mention—"

She broke off when she saw Diana and hurried to her. "How do you feel? Sit down. I'll get you some breakfast. You should have waked me up. Let me see your feet. Walt said you cut them real bad. I don't suppose he had sense enough to clean the cuts or bandage them. When did you have your last tetanus shot?"

She had pushed Diana into a chair and whipped off her sandals before the latter could get a word in.

"I fell asleep before he could do more than wash off the dirt," she said, yawning. "Don't fuss, Mary Jo. I'm in better shape than either of them."

Walt's eye was slightly puffy and Andy's lower lip had swelled, giving him the look of a pouting baby. The nastiest wounds were the ones she had inflicted: a row of inflamed parallel lines from Walt's cheekbone to his jaw.

"Serves them right," Mary Jo muttered. "That's men for you; their solution to any problem is to punch somebody."

She insisted on painting Diana's feet with antiseptic and plastering them with Band-Aids. When she turned to Walt, waving the bottle purposefully, he put up his hands and backed away. "Oh, no, you don't. Not Mercurochrome. Nobody uses that anymore; you just want to make me look like a damned fool."

"That's what you are." Mary Jo sat down suddenly. Her face crumpled. "I don't understand you. Fighting like snotty-nosed kids and now joking about it . . . Don't you realize what could have happened to her?"

"She might have fallen or bumped into a tree," Andy said. "Nothing worse. There aren't any cliffs around here to walk off."

His attempt at comforting Mary Jo failed. "What do you mean, there's nothing worse? He's still out there somewhere—Larry—"

"He wasn't here, though." Walt's brows drew together. "He can't be everywhere, for God's sake! You talk about him as if he were some kind of superhuman comic-book villain. He's not. He isn't even particularly bright. You're not the only one, he's got us all starting at shadows and looking over our shoulders. I tell you, we're giving him credit for more intelligence and a helluva lot more balls than he's got. I've had it up to here with Larry, and I'll be damned if I'm going to let him intimidate me anymore."

Andy's eyes widened. He stared at Walt as if he had sprouted horns, or delivered an oration comparable to the Gettysburg Address, but he did not speak.

"Three cheers for you," Mary Jo said, unimpressed. "If you're through flexing your muscles, how about making Diana some toast?"

"That's women for you," said Walt. "Their solution to any problem is to feed somebody." He glanced at Andy, who nodded appreciatively, and went on before Mary Jo could reply. "Wasn't that detective supposed to call last night?"

"Or early this morning," Diana said. "I wonder what he meant by 'early.' It's after nine."

"Call him," Andy suggested.

"What's the use? He promised to let us know as soon as he had any information. One can only assume that in this case no news is bad news."

They were still at the table when the phone rang. Andy made a dive for it, but Diana reached it first. "Yes? Yes, Mr. Bellows. We've been waiting to hear from you."

He spoke quickly and urgently, without giving her a chance to answer. She could feel the very skin of her face changing, hardening, forming new lines. Finally she said, "I understand. Yes, all of it. Yes, of course. No. No, I won't. Thank you."

She hung up the phone and turned to face them. Three pairs of eyes met hers with the impact of separate blows. No one so much as blinked.

"They found him," Diana said. "Mary Jo—he's . . ."

"Dead?"

"Yes. They're calling it suicide. They found a note."

Mary Jo nodded. Her face was quite calm, though she had paled a trifle.

"That's not all," Andy said, his eyes intent. "What is it?"

Astonishing, she thought, how a single short sentence could alter perception so drastically. Even their faces looked different—Andy's crafty and calculating instead of good-natured, Walt's hard and hostile instead of strong. Mary Jo . . . No, not Mary Jo. She had never believed it of Mary Jo. She wouldn't believe it now.

"He's been dead for some time," she said. "At least three days."

Bellows had wanted her to leave the house. "You realize what this means, don't you?" he had asked, and had then proceeded to tell her. If Larry had been dead for three days, and there was little doubt of it, he could not have been the one who left Brad's watch.

"There are several harmless explanations for that," Bellows went on. "But there's another possibility that isn't so harmless. I don't think it's likely, but it can't be ruled out altogether at this time. So don't take chances. If you're determined to stay on, watch yourself and be careful what you say."

He had not needed to warn her. All the doubts she had harbored at the beginning, before Larry made himself such an obvious and convenient suspect, flooded back into her mind. She had to fight a silent, invisible battle to keep them hidden from the others.

She was not certain she had succeeded. The implications weren't that obscure, she told herself; they were surely as evident to the others as they had been to Bellows and to her. Andy kept looking at her oddly; Walt avoided her eyes altogether. Mary Jo was the only one who behaved normally—normally, that is, for a woman in a state of shock.

"I can't believe it," she kept repeating. "Is he sure? Is it really true?"

Finally Walt said bluntly, "Why can't you believe it? You're afraid to—or you don't want to?"

The color returned to Mary Jo's face. "I'm not grieving over him, if that's what you mean. I'm only sorry because—because I can't grieve."

Diana was holding her hand, feeling helpless and ineffectual because she could offer no better comfort. "You'd be a fool to feel otherwise, Mary Jo. It's over. That's what you have to concentrate on. It's all over now."

Andy's chair creaked as he shifted position. He spoke so softly that Diana barely heard him. "Is it?"

"Suicide," the sheriff said flatly. "No doubt about it."

The squad car had arrived shortly after Bellows called. Diana was sourly amused to see that certain conventions still held good; a nervous young policewoman accompanied the sheriff, presumably to offer consolation to the bereaved . . . What did you call the ex-wife of a dead wife-beater?

Relieved. She'd have been crazy to feel any stronger emotion, and Mary Jo was eminently sane. She could not even feel regret for what might have been; the patterns, for both, had been set long before they met, and they could never have matched.

But patterns of behavior, habit, even hereditary predispositions, weren't shaped of steel. Mary Jo was breaking through the barriers that had held her back from achievement. The choice was there, sometimes easy, sometimes unendurably difficult. Perhaps for some it was just not possible.

The sheriff had been visibly put out by finding he was not the first to break the news, but pleased to learn they knew little beyond the bare facts. "Yep," he repeated. "He left a note. Said he was sorry, he didn't mean to do it."

"Do what?" Andy asked.

"Why—uh—kill that kid, what else?"

"Could be he regretted what he'd done to his wife," Andy said.

"It'd be the first time, then. He never was sorry before." The sheriff glanced at Mary Jo, whose lips had formed a tight, white-rimmed line, and then turned to Diana. "Not that we ever suspected he'd committed a murder. There was no way we could've known. If you'd come to us, ma'am, instead of—"

"You wouldn't have believed her," Walt interrupted.

"He's right," Diana said, though she appreciated Walt's coming to her defense. "I should have."

"Oh, well, it all turned out for the best," said the sheriff, blissfully unaware of tactlessness. "And that private detective you hired wasn't worth shit, ma'am, if you'll excuse me. It was plain routine police work that found him."

The inaccuracy of this claim became evident as he explained further. Diana felt sure Larry's buddy would not have betrayed the existence of the long-abandoned cabin to the police; it had taken Bellows's persuasion, and the prospect of a reward, to extract that information. Nor would the sheriff have expended so much manpower scouring the woods after a search of the cabin showed Larry had been there recently, if the accusation of murder had not been made. A wife-beater didn't rate that much attention.

Mary Jo insisted on having all the details, and the sheriff was happy to oblige. "He was lying under a tree about fifty feet from the cabin. There was an empty bourbon bottle next to him. I figure he drank the whole fifth; that's what I'd have done if I was figuring to blow my head off. Could've been an accident, I guess, but there was the note, he'd left it on the table in the cabin. It was his own gun—both barrels, square in the—"

It was Diana who exclaimed in protest, not Mary Jo. "That means a closed coffin, I guess," she said stoically. "When are you going to release the body?"

"Maybe tomorrow, most likely the day after. Takes a while to finish the paperwork. Like formal identification."

Diana's horrified objections had no effect on the sheriff or on Mary Jo. "Somebody's got to do it, and make funeral arrangements. His Aunt Bertha is so cheap she buys her kids' clothes at Goodwill and she never could stand Larry."

Like a rock, like a brick wall. "I'm going with you," Diana said.

"You can't. Your dad will be here pretty soon. Don't worry about me. I've done worse and seen worse."

"He's not my dad," Andy announced. "I'll trail along if that's okay with everyone."

Walt said nothing. He just went.

It felt strange to be alone in the house, and to realize that she could go out if she liked—visit the rose garden, walk across the meadow—without fearing attack. Though she was so restless she could not sit still, so on edge her skin prickled, Diana was reluctant to leave the protection of the house. Mary Jo's ordeal was over. Hers was not.

If there were a foot-in-the-mouth award, Sheriff Whittenhouse would have been a leading contender. "Too bad Larry didn't see fit to mention where he put your brother's body. But don't worry, ma'am, it'll turn up sooner or later. Kids exploring in the woods, or dogs—"

Andy had propelled him out the door before he could finish the sentence.

"Later" seemed more likely than "sooner," and "never" was equally possible. The bones under the floor of the barn had escaped discovery for a century, give or take fifty years. The wilderness area covered hundreds of acres; it was unlikely it would be opened for development in the near future. If the grave had been dug deep enough, dogs or children wouldn't come across it by accident.

Sitting in the sunny kitchen with Baby's head resting on her feet, she faced the fact that Larry's death had not answered any of the questions that had brought her here. There were too many imponderables remaining. His death could have been a drunken accident, the scrawled note an unfinished plea for understanding and forgiveness. "He was always sorry afterward," Mary Jo had said. If he had meant to take his life, after confessing to murder, why hadn't he directed them to the spot where Brad was buried?

Because he was drunk and irrational and because he wasn't the kind of man, drunk or sober, to care about the feelings of other people. Diana could accept that, just as she could find reasonable explanations for the other anomalies that cast a doubt on Larry's guilt. He could have given the watch to a friend or lover, saying that he had found it or that Brad had given it to him. The watch had not been returned until after word got out that Larry was suspected of having murdered the original owner—until after Larry was dead, in fact. But the person who had the watch might not have known that, and he would be anxious to get rid of such an incriminating object. Some buried streak of decency could have prompted him to return the expensive jewel instead of destroying it.

Diana tried to cling to that explanation, but it didn't convince her. Larry was such a convenient scapegoat, incapable of defending himself adequately even if he had been captured and brought to trial. Why not pound an extra nail in his coffin by delivering that damning evidence? Larry could not have delivered it—but no one knew that at the time. How easy it would have been for someone living in the house to open the front door and leave the paper bag on the doorstep. The dogs wouldn't bark at one of them.

She was still sitting at the table when she heard the sound of a car approaching. Startled, she looked at the clock. He was early, but not by much. She had been trapped in an endless circle of thought, like a hamster on a wheel, for almost an hour.

She hurried to the front door. After struggling ineffectually to open it she realized she must have locked it. Habit—or an acknowledgment of continuing danger she was reluctant to admit consciously?

Her father's face wore the expression that was as close to a smile as he permitted. He must have heard the news. The corners of his mouth straightened as he glanced at Baby, pressed close to Diana's side.

"What in heaven's name is that?"

"I forgot you hadn't met Baby." Diana got a firm grip on the dog's collar before she unlatched the screen door. "She's perfectly harmless. Come in. Maybe I can get her to go out."

Baby preferred not to go out. She was fascinated by the newcomer, for reasons that eluded Diana—and perhaps Baby herself. John Randall accepted the moist snuffling and the transfer of copious quantities of hair to his trousers with better humor than Diana had expected. "She seems to be an excellent judge of character," he said gravely. "We'll keep each other company while you change. I'm a little early, I know."

Diana glanced at her reflection in the hall mirror. Her shirt was clean and pressed, she was wearing a skirt instead of pants, and sandals instead of dirty sneakers. She had twisted her hair into a loose knot and fastened it with a silver clasp, and put on lipstick. Compared to the image she had become used to seeing, this one was positively soigné.

"I'm wearing shoes and I'm not bare-chested," she said. "That's all Bettie requires of her customers. Let's go."

Her father didn't insist that she change, but he did draw the line at Bettie's. They drove twenty miles to a restaurant he had noticed on the way down; the food was no better but, as he pointed out, it had the advantage of being less popular and farther away. The town would be buzzing with gossip and they would attract unwanted attention at Bettie's.

"So long as we don't go too far," Diana said. "I want to be there when Mary Jo gets back. She'll have had a ghastly time."

"She struck me as a very tough woman, Diana. You mustn't attribute sensitivities like yours to these people."

"For God's sake, Father, she's had to identify the mutilated body of a man with whom she shared the most intimate of all human relationships. One needn't be a shrinking violet to be shattered by that experience."

"You haven't had an easy time of it either." He gestured at her glass. "Drink your wine and try to relax. I'd like to take you home with me tonight. The sooner you're away from that house and its painful memories, the better."

Diana shook her head. "I can't walk out on Mary Jo. We're friends, Father. And I promised Emily—Mrs. Nicholson—I'd stay till she got back. Even if I didn't feel an obligation, it would be cowardly of me to sneak away without explaining why I took advantage of her, and asking for her forgiveness."

"Aren't you being a little melodramatic? It's understandable, considering the strain you've been under," he added quickly. "Your behavior may have been foolish, but it was not culpable, and the results of our inquiry go a long way toward justifying your action. You hardly know these people. Why do you care what they think?"

"They're nice people," Diana mumbled, only too well aware of how banal it sounded. "It's not just what they think of me, Father; it's what I think of myself. You've always told me that living up to one's own standards was the most important thing."

A tilt of one eyebrow acknowledged the justice of her reply. "Fair enough. How long do you think it will take to satisfy your opinion of yourself?"

"A few days—a week—"

"That's absurd, Diana. You have other obligations, including an excellent position which you will jeopardize if you prolong your absence. I've explained the situation to Howard; he's been most understanding, but you can't expect him to keep covering for you indefinitely on a day-by-day basis. There are cases . . . "

He stopped talking as the waiter approached with their entrées. Diana decided this was probably not the time to tell him she might never return to the law firm and the "excellent position" she owed in large part to his influence. Once the waiter had gone, leaving her father staring dubiously at his grilled bluefish—it was criss-crossed with dark lines, like a surveyor's grid—she said, "He'll have to go on being understanding. I can't just tip my hat and walk off into the sunset."

"No one is asking you to do that. But for your own good you must forget this unfortunate interlude. It's over now—"

"How can you say that?" The rising impatience in his voice sparked an answering flash of anger. "We still don't *know,* Father! I came here looking for Brad. I haven't found him. I'm no closer to finding him than I was three weeks ago!"

"Please lower your voice. People are staring."

He waited until her breathing had quieted before he went on. "He's dead. Can you accept that now?"

"I . . . Yes."

"Then you've found out what you most needed to know. As for finding . . . him—that will happen eventually. I intend . . . What is it?"

Sooner or later—kids or dogs . . . Diana forced the grisly image from her mind. "Nothing. What do you intend?"

"To instigate a search for Brad's body, of course. The police will have to take action now, there is sufficient evidence to justify it. We'll hire extra manpower if that seems advisable. Something may turn up in the fellow's apartment that will give us a clue. Or he may have boasted to one of his friends."

He was eating with good appetite. Diana pushed shrimp and bits of crab around her plate. "Good."

Her father put down his fork. "My dear, I agree the food is abominable, but try to eat something."

The kindness in his voice was more demoralizing than his disapproval, and his next words drove a great gap through her defenses. "If I sounded dictatorial, it was because I care very much about your happiness. You are all I have left now."

She could only stare at him, her eyes blurred by tears. She expected a gentle remonstrance—public displays of emotion were anathema to him—but instead he smiled. "Trite, I agree; but in this case it is a simple statement of fact. There is no other woman, Diana. Not one I care about. I don't want to make the same mistake with you that I made with Brad. Stay here as long as you like, do whatever you think best. I'll back you up in anything you choose to do—" He paused, thought for a moment, and then said anxiously, "Are you . . . You aren't seriously interested in that young man, are you?"

"Which young man?" Diana asked.

He studied her for a moment; then his mouth twitched. "That would be a genuine test of my sincerity, wouldn't it? All right, you win. Either of them. I'll hire him, adopt him, give you away to him. On the whole, I think I'd prefer the strong silent sullen gentleman with the muscles to the loquacious youth with the garish taste in haberdashery."

Diana laughed and wiped away the last traces of tears. "You knew Andy was making fun of you, didn't you?"

"Of course. I found him rather amusing, but I'm afraid twenty or thirty years of it might get on my nerves."

"Don't worry. I'm not seriously interested in either. Nor vice versa."

"I find that difficult to believe. Tell me about them. Not that I don't believe you, but I like to be prepared for all eventualities."

He wasn't really interested, he was only trying to find a less distressing topic of conversation. Diana was perfectly willing to comply, but it was impossible to avoid mentioning Brad; Andy's penchant for collecting antique cars and large dogs led her to talk about his other interests, such as roses and poetry, and that led to the story Andy had told her about his conversation with her brother. Again, her father deftly turned her to a less emotional subject.

"You seem to have become quite interested in horticulture. I deduce this not so much from the information you've acquired— you always were a quick, thorough study—but from the dirt under your fingernails."

She could have sworn his eyes were twinkling. "It's not dirt," she protested with a smile. "The local clay leaves a stain."

They lingered over coffee and dessert, talking easily and without constraint. The mood held until they had almost reached the house. The sun had vanished behind a bank of gathering clouds, and a corresponding shadow enveloped Diana's spirits. She let out a sigh. Her father gave her a quick sidelong glance. "Are you sure you won't come back with me tonight? We can send someone for the car later—"

"No, that would be silly. Why don't you spend the night? The weather looks threatening, and it's a long drive."

"As you know, I like to drive, especially at night. Less traffic. Don't worry, I'll stop somewhere if the weather worsens." He stopped in front of the house. "I don't see any vehicles. Your friends aren't back yet, it appears."

"They'll be here soon, I'm sure."

"It's a handsome old place," her father said, studying the facade. "How old did you say it was?"

Diana obliged with a brief history of the house. Her mind wasn't on what she was saying; she dreaded being alone in a house full of shadows with a storm on the way—and with her own thoughts. Finally she said, "You've never really seen the house. Would you like a tour? I shouldn't keep you, though."

"I'm in no hurry. It's only a six-hour drive, and I don't have to be at the office until after noon."

He had never shown any interest in historic houses before, but it was not until he asked to see the upstairs that she began to wonder. Had he sensed her own uneasiness, or did he, like herself, harbor suspicions he was reluctant to share for fear of worrying her? Surely not, Diana thought. He wouldn't leave me here if he believed there was any danger. He'd use that argument to convince me I ought to go with him.

They ended up in the library, where Diana displayed the new mantel and described Andy's exploration of the concealed staircase. Her father was amused, but he shook his head disapprovingly. "Foolhardy and childish." He turned his head, listening. "That sounded like thunder. Shall I close the windows?"

"You're just trying to avoid Miss Matilda," Diana said, scooping up the cat that was advancing along the back of the sofa toward her father. "Cats always pick the laps of the people who don't like them."

"I don't dislike them." Her father got up and went to the window. "Indifference is the most accurate— Excuse me. Frog in my throat. May as well lock these; where is— Ah, I've found it. I guess it's time I was leaving."

"I'll go to the door with you."

"Don't bother, you look very comfortable with the cat on your lap." He leaned over to kiss her. "You'll be all right?"

"Of course. Drive carefully."

"I always do. Good night, my dear. Sleep well." He left the room; after a moment she heard the front door close.

Sleep well— Would she sleep without dreaming, now that "it was over"? Or would her unconscious body rise and walk, searching for the thing she still had not found? She could not tell her skeptical, rational father why she was so certain Brad was dead. Some sense other than sight had allowed her to witness his murder. Some sense beyond the normal senses had tried to lead her— where? Not toward the barn, Andy had said. Those poor scraps of mortality had not been Brad. Strange, though, that another man, a young man, had met a similar fate—a violent death, a secret burial.

Not Brad. She fastened on that; her head felt as if it were about to split open, not with pain but with an eerie pressure. Not Brad, not toward the barn. Toward the rose garden and the stream. Toward the place she had seen dimly in the darkness of a dream.

Diana's dilated eyes went to the cat curled on her lap. Miss Matilda let out a squeak of protest as Diana snatched her up and put her aside. The bolt on the window was stiff, she had to wrestle with it, her fingers slippery with sweat, before it yielded. Leaving the window open, she ran.

She was gasping for breath when she reached the glade. An early, unnatural dusk cast gray light over the spreading branches and the silent stones. One of them lay face-down, as usual. Next to it the quiet earth had been violated. A heap of dirt and a hole, six feet deep—and Andy, holding a stained shovel in his hand. He was breathing almost as heavily as she.

The silence seemed to last for an eternity. Then he spoke, though she would not have known the voice was his if she had not actually seen him. "How did you know?"

CHAPTER NINETEEN

See the last orange roses, how they blow
Deeper and heavier than in their prime,
In one defiant flame before they go,

—Vita Sackville-West

She hadn't known, not for certain. Not until that moment.

Diana's lungs strained for breath. The air was thick with heat and the moisture of the hovering storm. It was so dark under the trees she couldn't see Andy's features clearly. He had tossed his shirt over the other stone, the one belonging to George's wife Amaranth, and he looked taller, heavier than she remembered. For one wild instant she saw another man, a stranger, confronting her, with a sharp-edged spade in his hand and her brother's body under his feet.

"You couldn't have seen me," Andy went on in a conversational tone. The voice at least was unmistakably his. "I left the van in the back pasture and walked to the toolshed."

"I didn't see you."

"Then how—Well. Irrelevant and immaterial," he said with forced jauntiness. "Go back to the house, Diana."

"Why?"

"You don't want to see this."

"You mean—" Her breathing was almost normal now, but she had to take a deep breath before she could go on. "You mean you don't want me to see it."

"What are you—"

"I'm not leaving. I have to know."

He moved with startling quickness, swinging the shovel up, his feet silent on the carpet of pine needles that cushioned all sound.

He was not quite quick enough. The stick thudded against the upraised wooden haft, knocking it out of his hand, and struck his temple. The back of his head skimmed the edge of the standing stone as he fell full-length beside the open grave.

Diana pushed the other man out of her way and knelt beside Andy. The storm seemed to be blowing away; there was more light now, and wind rattled the branches overhead. Her hand found the pulse beating slow and steady in Andy's throat and then moved to his head, feeling the sticky seepage of blood. He stirred a little when she touched him and muttered unintelligibly. The sound was barely audible over the murmur of the pines.

Then she looked up at her father.

"He isn't dead."

"Get away from him, then. He's already tried to kill you."

"You know I don't believe that."

"He was about to—"

"He was trying to defend himself. He saw you raise the stick. If he hadn't managed to deflect the blow it might have crushed his skull. The knob of that stick is gold. Heavy metal."

Her father said nothing. He was in his shirt sleeves, his tie loosened. It was a relaxation of standards he only permitted himself when he was hard at work, alone in his office. His face had the same intent look of concentration she had seen on those few occasions when she had ventured to intrude on him there.

Finally he said quietly, "Is that where Brad is buried?"

"Yes."

"How did he"—the stick swung, indicating Andy—"know it was here? Why didn't he tell the authorities of his suspicions instead of creeping here like a grave robber?"

Diana sat back on her heels. So this was to be a battle of wits—at least in the beginning. It was the kind of battle at which her father excelled and, win or lose, she was certain to lose in the end. That seemed unimportant now.

"That argument would have considerable weight with a jury," she agreed. "But his explanation may be equally convincing—assuming he is alive to make it. Your other question implies that he was afraid the grave would be found and he wanted to make certain he had left no incriminating evidence when he buried Brad. That same implication could be used to make a case against me. Or against you, Father. Why did you come back?"

"I was worried about you. The weather was threatening."

Like an ironic commentary from some higher authority, a feeble shaft of sunlight straggled through the branches. Andy was mumbling and trying to move; shadows shifted across his twitching face.

"You came back," Diana said, "because when you went to close the window you saw Andy crossing the pasture, carrying a shovel. He might have been planning to plant something; Andy's nutty enough to start a project like that with a storm coming on. But you don't know him that well, and you did know something else. You left rather abruptly. I suppose you drove a little distance and then left the car and walked back—straight to this place. How did you know where it was unless you'd been here before?"

Andy sat up. "Listen, Di," he croaked, "this may not be the best time to—" His eyes rolled up and his head fell back. She managed to catch him in time to avoid another uncomfortable encounter with a tombstone, throwing both arms around him and pulling his head against her breast.

"He's right, you know," her father said coolly. "This is all conjecture. I may have been mistaken about the young man's intentions, but no one could blame me for misinterpreting them or for trying, as I believed, to protect you. We know who killed your brother—"

"Oh, yes. We do, don't we? I always doubted Larry was guilty. I just didn't want to face the possibility that it might be—someone else. He was capable of killing Brad in a fit of rage, and of concealing his body, but stealing that watch was out of character for him and for the type of crime we had postulated. The postcard from New York was the major stumbling block, though. I found it hard to believe Larry would be clever enough to think of laying a false trail, or of carrying out the plan with such cold-blooded thoroughness.

"I never thought of you, Father. I should have. You jeered at my suspicions and kept trying to turn my attention back to New York, until Larry presented himself as a potential killer. Then all of a sudden you were on my side. You had hoped Brad's body would never be found, but there was always a chance it might be. This was an even better solution—a man who had a motive and who had demonstrated his capacity for violence. You knew Larry would never be able to prove his innocence. It was unlikely that he could produce a valid alibi; few people can remember what they were doing on a given night eight months ago, and after such a long time it would be impossible to tell exactly when Brad died. You may even have counted on badgering and bewildering him into confessing. You're good at that."

She stopped speaking, straining to hear. Was that a voice, calling her name? Mary Jo and Walt should be back before long. Blood had soaked through the sleeve of her blouse; she felt it sticky against her skin, and she also felt the warm, steady rhythm of Andy's breath. He lay quiet in her grasp, but the muscles of his back felt like stretched rubber. He was hoarding his strength, waiting for the right moment. It might come to that, but not until after she had used every other weapon in her arsenal. Her father had helped provide and hone those weapons. He ought to be proud of her skill in using them.

"This was how it happened the last time, wasn't it, Father? Did you use your stick on Brad too? It wouldn't have been necessary; a blow or even a push could have done the job, if his head struck one of the stones. Oh, I can believe it was an accident. But what you did afterward was no accident.

"You could have carried him into the woods. It's hard to dig there, though, through tangled roots and rocky soil. The ground here is soft under the pines, and you thought this was an old cemetery, didn't you? That the stones marked graves. Much easier to dig where the ground has already been disturbed. I'd like to believe you were also moved by some moribund streak of senti-ment—some idea of laying him to rest in consecrated ground."

Her voice, which had been so abnormally steady, broke. Andy stirred; she tightened her grip, holding him down. She hadn't used the ultimate weapon yet. That last shaft had gone wide; her father's face was unmoved, cold as ice.

"You went back to the barn and got a shovel. After you had— Afterward, you packed Brad's things. There weren't many; he traveled light. The only person who might have seen you was poor old Miss Musser, and you weren't worried about her; she was too old and feeble to interfere with you and nobody would have be-lieved her if she had told them. Everybody thought she was senile. You knew that; you had read Brad's letters, after I passed them on to Mother. How could I have supposed you wouldn't? You always have to know everything. 'Knowledge is power,' you used to say. You couldn't just ask to see Brad's letters, that would be confessing how much you cared about him. You were too much of a coward to do that."

Finally, a shaft struck home. His mouth twisted, with pain or anger, she could not tell which. She went on without pausing, keeping up the pressure—as he had taught her to do.

"The only thing I'm not sure of is why you came to see him. I can hazard a guess, though. That last letter of Brad's mentioned his suspicion that someone was taking advantage of Miss Musser. Another of the letters contained a disparaging remark about her lawyer. If he suspected that kind of misconduct, whom would he consult? He couldn't have reached me; I was in Europe last August, on vacation. He called you, didn't he? He cared more about a helpless, senile old woman than he did about preserving his pride.

"How you must have reveled in that! You wanted him back. You had hoped he'd tire of wandering and working, that he'd come crawling to you admitting he was wrong and asking for forgiveness. He didn't do that, but at least it was he who made the first move. Your pride was intact, and your monstrous insensivity misled you into believing what you wanted to believe—that his request was only an excuse for a rapprochement. You came here hoping, expecting, to take him home with you. If you had pleaded with him—told him you loved him, begged his forgiveness—"

She had to stop again to clear her throat. "You didn't though, did you? What in God's name did you say to him, to bring on such a terrible ending? Did you threaten him? 'Come back, be my docile obedient son, or I'll throw your mother onto the trash heap and beget more sons on another woman'?"

The wind roared through the branches, and the shadows danced along the ground. It was not shadow that changed his face so horribly, though. The struggle of conscious will to maintain control, against the inner agony that twisted muscle and flesh, told her she had won—and that winning might have been the last mistake she would ever make.

Andy lifted his head. Slowly, as he would have moved in the presence of a feral animal, he shifted position until he was sitting upright, knees bent and feet braced. "Watch it," he said under his breath.

She couldn't stop, though. She had waited for this all her life—

wanting it and dreading it at the same time. "I wonder how you felt when you realized he was wearing the watch you gave him," she said. "I thought he'd taken it to hock it or sell it. He could have used the money. But he kept it. He had a picture of you too—the one he took at my graduation, you and me and Mother. Is it still in his wallet, or did you—"

"Diana." Even knowing him as she did, she would not have believed he could do it. His face shone with perspiration, but it was the familiar, rigidly controlled mask and his voice was—almost—steady. "You have been under a considerable strain. I don't blame you for letting your imagination run away with you. Stop a moment and think. Even if your wild theories were correct—which of course they are not—what possible good could come of expressing them? You have no case. You know that. Nothing can bring your brother back. If you want to cause me pain, as is evidently the case, the publicity, the shame, and public exposure will also hurt you, and God knows what it would do to your mother. Is it worth that?"

"That depends on what you mean by 'it,' Father."

Only the sibilant murmur of the trees broke the silence for a time. The wind had subsided and the sun had broken through; one ray shone like a spotlight on his ravaged face. Incredibly, his lips curved in a smile. "Ah, yes, I see. I can dimly remember believing in it myself once. A long time ago."

"They're back," Andy said suddenly. "I hear Mary Jo calling."

"In that case," said John Randall, "I had better be off."

Andy let out his breath. Randall gave him a quizzical look. "You didn't think I was going to commit double homicide, did you? That was never an alternative. Diana has now removed the only one remaining." His eyes went to her. "I hope you will allow me the privilege of carrying out your wishes in my own way. Goodbye. My dear."

He left the way he had come, in the concealment of the trees. The sound of his passage was hidden by the rustle of foliage.

Andy got to his feet and gave Diana a hand to help her up. His hair bristled with pine needles and clotted blood and the rest of him didn't look much better. Wordlessly he held out his arms.

For a time she was conscious of nothing except the warmth and strength of him, the comfort of his grasp and his silent, passionate sharing of her pain. She could hear the steady beat of his heart against her cheek, feel the touch of his lips on her hair. It was enough to keep the demons at bay for a while—long enough to gather strength, from him, in order to face what had to be done.

Andy's arms tightened. "Oh, my God," he whispered.

Diana raised her head. "What is it? Are you—"

Andy had gone pale. "That's not Mary Jo. That's my mother!"

"I will never forgive you for this!" Emily exclaimed.

She meant it, too. Diana would not have believed she could look so formidable—eyes snapping, teeth bared, cheeks flaming with anger. She thanked heaven Emily's fury was not directed at her.

Andy had rolled himself up into a defensive ball like a porcupine. "Ma, I was only trying—"

"This time you've gone too far, Andrew Davis! Of all the arrogant, cocksure, conceited men I have ever encountered, you are the worst. Trying to protect me! I'm twice your age and fifty times your superior in everything worth mentioning, including common sense! How the hell do you suppose I managed all those years, supporting you and trying to raise you right—an endeavor that obviously failed miserably—after your no-good father walked out on me and before I met Charlie? Charlie doesn't try to protect me!"

Andy looked involuntarily at his stepfather. Charles's face remained impassive, but Andy must have seen something no one else saw, for he uncoiled himself and sat up, squaring his shoulders. "Now look, Ma—"

"And this poor girl!" Emily pounced on Diana and threw both arms around her. "Keeping me away from her, when what she needed was the sympathy of an older, more experienced woman. And that poor girl—" She released Diana and ran to Mary Jo. "She needed me too. Me and Charles. Whatever possessed you to suppose you could handle this dreadful situation by yourselves?"

"Uh—Mrs. Nicholson," Walt began.

"You're as bad as Andy!" Emily whirled and shook a finger under Walt's nose. "You be quiet. Be quiet, all of you. I have to start making plans. Thank goodness I called Barbara Williams this morning to ask her if she wanted me to bring her some perennials. She told me everything. She was shocked when she found out you hadn't told me. Shocked!"

Diana looked at her clasped hands. Emily was going to be even more shocked than Barbara Williams (president of the local garden club) when she discovered that she still didn't know everything.

Brad's grave was empty now. The police had come and gone. The news of that discovery had stunned Emily into silence for a while, and concentrated her monumental gift of sympathy on Diana. It had taken two more hours—thanks in part to Emily's constant interruptions and shrieks of rage—to bring Charles and Emily up-to-date and fill in the missing pieces of the story.

All the pieces except one.

Diana's eyes focused on her watch. Nine o'clock. He was well on his way by now. She wondered how and when it would happen, and how she would feel. So far she had been remarkably calm. Shock, Emily called it, and tried to stuff her with food, disgustingly sweet tea, and various alcoholic beverages. It wasn't so much shock, Diana thought, as paralysis—a complete blockage of emotion.

Andy was watching her. She knew what he was thinking; she would always know what Andy was thinking. He was going to leave it up to her, to speak or remain silent.

Justice of a sort would be served if—when—her father did what he had implied he would do. Justice or retribution— Was there a difference? It would serve no purpose to make the matter public, but Mary Jo at least deserved to know the truth. Diana had no idea whether it would matter to Mary Jo, but she knew she had to offer that possible solace.

Not yet, though. The situation was complicated enough. Emily was still trying to cope with the complications. The spectacle of a small, fluffy infuriated lady bellowing at her tall cowering son had offered some moments of welcome comic relief, but Emily hadn't intended to be funny. She was genuinely distressed, and the warmth of concern that enveloped Diana reminded her of those moments in the glade when Andy had wrapped her in his arms and in his caring. A hereditary trait, obviously.

They had moved to the library after a hodgepodge meal no one felt like eating. Now Emily sat down on the sofa next to Diana. Her face was pink and crumpled with sympathy. "You poor child. What can we do for you?"

"You can yell at me if you like," Diana said with a faint smile. "After what I did to you—"

"Oh, that." Emily patted her hand. "I think you were wonderfully brave and clever to think of it. Forget that. What can I do to help?"

"You could change the subject, Ma," said Andy, now sprawled at ease on the other sofa with two cats on his stomach. "Everything that can be done has been done . . . for now. Maybe she'd like to forget it for a while. You haven't complimented us on the new mantel, or the drapes, or any of that stuff. We worked our tails off. Especially Walt."

"It does look nice," Emily said. "And I do appreciate all you've done—all of you. But I want—"

This distraction having failed, Andy put his life on the line with heroic gallantry. "Let me tell you about the hidden staircase."

It succeeded only too well. He must have expected Emily to respond as she did; her imagination was quite as exuberant as his. He must also have known how Charles was going to react, not only to the wanton destruction of his property, but to the enthusiastic response of his wife.

"But Andy, darling, how fascinating," Emily exclaimed. "We'll have to search the rest of the debris. You couldn't have found everything . . . What did you say, Walt?"

"Nothing, ma'am," said Walt.

"Outrageous," Charles sputtered. "Smashing walls, breaking down doors—"

"Now, Charlie darling, don't be mean. If you had found the staircase, you'd have done exactly as Andy did."

"Like hell, I would," said Charles. "Dangling on the end of a rope, smashing—"

"That was foolish," Emily agreed. She ran a considering eye over her son's long frame. "You do look a little the worse for wear, Andy. If you were eight years old instead of twenty-eight, I'd suspect you'd been fighting."

"Not me, Ma. You know I'm a pacifist at heart."

There was a brief silence, while Walt tried to look inconspicuous and Andy tried to look like a pacifist and Charles looked suspiciously from one of them to the other.

Mary Jo cleared her throat. "Guess I'd better pack my stuff. It's getting late."

"You aren't going back to that nasty little room of yours tonight," Emily said calmly. "Nor ever, if I have anything to say about it. When is the funeral?"

"I don't know yet. Everything is arranged, though. I talked to Reverend Layton today, and the funeral home. And I picked out a casket."

"What a horrible day you had," Diana murmured, thinking of the days she had yet to face.

"I wanted to get it over with," Mary Jo said briefly. "I've got that exam tomorrow."

Andy shifted a cat that had settled on his face. "I talked to the Reverend too, Ma. About the bones in the barn. It's all set. We'll have to pay for a plot—"

"Of course. I'm so glad you thought of it, darling. I hope you found a nice place for the poor thing."

"I thought I'd leave the decision up to you. There are several empty places."

Emily's brow wrinkled. "That's the Episcopal church, isn't it? I hope he won't mind. What if he was Catholic or Jewish or Moslem or—"

"We'll just have to do the best we can, Ma."

"True. He'll know our intentions were good, at any rate. I wonder if we'll ever know who he was and what happened to him."

Lying awake in the darkness after midnight, Diana heard the distant ringing of the telephone. She had been waiting for it.

Emily had insisted on tucking Diana into bed and giving her a sleeping pill, which Diana had politely accepted and quietly dropped into the wastebasket after Emily left the room. She had intended to creep downstairs and wait for the call in the library, after the others had gone to bed; but Emily hadn't gone to bed. She and Charles were still in the library, talking. They had plenty to talk about. Never, perhaps, had an innocent couple gone off for a harmless vacation and returned to find such a horrendous set of problems on their hands.

After a while Diana heard the footsteps outside. She had left her door ajar; when it opened wider she sat up and switched on the light. "Come in," she said. "I'm not asleep."

Emily's eyes moved from her face to the suitcases, packed and waiting, by the door. "You expected this," she said quietly.

"Yes. I'm sorry you were disturbed."

Emily trotted to the bed and sat down, taking Diana's hands in hers. Andy took her place in the doorway. Diana realized she hadn't been the only one to lie awake waiting for a telephone call.

"Tell her, Ma. Don't try to soften it."

"Of course." Emily gave her son a hard stare before turning back to Diana. "He was killed instantly, Diana, they are sure of that. He drove into a concrete bridge support—it happened on Route 95, a few miles past Wilmington. Witnesses said he was going fast, over eighty. The police think he had a heart attack or fell asleep; his foot must have—"

"It wasn't a heart attack," Diana said. Straight into a concrete slab, fully conscious, seeing it loom up, seeing the windshield splinter . . . He could have found an easier way. Was it because she had called him a coward?

Emily's hard little hands tightened. "I wondered if there was something. Do you want to tell me?"

Andy moved aside to admit Mary Jo. She had been asleep; her hair was rumpled and she was rubbing her eyes. Their voices must have wakened her.

"He killed Brad," Diana said. "It wasn't Larry, Mary Jo. When he said he was sorry, he meant—"

"He was always sorry afterward." There might have been kinder epitaphs, but none more appropriate. The distress on Mary Jo's face was not for herself. "Diana, are you sure?"

"Yes. I'd better get up."

"There's nothing you can do for him now," Emily said, her eyes luminous with the tears Diana was unable to shed. "Wait till morning."

"The nurse won't wake Mother at this hour, but she'll find out in the morning. I have to be there."

"Oh, good Lord," Emily murmured. "I didn't think . . . You are not going alone, Diana."

"No," Andy said. "She's not going alone."

CHAPTER TWENTY

Une rose d'automne est plus qu'une autre exquise.

—Théodore Agrippa d'Aubigné

*T*he banner hanging above the front door had been painted on an old bed sheet by someone who was completely devoid of calligraphic talent and/or high on some illegal chemical substance. One of the lower ends had come loose and was flapping in the breeze, but the message was legible. "Welcome home."

Diana got out of the car and stood looking around. Walt must have worked his crew to the point of rebellion; she wouldn't have believed so much could be done in less than a month. The lawn glowed as smooth as green velvet in the rays of the afternoon sun; two giant magnolias raised stately branches above flower beds filled with bright blossoming annuals.

Then the front door opened and they came spilling out, jostling one another in their eagerness to be the first to greet her, all talking at once. "You're late! We were beginning to worry. What took you so long? It's so good to see you . . ." All the things people said to a loved and long-awaited guest.

Charles was the first to reach her, his blue eyes warm with welcome. He took her hand in both of his—no cheap, sentimental embraces for Charles—but Emily was close behind him and she had no complexes about hugs and kisses. Andy waited till his mother backed off before throwing a fraternal arm around Diana's shoulders and planting a chaste kiss on her forehead.

"Where are Walt and Mary Jo?" she asked, as Emily tugged her toward the house. Andy followed with her suitcases.

"They had to make a quick trip to the store. The icemaker broke down—you might know it would, just when I want to give a party." Emily saw her face and added gently, "It's just us, Diana. None of us wanted outsiders."

They led her in ceremonial procession to the library, made her sit down, put her feet up. "Something to drink," Emily said. "What would you like? Iced tea—"

"There's no ice, my dear," Charles reminded her.

"How about some brandy?" Andy grinned at her.

She smiled back at him, remembering those unspeakable days when his presence at her side had been the only stability in a shaking universe, and his silly jokes had broken the tension when it peaked into unendurability. He had been particularly good with the press. They had swarmed like insects, attracted by the drama of it all—the courageous young seeker after truth and the sorrowing, broken mother, their loss of brother and son compounded by the tragic death of father and husband. John Randall's death was attributed to grief for his son. ("Tears blinded him," as one of the tabloids put it.) Fortunately the discovery of seventeen mutilated bodies buried in a backyard in Cleveland distracted the ghouls after only a few days.

She had walked steadily through those days as if enclosed in a shell of transparent glass, conscious of Andy not as an individual but as a source of strength and comfort. She had not broken down until the day of her father's funeral, when she had opened the door in response to a peremptory knock and found one of the security guards looming over a smaller, slimmer form.

"She made me let her in," the guard said in some confusion. "Wouldn't go away. Sorry if I did wrong, but she wouldn't . . . "

Mary Jo took a firmer grip on her shabby suitcase. "Emily made me come. Not that I didn't want to. I thought . . . But she said . . ."

"I didn't dare ask you," Diana said. "How was the exam?"

"Not one of my better efforts. But I passed."

She was wearing black—a cheap new polyester knit suit and a shiny black straw hat with a wide brim. Mary Jo wearing a hat . . . It was proper. It was what you wore to a funeral. Diana felt something crack, deep inside her.

"She said she was a friend of yours," the guard said anxiously.

"She is." The cracks spread in a widening network and the crystal enclosure shattered; the tears she had not been able to shed spilled out.

They had to put Mary Jo's suit jacket in the dryer before they left for the service.

The sound of voices brought Diana out of her reverie. Mary Jo and Walt had come back; they were, as usual, arguing. "What'd you have to take it out of the bag for? It's dripping. Get out of here. Put it in the kitchen."

"I was going to! Why do you always—"

"Just shut up and do it."

Walt did not shut up; his comments reverberated down the hall until the slam of the kitchen door cut them off. By that time Mary Jo was sitting on the sofa beside Diana.

"You made it. We were getting worried. You should have let me stay and drive you down."

"You had other things to do—and so did Andy."

"Him?" Mary Jo turned a disparaging eye on Andy. "I don't know what. He hasn't worked since—"

"Don't start on me," Andy mumbled. "Beat up on Walt, he's used to it."

"I better see what kind of a mess he's making," Mary Jo said, jumping up. "We'll bring some ice and something to drink. You just sit still and rest—you too, Emily, we've got everything under control."

"She's been like this all day," Emily said disapprovingly, as Mary Jo trotted out. "Cleaning, cooking, fussing. I keep trying to tell her it's really her party but she won't stop and be guest of honor."

Mary Jo reappeared in the doorway. "I forgot. The barbecue. Andy, you go start it or the coals won't be ready in time."

"I'll do it." Charles rose hastily. "He'll dump a can of lighter fluid on it and set fire to the house."

"A vile canard," said Andy, stretching out on the sofa. A cat promptly advanced, walked the length of his body, and settled down on his chest.

For a time the silence was broken only by the rasping purr of the cat. Then Emily said gently, "How is your mother?"

"Better. That's all she'll ever be, I think—not well, but better. An old friend of hers, someone she knew in college, recently lost her husband; they're talking about setting up housekeeping together."

"That would be wonderful. And you. You're all right now, aren't you?"

"Better," Diana said. "Better all the time. I'm not dreaming now. Andy told you, didn't he?"

"The whole thing. I hope you don't mind."

"I thought you'd get it out of him."

"I felt her myself," Emily said. "Not as intensely as you did, only as a faint presence that came and went. I never heard the music distinctly, just the suggestion of sound beyond the range of hearing."

Diana shifted uneasily. "I don't believe it, you know. Everything that happened can be explained in terms of autosuggestion and collective hallucination. My state of mind was abnormal—"

"And therefore receptive," Emily broke in. "She wouldn't come to me; there was no need. Your arrival struck the spark that crossed time and dimensions because the pattern was the same—loss and grief and uncertainty. She couldn't communicate in words, or even control the feelings and sensations she projected. That, I think, is why you received such bewildering, contradictory impressions— tenderness and horror, yearning and fear and doubt. Especially doubt. She went to her death not knowing what had happened to him. They probably told her he had gone away—abandoned her."

"He," Diana repeated. "You're thinking of the remains from the barn, aren't you? I don't mean to cast cold water on your theory—"

"You mean my wild fantasy," Emily said placidly. "It may be no more than that. But it makes a nice logical story, don't you think? Only a resident of the house could have—would have— buried him there. He meant something to someone who lived here. He wasn't a member of the family or he would have been given a proper grave and tombstone. He has them now—well, not the tombstone, it isn't finished yet—but I'm sure she's pleased about that."

" 'We buried him in the old churchyard,' " Andy crooned.

" 'And laid her there beside him.' " Emily sang in a sweet cracked voice. "Only it was the other way around, of course."

"What are you talking about, Ma?" Andy pushed the cat's tail off his face. "We don't know where she's buried. You put him next to—"

"Well, of course," Emily said. "Why do you suppose I insisted on that plot? She was the last of the family, so there was plenty of room. Her father probably thought she'd marry and have lots of—"

"Ma." Andy sat up. "What are you up to now? This is Martha's long-lost lover we're talking about. At least you and I are talking about him . . . Aren't we?"

"I thought you'd have sense enough to figure it out for yourself."
His mother looked at him reproachfully. "Martha Fairweather
died almost two hundred years ago. Professor Handson told you
he'd been there for a century, give or take fifty years; you didn't
want to believe that because you were fixated on your own romantic fantasy."

"Pots and kettles," Andy muttered, staring wide-eyed at his
mother.

"At least my fantasy doesn't contradict the facts. I suppose I
can't blame you for being so stupid. You young people can't believe
that everyone was young once. *Everyone.*"

Andy continued to stare, his mouth opening and closing. His
mother made clucking, exasperated noises, and went to the library
table. "It's so obvious! The clues were piled up so high I can't
believe you overlooked them. Neither of you bothered to read *The
Rosebud Girl,* did you?"

"That corny old book by Miss Musser's friend?" Diana gasped.
"No. You don't mean—"

"It's dedicated to her." Emily opened the book. "To Miss Matilda Musser, the original 'Rosebud Girl.' Miss Matilda loved roses.
The garden was hers; roses are astonishingly tough, but those had
obviously received recent care." She put the book down and picked
up another volume, bound in purple plush. "You looked at the
photos—some of them. Obviously you didn't see this one."

The face was that of a young girl, smooth cheeks delicately
curved by the smile that displayed small white teeth. Luxuriant
dark hair crowned her head; a rose nestled in the ruffled lace at
her slender throat.

"She was seventeen when this picture was taken, in 1915," Emily
said. "A century ago—give or take twenty years."

Diana's memory supplied an image of another photo—that of
a hard-faced rigid old woman leaning on a stick. Sometimes life
could be much crueler than death.

Emily turned pages. "They were still using horses and wagons,
buckboards, carriages, before World War One, especially in rural
areas. Matilda's father was conservative; he didn't buy his first car
until 1928."

Andy was struggling with disbelief. "How do you know it was
the first?"

Emily deftly slipped the photo from the grip of the old-fashioned
paper "corners" that held it. "It's on the back. 'Papa's first au-

tomobile.' " Replacing the picture, she turned more pages. "Here's the one I wanted to show you."

They joined her at the table.

"I saw that one," Andy said. "It's a good shot of the barn. Must have been taken by a professional photographer."

"It was taken to commemorate the completion of the barn," Emily said.

"That's on the back of the picture too, I suppose," Andy muttered.

"Mmm-hmmm. Along with the names of the people." Emily's forefinger indicated the man in the middle of the group that had been lined up in the foreground. "That's Papa—owner and proprietor. His wife next to him—one step behind, of course, as was fitting—and Matilda on his other side. The little boy was Matilda's brother. He died of influenza a few years later—that terrible epidemic that swept the country after World War One. And these were the servants and hired hands."

Her finger moved along the line of stiffly posed figures—white faces and black, cook and maids and farmhands—and stopped. "His name was Tadeus Waranowski."

"On the back," Andy said, like a parrot.

"All on the back. His name was underlined and marked by a little star. Here."

She handed Diana a magnifying glass.

Under the lens the face jumped out, a little blurred by magnification but boldly distinctive. The self-consciousness that had frozen the other faces had not affected his; under the drooping black mustache white teeth gleamed, and his nose jutted out like the prow of a ship. He looked very young. The mustache might have been designed to conceal that, but it did not succeed.

"He was a carpenter's assistant," Emily said. "That's on the back too—but I think Matilda was exaggerating just a little when she called him that. He was a handyman, a workingman. Itinerant, possibly; there's no record of that last name in the county records. A foreigner, perhaps. An unsuitable match for the daughter of the house, certainly."

Andy put up one last feeble objection. "How did he end up under the floor of the barn he helped build? Hey. Maybe it was one of the other workers who did him in. Hid the body—"

"It's possible," Emily said. "But I don't think so. She was stealing out at night to meet him, if Diana's visions were accurate. Sooner or later—if it hadn't happened already—the delicate flower of a maiden's most precious possession would have been given up to him. That's how Papa would have put it, and how do you think Papa would have reacted if he found his blossom of Southern womanhood in the arms of a dirty foreigner?"

Diana moved the lens. Papa scowled back at her; he hadn't bothered to smile. The arrogance and consciousness of power that marked his face must never have been questioned, least of all by the women whose lives he controlled as completely as did any oriental tyrant.

Andy stiffened. "Listen."

It was faint and slow, too slow for dancing. Crystalline as drops of water falling into a pool, gently, sadly.

"Finally," Walt said, entering with a tray. "Sorry it took so long, Mary Jo kept nattering at me about—" He broke off. The last phrase of the music faded into silence. "Pretty tune," Walt said. "One of those music boxes, huh? Oh, hell, what does that damned woman want now? Back in a minute."

"He heard it," Diana whispered. "He heard it too."

"Music," Andy said in a strangled voice. "Music . . . box? Oh, my God! Why didn't I . . . Where is it? Where'd you put it, Ma? It was in this drawer."

"No, it was not; it was, and still is, in the bottom drawer," said his mother in exasperation. "Stop throwing everything out on the floor. Honestly, Andy!"

The contents of the bottom drawer followed those of the other. Andy pulled out a brown paper bag and turned it upside down onto the table. The doll's head rolled and came to rest face-down; the fragments of its body were tossed aside. Andy snatched up one of the bits of rusted metal.

"Music box," he said again. "That's it. Look. This was a cylinder before it got smashed and flattened. These little knobs produced the notes as the cylinder rotated over a sounding board. Plucked, I said. Harpsichord, I said. Maybe even a guitar, I said. Where's the rest of it?"

"This bit of painted china may have been part of it." Emily plucked the fragment out of the litter. "Bavarian or Austrian, by the look of it. He must have given it to her. A family heirloom? That was her little box of treasures you found, Andy. She was the last person to live in the house before we came. She had years in which to find anything else that might have been hidden—years to brood on his defection, as she thought it, to become cynical and soured and old. She hid the follies of her youth away and painted them shut. That was another clue you missed," she said smugly. "Now put those things back in the drawer."

Diana picked up the broken bit of porcelain. The faded shape painted on it seemed to be a flower.

Summer had come early that year. The roses were in full bloom— the marbled pink-and-white of Rosa Mundi, Rose of the World; the white petals of the Rose of York enclosing a golden heart; the opulent tight-curled pink of the Autumn Damask in its first spring, filling the air with perfume. Marveling, Diana wandered from bush to bush. She felt as if she were meeting old friends, or rather, meeting for the first time people whose names and histories had been long familiar.

"This must be Baron Girod de l'Ain; even I know him, he's unique, with the white rimming the crimson petals."

"A rose that wasn't introduced till 1928." Andy made a sour face. "I should have seen it, I guess. But hell, I knew the garden had to have been cultivated throughout the years, and new plants introduced."

"You're a convert, then."

"I hate to admit it. Ma will gloat for months. And you? You still won't believe it, will you?"

Diana turned to face him. "What difference does it make? Let me enjoy a condition of receptive skepticism."

The boxwood hedges had been clipped and thinned. Faintly in the distance they could hear the sound of voices from the patio by the pool—another of Walt's recent achievements. One voice rose in insistent commentary; Andy smiled. "You think those two will get together?"

"I doubt it."

"He's crazy about her, you know."

"She won't let another man, however crazy about her, deflect her from what she means to do. At least I hope she won't. Why does a happy ending have to be two people falling into one another's arms?"

"It's one kind of happy ending. Does that mean you're planning to jilt me?"

"Where do you get these archaic notions? I never said—"

"You introduced me as your fi-ant-see."

"Well, what the hell was I supposed to call you? There was enough scandal and innuendo as it was; people like my mother—and yours—are old-fashioned about such things."

"I suppose 'friend' has lost its meaning," Andy said quietly.

"Not to me. Andy, I never thanked you properly—"

"You're trying to change the subject. Does this mean you refuse to live with me and be my love, or my significant other, or my wife or something, and support me while I go to law school?"

Diana gasped. "That is probably the least romantic proposal any woman ever . . . Are you serious? About law school, I mean?"

"It's about time I settled down to something."

"But why that?"

"So I can rob the rich and grind the poor and make lots of money. Why else? So you won't assist me in this worthy endeavor?"

"Certainly not."

"It's just as well I managed to save some money, then." His impudent grin faded. "That wasn't my only reason for suggesting the idea."

"No?"

"You may have noticed that I never made the ghost of a pass at you.

"I did notice."

"You didn't hear the shower running for hours at a time? Or notice how many long walks I took?"

"Andy, don't make me laugh. It isn't funny."

"Damn right," Andy said emphatically. "It's all Ma's fault. She was born in Nebraska, but she's a Southern lady at heart and she pounded it into me from an early age. 'A gentleman doesn't take advantage of a lady when she's vulnerable.' You were very vulnerable, Diana."

"Don't, Andy." She turned away from his outstretched hand. "Not now. Especially not here. I don't object to romance, but a rose garden at twilight is just too damned much."

"That's what I told Ma, but you know her. Are you ready for it, Diana?"

His hand still reached out to her. Wordlessly she took it and let him lead her along the path.

Dying light filled the glade with a luminous afterglow. The ground was carpeted with flowers. The violets were gone, but their heart-shaped leaves gave promise of another spring. The tiny azure blossoms of forget-me-not covered the area that had been her brother's grave.

She sat down on the simple wooden bench that had been placed under the trees. The stones had been moved closer together and propped by stakes.

"Ma decided to leave them here." Andy remained standing. "We'll put up some kind of simple shelter, a roof to protect them from rain and sunlight, and a more permanent support to keep them from falling." He went on without pausing, and in the same quiet voice. "Was that how you knew?"

"George's stone, you mean? It was partly that. I remember thinking, weeks ago, that the ground under it must be undermined by animal tunnels or . . ." She wasn't ready for that yet. Perhaps she never would be. "I didn't know for certain. It was no one thing, it was a gradual accumulation of them. This was the place I saw in my dream—not the darkness of an enclosed space, but night under the trees, and the shapes of the stones. I heard the sound when his head hit one of them. And don't tell me I'm being inconsistent, denying the validity of those experiences in one breath and then using them as evidence!"

"Not me, kid," Andy said. "I'm all for inconsistency."

"I sat there in the library after Father left," Diana went on. "Thinking how he'd changed. He'd been so kind, so sympathetic; he even made little jokes. And then—oh, God, I don't know, I can't begin to explain it—it was like a sly soft voice far back in my mind, whispering, 'He never behaved that way before. He never does anything without a reason. What reason could he have for wanting your love, your allegiance—now?' All the pieces seemed to snap together—my doubts about Larry's guilt, Brad's watch, Father's sudden change of heart. He knew where Mother kept Brad's letters. I remembered my dream and the fallen stone and . . . I can't explain how I knew. Maybe it was Miss Matilda forcing knowledge into my head. That makes as much sense as any other theory. I just got up and ran mindlessly."

"Lucky for me you did."

"I don't know what he would have done," Diana said slowly. "I don't want to know. There was nothing to incriminate him, after all, was there?"

"No. He couldn't be sure, though. He—even he—can't have been in control of himself when he buried his only son."

"What made you go to look? You didn't know what I knew."

"I wasn't sure either. That's why I sneaked out there alone; I didn't want to get you upset for no reason. It was something Reverend Layton said that started me wondering. I went with Mary Jo to see him, and after she'd made her arrangements I figured I might as well talk to him about the disposal of the bones. He approved, of course, told me what a fine, pious young man I was, and took me out to look at real estate and, incidentally, show off his preserve. The Musser monument is the pride of the cemetery— ugliest damn thing I ever saw, all mourning cherubs and weeping angels and junk—and while I fought down my nausea and made the proper admiring remarks, he started talking about the old lady. The tragedy of old age, the decay of a once-fine mind—that kind of thing. As an example of how dotty she had become he told me something that made my hair stand up. It seems Miss Musser had sent for him one day last fall. She was in considerable distress but at first she couldn't remember why, or why she'd called him. Finally she told him some rambling story about seeing a dead body, and someone digging a grave. She described the location accurately enough, but everything else was all mixed up; one minute she seemed to be describing an event that had occurred recently, and the next she was talking about George Fairweather, and then about some man falling off a horse into the water . . . You couldn't blame him for failing to take her seriously, but by the time he got through, my scalp was prickling. I told Walt to take Mary Jo out for a drink and headed back here."

Diana nodded. The shadows gathered in. After a while Andy said, "Are you ready to go back to the others? It's getting dark."

"You give up pretty easily, don't you?" She rose to her feet.

"Oh, no." He backed away. "Don't do this to me. Not unless you mean it." He put out a hand to hold her off. Diana caught it in hers and brought it to her breast. Andy let out his breath in a ragged gasp. "I have a delicate temperament, I can't stand ups and downs. Oy. What made you change your mind?"

"I didn't. It was always you."

"Why me?" His other hand went to her waist, fingers curling with delicate precision around the curve of her ribs.

"You make me laugh."

"So does Zero Mostel."

"You prop me up when I start to fall."

"So does Walt. Damn his eyes." Andy's hand slid slowly across her back, pressing harder, pulling her to him.

"He picks me up. I don't want to be picked up. Just a little shove now and then when . . ."

"Good reasons. But not enough." His warm, uneven breath moved from the hollow behind her ear to her closed eyes.

"Give me a better one."

"Conservation. All that water wasted."

Her lips were eager and waiting, parted in laughter, when his lips found them.

About the Author

Barbara Michaels is the pseudonym of Barbara Mertz, who has a Ph.D. in Egyptology from the University of Chicago. Under her own name she has written two nonfiction books on ancient Egypt. She also writes traditional mysteries under the name of Elizabeth Peters; these are now published by Warner Books. The winner of numerous awards for mystery writing, Ms. Mertz has been awarded an honorary degree by Hood College for her contributions to popular literature and women's studies, and is currently the president of the American Crime Writer's League. She is the mother of two and the proud grandmother of three. Born and raised in Illinois, she now inhabits a historic farmhouse in Frederick, Maryland, along with two dogs and six cats.

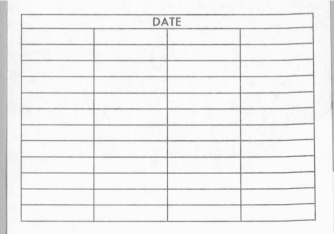

DATE		